IT COULD ONLY BE CHEMISTRY

Leanna heard him speak her thoughts. Beautiful. Absolutely beautiful. His heartbeat was a steadying rhythm and she nodded against his chest, holding tight to the magic she'd discovered in this night, in this man. She wanted more—to be held forever, safe in his arms while she explored this wholly new awareness. Every moment next to him created a need and her body demanded more. To kiss him was entering a realm of existence she hadn't known to be possible—warm and soaring, unimaginable until a few minutes ago. This, surely, was how it should be between two people.

Her dear, conservative father had urged her not to settle for less. Less was already in her life. Not to see was less; she knew that to return to feeling less was no longer possible. He had warned her that he would soon leave for Chicago; it was more than likely she'd never see him again. Maybe this evening could change that, but if it had to happen, she had every intention of having him leave on her terms.

Also by Jeane Renick

Trust Me
Always . . .

Available from
HarperPaperbacks

PROMISES

Jeane Renick

HarperPaperbacks
A Division of HarperCollins*Publishers*

This is a work of fiction. The characters, incidents, and dialogues are products of the author's imagination and are not to be construed as real. Any resemblance to actual events or persons, living or dead, is entirely coincidental.

HarperPaperbacks   *A Division of* HarperCollins*Publishers*
10 East 53rd Street, New York, N.Y. 10022

Cover illustration by Jim Griffin

First printing: May 1994

Printed in the United States of America

HarperPaperbacks, HarperMonogram, and colophon are trademarks of HarperCollins*Publishers*

❖ 10 9 8 7 6 5 4 3 2 1

Nothing destroys
like promises broken;
nothing so joyous
as promises kept . . .

For Jim and Annie
whose memories remain,
strong and welcome,
and my family. . . .

1

Promise to love and to cherish . . .

Leanna knew from the angle of warmth against her skin that the sun was settling just above the treeline on the far shore of the lake on her father's estate; and when the breeze was up the way it was this afternoon, its reflection would burn across the chopping water in a glistening row of banners all melting together in a shiny path. As a child and still a free spirit, she'd believed the splinters of light breaking off the waves were faeries dancing along the surface. She turned her face squarely into the sunshine and closed her eyes, intent on commemorating her feelings.

There was a slight give in the bench a few inches away from her; the wooden slats were adjusting to Curt's weight. She heard the liquid slap of water against the dock pilings beneath their feet as she added this day to the other special memories in this place. The summer she was fourteen George Woodruff's team of Belgians had splashed along the shallows, pulling a loose raft of logs through the water to this site. One of her last and favorite summer memories was the precision of those beautiful horses, their huge hooves tossing water high in the air.

Her final view of the world had been a rainy morning the following spring, under the angry, oyster sky of a late April storm. That day her life had split in two to become the then and the now, and her memories had evolved into an eerie gallery of familiar portraits with vivid impressions of two kinds of people: those she'd known before, interspersed with the haunting black spaces of those who'd come after.

Curt's portrait was a black space that contained impressions of his firm and powerful body, a lingering cologne, brisk and expensive, and confident arms that ended in smooth hands with soft, blunt fingers. His voice reflected a pleasant, if slightly driven personality, and he'd described himself indifferently as having light brown eyes and dark brown hair. Raised with sight and certain female expectations, she longed to know if he was handsome. No one in her family had been able to give a description that met her satisfaction, so she assigned his eyes the color of pecan shell and his hair the rich brown of bottomland, and Han Solo's features.

Fingering the solitaire engagement ring in her palm, its arc of metal smooth and cool in the center of her hand, she realized that she'd sensed for weeks that Curt had been different. However, a proposal of marriage was completely unexpected. What should she say to this man who'd become so important in her life these past months?

"It's a carat and a half, perfect blue-white in a platinum setting," Curt's voice described to her, close and caressing as the humid air. She wished desperately to see his face.

She had painted the dull green of the lake and the brassy glow of the late afternoon sun; she knew the precise ripe-wheat color of Thumper's hide, the gold-and-ivory depths of the mare's keen eyes, the grasshopper green of the drying grass, the whitened poplar leaves, and a thousand other details of Ohio life in August. But it was hard to re-create a blue-white diamond, something she'd had little interest in at fourteen. Everyone knew they sparkled, but there was no portrait in her gallery to call on. She was left with the soft silver glow of candlelit tableware and the white-blue shine of swimming-pool water. And the shards of light from the dancing faeries.

Unbidden, her ears brought heightened sound: the snuffling of the horses patiently awaiting their return to the stable and grain, a screech of saddle leather straining against a girth, the chain clinkling on Thumper's bridle, and the crunch of the mare's teeth occasionally pulling grass a few feet from the dock. There was a sudden wash of wind through the near stand of poplars; she heard the whispered rush as it moved toward her through the thick grass. It hit her, restless and warm, tossed her hair, riffled along the edges of her skirt, tickled the fine hair on her arms, and moved on, carrying away the tick of her watch.

Marriage. Her heart tightened at such an important commitment. She assessed her knowledge of Curtis Baylor. Unlike other men she'd dated in the past, in all the time she'd known him he had never taken advantage of her lack of sight, not one wrong gesture—not even alone in the stable the night of her birthday, when she'd tried to signal her feelings and a deep yearning to experience more with him. It had been the one occasion in her life when she'd felt wanton and reckless and . . . what, she wasn't entirely sure.

When he'd kissed her that night, she'd opened her mouth to kiss him back. She'd pressed her breasts and her body against him, something she'd never done before, excited at daring to bare her need and aware of opening a secret, inner door to feelings that were new and important. He'd held her close, and the hard outlines of his body had been keen and exciting; she'd strained even closer, but after a moment he'd pulled away and she'd kissed only the tips of his fingers held against her mouth.

"Let's not promise what can't be delivered." He'd kissed her again, but lightly, without the emotion of seconds before. Feeling clumsy and awkward, unsure how she'd failed, she'd walked with him back to the main house, where he'd gone inside to say good-bye to her father, then kissed her a chaste good night before driving away.

Afterward she'd tried to talk to her brother about what had happened—more to the point, what hadn't happened—but Parker's response had been equally disconcerting; they'd never shared intimate details of their romantic lives, but it was an open secret that he was sleeping with Jolene Llowell those nights he didn't come home. Parker had never endorsed Curt. She loved her brother and valued his opinion, and his reserve had nagged at her. "You'll know when you're in love," he'd said, sidestepping her. "If it's right, no one will have to tell you."

She was drifting. On this most important occasion, she was drifting.

She shifted on the bench and focused herself on this life-altering decision. Marriage was taking a partner forever, and children, and getting old together. Decisions so large demanded much thought and consideration. Blind her entire adult life, was she qualified to make such a huge commitment? She tried to examine her feelings.

What if she said no?

What if she said no and was desperately wrong?

What if she wrecked it all on some vague notion that she should be feeling more? Her mind sped through the argument of her age. More what? Excitement? Kissing Curt had been very exciting. But was it love? Did it equate to marriage? What precisely defined being in love that no one had to tell you? Did sighted people know? More feeling good? More unexplainable, possibly nonexistent . . . what?

Maybe it all came down to avoidance. Maybe she was looking for this whatever-it-was because she was frightened of entering into a lifetime contract with a man she couldn't see. For a moment she imagined her world without Curt, and a cold wraith of fear settled in her stomach.

"Listen to your feelings," Parker had said. Right now her feelings were rattling with alarm, and she was terrified suddenly that Curt would walk out of her life. Perhaps love was really just as simple as the safety of marriage, and sex would be a part of that haven. Staying a little girl, helpless in her blindness, was the unnerving alternative, and she'd sworn every day of her life that she'd never let that happen. If marrying Curt could provide the answer she was searching for, she'd be an absolute fool not to go forward.

To remind her he was waiting, Curt continued softly, "It belonged to my mother. Say yes, Leanna," he urged. "I promise we can make it work, I know we can."

She tried to listen with her heart and not with her head; to feel as she had as an artist when responses had flowed onto her canvases from emotion and feelings.

"If you can't say yes, I'll understand, I really will," he went on. "And I won't want it back. But I have to say this, and I want you to understand." The smooth inner palms of his hands sandwiched her face and turned her toward him. He was silent until she opened her eyes. "I'll owe it to myself to stop seeing you unless there's some possibility . . . It would hurt too much, Leanna."

She felt the soft touch of his lips on her own for a brief moment, so good, so caring.

"I want to marry you. Please say yes."

Curtis Baylor read the confusion in Leanna's face. The clarity and depth in the still, gray eyes that did not see amazed him for the thousandth time. It had taken three days to separate her from the dragon lady, and he'd taken a huge gamble this afternoon by giving her the ring while her father was out of town. He was frustrated at her inability to see him, to witness his sincerity so he could will her agreement. For he was absolutely sincere. Her blindness posed no problem he couldn't overcome.

He ached to grab her shoulders and shake her until she agreed. Instead he built the pressure for an answer by running his fingers soothingly up and down the butter-soft skin of her forearm. She was beautiful in a tomboyish sort of way, with her skin deeply tan from the summer sun and her brown hair bobbed in a chin-length cap that moved pleasantly in the summer breeze. She was the right age next to his twenty-six, and he had no doubt that she loved him. *Answer me,* he commanded silently.

"Yes." Her voice was husky with emotion.

Relieved, he took the ring from her palm and guided it carefully onto her finger. He checked his watch. It was a little after midnight in France. "Let's call your father.

He'll want to be the first to know." The emotion in his kiss was real, and Leanna's doubts were lifted as she returned his embrace with joy.

Sam Bowmont stared out his eighth-floor window at the city of Paris, sleepless despite his medication. The famous lights still glistened at this hour. If Dr. Edgar concurred, it would be official that he'd run out of time. The consensus of medical opinion to date was six to eight months. In all probability the specialist would confirm that as well.

Surely fate had had this punishment in mind in the design of his life from the very beginning. If indeed there was a God to call him into account, there was little enough he could point to as having accomplished. True, he had achieved, by most standards, extraordinary wealth, but most of it quite by accident. It had been as random and as life-altering an event as the automobile crash that had disfigured his face and body at eighteen.

He dropped the heavy drape into place and prepared to return to bed. When the phone sounded its peculiar double ring, he picked up the receiver to talk to his daughter.

"Daddy, Curt's asked me to marry him." He heard a joy and excitement in Leanna's voice that shook his father's heart. So, it had happened.

"And, I'm glad to say she's agreed." Curt's voice was strong and confident on the extension, which told him that Leanna was calling from the library, with Curt using the phone in the foyer. "We wanted you to be the first to know, sir."

Sam was moved to tears and profoundly aware of his relief. The young man had called him aside the night of her birthday to declare his intentions. He knew in his heart that he had glossed over his reservation about the match, but with each concurring medical opinion, Leanna's welfare had grown to an all-consuming proportion. Annoyed that Curt had waited until he was out of town, he wished himself home so he could see her face and be certain. Nonetheless, he told her heartily, "Well, I think that's fine. You have my congratulations, honey."

"We haven't set a date, yet." Curt's voice was equally hearty. "Soon, I hope. I intended to wait until you were home, sir, but I have a job interview in Chicago next week, and, well, I'm sure you understand."

"Of course." Sam dismissed his annoyance as unimportant. "Looks like I'll need a picture to run with an engagement announcement," he said teasingly, and was grateful to hear Leanna's delighted laughter.

"Daddy, I really don't want a fuss." She hadn't been comfortable having her picture taken since the accident, but he could tell from her response that she'd allow it, to please him.

"If my daughter's getting married, I'm going to tell the world. Curt, you arrange a sitting and pick out something suitable for the front page."

"Yes, sir. I'll take care of it tomorrow."

"Alice Faye's right here," said Leanna. "We wanted to tell you both at the same time. She wants to talk to you."

I'll just bet she does, he thought with the shrinking sensation in his stomach that only his unhappy wife could generate. Alice Faye, nearly twenty years his junior, would see this marriage in terms of becoming a grandmother, and that title at forty-five would be appalling. "All right, sweetheart, in a minute," he stalled.

"Welcome to the family, son. If you don't mind, I'd like you to hang up now so I can say good-bye to my daughter." He waited for the click that told him Curt had replaced the receiver, then as lightly as he could manage, he asked, "Are you sure, honey? Is this really what you want?"

In the foyer, Curt covered the bottom of the phone with his hand. He depressed the connection, then lifted it immediately to hear the last of Sam's question and Leanna's response.

"I think he loves me, and yes, I'm pretty sure."

"Do I hear room for doubt?" Sam needed to be certain; the last thing he wanted was the specter of an unhappy marriage haunting his final days.

"I don't think it's doubt. It's just . . . It's very new, that's all. How soon are you coming home? I miss you."

"I miss you, too, sweetie." Sam's sigh filled the lonely bedroom in the hotel suite. "I should have been there. I'll be home as soon as I can, I promise," he said guiltily. "I love you, now let me talk to Alice Faye." The clatter of jewelry came through the line, then silence. Alice Faye had taken the telephone, and he knew she was waiting until the two were out of hearing.

"She's too young, Sam." All hell knew she was not pleased, and her anger was palpable.

"Alice Faye, you were younger than she is when we were married." Sam knew this would not sit well with his wife, but truth was truth.

"You know what I mean. She hardly knows him."

"What you mean is, she's blind." He was too tired to fence with words.

"Yes, and lots of little boys will be happy to fall in love with rich little blind girls," she responded tartly.

Sam said nothing and sent his disapproval across the

distance. Leanna was one of the few areas in which he would not be pushed around. He let the silence build to a standoff.

Alice Faye went on the attack. "When are you coming home?" she demanded.

"Soon. I have a couple more meetings on this matter—this Tuesday and one the following week. Then I'll be home and we'll talk."

"I want to talk about it now."

"Alice Faye, they're not getting married tomorrow. Can we please discuss this when I get back? If we talk about it now, we'll fight. I'm tired, and I don't want to argue."

Thinly mollified, she relented. "All right. But I am not, repeat, *not,* planning a wedding until I'm satisfied he's in love with her and not Bowmont money."

"If she loves him, it's all that's important," he said tiredly. The muscle in his eye socket began to throb. "Please say good night."

"You're right, of course. It's late there. Get some sleep."

Sam replaced the receiver. Ordinarily he knew and respected Alice Faye's assessments, but in this instance he held insight that she did not have. He knew what it was like to lose the ability to see. He'd spent nine days of terror after his automobile accident, totally dependent on others. The fact that sight had eventually returned to his right eye was the greatest personal gift he'd received in his life, and he lived in hope that some miracle would occur for Leanna.

That his daughter had adapted so well had astounded him. He'd been devastated and dispirited at the ruin of his once handsome features and for all practical purposes had denied his loss and come out of the hospital only to go into hiding. Unable to face college with a physically limited future, he had joined Midland Insurance immediately after graduation. He'd married loyal, adoring Louise Mitchell two years later. Most of his face had since been reconstructed, but the ache where his left eye had been was chronic. Rather than deaden the nerves permanently, he lived with it to this day, and unfortunately, the pain had covered the symptoms of his illness.

Louise, the antithesis of Alice Faye, had been an unassuming, shy lady who undressed in the dark the entirety of their married life, and he took some small comfort in the fact that he had genuinely cared for his first wife—indeed, depended on her serenity—and for fifteen years they had been quietly happy in an orderly life. They had discovered her pregnancy when she was thirty-five, and at the time his world had been stricken daily with new and jarring events, every pattern thrown into disarray, every routine disrupted.

He smiled in wry amusement at the memory and at the massive changes in his life since then; looking back, it seemed to have been a harbinger of the strange events transpiring over the next several years. How odd that the most innocent of things, a trip to Chicago to attend an insurance convention, had started his life down a short path of unrelenting chaos. He knew now that his subsequent marriage had changed his psyche and reconnected him emotionally with the world and his feelings. Since then he'd lived more lies, more deceptions, and more pain in one lifetime than most men did in three.

Six months after Louise's astonished discovery and following forty-two hours of difficult labor, his pale, fragile daughter had arrived. Mystified at the magic of her, he had instantly adored all four pounds seven ounces of her existence and named her Leanna Faith. Louise never recovered from the trauma of Leanna's birth and was unwilling thereafter to share her bed with him; chagrined at being relegated to a distant second in her life, he had quietly withdrawn.

The spring following Leanna's first birthday, Louise had suffered a massive heart attack; thirty-nine and a widower with a child, he'd given in to grief and stumbled through funeral arrangements. Louise was buried in her family's plot near Fort Wayne, Indiana.

Early in April, before he could put things right, he'd met Alice Faye Marshall, a fateful turning point in his life. Lost and obsessed, he had never wanted anything so totally in his life—and he had the only thing that would make her available. Money. Within two months they became engaged, and he climbed aboard an emotional roller coaster, not caring that she was leveraging her youth and beauty at twenty-two in an unabashed sellout for his wealth—prenuptial agreement and infant daughter notwithstanding.

From that moment, his world became a living hell; hailstorms of fear had pelted him daily, of being discovered, of being destroyed. To this day he had not discussed with any living soul what it had cost him, but on September first of that year he had walked down the aisle of the Walden City Community Church to marry Alice Faye Marshall.

And now his daughter was to be married. Life had come full circle.

2

Old promises . . .

    A few minutes past two A.M., in her mother's parrot green bedroom with its parrot green padded-silk walls and matching drapes held back with knotted silk cords, Jolene Llowell lay on her back on a beach towel on her mother's bed and surveyed the parrot green silk faille canopy covering and matching trim. "Madeline Llowell can't possibly be my mother," she said idly. "I hate green."

    Her parents had flown to London yesterday, and this was the first night of a four-week sabbatical for her doctor father. Lying on the towel to protect the duvet from the sweat of her naked body, she looked at the massive Baccarat clock on the night table; it was set to London time and read two minutes past seven in the morning. The phone rang for the fourth time in the past two hours, and this time she picked it up.

    "Morning, Mother. Oops, hi, Daddy . . ." She rolled away from an equally bare and sweaty Parker Bowmont, closed her knees, and concentrated on her father's voice. "Are you sure? I've been in all evening. I took a late swim." She grinned at Parker. "And a shower after. I probably didn't hear the phone." He left the bed, and she followed the jiggle of tennis-firm cheeks appreciatively as he headed toward the kitchen, then shifted her attention to her father's rumbling list of possible birthday gifts.

"The only thing I want from Scotland is cashmere—a full-length cape. Camel," she instructed, and made a face at the room. "Tell Mother if she buys anything else, please, any color but green."

"Your mother picked out a beautiful onyx pin—"

"I hate onyx, and I hate pins. You promised me anything I wanted for not being here on my birthday," she accused.

"Cashmere it is," responded her father. "Hold on, here's your mother."

"Daddy, I . . ." Jolene gritted her teeth and impatiently answered a barrage of basic parent questions. Parker's insolent saunter as he returned to the bedroom with a couple of beers held far more interest. "Tell Daddy I talked to Jillian yesterday," she broke in. "By the way, in case you're still looking for something for her birthday, she loves onyx and . . . Right, and she'll be here on schedule, so I'm perfectly fine."

Jolene took one of the opened beers. "It's been lovely having the house to myself for a change." She deliberately turned to kiss Parker, half listening to her mother's voice. "I promise," she said. "Let me say good night to Daddy, bye." After a moment: "Hugs and kisses, Daddy. Don't forget. Nothing green unless it's emeralds. Good night."

"'Hugs and kisses, Daddy,'" mocked Parker. It was no

secret that Jolene enjoyed her position as favored child in the Llowell family and openly relied on her father's tolerance. To date, in his hearing, *no* had never appeared in Dr. Llowell's vocabulary relative to Jolene. Her relationship with Madeline Llowell, on the other hand, was generally less than cordial but never quite rude. "What'd you promise your mother?" He took a sip of beer.

Jolene laughed. "To be a good girl."

"Well, that's safe." He lazed his naked body next to hers and gave her a beery kiss designed to get back to business. "Want me to tell her how good you are?"

He licked her nipple with his cold tongue until it was stiff, and Jolene watched him harden. "I see definite interest here," she teased. Parker was a terrific lover who made sure she was ready before he put it in, and she savored the knowledge of the pleasure to come. Her body tightened, and a pressing sexual urge began to build as he aggressively sucked the nipple into his mouth and traveled his hand from her breasts to her navel, working his way lower.

The phone rang again.

He moved onto her body and pushed the tip of his tongue into her ear. "Don't answer it," he whispered.

"What if it's my parents again? They know I'm up—"

"Yeah, but do they know I'm up?" Parker gave her a bawdy grin and waggled his brows.

She kissed him and deliberately picked up the phone. Her sister's quiet voice sounded in her ear.

"Hey, Jo, it's Jillian. Sorry it's so late, but I just talked to Mom."

"Yeah, they just called here. What's she want now?" Jolene smacked Parker's hand, then covered the phone to whisper, "I'll make it fast, I promise."

"So will I," he threatened. It became a contest of wills as he put his beer aside to deliberately increase his attentions to her body.

"She asked me to come home a few days early. I was thinking about it anyway, honest."

"Okay, whatever. When?" Unenthusiastic, Jolene rushed her end of the conversation, eager to complete the call and take advantage of Parker's attempts to separate her knees.

"Saturday."

"What time?"

In New York, Jillian began to grasp the situation: her sister was entertaining, probably in her mother's bedroom. It wouldn't occur to Jolene that including her via phone without her consent was completely against the rules. She felt herself flush as her imagination, of course, provided the one person she didn't want to be in bed with her sister. "I'll see you around three?"

The need to know was overwhelming. Jillian bit the inside of her cheek. What if it was Jay—what if he was home and . . . She pressed the receiver to her ear so hard that it hurt, but no second voice carried through the line, and she desperately wanted to end the call before it did. And she desperately wanted to know who was there. Above all, she didn't want to be the humiliated part of the triangle.

Jolene went crashing on as Parker intensified his efforts. "That's fine with me. Uh, so you know, Parker's here, so if you change your plans, make sure I know it. Bye."

"Jo, what about—" Jolene was gone. The air went out of Jillian's body, and she relaxed. Parker. Not Jay. Suddenly life was a thousand percent better. She hung up the phone and walked restlessly around the room in her underwear.

On the sixth floor of an old building on the Lower West Side of Manhattan, the minuscule apartment lacked air-conditioning; all her windows were open to the stifling heat and near hundred percent humidity. Even at this late hour, steam emanated from manholes in treeless, sunbaked streets, and there was a heat saturation in the brick and concrete of the city that only New York could generate this time of year.

She wet a washcloth at the kitchen counter and held it in front of an oscillating fan. On the wall next to the phone was a modestly framed four-and-a-half-year-old photograph: she and Jay Sprengsten were leaning against somebody's old green sedan. His ribs were countable on his bare chest at a scrawny seventeen. Sweaty from a track meet, he had one arm around her waist and was leaning over to kiss her, a geeky teenager in twin ponytails, with hideous freckles. It had been a real kiss, not on the cheek, and her very first.

Jolene, heartlessly secure in his life, had laughed and taken the picture purely to embarrass her. Tucked inside a corner of the frame was a wallet-size portrait of Jay in his army uniform with a skinned haircut and the sober stare of youthful responsibility. She waved the wet cloth to aid its cooling process, then draped it around the back of her neck.

She smiled again at the ridiculous picture. She'd stolen it from Jolene with every intention of destroying it but over the past five years had been grateful a hundred times that she hadn't. Jolene had never missed it, and she doubted her sister remembered that it was ever taken.

She'd been in love with him, desperately, secretly, and the excitement at his attention had held, along with the burn of his mouth on her lips, the rest of that summer and long after she'd hidden, miserable with tears, at the train station to watch him kiss Jolene good-bye. When she moved to New York to go to college, she'd sent him a note with her address. To her joy and surprise, he'd written in response: nothing special, just a big brother kind of thing—thanks for writing, and he hoped things were going well for her in the Big Apple. After that, she'd written as often as she'd dared, deliberately chatty, innocent of feelings, describing college life in New York and her part-time job at a small newspaper publication in SoHo.

"You promised me a dance. . . ." A harmless joke between them, but he'd remembered to say it each time he wrote. Her hopes had been buoyed by his letters and by Jolene's two-year-long attention to Parker Bowmont.

Her sublet was up at the end of October, and the owner was reclaiming the apartment; she would have to make a decision soon about finding another place. She folded an ice cube into a dry dishtowel, rapped it smartly with a knife handle, and put the chips in her mouth. God, it was hot.

Dating in the hard hustle of New York hadn't produced anyone who'd stirred her feelings like the skinny boy in the photo. She turned the cooler side of the washcloth against her skin. After five years, surely her feelings for Jay were no longer an adolescent crush. The only way to know was to see him, which meant going home. She'd promised her mother that she would be there for Jolene's birthday and stay until her parents returned from Europe. Lingering beyond that time would be to risk stepping back into the pain of living in her sister's shadow.

"I'd know the minute I saw him," she reasoned. She turned the cloth again. He'd be home from the army soon. "Stay in love with Parker," she murmured to her absent sister, and moved her thumb over the image next to the green Ford sedan.

$\overline{3}$

Traxx promise . . .

Four miles east of Walden City, in the hard-scrabble community of Wellington Flats, Charlene Sprengsten was hidden in Annie Chatfield's tree-house. High in the crotch of an ancient maple tree in Annie's backyard, it was a solid, wooden square of a room built by her father and brothers before Danni was born. She had been there for three hours getting up her nerve. Aunt Jessica had given an ultimatum and was refusing to budge, and Charlie was equally dug in.

Under the glare of a light bulb, she stared into a fragment of mirror at the purple streaks in her hair that had caused the crisis. Three months ago, Jack Myers, who was a big, overgrown bully of a sophomore, had cornered her in the gym and tried to kiss her; he'd felt her chest and bragged to the other boys about how much he liked cute little girls with long blond hair and "nubbins."

Humiliated, furious, Charlie had bagged him good, called him a lying asshole in front of half the school. She knew she'd hit the mark when he got all red and embarrassed, but Wellington Flats wasn't that big, and he'd been following her around all summer, hassling her every chance he got. Plus, he'd started a bunch of lies about her, hooting and carrying on with his friends about what a wild time he was having with the "bombshell with the temper" and the "nubbins."

She'd tried to cool things by raiding Jay's storage boxes and wearing some of his old clothes. To top it off, she bought a bottle of hair color to streak her sun-bleached hair a blatant purple. Aunt Jessica had had a heart attack over her appearance and accused her of deliberately taunting her authority. She'd demanded that Charlie dress normal and wash out the dye. Only it hadn't come out.

After the color remover she bought at a beauty supply transformed the dull, dark purple streaking to huge, hideously neon-bright splotches, she broke her word and ran away rather than face off with Aunt Jessica again. She looked sideways into the peeling mirror; it would cost forty hard-earned dollars to fix it at the beauty shop. When Jay got home the family would need the money.

Finally she picked up the scissors. She had promised her brother she wouldn't cut her hair until he got back, but no way she'd let him see her like this. After the first handful fell away, she became absorbed in the process and worked from either side around to the back of her neck. It didn't look too bad, she decided, if you didn't count the ragged place around one ear where most of the dye had congregated.

Trying to adapt to the odd, weightless feeling about her head, she froze when she felt the subtle vibration of someone climbing the ladder. If it was Jack, she was trapped. Her heart pounded its way into her throat, and she wasn't sure what to do.

Without moving or making a noise, she gripped the scissors and tried to see through the cracks in the wooden walls, but it was too dark. "Who is it?" she challenged. If it was Jack, she was going to draw first blood and holler her head off. Annie was home, and no one, not even mean old Jack Myers, wanted to deal with Annie Chatfield if she got on the warpath.

Stephen's quiet voice drifted up the ladder. "It's me."

Charlie released her breath and grabbed at the pile of hair in a belated effort to stuff it out of sight. Then she realized that trying to hide the evidence was pretty dumb—all her brother had to do was take a look at her. Knowing it was too late to do anything but tough it out, she waited defiantly, hair in one hand, scissors in the other.

Stephen stepped into the treehouse, silently assessed the destruction to his sister's beautiful hair, and her pain, and judged the situation past discussion. Whatever her reasons, it was done, and no amount of conversation would alter the damage.

Charlie broke the silence. "Hi."

As was usual with Stephen, there was no reply. Charlie dropped the hair and scissors to take the knapsack he held out to her. "Thanks for the care package."

She gave his wiry, sixteen-year-old body a hug, which he did not return. Along with unnecessary conversation, Stephen had stopped hugging people a long time ago.

"Aunt Jessica called you, right?" She unwrapped a sandwich. "Hey, peanut butter, thanks! Does she know I'm here?"

He gave her a brief nod.

"You're unquestionably my best brother, you know that?" Charlie's words were muffled in sandwich. "No one else ever listens to me."

Stephen dug into the pack for a bottle of apple juice. Charlie could feel his mood, and he was too quiet, even for Stephen.

"You hear from Jay?" She saw him shake his head in the negative and studiously avoided his eyes. "Some-times . . ." She paused to rip open the king-size package of potato chips and filled her mouth. Potato chips were expensive and hard to come by. "I think you don't talk just to make me crazy," she finished.

The intensity of his silence finally broke through her defenses. "Okay, what? You already know I ran away. If it's about my hair—"

"You hitched to Walden City." Stephen's voice was calm, as always, but deadly.

"So?" Damn, George Woodruff had ratted her out. Her defensive posture was hard to maintain against Stephen's icy silence. A three-alarm fire wouldn't melt this one. "George's like family. I wouldn't get in a car with somebody I didn't know. Don't worry, I'm not gonna be a body on the landscape." Her rationale wasn't cutting the ice. "Came back by bus," she muttered.

Stephen stared her down. Then in a calm but lethal tone he nailed her. "No hitching. You know that. I don't care where or when or why. Not one more time. You need a ride, you call me. You call Tommy. You can't get us, you call Aunt Jessica. You got it?"

This was a major speech from Stephen, not to be

taken lightly. Charlie's defenses slipped again. "I got it."

Stephen watched his sister while she fought the remaining fight, clinging to her position with a stubborn tenacity.

"I got it!" she declared again, and abandoned the chips.

It was a contest of wills in which he would wait forever, and she knew it, for the unbreakable promise. Abruptly she gave over. "I miss Mom."

"Me too." Stephen allowed the ice to disappear; the waiting did not.

"Traxx promise. I won't hitch." She gave him another hug which he did not return, but in which he allowed relief. "That's from Mom," she told him.

He folded himself onto the floor. This was the third time in two years Charlie had run away. Both times before, he'd found her in the treehouse. He and his brothers lived in fear of the day she would not be here. "Aunt Jess told me about your hair," he said.

The dam broke, and Charlie paced the small space with pent-up emphasis. "You guys don't know what it's like. You live with families—even if they get paid to keep you, they're still families. I mean, they know you're there, they talk to you and treat you okay. Just because I'm a girl I had to stay with Aunt Jessica."

Stephen listened in silence, allowing her to blow the steam. This ground had been covered extensively over the past four years.

"It's Danielle this and Danielle that. She's only a little kid, for cripe's sake. Everybody knows she only wanted Danni. She only took me to get her. She doesn't even see me half the time."

He had no reply to this. It was true, and everyone in the family knew it. In her devotion to eight-year-old

Danielle, Jessica Sprengsten had failed miserably to care equally for Charlie.

"Then Danni gets upset when I fight with Aunt Jess. It's just that Jay's been gone so long and I never see you and Tommy, and now all the time I'm—"

Charlie stopped in midsentence, and Stephen saw her switch gears. "Is Jay coming back for sure next week, Stevie? For sure? No lie?" Her passion ebbed as she admitted to her worst fear. "I mean, the army won't screw it up and not let him out or anything?"

"He'll be here." What she'd pounded out had held the ring of truth, but Stephen sensed something underneath her frustration, a deeper anxiety. "You're what?" he prompted.

For a split second, Charlie was tempted to lay it out and tell him that she was terrified of going back to school—that unless she hid from him, she could expect day in and day out hassle from Jack: about being humiliated every time he talked about her "nubbins"; about never sitting next to an empty chair in study hall because he'd sit down and try to grab her under the table; about always making sure she was near a teacher if he was behind her in the hallways; about constantly watching out for him in some sort of relentless, adolescent battle.

But at the last instant something told her to wait. When Jay got home they could handle it together. Jack was a football player and almost six feet, and Stephen might get hurt, and she couldn't stand it if Stephen got hurt on account of her. She threw herself on the bunk and rooted around in the knapsack.

"I'm hungry. You know I'm horrible when I'm hungry. Hey, apple juice!" Knowing the answer, she asked, "You got any dollars? I'm down to three bucks."

Stephen decided to let her sidestep him and dug into his jeans to locate a twenty-dollar bill and a couple of fives. He handed her the twenty.

"No, five's enough. I'll just spend it on bus fare."

He watched her smile at her successful dig and traded her the twenty for a five and stuffed the second five in the knapsack.

"We're gonna need every cent when Jay gets home," she objected, but she left it in the sack and sat down next to him with the scissors.

He took them from her and began to even up the hacked line of her hair. "Annie know you're here?"

"No, she'd just call Aunt Jess."

He paused while she jumped up for the mirror and returned to submit to his barbering. "If you stay here, Aunt Jessie'll call Jay," he said quietly. "He doesn't need the aggravation right now."

"I know. I'll go back in a couple of days," she conceded.

Stephen said nothing. He finished trimming her hair and reached up to put the scissors back on the shelf.

Uncomfortable in his silence, she was more specific. "Tomorrow." He looked at her to let her know he had no plans to let her off the hook, and she gave in again. "Traxx promise. Enough already."

Satisfied at last, Stephen stretched out along one wall and prepared to go to sleep. Traxx promises could not be broken. They had evolved in the family by way of Traxx University. Mom used to joke that they ought to be the Traxx family because all the kids left muddy tracks whenever they came into the house. They'd all promised not to do it, and eventually it had been incorporated into the name of their business, Traxx Jobbing, because in business and in life, you had to be

as good as your word. If she'd made a Traxx promise,
Charlie would go home tomorrow. The next step was
to extract a Traxx promise that she wouldn't run away
again.

Outmaneuvered and mystified, she poked him with
her foot in annoyance. "How do you do that?"

Unseen by his sibling, Stephen almost smiled; he
genuinely had no idea how he managed to corral his sister and fervently hoped it would be the last time before
Jay returned. Squaring off with Charlie was hard work.
He closed his eyes to the instant sleep of youth.

Secure in his presence, Charlie covered him with an
ancient afghan, one of Annie's discarded treasures, then
settled onto the bunk to feast on potato chips. At least
Aunt Jess couldn't hassle her tonight, she decided. She
blew out the candles and wrinkled her nose at the
scorched-wick smell. "Hah. Wait 'til she sees the new
look," she said to herself. "That'll cap her." But her satisfaction was bleak.

At 2:15 A.M., the screen door to Annie's apartment
was nursed past the point at which it had screeched for
years. Jay Sprengsten stepped inside her kitchen. Annie
Chatfield hadn't locked a door in sixty years. "Nothing
here to steal," she'd declare. "Hell, they ain't room for a
cat. Anybody that wants in is welcome."

He parked his shoes under his duffel next to the wall
and padded across the floor in green army socks to pat
the pot of coffee; it was still warm enough to drink.
Grinning, he half filled an old blue mug, his since high
school, and headed toward the vintage Kelvinator for
milk. Just this once he was going to get one over on
Annie.

Inside, on the shelf, was a carton with a note taped to its side: WELCOME HOME, SMART ALECK!!! He laughed out loud and grabbed the milk as light flooded the kitchen, and he turned in time to intercept Annie bearing down on him, robe flapping, house slippers slapping, to crunch him in a bone-testing hug.

He crunched her back, milk and all. Over the years, gravity had reduced Annie's ample frame to five feet ten, and she was a stocky armful. For the first time in his life he could see over the top of her head.

"Jay Sprengsten, you ought to know by now you can't put anything over on me. Welcome home, you big handsome thing. I had a feeling all day." She beamed at him. "Got the cot all made up."

"I didn't know until today they were letting me go." He crunched her again. "God, Annie, it's good to see you."

Annie gave him a huge, ribaldly innocent kiss. "And me without my wig on, even. . . . Honeybun, you put your butt on that chair over there and tell me why you didn't let us know you'd be home tonight."

He poured milk into his coffee, knowing that Annie, of all people, would understand. "I guess I've waited so long for this—I couldn't wait one more minute. Afraid something would go wrong, I guess."

"Now, nothing's gonna go wrong, dear heart. You worked your fanny off so you could get those kids, and by golly, it's gonna happen."

Annie put heat under the coffee, poured herself a cup, and plunked herself onto a kitchen chair. A short silence descended on the room.

Jay began to relax into the smells of Annie's kitchen —honest coffee and Pine-Sol, home-baked pies. "Just like old times," he said. "God love you, Annie, I couldn't have made it without you." His eyes stung at the thought of his mother. "You got any pie to go with this coffee?"

She was already moving, and he watched her chug about the kitchen in her comfy slippers. Annie'd been here since his family had moved in next door. If he let himself, he could remember how it was before his mother died. His father had been good as new—his long, painful recovery behind him. Out of the wheelchair and using a cane, he'd started back to work as a construction site supervisor. Life had been full and possible.

His parents had started laughing again, and the kids, except for Stephen, were sassy and energized. There'd been picnics in the backyard with gallons of Mom's orangy lemonade, and all-night Monopoly sessions—Stephen was even starting to hold his own as the banker. Finessing the rights to a cooking pot sticky with warm, homemade fudge, Danni would lick the spoon and smear chocolate all over her face. They'd wake to the smell of French toast for breakfast on Sundays instead of the incessant oatmeal.

He'd been good to excellent in track with graduation around the corner; his grades were solid and tacked up in his bedroom there'd been an A list of colleges with an interest in him. And sex, oh, God, sex with Jolene Llowell. As soon as he was halfway through law school they were going to get married. She was gorgeous, and making love with her was three feet higher than heaven.

At night in the barracks he'd remember the tight, silky feel of her skin, and it used to keep him awake when he let himself think about it. They were going to bike through Colorado that summer and make love in the desert under a million stars.

Then the bottom had dropped out of his life. Mom had had a stroke. He hadn't even known what a stroke was. Then she'd had another one. That time he'd known, and it was bad. He'd gotten to the hospital to see her before she died. Mom. Jesus, he missed her so much. Her shining laugh, arms reaching out to bring him close. Messing up his hair. All sons think their mothers are beautiful, but she really was. No wonder his father had adored her.

After the army had beaten him through basic training, he'd had plenty of time to think, and it was suddenly as clear as if she'd spoken from the grave: his dad was losing it, and she knew it. That's why she'd made him promise to take care of the kids and keep them together, why she'd had tears in her eyes the minute he came into the hospital room. She'd known what she was asking, but she'd had no other choice.

Then, in a terrible giving up, she was gone. Unable to hear, in too much pain to cry, he'd closed her eyes. Touching his mother's face hadn't helped at all. It had hurt like God-awful hell. And *nothing* the army had done to him had been worse than having to leave his family. But now he was home, and he was going to keep his promise.

Annie slipped a giant wedge of pie onto a worn china plate and located a fork.

"It so happens I have a peach pie," she told him. "Baked it this morning. Can't have you coming home without a peach pie waitin'." She smiled into his reverie; fully aware of where he'd gone, she added more coffee to his cup and refilled her own. They each offered a toast.

"Here's to you, Annie. And to Mom. The two best people I know."

"Welcome home, darlin'. It's been a long time comin'."

Their peace was shattered when Charlie came crashing into the kitchen, all arms and legs, squeals and kisses for her big brother, who managed to jump up in time to prevent a collision with the kitchen table. He swung her into his arms. "Charlie?"

"I knew it. I knew it was you. Why didn't you tell me?" she accused.

"I didn't even tell Annie, I swear. Tell her, Annie."

Annie stopped short, stunned at the sight of Charlie's shorn hair. "Found him sneaking around my kitchen about ten minutes ago. Now sit yourself and stop waking the neighborhood. My land, child."

Charlie, entirely too excited to sit, clung to her brother's arm and jiggled with energy. "I knew it. I just knew it."

Jay held her at arm's length to take in the ragged haircut. "What the hell happened to you? She looks worse than I did when the army skinned me," he said to Annie. "And why is it . . ." He held his happy sister under the light to be sure. "Purple?"

"It's just junk stuff. All the girls are doing it."

"How long has she been like this?" Jay studied his sister with concern. Her hair had been her pride and joy.

"The color's been around a couple of weeks, but she had a lot more of it the last time I saw her," Annie said mildly. "I'm surprised Jessica hasn't burned up AT and T's wires letting you know about it."

"Jesus, Charlie, it's almost three o'clock in the morning—what are you doing out at this time of night?"

"Your aunt Jessie's probably having a cow. You in the treehouse again?" Annie wasn't overjoyed.

"Don't worry about Aunt Jess." Stephen stepped through the door with a rare, genuine smile for Jay. "She called me about Charlie." He endured a huge hug from his brother and thumping raps on his back. "Welcome home, Jay."

Annie automatically reached for two more plates and cut pie wedges for Stephen and Charlie, shaking her head. "You both out there?"

Charlie danced around the kitchen from sheer exuberance. "Yeah. You don't care, do you, Annie?" Jay was home and her hair would grow and everything was going to be *all right*.

"I don't mind as long as I know it," Annie answered with mild reproof.

Jay's disapproval was stronger. "I thought we had a deal, Charlene."

"We did have a deal. I promised I'd stay with Aunt Jessica until you got home from the army, and you're home. Deal's off." Charlie plopped herself onto a chair to take a large swig of milk.

"Draw," umpired Stephen. He settled himself at the kitchen table, waiting for and receiving Annie's bear hug, which pinned him onto the chair while she ruffled his hair. Content to referee the struggle of wills, he abandoned his customary silence in celebration of Jay's return. "She's going back tomorrow."

"Traitor." Charlie, having glimpsed light at the end of her long struggle with Aunt Jessica, was too happy to put up a proper fight.

"Well, we oughtn't to wake your aunt this time of night," judged Annie.

"Danni, either. I'll call her and Tommy tomorrow,"

said Jay. "It's late, we got to let Annie get some rest."

Annie kissed each of them in turn. "I'm an old lady and I need my beauty sleep. Lights out in five minutes, darlin's." She slapped her way out of the kitchen.

Charlie wiggled her way onto Jay's lap, suddenly an exhausted little girl. "Are you really home?"

"I'm really here, kiddo," he answered, and looked across the table into Stephen's still-smiling face. "And we're gonna be a family again, just like I promised."

Let's not promise . . .

In her bedroom on the third floor of the Bowmont mansion, Leanna started awake with her heart beating hard against her ribs, trying to fly its way out. In the dream she could see again, which always made it worse. Opening her eyes to nothing, she sought the calming breeze off the lake as it flowed through her open window and took a moment to reorient herself to the safety of her room.

Pushing past the pillows of the familiar sleigh bed, her fingers searched for the wrought-iron oak-leaf inserts in the pine headboard. Centered, she found the embroidered edges of the top sheet and carefully lifted it aside to slide out of bed. Mentally she repainted a picture of the room—delft blue and cream, with her favorite midnight blue velvet armchair sitting by the table in front of the window; under her feet, the white cotton rug with the acorn pattern she knew by heart. The strands of yellow crystal beads that fringed the silk lampshade tinkled faintly with the movement of air. Waking up to sunlight streaking through them was gone forever, and the table lamp had no use, but knowing it was still there brought reassurance.

The unaccustomed weight of Curt's ring felt odd on her finger, and she worried it back and forth. Anxiety tightened its way up her spine and spread into the muscles across her shoulders, coiling into hurtful knots. Life here was going to end. Time was slipping away. Accepting Curt's ring had brought her closer to the eventuality of leaving the safety of this house.

Marriage was supposed to be normal in the course of events, a forward motion in life, but alone in her room she was suddenly unsure. From the moment she'd given Curt her answer, change had gnawed at the edges of her mind. The excitement had held until Curt kissed her good night; but now, in her father's silent house, with him so far away in Paris at this middle-of-the-night hour, change held little promise.

She discovered that she was truly frightened. The prospect of moving away from her family surrounded her, clawed at her with hard and desperate intention. She didn't want her life to be different. Not again. The last time had taken years.

In the dream she'd felt the young horse falter and lose his footing on the path, as if it were happening all over again; too late, the realization that he was going down. Tonight, she'd come awake trying desperately to throw herself clear so he wouldn't land on her; then, her next memories had been sick with pain. Wrenched and punished muscles throughout her body had spasmed, excruciating, in retaliation for the trauma they'd sustained. When she'd regained consciousness in the hospital her father's hand had been clutching hers so hard that it, too, had hurt.

They told her that her skull had been fractured at the point of impact and three ribs were broken, as well as her collarbones; that her head had smacked against the trunk of a sapling, and it was a miracle her neck hadn't broken on impact. Worse than the pain was the void where her sight had been—an incessant inky blackness that melted over everything and reduced her life to tastes and smells, and those things she could decipher by hearing or touch. She'd been trapped in the hospital for what seemed like forever, and to this day antiseptic odors made her feel faint.

Hideous months had followed as she had been forced to adjust to life in a relentless, lightless hole that enveloped her being and wouldn't go away: learning to eat again, neatly; regaining her balance when she was finally able to stand and walk; dressing herself in a darkness so total that it held no gray or shape. It had seemed that up was suddenly down, or sideways, or something new, or no longer possible.

Dependent overnight on someone to tell her if it was morning or night—and as an artist and painter, doubly mourning the loss of color. Everything was gone: from sherry-crystal sunrises to the milky purple blues of twilight, and all between. In its place, a braille watch.

Eventually she had righted herself and come home to the world that was her father's house. Using her artist's training, she'd been able to adapt spatially within a reasonably short time, according to her doctors. For her, it had seemed an eternity.

In addition to her bedroom, she'd re-created the rest of the house inside her head, adding the colors she remembered, the rich grays and creams, bold carmines, crackling yellows, and the textures of fabrics—silk jacquards, corduroys and velvets, poolside canvas, terry cloth, bedroom lace and smooth cotton sheets; parqueted wood floors, crisp carpets and soft suedes and leathers, cool crystals and porcelains, all blended with the hollow sounds of hallways, the low crackle of burning logs in the fireplaces, and the dull air of books in her father's study, the room that held marvelous paintings she could no longer see and shelves of rich volumes she could no longer read.

Housekeepers had carefully stacked or hung her clothing in braille-coded rows in her bureaus and closets—sweaters in winter, T-shirts in summer. Outside, there were various masses she learned to sense as barriers using "facial vision", while she savored the feel of the sun and sounds of the trees. Food odors signaled meals, and during the daylight hours, vehicle motors, the whir of hand-pushed lawn mowers, the *thwack* of tennis balls and their slap on the clay court when Parker was practicing his serve, the faint, hollow roar of jet planes arcing dully overhead, barking dogs and the activity sounds of all sorts of day creatures spoke to her, and after dark, the night dwellers: crickets and tree frogs. Rain on the roof and tumbling thunder, the spitting crack of lightning.

Trilling songs of meadowlarks and the calls of robins and cardinals announced spring with its blossom fragrances of dogwood and apple trees, lilacs and peonies, roses; the rich warmth of the summer sun on her face told her that wild raspberries would soon be ripe along the fence rows and county roads. In fall, a crunching under her feet signaled that dew had frozen on the grass during the night; a peculiar muffled stillness on crisp winter mornings whispered that snow had fallen. Sometimes she could feel snowflakes against her face and, if it was really cold and she moved quickly enough, the moisture of her breath as it hung frozen in midair.

Getting around Walden City on Thumper, she had stubbornly managed to eliminate the slender fiberglass cane she knew was white with a red tip, as well as the monotonous pattern of hollow taps she loathed on the wooden floors of the house, the graveled courtyard, and the concrete walk to the stable. After Suli died, she refused to become dependent on another seeing-eye dog and used the cane until she memorized every walkway, every obstacle in her world; eventually she expanded it to the one her artist's eye remembered. It had taken years.

Unless they lived here in her father's house after their marriage, she would have to start over and build everything again—this time with no past knowledge to call on. The thought was overwhelming.

Being Curt's wife would be a more personal change, also frightening in its intimacy and equally permanent. She hadn't made love with him—or anyone, for that matter—and that prospect was unsettling as well. There was no coming back for anyone to not having sexual knowledge, she realized, but the crossing for a blind woman had a greater and more enduring significance: the taking on of maternal responsibility and the possibility of bringing children into the world they could see and she could not.

Then there was the reality of learning to function as a wife, of making Curt proud of her. In her mind's eye, permanent and unchanged as her family, was her last memory of herself: stick thin with a gangling body, too large gray eyes—not the prized blue like Parker's that would make her hair more interesting, or even a sparkling saucy brown like Jolene Llowell's, but verdigris: somewhere between a muddy green and a battleship gray. Cat's eyes. Sage.

Her nose was okay, but she had an ordinary mouth and, the final indignity, braces wired around half her teeth. The braces were long gone, thank God, and she had gained breasts, but they were not large and she often went without a bra. Despite assurances from her father that she was beautiful—which didn't count and, if anything, his insistence added to her uncertainty —the immutable images remained.

She was one of the "then" portraits, and endless examinations of her features gave no peace and no indication as to why Curtis Baylor would fall in love with her.

Boys hadn't been interested before the accident, and since she'd recovered, she hadn't had much experience. Not knowing the why of interest from young men had only fueled her suspicion that her father's wealth made her attractive, and little else. Certainly it was Alice Faye's opinion, written in her voice and sometimes none-too-subtle comments.

Leanna wasn't a fool: she hadn't been beautiful before the accident, and she wasn't beautiful now; but Curt's interest had come before his knowledge that she was blind. She had examined his attentions at great length and she was sure of it. Since it was no longer possible to verify with a look whether someone was honest or fooling, or wise, or shy, she'd relied on his voice and his willingness to reveal himself. They'd met at the Soda Shoppe in Walden City. All the village streets had been paved by hand during the Depression with old-fashioned bricks; their worn, lumpy surfaces made it easy to count her way whenever she crossed, and she hadn't been using the telltale stick. She'd left Thumper at the hitching rail and waited for Art to pack her a quart of strawberry ice cream. Curt had stopped her at the door to introduce himself as a fellow rider and a transfer student from Texas, a chemistry major at Traxx University. He followed her to the rail to ask permission to accompany her home so they could get better acquainted. Riding side by side, serious one moment, joking the next, they were nearly home before he finally asked her out. She put off any response, prolonging her joy at his attention.

Eventually they reached the house, where he met Alice Faye, who bluntly told him that it was pointless to take Leanna to a movie because she was blind. She cringed inside, desperate to see his reaction. It turned out he was surprised but not put off, and he didn't retract the invitation. He took her to a concert instead. And asked her out again.

Word had sort of gotten around since then, and other boys had stopped calling. But Curt had stayed, surprising her with thoughtful gifts, pacing her as she swam in the pool, patiently describing television shows and rental movies. They'd never had a cross word or a misunderstanding, and she'd become comfortable with him where her blindness was concerned. She had a sense of his strength, in body and in decision, and she was no longer self-conscious in his presence. When she reached out, he was always there.

During the summer, her feelings about him had evolved to something a great deal more complicated, and sometimes the liquid black of her life was close to being more than she could stand. To never know at a glance if he was smiling or thoughtful, to never be aware if he was following her with his eyes, looking at her, to never be able to guess at what he was thinking or feeling. If she could just see his face, she would know so much more, she was sure of it. She fingered the ring and the diamond's sculptured surface and fought a tide of confusion. Had she made the right choice?

He'd convinced her that lacking sight was truly unimportant to him. Whenever her doubts came to the surface, he inevitably answered her requests for assurance with the same response. "If you could see how messed up the world is, you wouldn't consider sight so important." His opinion had never wavered, she reasoned, and began to relax. If Curt could take it on faith that she could be a good wife, it must be so. After all, he could see and had all of life's choices.

He had asked for her hand in marriage. Wasn't that testimony to his belief in her? To enter, with her, into a mutual promise to love, honor, and protect one another. Her father had placed his blessing on their union. His response had been of crucial importance; if anyone in her life was protective, it was her father, and he had been happy for her. Alice Faye had never made a secret of her distrust of Curt, but her father's reaction outweighed her stepmother's suspicion. And Parker's hug and immediate congratulations had been sincere; he'd been openly happy for her, too.

Maybe it was all about sex after all, and the fact that she was largely ignorant of the sorts of intimacies marriage would call forth. If she just had some sort of proof, some assurance, some *something* to assuage her suspicion that not having sight had taken away an ability to be passionate and responsive like other women.

His cryptic comment rose again in her mind. "Let's not promise what can't be delivered." What was it that Curt had accepted that couldn't happen?

5

A promise is a promise . . .

Wig securely in place, Annie hummed contentedly along with Paul Simon. Thank goodness for oldies stations. The shouting cadence of hip-hop rap just didn't have the right rhythm. After energetically whopping half a dozen eggs into milk and buckwheat in her mixing bowl, she paused to turn up the gas under a cast-iron griddle. Then she moved to an ancient skillet to shake up a dozen sausages before picking up her wooden spoon to catch up with Julio and Mama Pajama. Things would get started soon. Jay was home.

The coffeepot blurbled its last bit of water through fresh-ground coffee and completed its morning assignment with a long steamy sigh. Tommy Sprengsten tapped on her back door and screeched through the screen into her kitchen. Annie gave him a smacking kiss on the cheek as he eyed her activity.

"Pancakes," he said approvingly. "Obviously I've done something wonderful to deserve pancakes. And whatever it is, I promise to do it again." He tossed a *Bowmont Herald* onto the kitchen table. "You making real syrup?"

"I thought you Zen types didn't eat all this sugar and carbohydrate stuff," she teased. "What happened to pure water and raw carrots?" She added another dollop of milk to the mixture and beat it some more.

"Water, yes, but I can be bribed," replied the fair-haired seventeen-year-old, exhibiting his father's charm. "It is a bribe, right? You've got some rotten job you want to soften me up for. And I'm the guy with a brother just dying to do it."

Annie let the batter rest long enough to select a handful of knives and forks from a drawer and a stack of Melmac from the cupboard. "Here. Make yourself useful as well as ornamental. You got all Sam Bowmont's papers delivered already?" Tina Turner was revving up on "Proud Mary," and Annie started whopping again.

"Yep. And, his personal *Wall Street Journal*." He placed two of the plates on her kitchen table. "You want all these?"

"All of 'em." Annie's face didn't give him a clue.

"And his *New Yawk Times*," he drawled. "I guess he gets a kick out of reading his competition." He opened the paper and sat down to thumb through to one of the pages. "It's in the *Herald* this morning."

Annie paused to read the ad. Then, over his shoulder, she watched Jay pad toward the kitchen, barefoot. "Well, I got a surprise for you, too, honeycakes."

"You heard from old man Hartford," Tommy teased hopefully.

Jay sauntered past and casually gave Annie a kiss. "What about old man Hartford?"

Tommy leaped up and grabbed his brother, joyously

pounding him on the back. "Hey, no wonder she's makin' pancakes! She never makes pancakes for poor little me." He dodged Annie's swipe at this outrageous lie and beamed at his older brother. "You're out. We gotta have a party."

Jay poured himself a cup of coffee. "We can't afford a party."

"So, we'll have a cheap party."

A sleepy Charlie, followed by Stephen, came through the screen door. She yawned greetings, eyes on Jay, and headed for the counter to get the carton of milk.

Containing his shock at Charlie's hair and honoring Stephen's quiet signal not to mention it, Tommy was suspicious. "You guys look like you already had your party. What am I, the last to know?"

Annie skated a spoonful of oil around the hot surface of her griddle and poured the first pancakes. Stephen automatically took over frying the sausages.

Charlie added milk to Jay's coffee and barnacled herself against him. "You talk to Danni yet? She has a ballet class at seven-thirty," she warned.

Tommy grabbed the phone. "Like Danni's going to care if we get her out of bed."

When the telephone rang, Jessica Sprengsten was annoyed. A call this early could only be trouble, and it was probably about Charlene. The girl had been gone nearly thirty-six hours, and Danni was upset to the point where she was barely sleeping. "Hello, Tommy," she said shortly.

Danni abandoned her cereal and approached the phone hopefully, annoying Jessica further; the child should be allowed to eat her breakfast in peace. The tiny little girl looked up at her, waiting in solemn anticipation.

"Is Danni up?" Tommy's voice was neutral.

"Who wants to talk to her?" Jessica was in no mood for games, and if it was Charlene, she would first apologize and explain her absence.

"Jay got home last night and he wants to surprise her."

A tide of dread spread through her body. "Why didn't he call when he got in?" she stalled, fighting for a moment to think. But it was too late. She saw the change in Danni's face, and the little girl began to dance in expectation.

Jay came on the phone. "Hello, Aunt Jessica, how are you? Can I talk to Danni, please?"

Jessica's jaw tightened in resignation. "Of course, Jay, she's right here."

Danni grabbed the receiver. "Jay? Are you home?"

Excitement lifted the little girl's voice, and Jay's heart sang. "I'm sitting right here in Annie's kitchen, Danni-bug, and I'm getting ready to come see you. You gonna wait till I get there?"

"Sure! Are you coming now?"

"Charlie says you have dance class."

"I won't go today. Is Charlie okay?"

"She's fine."

"You coming right now?"

"Give me ten minutes to eat some of Annie's pancakes?"

"Okay. I'll be waiting. I'll be here. Aunt Jess wants to talk. I'm going to change, bye. I love you, bye."

Jessica Sprengsten took the telephone. It was starting already. Her meager budget was strained to the hilt, and the sole luxury she allowed in her life was

Danielle's ballet class. Wellington's budding young dancers were confined to waiting lists for months to enter Dolly West's classes, but Dolly had agreed to take Danielle as soon as she'd seen the little girl dance, and Jessica had been overjoyed. The only sessions she'd missed had been due to a bout of chicken pox two years ago. Now, without warning, today's class would go by the boards, and it would have to be paid for. She sighed, angry and impatient. Jay hadn't been due for another week.

"I'm sorry I didn't let you know sooner, but it was too late last night."

"I appreciate that, at least. About Charlene . . ."

"I'll be over to get Danni in a half an hour. Charlie's here at Annie's, and I'll be bringing her with me. I hope that won't be a problem."

"Well, actually, Jay, it is a problem." She took a deep breath and bit the bullet, speaking carefully in front of Danielle. The little girl had already skinned out of her leotard and was standing in her underwear, eating her breakfast as rapidly as possible. "It's something we have to discuss, and the sooner the better."

"Surely it can wait till I see Danni."

"Certainly." Angered that she had handled it badly, Jessica cut the connection before he could respond.

In Annie's kitchen, Jay said good-bye to a dial tone. Not a good sign. A confrontation with his aunt had been brewing for at least two years, but he didn't want it today. This was Danni's day, and just talking with his little sister made him miss her so much that he could hardly stand it. He caught up with Tommy's conversation with Annie.

"I think you ought to call her. Jay's home now and we can move on this."

Annie plunked a platter heaped with pancakes onto the table. She watched the boys and Charlie spear them onto their plates and pass around her homemade syrup; Stephen brought the sausages to the table, seated himself, and took the last two pancakes. The kid was gaunt and at that age when a dozen wouldn't fill him up, but she couldn't remember the last time he'd asked for more. She moved to the stove and began pouring batter.

"Darlin', I told Iris I had a buyer for the old Hartford place and not to sell it until we had a chance to talk to her," she said.

Jay was confused. "That place has been boarded up for years. What about it?"

"We were saving it for a surprise." Tommy spoke around a mouthful of syrup and pancake. "Apparently Alan Hartford's decided to sell it now his grandmother's dead."

"Iris Cox works for the real estate agent, and she called a few weeks back to let me know it was going on the market," Annie filled in.

"The ad came out in the *Herald* today. Annie says we can afford it." Tommy waited expectantly.

"You're kidding. There's no land to speak of, but it does border the Bowmont lake. That old place must have at least six bedrooms in it." Jay was beginning to get excited.

"Nine," from Stephen. "Plus servants', Charlie and I checked it out."

Charlie put down her fork to count on her fingers. "You, Tommy, Stephen, me, Danni, and Annie makes six. And one for Dad when he comes home." She sneaked a look at Jay from the corner of her eye.

"We'd have three bedrooms and the servants' quarters to rent out to boarders." Annie spoke over the lull created by mention of their missing parent; Jay had been known to go ballistic over comments about his father, but this time he let it pass.

Jay drained the blue mug. "Nine bedrooms, plus servants' quarters?" His inherent caution kicked in from their silence. An old house that size ought to be slow moving in the current economy even with the lake frontage. Something about their behavior didn't jibe. "What's the catch?"

Everyone waited that one out. There was a catch, and it was a great big one. Finally Annie fielded his question. "We just have to convince Mr. Hartford to carry half the paper and let us buy it instead of selling it to Bowmont properties."

"Got any other mountains you want moved this morning?" he said good-naturedly.

"No, just that one." Annie was serious. "You don't know 'til you try."

"I'm going to go see Danni." First things first in the real world. "Come on, Charlie, let's not keep her waiting." The two of them disappeared out the door.

"What do you really think, Annie? We have a shot?" Tommy drew a glass of water and paced the kitchen, too intent on his hopes to drink it. "If he's got enough severance, you think old man Hartford'll take the deal?"

"Lord, I don't know, Tommy. We got as much chance as anybody, I guess."

Stephen's quiet voice was barely audible as she pushed more pancakes onto his plate and added the last of the sausage. "We can't outbid Bowmont." He looked steadily at Annie, having said what they all knew was true. "But Bowmont can't buy everything." He bowed his head and dug into his pancakes.

*   *   *

At Jessica Sprengsten's immaculate apartment, Danni, now T-shirted and jeaned, opened the door with a shriek of joy and was swooped up in her brother's arms so she could smother him with eight-year-old kisses. The little girl was incandescent, and Jessica's heart tightened with resentment. After four years of caring for her, loving her, Danielle had never greeted her with such love. It wasn't fair.

When her excitement reached manageable proportion, Jay slid Danni onto his hip and carried her around the apartment while she clung to him for dear life. She was small for her age, closer to the size of a six-year-old. Charlie came in to sit quietly on the sofa, refusing to meet her Aunt Jessica's glance. "You look weird, Charlie," was Danni's sole reaction to her sister's butchered hair. Charlie stonewalled it for a few more moments, then escaped to their room.

Jessica Sprengsten was horrified at Charlie's drastic solution to their impasse. "She brought it on herself," she justified to Jay. "There was simply no reason to do such a thing. It could have grown out or Charlene could have paid for it from her own money. Either way she has, hopefully, learned a lesson from the experience."

If anything, it was more proof that the girl was impossible. She could not contain her frustration. "It's just too much, Jay. First it was wearing boys' clothing. She absolutely insists in spite of anything I say. I take them away from her, and she gets more somewhere else. What she's done to her hair is appalling. Now she's running away again, the hoarding . . . It's just too much. She's becoming incorrigible, and I won't have it. She upsets Danielle's life, and mine, without any consideration."

Jay stooped to put Danni's reluctant feet on the floor. "I want to talk to Aunt Jess," he told her. "Go see Charlie." The little girl fled the room, and he turned abruptly to his father's sister. "I thought this could wait, but apparently it can't. I know it hasn't been easy, Aunt Jess, but it hasn't been easy on them, either. I'll have a job with Milbrook starting next week, and I'll take them off your hands as soon as I can."

Jessica plunged into an appeal. "Leave Danielle with me. Please, she's—"

"No way." He walked out the doorway and into the hall.

"Jay, be reasonable. She's still a little girl, she needs a mother."

"Mom's dead and she knows it. What she needs is a family."

"I won't fight about this. But I will tell you that if I have the slightest suspicion that leaving me is not in her best interests, I'll . . ."

Jay was surprised at her unusual outburst and tried to head her off. "Aunt Jessica, I know how much you love her."

Undeterred, Jessica Sprengsten burned all bridges. "I'll move for custody. She's my brother's child, and I have rights."

He stared at her, frozen. Would she do that? Could she? Certainly she was determined enough to try. He searched for a diplomatic answer to defuse the situation. "I know you love her," he repeated. "We all do. And you know, when you think about it, that I wouldn't do anything to hurt her." He moved toward the door to the street. "Now, before this gets out of hand, just give me a chance to prove to you that living with us will be good for her." As much as it galled him, he invoked the name of his father. "I think even Dad would want that."

The mention struck home, and Jessica paled. "It's just that I've tried so hard."

"I know you have. Now let me try for a little while."

Peace relatively restored, Jay sent his voice down the hall to his sisters. "Hey. Who's up for ice cream?" He listened to the scrambled replies and the pounding of little girl feet.

Jessica's maternal instincts contracted once again. "Jay, really. It's not even eight o'clock in the morning." Then she gave up. "Oh, never mind. Just have her home by bedtime. Please?" It was a double plea: her, not them.

Jay cringed for Charlie. "I promise."

6

Promise of a lifetime . . .

  Curt Baylor's alarm clock ticked stolidly on and passed ten o'clock. He was sleeping late in celebration, dozing luxuriously and reliving the satisfaction of his engagement to Leanna Faith Bowmont, richest little girl in Walden City. He chuckled to himself. Life was clockwork. It was all a matter of timing.

  The ring had worked like a breeze, and no one could even suspect that he'd extracted it six months ago from a lowlife named Mickey Scolari. It had proven a wise decision; Mickey had checked out on a payload of horse tranquilizer, still owing the balance of the money, and now the ring was circling Leanna Bowmont's finger.

  Of course, he'd had it appraised and hadn't been surprised that a mediocre diamond had at some point replaced the original stone, but the setting was platinum and expensive. It had gotten by Leanna's stepmother, one of the rich witches of the world. He'd financed a new diamond, using the proceeds from his last deal, and the carat weight was just respectable enough, he judged—not large enough to be anxious or showy, not too small for a rich man's daughter.

He'd purchased it at the wholesale mart in Chicago last week with the full understanding that the stone was returnable. It was written on the receipt. If she didn't go through with the marriage, Leanna wasn't the type to keep the ring; women with money had a different set of rules.

The telephone rang its way into his delicious morning, and he answered it with unaccustomed charm to discover he was talking to Christie Scott. She was based in Chicago but spent her layovers in Wellington and, thanks to his vigorous appreciation of her body, usually in his bed. "Is this the lively, lovely Christie, airline stew from Mississippi, getting me up this morning?"

She laughed in his ear. "Oh, hi, Curt, honey, I'm sorry to wake you, but I have a run to Houston this morning and didn't want to miss you, you-all want to go see a play in two weeks? I just got tickets from a friend of mine, she cain't go."

Christie was Dallas cheerleader material who ran all her sentences together and was just flaky enough to be really interesting in bed. He had a morning hard-on and didn't give a shit about a play. "Where are you?"

"Chicago. Two weeks from tomorrow night, you want to go?"

Hell, Chicago didn't do him any good this morning. He rolled over, considering. He'd probably be making a delivery there in a couple of weeks and he could always bail out on her if something better came along—like dinner at the Bowmonts.

"What's the date?" he said, bored already with the idea. He circled a Saturday on his wall calendar with a red pen. Christie was red, Bowmont was blue. "I'll take you to dinner, too, as long as you're dessert," he said lazily. She laughed, and he hung up the phone. A couple of minutes later he hit the head and relieved himself, then turned on the shower.

Things weren't all that bad for Wendy Baylor's little boy from Aberdeen. "Smart." He grinned at his image in the mirror. "Handsome, ambitious, you got a big future, boy. Sam Bowmont's approved choice for his little girl. Tom Cruise got nothin' on you."

In the year he had courted the future Mrs. Baylor, he'd scrupulously kept their relationship out of the bedroom; he'd scoped Samuel Bowmont in a hot instant and realized he couldn't threaten the daughter in any way or the old man would toss him out quick as a tick on a prize dog. The brother he'd ignored: a snotty rich kid with too much weight being piled on by his mother. Parker wouldn't be a problem. Once the I do's went on record, he could be handled.

The dragon lady was a whole other story. Sexy Mrs. Bowmont thought she had his number. She'd trotted out all her whooptee-do necklines and string bikinis on that overexercised body all summer and was waiting for him to trip over his dick. But he was biding his time. Greed, sexual or otherwise, never paid off.

He hadn't successfully worked his way to an engagement by staying out of Leanna's rich little underwear for nothing, and he knew he could take her to bed whenever he wanted. She was ready. When she'd gotten all hot and bothered the night of her birthday, he knew it was time to pop the question. He could have had her right there in the stable if he'd wanted to. But he'd played it smart. He'd come much too far to get caught in a pile of hay with his pants down.

As soon as they were married, getting her pregnant

with Bowmont's grandchild would be the absolute first order of business: a nanny for the kid, a housekeeper to see to the details of everyday life, and a driver for Leanna, maybe a cook. Bowmont money was going to deliver it all. Life was going to give him everything he'd ever wanted, plus a few things he hadn't thought of yet.

And he had been faithful to her by keeping himself satisfied with the fresh little stew, who was not only accommodating sexually, but content with an open relationship. He'd probably eliminate that situation once he'd said "I do"—assuming his rich wife wasn't terrible in bed. A virgin bride would certainly be a novelty in this day and age. No threat of AIDS, at the very least, and he could arrange his sex life with her any way he wanted it, which had fascinating possibilities.

He might even learn to love her; for the chunk of Bowmont money he anticipated, he'd learn to love her a lot. And, come to think of it, now that the engagement was public, getting her pregnant would sure hurry up a wedding—maybe the best way to go. Hell, he'd always wanted a kid. He stepped into the shower to give it some thought.

Alice Faye, cool and elegant in the sultry morning heat, launched her campaign over brunch. "What do you think of the sudden engagement?"

"I think it's terrific." Parker's scanner where his mother was concerned began burping out warning signals. "Since when do you care what happens with Leanna?"

"I care a great deal about Sam's daughter. If it happens, it's going to put a new player in our midst. A very ambitious one." Alice Faye reached for a slice of dry toast. "Is she sleeping with him?"

He ignored the question. "Dad's probably checked him out seven ways from Sunday. If she loves him, what makes the difference?" Uncomfortable, he drank a small glass of tomato juice. He wasn't too hot on the guy, but it was Leanna's decision, not his. And certainly not Alice Faye's.

His mother reached for the crystal juice pitcher and refilled his glass. "Next thing you know, you'll be an uncle," she said pointedly.

He drained the second glass, and she refilled it again. It was going to be another one of her money and responsibility lectures. "So what's wrong with that?"

"I'll tell you what's wrong with that. Your father's not going to live forever, and if Curt moves in on him the way he moved in on your blind little stepsister . . ."

"I prefer sister," he said automatically. "Leanna's my sister." It was an ongoing battle between them and one he occasionally won.

Alice Faye barely paused. "All it's going to take from your *sister* is one grandchild. And you can bet it will arrive with the speed of light. So stop ducking the question. Is she sleeping with him or not?"

"Not as far as I know. Give her a little credit, she's not about to—"

"Of course she is. Are you still seeing that Llowell girl? What's her name?"

"Jolene."

"Lovely girl. Just how serious is your relationship?"

"We're not approaching marriage, if that's what you're pushing with the tomato juice."

"Don't be surly with me, young man. I'm just pushing a few facts of life, and I don't appreciate your attitude. I love your father dearly, but he's a businessman first, a family man second. Businessmen look for successors.

And successors," Alice Faye imparted coldly, "plan ahead. I assure you, my dear, that Curt Baylor is planning ahead while you're sitting here giving me a smart mouth. You think about that."

His mother stalked off the patio.

Parker sighed. How his father held his own with her escaped him. They never appeared to fight, and she inevitably wound up with everything she wanted; being her son had given him no special privilege in coping with her iron will and unsparing determination. As a child, he'd lost sight of the number of people employed in their home, as over the years, one by one, they'd thrown up their hands rather than deal with her. He estimated there must have been at least five a year for the past ten years, and who knew how many before that. When he was younger, she'd been in and out of his life like a yo-yo, coming home long enough to remove the latest group of people hired to take care of him and Leanna.

Until he was twelve, Leanna had been a surety and a constant, acting as buffer between him and his mother. But after her accident, he had reversed his role to become protector to his sister, to be the invariable in her life and the one person who was aware of the fear she would not show to anyone else.

Since he could remember, and never in front of his father, Alice Faye had insisted on his being prepared for dual oncoming responsibilities: his family's wealth and the long-term care of Leanna. He'd been shoe-horned into a fancy prep school to prepare for a business major at Traxx University. While he agreed with it in principle, the first year, with the dullest of subjects—math, management, and accounting—and Alice Faye's incessant warning shots about gold diggers, had so overwhelmed him that the freedom of being young and rich and good-looking had all but disappeared. Then he'd come home and started getting it on with sexy Jolene Llowell, and they'd been steady for the past couple of years.

Jolene's being the daughter of prominent Dr. Carter Llowell had evidently satisfied enough of his mother's social register requirements to be acceptable as his girl-friend; with the advent of Leanna's marriage to Curt, she had suddenly been elevated to prospective daugh-ter-in-law. Alice Faye must be really shook over this Curt guy.

There was no reason to consider marriage to Jolene; he wasn't ready to get married, and kids were totally out of the question. They'd made love all night last night, and he could not conjure up Jolene's saucy tits and cute round ass, not to mention that smooth, firm tummy, all swollen out of shape with a baby. Not Jolene, who insisted on putting a rubber on him before she'd let him inside, let alone come. He was getting hard just thinking about her.

He looked at his watch. Jolene liked a morning swim and he liked doing it in the pool; there, he could deal with Hartford's broker without Alice Faye standing over him. He decided that his mother would just have to adapt and he would have to trust his father, because he was going swimming.

An hour later he was sitting nude in the Llowell pool house, on the phone with Hartford's real estate agent checking a couple of details and watching Jolene's pert nipples point skyward as she sighed and lifted her hair off the back of her neck. They'd done it once in the pool, and he knew she was hinting to go upstairs to the icy cool, air-conditioned pleasure of her bedroom. He couldn't deny that it was too humid to be outside, even stark naked under the pool umbrellas.

The radio said thunderstorms were due, and he hoped the weather would hurry up and break. It had gotten so breathless in the last hour that it was too sticky to make love anywhere except in the pool. Jolene stooped behind his chair and reached around into his lap. The agent came back on the line and gave him the information. "The offer's contingent on a September closing," he insisted.

As he talked, Jolene put her fingers in motion; ordinarily, it never took long for her to take his attention away from business, but this was important, so he stopped her hand. "Fine. The acreage borders the shoreline of our lake, so you understand I'll want the opportunity to match any offers on the place."

The purchase of the Hartford property was the first matter in which Sam had given him total authority, and he was determined not to disappoint his father. "I'll expect to hear from you by the first of next week."

He kissed Jolene's fingers and released her hand, hung up the phone, and tweaked her nipples in encouragement. She could get him hard incredibly fast, and he opened his thighs to give her better access. One of the things he liked most about her was that she never seemed to get enough sex. "It's a huge old barn of a place." She was doing it right, and he could feel the surging ache as he stiffened under her fingers. "The value's in the frontage." He matched her motion for motion, turning her on the way he was getting turned on.

"Yes," she countered. "The frontage." He stood and she stood, and they walked in dense heat: he was rock hard when she put the rubber on him, and they got into the water to make use of the shallow end of the pool.

7

I promise you this . . .

"*I know it's complicated,* Iris, but Alan Hartford don't need the money and it's just possible he'll find it interesting enough to accept. . . . Well, let me know what he says." Annie replaced the receiver and heaved a sigh in the heat. Dog days just about wore her out.

"With a down payment this low, it's going to take an act of Congress to compete with Bowmont Properties." Jay saw her disapproving face. "I know," he said. "Don't roll over 'til it's over." He gave her a sticky hug on his way to her kitchen. "I start at Milbrook on Monday. Once I'm employed maybe the bank'll tilt sideways and give me a loan, you never know."

Annie followed him, her mind no longer on the Hartford property but on the letter in the bottom drawer of the TV cabinet. Sooner or later it would have to come out. She poured coffee over two glasses of ice and satisfied herself one last time of Jay's determination. "Once it's done, honey, you're gonna uproot five other people and take on an enormous responsibility for someone your age. Your mother would understand if you decide it's too much to handle."

He stopped her. "Not up for discussion. I promised Mom." He shifted toward her on his chair. "Annie, I was stationed in countries where people have less than nothing. Men and women walk around in rags in order to feed their kids. And you know what I learned? I learned that life doesn't owe me anything. It's up to me to make something out of it."

He drifted impatiently toward the window and looked out. "Besides, you don't walk away from your word. That's who you are. If I left Tom and Stevie in foster homes so I could go to law school, I'd hate myself. I wouldn't last five minutes. They're my family, you and Charlie and Danni, Aunt Jess—we're all family, and that's what's important." He rejoined her at the table and sipped the iced coffee, savoring its cold. "What about you? Are you having second thoughts?"

"Not on your life, cutie. I been waiting on this for a long time. Been reading up on it and everything. We got to get certified and insured and approved by the state as a bed and breakfast. The papers're all waiting. We just need the house."

"Well, if we don't get this one, we'll get one just like it."

"Have you talked to Jolene?" she asked, watching him carefully. "Living with your brothers and sisters don't strike me as something that'll fit in her life."

"Jolene isn't a factor, Annie. There's nothing I can offer now that's any different from the last time I saw her. She promised to wait, she didn't. I don't want to open that particular door in my life again. I don't need any losses right now. None of us do."

Satisfied he was set on it, Annie let it go. One thing for sure, the letter in the cabinet was a definite loss. Right now, the boy's family was his priority, as it should be. The letter would wait. It would be hard upsetting him with what she knew, and that would come soon enough. If there was any justice, Alan Hartford would at least consider their offer. She got up to make a fresh pot of coffee.

Despite his intentions, talk of Jolene inevitably pulled Jay into the past. From the moment his father had learned of his mother's death, Jim Sprengsten had given up and begun to go away. He wondered if he'd been too young at the time, in too much pain, to see that it was a prelude to his father's departure from their lives or if, as he remembered, there'd been no outward sign. Looking back, he decided it was probably both.

After Mom's funeral, it had been left to him and Annie to organize the rest of the kids, make sure food was purchased, meals prepared, get everyone to school. He had shared his grief with her and his brothers and sisters, but his father had been out of reach.

When his dad disappeared, Jolene's support began to waver. He hadn't seen the scope, not then. But he'd had a lot of time since to reflect—too much time, maybe. He'd been so consumed with the void created by the loss of his parents that half the hours he'd spent with her he'd been on the borderline of exhaustion, unable to concentrate on her or their future together. Too tired to make love.

There'd just been the two awful empty places at the table, the lack of their voices, the nonpresence, the gone-ness of his mother and father, that couldn't be conveyed. That and the unconscious searching, the hours he'd spent scanning each face in a crowd, arguing with the police that his dad could never have walked away, fighting the fear that something had happened to him. Endless time. It became second nature to assess the backs of men's heads, double-check the workers at construction sites, deal with the ever-present awareness of men his father's age or build, in any city, even overseas. He caught himself doing it occasionally to this day.

When his dad had been gone eleven weeks, the police notified him that the family car had been located in Chicago. The description of the seller had fit his father; a few days later the pink slip for the battered old truck and a cashier's check in the amount of two thousand dollars had arrived in the mail. There was no letter, no note of explanation, just the Chicago postmark. The message was clear: Jim Sprengsten wasn't coming back. Finally, he and Aunt Jessica inventoried the family cash and possessions. Net revenue, including the income from yard sales disposing of everything they couldn't use, was a little over four thousand dollars, and the truck.

The costs of his mother's funeral and immediate debts wiped out a meager life insurance policy, and the money drained away. At seventeen he couldn't earn enough to support himself, let alone four other people, and had been forced to accept that he couldn't keep the family together.

Inquiries about public assistance sealed the decision. Their assets were below the necessary minimum. It would be foster homes for all of them until he could support the family. He knew that it was only a matter of

time before some public agency or other would be in
their lives, and after an agonizing examination of the
options and many cups of coffee with Annie, he decided
to join the army, complete his education, and be out in
four years with a job skill. His brothers would go into
foster homes, stay in school, and if something happened
to him, they'd have to be ready to take over. Aunt
Jessica would keep the girls.

He and Jolene had shared one final, wonderful night
together at the bluff, then he'd gotten on the train.
She'd written once during the first two months, once
again in the next three, and then there had been a long,
long silence. Early in his second year, on a precious, last
minute leave before being shipped overseas, he waited
an eternal two hours for some jock to bring her home
from a date after a football game. He'd grown up in a
hurry that summer.

They'd gone to a motel, but for him it had been little more than physical relief, angry sex mixed with
ambivalence and frustration with one eye on the
clock; but worse, not making love the way he'd
dreamed, the way he'd needed to keep his hope alive.
She'd driven him to the airport in her new convertible, promising that she'd wait for him, promising that
she'd be there when he got home next time—just to
let her know.

He knew when he kissed her good-bye that it was
over. There'd been no correspondence from that time,
and he hadn't been surprised when a letter from
Tommy a few months later confirmed that she and
Bowmont were a couple. He had long since added the
loss of Jolene Llowell to his rage against his father.

It was too hot to sit and dwell on the past. He got up
to go for a walk.

°   °   °

George didn't return his nod, and Stephen saw that the blacksmith's face was twisted in pain; he stepped inside the farrier's shed and laid his shirt across a stall partition, then changed his mind when the Belgian yearling named Gondolf reached over to inspect the intrusive item with his teeth. The black gelding, already bigger than a full-grown quarterhorse, had been known to take a bite out of anything he didn't approve of in his stall.

"This'n's memorable," mumbled George through clenched jaws. "Leanna Bowmont's bringing her mare. Loose shoe. You fix it. Don't do nothin' else." He stopped for a moment to allow the pain from his broken tooth to subside. "She's blind, so don't move anythin'. Does just fine 'nless you put somethin' in her way. See you don't embarrass her."

George stalked off to the hated dentist's while Stephen looked around the shop at the disarray. He debated about moving the tackle hanging down from the eave, but George had been clear in his warning, so he left things as they were.

Outside, he heard the *kling* of metal shoes on the bricked street. He looked out to see a young woman riding bareback in worn blue jeans and a bright yellow T-shirt; her horse, an old palomino mare, brushed and in fine condition, stopped at George's hitching rail. Even without makeup the girl was pretty, with a great, lean, twentysomething body that gave his hormones a rush.

He put on the shirt and tried not to stare. "Leanna? I'm Stephen. George's at the dentist. Said you had a loose shoe."

She slid without hesitation off the horse's back onto the sidewalk. "It's so hot, I almost didn't come."

The old mare stood alert and obedient while she lifted its left foreleg, then ran a finger around the edge of the hoof to point out the problem. The frog was clean, and there was no need to pare. It would be a simple matter of renailing the shoe, and he told her what he planned to do.

The girl led the horse confidently up the ramp and into the shop, ducking automatically under the tackle dangling from the eave. Prepared to guide her, Stephen watched in amazement as she negotiated the horse into position and fearlessly put out her hand to pat the Belgian yearling.

Leanna held Thumper's bridle and concentrated on defining this person, Stephen; she was certain George had warned him she was blind. Too bad. She hated people knowing before she met them. The aroma of well-oiled harness mixed with the dry, waxy smell of fresh straw and a pungent odor of fresh manure emanated from Gondolf's stall into the silence. She listened to the dull clack of a hammer against the metal shoe while her curiosity worked on her. "Are you a student?"

"And handyman. My family owns Traxx Jobbing."

"Really." She'd never heard of them. "You do repair work? Like that?"

"Roofing, painting, just about anything."

She stood at Thumper's head, pondering. He wasn't asking the usual awkward questions; maybe he didn't know. The voice was young, sixteen or seventeen, and came at her from about her own height; he was slight because Thumper was very close to Gondolf's stall, and he hadn't shifted the mare to make more room for himself to nail the shoe in place. She heard him circle the horse, checking the rest of the shoes. "They should be okay," she said.

Stephen was suddenly aware that she'd been monitoring his movements around the horse. "They're fine," he confirmed.

"We're painting our stables in a few days, and Thumper kicked a couple of boards out of her stall. Why don't you come over later and give me an estimate?"

Stephen stood ready, but it wasn't necessary to help her back the horse down the ramp. It was apparent the animal would have allowed her to walk it into fire, the trust between them was so complete. He waited in the doorway while she stepped carefully onto a small wooden bench and slid with ease onto the mare's back once again. Even his unpracticed eye could see that the animal was grayed and aging, but it stood, ears alert, waiting for the girl's signal.

"I'll see you in a couple of hours." She gave him the address and urged the mare into a lazy canter, heading toward Main Street, her body moving in perfect rhythm with the horse's rocking gait.

Turning back to the shed, he closed his eyes and tied a rag into a blindfold around his head; he tried to remember the layout of the workroom and succeeded in walking up the ramp, but one of the hanging bridles rapped him in the forehead; he ducked instinctively and banged his arm into Gondolf's partition. The startled gelding whickered in complaint and made a grab for the rag with its teeth. Stephen elevated his estimation of the girl's ability. She obviously hadn't been to the shop in months and had remembered every obstacle.

He stopped by the Bowmont estate on his way home, and Leanna answered the door. She accompanied him to the stables to show him Thumper's stall and the damage, walking as confidently as a sighted person. He gave her a quote and a completion date and bicycled to Annie's for dinner.

After Stephen left, Leanna found her brother in the study. "Before I forget," she said, "I just arranged for someone to do the work on Thumper's stall. His name is Stephen Traxx. Traxx Jobbing. Will you tell the painters to keep the stall till last?"

He agreed, and she hesitated. "Park, can I talk to you for a few minutes? It's about me. And Curt."

His voice thickened, suspicion coating every word. "What's going on?"

"Why don't you like him?" she bridled. "I thought you'd changed your mind about him, but you haven't, have you? What is it?" She knew by his silence that he was searching for an adequate answer.

"Probably that he's not good enough for you. I doubt if anyone would be, I guess. Ever the protective brother." His voice was joking, but he was serious. "I just want the best for you, and I'm not sure he's it, that's all."

The assessment hurt. "I think he's very good for me." She could hear defensiveness in her voice and hated it.

"Yeah, well, that doesn't count. You're gonna marry him."

Parker's casual acceptance of such a profound decision in her life was painful, too.

"Is that what this is about?" He took her arm and walked her to her father's huge leather reading chair. She sat on the seat and he perched on the arm, like old times. They'd spent hours in this room, studying together, him reading text and answering her questions.

"Nothing in the rules says you can't change your mind. You know that."

She heaved a reluctant sigh, but the door was finally open and she desperately wanted to air her doubts. "Are you and Jolene thinking about getting married?"

"What is it?" her brother challenged. "Why all the sudden interest in me and Jolene?"

"It's not exactly a secret about you two." Leanna paused awkwardly, unsure how to proceed. "If you decide you want to get married, you already know about that part of your relationship and you don't have to wonder if it's going to be all right." Why was it so hard to talk about such things?

He moved off the chair's arm, and she heard his shoes scraping lightly on the carpet as he paced the study.

"Oh, God. You want to know if you should sleep with him first."

The scraping stopped at the fireplace, and his voice was dully amplified in the still air.

"I don't know, it's different with a guy, Sissie. And it's different with Jolene."

"Why?"

"It just is. Look, I wasn't the first guy with her. If Curt's your husband, then you love him and there's no reason to wonder."

"Is it really all that—" If Parker wouldn't tell her, there was no one else to ask. "I mean, some girls are a lot better at it than others, right?"

"Yeah, but mostly it's the same." She knew he was treading gently. This was delicate territory, and as much as he loved her, she knew it was hard for him to be dead honest.

"It depends on the person," he continued. "Not just

what they do or how they do it. It's really whether they
turn you on. Jolene turns me on. I just look at her and I
want to take her to bed."

"But you can see her. . . ."

He was at a loss for a moment. "Thinking about her
does the same thing," he said finally. "Just the idea of
her."

"Do you think you'll marry her?"

He was still defensive. "I don't know. We've never
talked about it."

"I'm talking about you. Have you considered it?" she
persisted.

"Look, sex can't be the determining factor in deciding about marriage. It's about whether you want to
spend your life with someone, whether you trust them
and believe in them. I've been sleeping with her for two
years and I know I like her in bed, but I still don't know
if I want to spend my life with her."

"But it will be part of making that decision?"

"Of course."

"How big a part?"

"Big, little, I don't know. Loving somebody is the
decision. Sex isn't that big a deal."

Leanna was upset. "How can sex not be a big deal?
I'm about to get married, and I'm walking around without a clue," she railed. "The one time I wanted to make
love with him, he said no. Maybe Alice Faye's right.
Maybe it's not me, maybe he is after Daddy's money."

Parker came back to her chair. "Mother is terrified of
becoming a grandmother. She's scared silly that she's
getting older, and she'd tell you he was a serial killer if
she thought it would put you off. Don't pay any attention
to her."

He stopped in frustration, and she knew he was at

the end of his ability to make clear what he himself obviously wasn't sure about. "You're the only one who can make this decision, Sissie. I wouldn't if I could. It's your life, and if you feel right about Curt, marry him."

He pulled her to her feet and gave her a gentle bear hug. "But I promise you this on my life. If you change your mind—and I don't care if it's in the middle of the church in front of God and everybody—you tell him to take a hike and I'll back you up. Don't forget it."

She smiled and hugged him back. He'd done his best. Even if it hadn't been an answer, it had helped. "I wouldn't have agreed to marry him if I thought it would come to that."

8

No promises . . .

Looking down, Jillian picked out Wellington High School and half a dozen other familiar landmarks as the small commuter plane circled for its west-to-east landing. From the air, Ohio in late summer was a patchwork: interlocking fields of dull green corn, dark green wheat, and the rich wet brown of fresh-plowed soil, sewn together with gray roads and streams and black fence rows lined with trees. After the concrete and glass pillars of New York's crush of skyscrapers, it looked wonderfully peaceful and inviting.

The connecting flight out of Cleveland had been rougher than usual, and according to the pilot, a major storm was definitely in the offing. Cathy was late, but it gave Jillian time to collect her luggage and corral it at the exit gate next to the taxi stand. Thunder muttered in the distance; the air was sultry and listless, and leaves hung motionless in the trees. Her T-shirt was damp from her efforts, and she was about to give up on her

former high school buddy when the familiar blue
Volkswagen banked toward the curb. Cathy leaped out
to give her a hug and eyed the stack of luggage. "You
moving home?"

"Maybe." Jillian popped the trunk and began tossing
suitcases into the maw of the ancient convertible.
"You've been driving this bug since you got your license.
You gonna put Nick Junior in here one of these days?"
she teased.

Cathy busied herself jamming a couple of smaller
bags behind the passenger seats. "So, how's New York?"
She looked at her watch.

"As hot as it is here," Jillian complained; she eyed the
ominous sky. "We are going to get wet."

By the time they were halfway to Walden City, angry
gray clouds were glowing here and there as bursts of
lightning streaked and danced in the sky; earsplitting
cracks assaulted their ears at shorter and shorter inter-
vals, followed by violent drumrolls of thunder. They
caught up to the weather, and conversation was punctu-
ated with the crash and rumble of an old-fashioned
thunderstorm.

"We're not getting married," Cathy announced suddenly. "It's over. He told me last week he wants to
keep it 'friendly.' I'm mostly okay about it, I guess, but
sometimes I get really down. After eight years, I don't
know what the hell he wants." She looked at her watch
again.

"Hey, I'm sorry." Jillian was at a loss. Nick and Cathy
had been steadies since the sixth grade. All their friends
had assumed they'd get married right out of high school,
but Nick's parents had insisted he go to college, and she
had stayed on as a secretary at Milbrook Construction.
Cathy had been planning her wedding as long as Jillian

could remember. "I'm really sorry," she repeated, doubly guilty about her Nick Junior remark.

"Yeah." Cathy was close to tears. "Well, hey, you know. So what's going on with you? Some guy in New York, or you still got it for Sprengsten? He's home, you know."

Jillian looked at her, her pulse gaining speed. No, she hadn't known.

"Yeah, he called my boss two days ago. He starts work on Monday." She glanced again at her watch.

They neared the bluff just outside Walden City when grape-size raindrops began to splotch the dusty windshield. Cathy stopped, and they jumped out to pull up the ragged top. Jillian saw in the valley below the graceful spire of the Walden City Community Church pointing skyward like a compass needle through the huge old trees of the surrounding village. It was her favorite view of the town. Partially hidden among the trees, the stalwart halls of Traxx University marched up the hillsides to the north, and the rest of the houses began to disappear into a murky gray-green wall of rain moving toward them through the valley.

After the initial rush of fresh, chilled wind, the rain reached the top of the hill and Jillian stood with her mouth open to receive the huge droplets, unconcerned that her hair and clothing were getting drenched. Jay was home. She would see him soon and either be washed clean of her feelings for him or be drowned in another storm. She laughed into the rain smashing her in the face and finally ducked inside the car when the thunder got too close. They stuffed the dripping holes in the canvas top with the plastic bags and paper towels that Cathy carried for the occasion, and decided to sit out the worst of the downpour.

"I saw him at the Soda Shoppe," Cathy confided, her knee bouncing up and down with a nervous rhythm. "Had his sisters with him. He's a little taller, and he's still cute. Wait 'til he sees you." She gave an exaggerated sigh. "You've really changed since you've been in New York."

"I doubt if he'll know me," Jillian responded wryly, a little embarrassed at Cathy's open acknowledgment of very private feelings; she craned her head to look into the rearview mirror at her wet, curling hair, newly lightened to blond. She'd had it weaved and permed and had to admit that she kind of liked it. Definitely a better frame for her dark brown eyes, but there seemed to be twice as much of it now that it had curl.

"It's ten times better than that dishwater brown it used to be. You think Jolene's going to stay with Parker?" Cathy checked her watch again.

Jillian shrugged her response. She genuinely had no idea. And until she saw Jay, she would have no idea if she even wanted her to. From there it was anybody's guess. To get Cathy off the subject, she pointed to a group of Guernseys calmly watching them from a small meadow. "It's going to rain all day, we may as well go."

"How do you know?"

"If cows don't seek shelter, it's going to rain a long time."

Cathy started the engine. "Yeah, well, you *look* like New York, but . . ."

Jillian skipped to the finish. "You can't take the country out of the girl. Do you have to be somewhere?"

"No, why?" Cathy stared at her.

"You've looked at your watch fourteen times. Are you meeting someone?"

"Nah, it's just habit, I guess. Nick was always late. Just a nervous habit." She got very quiet.

Rain was still pouring down when Cathy dropped Jillian under the portico in front of her parents' house. It was three o'clock, and Jolene's car wasn't in the garage. Jillian grabbed her suitcases. "Why don't you come in for a while," she invited.

"Nah—gotta get going. Got a few things to do." Cathy was fidgety. She checked her watch.

"Are you really okay about Nick?" Jillian asked carefully. "If you want to talk about it, I'm here. Any time."

Cathy laughed and gave her a bright smile. "I'm fine," she said. "Thanks. Same here if you want to talk about Jay." She wrenched gears, and the little car sped down the drive. Barely pausing at the curb, she be-beeped the horn and waved gaily as the VW charged up the street and was gone in the rain.

Jillian hung her clothes in the closet, took a quick shower, and had blown her hair dry by the time Jolene came in to sprawl across the bedspread. She openly studied Jillian's new hair color as she announced her arrangements with Parker.

"He's probably going to spend nights here, too, so don't go walking around with your clothes off unless you want to get seen," she instructed, and eased off the bed to examine a teal silk Donna Karan sweater. "Mmmmm, this is new." She draped it under her chin and looked in the mirror. "Bad color for me—too green. You wear it to work?"

Jillian watched tolerantly. This was an old game of her sister's, and Jillian was determined to remain detached.

"It's the last time we'll have before the fall semester, so we'll probably sleep in a lot. Try not to make any noise when you get up." Jolene carelessly hung the sweater back in the closet.

"Okay." Jillian fought the urge to rescue the sweater.

"He's got his own key. Don't panic if you hear some-one in the middle of the night." Jolene quickly inspected the rest of Jillian's clothes. "If you want anything special, just call Gibbs' and have it delivered. I can sign Daddy's name. Do anything for your birthday?"

"No. A couple of friends took me to dinner," she amended.

"Is that why you had the weave?" Jolene asked finally. She tossed her hair. "I've been thinking about having mine done, too, but Parker says he likes it this way." Her long honey-gold hair was styled beautifully, and she knew it. Jolene paused. "You remember Jay Sprengsten?"

Jillian heard a new note in her sister's voice. "Sure." Jolene's face was uncharacteristically thoughtful, and Jillian's heart did a slow rollover. Things where Jay was concerned were not going to be as simple as seeing him after all. "What about Parker?" she ventured. "I thought you two were pretty solid."

"We are, but that doesn't mean anything's guaran-teed. He could change his mind tomorrow. So could I."

"Does he know about Jay?"

"I don't care if he knows."

Parker's voice sounded suddenly from the hallway. "Knows what?"

Both women yelped in surprise.

A bottle of champagne was thrust through the doorway, suspended from Parker's fist. "Apologies and permission to enter?"

Jillian granted permission, somewhere between relieved and miffed. Neither she nor Jolene had heard him come up the stairs.

"Hey, Jillian." Parker kissed her cheek and settled onto the bed with the champagne. "I didn't know if you were here yet, and I was going to surprise Jolene. I promise to announce myself well in advance from now on."

"What's the champagne for?" Jolene gave him a small kiss.

"To celebrate Jillian's homecoming."

Jillian was silent. It wasn't a homecoming, yet. "I hear your sister's getting married," she said, to change the subject.

"He doesn't like the guy," observed Jolene.

"Hey, I'm not marrying him," Parker said lightly. "Maybe you one of these days . . ." He ran a finger under the spaghetti strap of Jolene's skimpy shift and traced the skin across her shoulder.

Jolene moved away, and Jillian knew she was trying to figure out how much he'd overheard. "You haven't asked me, yet."

Parker laughed and sprang off the bed. "This is getting warm. Shall we drink it now or chill it again?"

Jillian looked at Jolene. It was nearly six o'clock. "Now?"

Jolene shrugged.

Parker moved out of the room and bounced down the stairs. He hadn't meant to eavesdrop; he'd given in to a sudden attack of adolescence and was just going to make them jump. They'd been talking about Jay Sprengsten, and the subject evaporated into thin air the minute he arrived.

He was irritated with Jolene. Sprengsten was home and they were suddenly a "maybe"? The guy was a skinny, nothing nobody, as he remembered him. He wrestled with the stubborn cork and finally it popped loose from the bottle. Too warm champagne spurted onto the counter and spilled over the first glass. He grabbed a paper towel to mop it up. What the hell made her think she could put him on hold? For anybody.

She'd sworn she and Sprengsten hadn't been lovers, but he'd never bought it. Not really. Sprengsten had been stationed overseas for the past three years, so they couldn't have seen each other for at least that long. Jillian and Jolene came into the kitchen and he put the bottle into the freezer for a quick chill.

"Welcome home."

The three clinked glasses and drank.

"To your sister's marriage," offered Jillian.

"To marriage," Jolene echoed, and drained her glass, eyes on his face.

That night, he made love to her until she wouldn't let him anymore but couldn't reach his own climax. He'd gotten her there twice, and she was relaxed and totally unwound, nuzzling his chest with little moans of contentment. Hoping he could make her ready again before she went to sleep, he moved her hand between his legs to let her know he was still hard.

"Mmmmm, Jay," she mumbled. "That was the best ever." She sighed again and rolled away from him.

The pounding rain matched the roar in his mind. It was a long time before he slept.

9

Traxx promise . . .

Danni looked up with solemn eyes as rain beat onto the roof of the treehouse. "Traxx promise," Charlie said soberly. "You can't tell anybody about the hiding place or what's in it. Not anybody," she warned.

"I already did a Traxx promise," Danni reminded her.

Charlie retrieved the plastic bag that contained the cardboard core from a roll of paper towels and pushed the bunk back in place. "Do another one for what's in here," she demanded.

"Traxx promise, Charlie, I won't tell anybody. Not even Jay."

"Okay, because this is really secret." Charlie pulled a tightly sealed plastic bag out of the core. It covered a roll of money.

Danni's eyes widened. There were tens and twenties and all kinds of fives and ones, all neatly bundled together, with the numbers and the presidents all facing the same way. "How much is it?" she whispered.

"Two hundred and eighty-two dollars."

Danni's slow indrawn breath was music to Charlie's ears.

"Where'd you get it?" Danni was too overwhelmed to even touch so much money.

"Oh, here and there," Charlie told her. "As soon as Jay buys the house, I'm gonna give it to him." She'd been saving lunch money and bus fares and every coin she'd found since Jay had gone to the army. Whenever she got paid for baby-sitting or mowing lawns, it all got changed into dollars and went into the house fund. Every cent.

"Are we gonna get a house, Charlie?"

"Jay promised."

Danni's face was filled with cautious hope. "You think it's gonna be soon?"

"Yeah, I think so," Charlie answered with absolute confidence. She rewrapped the money and pushed it inside the core, then back in the plastic bag, and back in the hole. Danni helped her move the bunk, and they both made sure the hole didn't show before they went out into the rain to Annie's for lunch with Jay and Tommy.

All during the meal, their conversation seldom strayed from the point at which Jay had purchased a house that they were all going to live in. And Danni kept her promise of silence, but her eyes were filled with longing as she followed the faces she loved from Annie to Jay and Charlie and Tommy and back to Jay.

Charlie would grin and sneak a look at Danni, whose face would light up in delight; Charlie would laugh and Danni would laugh and Jay's serious face would break into a smile for a moment and Annie and Tommy would grin for no reason other than everyone was happy. It was almost like old times.

After his brother and sisters left, Jay paced Annie's apartment. Pouring rain hadn't let up all weekend, and Milbrook had called that morning to delay his start on construction until tomorrow, which was okay, but a few moments ago they'd called again with an update. The site had flooded, the foundation had washed out, and it was too muddy to do repair work until next week. All the other crews were full up. Sorry.

He had used the morning to work on loan papers for the bank and had slogged out in the rain to look at a couple of other houses, which were zeros. Charlie and Danni had driven him crazy at lunch, counting the minutes until they were all in the same house, and the loss of a week's work because of a stupid rainstorm was frustrating.

Trying to keep things level, he called Iris to see if their offer for the Hartford place was still alive, only to learn that the seller hadn't yet responded and to be warned that there was another offer on the table. It had to be Bowmont Properties. Damn the Bowmonts.

No sooner had he put down the phone than Stephen called.

"George wants me to cover the shop tomorrow so he can go back to the dentist, but I promised Leanna Bowmont I'd do their stable repair—"

Jay stopped him. "Bowmont, as in Sam Bowmont?"

"She's Sam's—"

"Yeah, right." He knew what everyone knew about Sam Bowmont. He had a young wife, owned the paper, and his real estate firm was probably going to outbid them on the Hartford place. And he was Parker Bowmont's wealthy father. He found a target for his anger, and Stephen caught the brunt of it. "I don't *believe* you picked up work from them!"

There was a short pause, then, "It's money, Jay."

The last thing he wanted to do was be anywhere near Parker bloody Bowmont, but Stephen was right. The day hadn't dawned when he could turn down money, and it made him angrier. "Okay, I'll take care of it." He reluctantly wrote down the phone number.

"Lumber's in the truck. You know about—"

He cut Stephen short. "Yes! I said I'd take care of it." He hung up the phone and fought the fury the rest of the afternoon; the more he thought about it, the less attractive working for the Bowmonts became. Finally he made himself dial the number. He'd simply delay the job a couple of days until Stephen could handle it. Mrs. Bowmont answered.

"This is Traxx Jobbing regarding the work on your stables," he said quickly. "We're having a few scheduling difficulties due to the rain—"

"The people the painters are waiting on?" she interrupted pointedly. "You will be here tomorrow?"

He sighed in irritation. "I just wanted to make sure you hadn't made other arrangements."

"Fine. We'll see you then." The less than charming woman hung up.

He skipped breakfast, drove the battered pickup onto the estate, and had the lumber unloaded by a quarter after seven. This was going to be the fastest repair in history, and with any luck he'd be gone before Parker rolled his royal ass out of bed. By eight he'd torn out the rotten post and four of the planks in the stable wall and tossed the debris into the truck. He was fitting a new post into the old posthole when Parker walked in. "Since when are you Traxx Jobbing?" he challenged.

"Hello, Parker." His attitude hadn't changed much from the sophomore he remembered in high school, still arrogant and demanding. Jay moved the post into position; when it refused to fit, he pencil-marked a place to plane the wood.

"Leanna said someone named Traxx was doing this work. Why are you here?" Parker was clearly agitated and not about to leave it alone.

"Stephen couldn't make it."

"No shit."

Jay ignored the sarcasm and set to work with the plane. Shavings feathered soundlessly onto the floor.

Parker moved into the stall, crowding him. "So when'd you get back?"

"Couple of days ago." He was annoyed and decided to needle Parker. "How's Jolene?"

"You ought to know."

Parker was fishing. Pleased that his dig had worked, Jay was deliberately innocent in his response. "I haven't spoken to her." A three-year-old wouldn't have believed him.

"That's odd. She was talking about you just a couple of days ago." Parker's caution was exhausted.

Jay hid his interest in this information and tried the post again. This time it fit. "What do you want me to say? I haven't seen her."

"I don't believe you."

Jay jammed the post into the hole and leaned all his weight against it. It was firm and didn't give.

"I said, I don't believe you." Parker's stance was hostile, and his challenge hung in the air.

Jay decided things had been pushed far enough. He stood to his full height and squared off in Parker's face. "I've already told you, Parker. I haven't seen her. I have no plans to see her. I'll be done with this in an hour and I'm out of here. So why don't we leave it at that?"

"Just see that you are." Parker brushed past him, nearly knocking him over.

Jay lost the hold on his temper. If Bowmont wanted to get physical, it was fine with him. "You got a problem with Jolene, you talk to Jolene. Don't put it in my face," he called ominously after Parker's retreating back.

There was no answer. A few minutes later the roar of Bowmont's Porsche sounded down the length of the driveway. The high whine of the expensive engine had barely died away when another voice startled him.

"Hi. How's it going?"

Unless the old man was a real cradle robber, she couldn't be Mrs. Bowmont. Plus, she didn't have an attitude. Jay blew out his breath and clasped her outstretched hand. "Getting there," he answered, his voice reflecting his curiosity. She was definitely attractive, but he didn't have a clue.

She cocked her head and stared past him at the partition. "I'm Parker's sister. And you're . . . ?"

"Stephen's brother, Jay. He's working another job. Glad to meet you." She was nothing like Parker in appearance, and she moved with a calmness of purpose that eased the tension in his gut. "I didn't know Parker had a sister. Older or younger?" he asked curiously.

"I'm twenty-four."

"Ah, boy. Too old for me," he joked, and returned to testing the wooden post.

"This is my new look," she said suddenly. "I'm having my picture taken in about an hour. What do you think?" She took off her glasses and turned to give him a profile.

She was very pretty, and her makeup was flawless. A shaft of light from a window in the haymow caught her hair and lit her features. She stood quietly, waiting for his response. "Looks great to me. Are you a model?"

She flushed at the compliment. "I've just gotten engaged, and it's for my dad's paper," she explained. "The announcement."

"Too young and too late," he teased. And too poor. He moved one of the planks into position and tapped a nail to hold it in place along the wall. "This is going to be loud, so don't take it personal."

He started hammering nails into the plank, and Leanna realized that Jay Traxx didn't know she was blind. She embraced the rare opportunity. It was going to be fun seeing how long it would take him to figure it out. She dropped Thumper's empty oat bucket, upended it, and sat facing him. "Your family from around here?"

He finished nailing the board, and she heard him pick up another one.

"Grew up in Wellington Flats. I got out of the army a few days ago, and I'm getting used to being a civilian again. Watch it."

She smiled in his direction as the board scraped into place along the wall. "Do you miss reveille?" she teased in return.

He laughed. "No, I sure don't. But I do miss taps. There was always something special about it."

More pounding, higher up on the wall. She sat trading idle information until he'd nailed the plank, then fingered her watch. She had about half an hour before the photographer was due and she had to get dressed, but she knew she'd won. He hadn't figured it out. She'd been listening very carefully to the rhythm of his work, so all she had to do was stand and leave. He'd never have a clue.

What she couldn't have known was that the last wooden board was not adjacent to the others but was lying crosswise in the wood shavings on the floor; when she stood, she rose directly into its silent path as Jay swung the heavy plank toward the wall. Nor did she realize that he had checked her position and adjusted his motions to clear her head, as he had all the others. The split instant he looked away was the moment she chose to move.

The heavy wood hit her squarely in the forehead and knocked her down. Jay felt the impact and looked back, horrified. She was on the floor. He threw the plank aside and knelt next to her. There was a sawdust mark on her forehead from the blow and she was out cold. Thank God he hadn't hit her glasses or there'd have been glass cuts, too. There had been a solid *thunk* as the back of her head hit the cement floor of the stable. Damn it all to hell!

He checked her pulse; relieved to find it steady, he sprinted for the house. By the time the paramedics arrived, she was beginning to regain consciousness and the cook had reached her mother on a car phone. Five minutes later Alice Faye met the ambulance at the emergency entrance to Traxx University Hospital to admit Leanna for examination. For the next twenty minutes Jay paced helplessly in the waiting room, trying to obtain information on the girl's condition.

Parker came flying through the door. He charged across the room, and before Jay could offer an explanation Parker's fist crashed into his face and knocked him to his knees. "You coward son of a bitch!" Parker raged. "Get out of here! I see you again, I'll kill you!"

Jay pulled himself to his feet and took another blow, this time in the shoulder. He faced her furious brother. "It was an accident."

"I'll see that you never work again, you bastard!" Before Parker could come at him a second time, several members of the hospital staff moved in to intervene. "I'll sue you within an inch of your life, you son of a bitch! Get away from me." He shook off the orderlies and stalked to the other side of the room, where he continued to pace and stared malevolently across the waiting room.

Jay approached the nurses' station. "Anything yet?"

The nurse shook her head. "She's finished the CAT scan, but we won't know anything for quite some time. Why don't you wait outside for a little while?" she suggested hesitantly, with a glance at Parker's ominous presence.

Jay paused in frustration. A split instant. One split second and his life had changed. Sam Bowmont's daughter. Christ, what if the girl was injured for life? "Where's a phone?" he asked finally.

The nurse indicated a bank of telephones around the corner and a short distance down a hall. He dug in his pockets for change and called Annie to report what had happened. "I don't understand it. She was watching me, she knew when I picked it up, I saw her. It's like she did it deliberately. Parker's screaming lawsuit, it's a mess."

Annie paused on the other end of the line. "Leanna Bowmont's blind, child, didn't you know that?"

Blind. He was shocked into silence as the information ripped through his body. How the hell could the girl be blind? She was wearing glasses; she'd walked into the stall carrying a bucket, shook his hand, stared straight at him, smiled. She hadn't reached out to touch anything or feel along the walls like a normal blind person. No wonder Parker was rabid. He'd be lucky if Sam Bowmont settled for having him skinned alive.

"Hell, I didn't know she existed, let alone she was blind." He groaned with the knowledge that Stephen had tried to warn him and he'd been too wired up to listen. "All they'll tell me is she's getting a CAT scan."

"None of them doctors is going to say anything until their butts are covered," said Annie sagely, "so don't buy yourself trouble. She could be perfectly all right and doctors won't admit to it for another six months, so don't expect any information."

"I can't believe I hit a blind girl." The enormity of the situation began to sink in and guilt washed over him like a wall of water. "I'm not leaving here until I see her. Then come home, I guess. I came over with the paramedics. Can you have Tommy pick up the truck?"

"I'll send him over to get you."

Jay hung up the phone, and the dead weight of responsibility settled onto his shoulders. A Bowmont was bad enough, but a blind Bowmont? Life had thrown him one hell of a curve today. He turned back toward the waiting room.

Parker was nowhere in sight, and the head nurse had also disappeared; he approached a young aide at the desk. "Leanna Bowmont's room?"

"Are you family?"

"I'm her brother," he said hurriedly. "What's the number?"

The aide scanned the charts. "She's been moved to four-oh-two. That's a private room."

"How's she doing?"

"I really don't know, I just came on."

A few minutes later, he found the room. The door was open, and conversation flowed in and out with various nurses and orderlies. A man about his own age arrived, probably the fiancé, and he heard Mrs. Bowmont's voice.

"Here's Curt, and Parker's gone to pick up a few things at the house for you and you'll stay overnight like a good girl."

He waited on edge for Leanna to speak and heard the man announce, "I'm canceling my trip to Chicago. It's nothing that can't wait, and you're more important. How're you feeling?"

At last Jay heard her voice, low and completely different from the girl he'd been teasing in the stable. No longer vital, nearly overwhelmed. The iron weight of guilt multiplied.

"It was a stupid accident." She gave a valiant attempt at humor. "I have a royal headache and a few bruises, but it's not like I can get any more blind. The CAT scan says I'm fine."

Jay felt a tidal wave of relief mixed with sorrow.

"I just want to go home." This time her voice held a plaintive energy.

"We don't know how you are yet." The girl's mother. "And I won't hear of her leaving until we're certain there's no cranial damage. Her father's not going to sit still for her leaving the hospital until he gets here, so don't even think about it."

He heard Leanna's energy wane. "I asked you not to call him. There's nothing he can do, and he'll be so upset. He knows how much I hate hospitals. Just staying overnight is going to convince him something terrible is wrong. What did you tell him?"

"I haven't reached him, but I left word at the hotel to have him call tomorrow morning." Mrs. Bowmont again. "Curt, she'll stay overnight, and if the doctors tell me there's nothing wrong, we'll let him know then."

"She's absolutely right, Leanna. You're not going home tonight."

It was said with finality, and the girl's voice admitted defeat. "All right." Then she rallied. "But I don't want you to postpone your trip. I'm not even on painkillers. I'd know if something was wrong."

Curt laughed. "I may as well go. Looks like I'm going to wait a little longer to tell the world about my fiancée because it'll be at least a week before those black eyes go away."

"Oh, God, am I awful looking?" Leanna asked woefully.

"Well, you're pretty badly swollen, but the ice packs should bring it down by tomorrow," said her mother. "We'll have some pictures taken, just in case."

There was a heavy silence in the room, and Jay's guard came up. Pictures for a lawsuit, no doubt. Wonderful. Just what he needed. Hopefully Annie had maintained Traxx's insurance or they could all kiss their futures good-bye.

Leanna spoke again in a low, tired voice. "I'm awfully sleepy, Alice Faye. Would you mind . . . ?"

"Of course. Let's go, Curt."

"I'll stop by later," he told her.

"And you'll take your trip?"

"I promise. Now you get some rest. I'm not going to kiss you because it'll probably hurt, but I love you, black eyes and all. Feel better."

Jay walked a few paces down the hall until Curt passed him by, then he returned to stand near the doorway of Leanna's room. Mrs. Bowmont was still lecturing her daughter.

"I haven't said anything to Sam, but it was only a matter of time until something like this happened. I want you to think about living at home after you're married, or you're going to worry your father to death."

"Accidents happen, Alice Faye. I'm probably the only blind person in this hospital."

"My point exactly. Just look at the horrible things that happen to people who can see. Life is dangerous enough for people with sight, let alone what happens to the blind. Maybe now you'll be more careful."

"I'm really tired, Alice Faye."

"Of course, dear."

Jay looked at his watch. It was noon. During the time he'd stood outside her room, these two had done more damage to Leanna Bowmont than he had managed with the board.

A few moments after her mother left, Jay slipped into the room and stood quietly inside the doorway. She did look a mess. Her face was swollen, and she was holding an ice pack to her forehead. Huge dark circles were forming under her eyes. When she moved the pack, a lump the size of a goose egg stood out on her forehead.

"Who is it?" she asked in a low voice. "I can hear you."

"It's Jay Sprengsten. I just wanted to be sure you were all right and to tell you that I am so sorry."

"You must be really worried about all this. Don't be. I'll explain to my father. . . ."

Right, and green elephants flew in Bangkok. He

approached her hospital bed with caution. "Listen, Leanna, I'm not trying to make excuses, but I had no idea you were blind. I talked to you for twenty minutes and . . . I still can't believe this happened. You don't act like a blind person."

"Really?" Her voice lifted with interest. "You couldn't tell?"

"I don't normally hit blind people."

"Mmmmph." Her face closed with pain. "I'll bet you do," she joked haltingly. "Every day of the week."

"Yeah, and twice on Sunday." She looked really beat. "I ought to be going. Like I said, I just wanted to make sure you were okay."

"Would you mind not leaving me alone? The hardest thing is being here by myself. I'm terrified of hospitals."

He began to object, then realized she'd exaggerated her tiredness to get rid of her mother.

"I need more water in this." She removed the ice pack from her forehead and felt along the headboard for the nurse's buzzer. "It's too lumpy and it hurts."

"I'll do it." He took the pack, unscrewed the top, and poured in some water from a pitcher on her bedstand.

"It's not your fault," she said slowly. "I should have said something. I just wanted to practice."

"Practice what? Getting whopped in the head?"

She explained. "When I meet someone who knows I'm blind, there's a difference in the way they treat me. With kid gloves, sort of. And if they meet me first and then find out, it's . . . it's like I'm a person first and a blind person second," she finished. "Now that I'm going to get married and move—maybe to another city, I wanted to practice starting off equal. The way I used to when I could see. You were my first 'opportunity.'" He handed her the ice pack, and she settled it gingerly against her forehead.

Jay thought about it. He'd have treated her differently all right. He wouldn't have hit her.

"Can you do this one, too?" She moved her head aside, and he saw a second pack on her pillow. He picked it up, quickly added the water, and replaced it so she could lie back.

She gave him a brief description of the accident that had cost her sight. "I know better than not to tell people," she continued. "It's not fair, but I knew what you were doing and that I had to be careful. I just had lousy timing. Don't worry about it. My father will understand. It'll all be okay, I promise." She paused for a moment, her face puzzled. "I thought your name was Traxx."

"No. We own Traxx Jobbing. You probably saw the logo. . . ." He stopped, enlightened.

Leanna's eyes closed, and her voice began to ebb with fatigue. "See what I mean?"

"I better get out and let you get some rest."

When she didn't argue, he took her free hand. "Anything else I can do?"

"Huh-uh." She was fading into sleep.

"Is it okay to call you and see how you're doing?"

"Sure. Besides, you have to finish the stable. I have painters waiting," she said sleepily.

Parker stepped into the room, and Jay let go of her hand. "I'm just leaving, Parker. Don't get crazy."

Parker's eyes were deadly. "How dare you come in here," he said furiously. "You are going to pay for this."

Leanna stirred. "It wasn't his fault, Parker."

"Great job." Parker's voice was choked with rage. "Did you get her to sign a waiver, too?"

"Parker, leave him alone." Leanna's voice was strained with effort. She made an attempt to sit up, and Parker took his attention off Jay long enough to move to her side.

"I'm leaving," Jay said quietly. "Get some rest." He stepped out the door and walked quickly into the waiting room. If she was going to call off the Bowmont dogs, she'd have to start with her brother. He paced the floor in agitation, expecting Parker to come flying at him at any second. Where the hell was Tommy?

He saw Curt come out of the hospital gift shop carrying a small bouquet of red roses and moved out of sight to the bank of phones; the last thing he needed was another confrontation in the lobby. He decided to check with Annie. Maybe she hadn't been able to find Tommy. A moment later, Curt rounded the corner and picked up a phone.

"I'd like to make this call collect from Curt."

I ought to apologize to him, too, Jay decided. He depressed the lever to disconnect his call, but before he could interrupt, Curt began his conversation. It was impossible not to overhear.

"Yeah, it's me. I just wanted to let you know that I'm taking a later flight and you can pick me up at Delta instead of American." Curt paused. "Any restaurant you want, honey, I don't care," he said indulgently. "Yeah, well I can't talk now. I'm visiting a friend in the hospital and it's a public phone."

Jay's gut tightened. Clearly this wasn't the time or place to admit knowledge of Leanna Bowmont. He turned his back and mumbled "Uh-huh" a couple of times to provide conversation of his own.

"Right. Me too. . . . Four o'clock. I'll be at the curb."

Curt disappeared around the corner, and Jay sagged

under the weight of this new information. A friend in the hospital? What kind of guy calls the woman he's engaged to a "friend"? It's what you get for eavesdropping, he told himself. By the time he'd filled Annie in on Leanna's condition, Tommy's worried face was a welcome sight, wheeling the Traxx pickup into the hospital driveway.

God, what a day.

10

Traxx promise . . .

Wednesday, Jay finished repairing the Bowmont stable and made a deal with the paint crew to leave a gallon of white to finish the stall. He was able to ascertain from one of the men that in exchange for Sam Bowmont's not flying home in a panic, Leanna had stayed an extra day at the hospital to assure her father that she was all right. He felt bad for her, knowing how much she hated being there.

The following morning he completed the painting and was cleaning the brushes when she came into the stall. Her face was no longer swollen, but there was an ugly bruise on her forehead. Yellow-and-purple splotches under her eyes matched his cheek where Parker had clobbered him.

"You washing the brushes?"

"You can smell the turpentine," he guessed.

She nodded. "Oil-base paint. I was an artist," she said, and immediately changed the subject. "Parker says you used to date Jolene."

"That's been over a long time." He rubbed the brush with a cotton rag to soak up the solvent and studied her battered face. She looked a little pale to him despite her tan. "Should you be out here?"

"The doctors say no major damage—just sore and probably very unattractive. They want me to get rest, the usual. I came out to give Thumper a couple of apples. She loves them, and I'm a few behind."

"What about your dad? I'll bet he had a few opinions about my ancestry."

She laughed painfully. "He was pretty nuts for a while, but he'll come around. He'll be home next week. You want to come over to dinner?"

"Yeah, right. Between him and Parker, I'll be the entrée. Barbecued Sprengsten." He was glad it hadn't escalated to an awkward situation between them. There was something basically decent and, actually, very nice about her. He found himself curious. "Is this going to interfere with your wedding?"

"No, uh, we haven't set a date yet."

Her swift answer alerted his interest. She was nervous about getting married. Probably normal, given she was blind and looked like the loser in a boxing match. "Well, if I was your fiancé, I'd tie the knot pretty quick. Every guy I know would fall over his feet to meet a girl as pretty as you are," he said honestly.

Leanna smiled at the compliment and wished with all her might she could see this man whose voice came at her from a tall place. There was something about him that emanated security and a steady assurance that reminded her of her father.

The sound of Parker's car came whining up the driveway, and she realized he would see Jay's truck. The Porsche came to a screeching halt, a door slammed heavily, and footsteps scraped along the walk. "Parker's still angry," she warned. "I can't get him past it. Are you about finished?"

"I'll be out of here in two minutes." He paused. "Can you get the paint? I'll carry the dropcloths and the turpentine. Shouldn't be left in a barn."

She held out her hand, and he positioned the wire handle across her palm. A blob of white smeared her fingers.

"I got paint on you," he explained, and used the cloth to wipe her hand.

Parker arrived at the stall in time to see Jay's attention to his sister. "I told you to stay away from her. I can't believe you were stupid enough to come back here."

"Please, Parker, he's leaving."

Jay screwed the lid onto the turpentine can before picking up the bulky canvas and his brushes. "Don't upset your sister, Parker, I'm out of here."

"Don't tell me how to treat my sister." Parker turned to Leanna. "You stay here," he instructed abruptly. "I want to make sure this jerk understands he's not welcome on Bowmont property."

Jay retrieved the can of paint from her fingers. "It's okay, Leanna," he said. "I'll call you in a couple of days, if that's all right."

"No, it's not all right." Parker shoved him toward the front of the barn. "You stay the hell away from her. You understand me?"

Jay knew Parker was waiting for the least sign of resistance to justify his rage and decided not to escalate the situation in front of Leanna, but any more shoving and all bets were off. He shot Parker a look that told him he'd reached the line. Outside, he tossed the drops into the truck bed and put the cans and brushes inside the cab before climbing heavily into the truck.

"Parker, I'm just trying to make things right." His voice was thick with frustration as he made one last effort at conciliation. "Just tell me what to do and I'll do it."

"Well, the first thing you can do is forget making moves on the poor little rich girl," Parker said violently. "She's out of your league. Just like Jolene."

Aware that if he answered Parker's insults, it was going to get bloody right there in the Bowmont courtyard, Jay ground his jaws together and restrained his impulse to gun the engine and throw gravel into Parker's knees. Instead he turned the truck around with care. In the side mirror, he saw Leanna standing in the doorway to the barn, the hurt still on her face. He came within an inch of stopping but realized there was little he could do. A few yards down the lane he tromped on the accelerator, unable to get out of the Bowmont domain fast enough.

Leanna stood, stunned. Never in her life had her brother referred to her as a poor little rich girl, and her mind was reeling with disillusionment. She tried to tell herself that he hadn't meant it, that he was just angry and determined to cut down Jay Sprengsten. But she knew now that deep in his heart it was what Parker really thought of her. You don't make up destructive things about one person to hurt another. Parker had resorted to honesty in the heat of rage, and it amounted to proof of her worst fear.

Jay arrived at Annie's apartment to learn that Alan Hartford had refused his bid for the property. Smarting from the encounter with Bowmont, he recklessly increased his offer and threw in the balance of his severance as down payment. Iris got an agreement from Hartford to reconsider and a promise to get back to them within seventy-two hours.

That evening, he was too depressed even to hope. "It's not going to happen, Annie." This time she did not disagree, which told him he was right. He watched her get off her couch to check on her roast chicken and decided the smell was the only good thing left in the universe.

The doorbell rang, and Annie detoured to the front door. "You expecting someone?"

"Madonna," he said testily. "Tell her she's early."

Annie opened the door.

"Is this Traxx Jobbing?"

"Yes, ma'am, it is. Come on in, honey." Annie held the screen aside. "I'll just bet those sunglasses are hiding a couple of black eyes I heard about."

Leanna gave a small self-conscious laugh, folded her stick, and stepped inside.

Jay came to life and hurriedly introduced the two women. "Annie's our accountant. What are you doing here?"

"You left without getting paid." Leanna searched in her purse and held out an envelope.

"Wha—" Jay was tongue-tied. "You can't—I can't take money from you."

"You did the work."

"No way. Not up for discussion." Jay was adamant. He walked away from her outstretched hand.

"Annie," she said stubbornly, "you're the accountant. You tell him it's good business to accept payment for services rendered."

Annie tucked the envelope into Leanna's purse. "I just rent space here, honey," she said jovially. "He's boss. Why don't you sit down? There's a chair about two feet to your left with nothing in front of it."

Leanna paused, having intended to give Jay the check and leave; she had anticipated a certain amount of resistance but was equally determined to see that he was paid. Parker had refused absolutely to consider payment to Traxx, and the hurt from his comment this afternoon was so fresh that she hadn't risked discussing it. Tears were too near the surface.

Inside this room were sweet aromas of roasting chicken and baking pies. She was so unexpectedly at ease that she followed Annie's instructions and found herself accepting a glass of iced tea. "Jay, would you mind telling the driver I'll call when I'm ready to leave?"

He went outside to dismiss the taxi, and Annie excused herself to check on dinner. Mouth-watering smells followed the squeak of an oven door, and Annie confirmed her identification of the pie aroma as peach.

"Almost burned my crust," she reported. Pie tin scraped against stove top. "But this bird's got more cookin' to do." The oven door squeaked and thumped lightly.

"We used to have a cook who baked pies," Leanna said appreciatively.

"Well, you're gonna stay for a piece of this one," Annie declared. "It'll be cool enough to cut pretty soon."

An hour flew by while the pie cooled. Meanwhile, Jay's brother, Tommy, and his sisters arrived for dinner. They were as comfortable with her as Stephen had been at the farrier's, and she was invited to join them; small clinks and clatters of plates and tableware sounded softly from the kitchen. At first her stomach rolled over in self-conscious concern that everyone would be watching her, but her nose and the promise of Annie's peach pie tilted the balance against declining. Neither Alice Faye nor Parker was home, so she left word with the cook that she was having dinner with friends and left a phone number.

Annie sat her at the kitchen table with Jay and described her plate. "White meat chicken at six, mashed potatoes with gravy mixed in at eleven, and applesauce at two o'clock. Salt and pepper at one," she added, and sat down to join them. Everyone else ate in the living room, coming in occasionally for seconds. Conversation ebbed and flowed with laughter, and when she removed her glasses, she accepted a good-natured razzing about her black eyes.

The peach pie was delicious. Dishes were quickly dispatched, and after hugs and kisses dispensed to and from Annie and shakes of her outstretched hand over polite good-nights, Tommy left to drive the girls home. A few minutes later, he returned to drop the keys to the truck with Jay and took his leave on his bicycle.

Her watch said eight-thirty, and it was time to go home. She reluctantly bade good-night to Annie, who gave her a huge hug and pressed a warm kiss against her cheek, then thrust a foil-wrapped wedge of pie into her hands. "'Night, honeybun," she said.

Leanna was silent during the drive home as Jay described the scope of his plans to reunite his family. "I didn't mean to bore you," he said after a few minutes. "I get carried away."

"I'm not bored," she assured him. "I'm . . . astonished, I think. I can't imagine being responsible for so many people. It would terrify me." After a short pause, she made a confession. "I had a great time this evening. It was a huge step for me."

He said nothing, but she was sure he'd turned to give her a questioning look.

"This was the first time I've eaten in someone's home without . . ." She searched for an accurate explanation. "Usually there's a person I know there who makes it 'safe.'" She sighed, elated at her discoveries. "For me it was a big accomplishment. Huge. In my life it is. But when I compare it with what you want to accomplish for your family, I see how sheltered I've been."

At a stoplight, she leaned her elbow out the open window into the cool night air and let the breeze hit her in the face. "I can't remember the last time I acted on impulse. I've learned to be so cautious and so safe all the time." She turned toward him. "This truly is very big for me, and I really don't want to go home right now. Do you mind if we just talk?"

He turned the truck toward the bluff. A few minutes later he pulled off the road and parked near the outlook. "There's a giant three-quarter harvest moon," he told her, "a couple of inches above high noon, and the Big Dipper's just to the right."

"Thanks," she answered, lifting her gaze politely, seeing nothing. "I lose track of the moon."

He set the brake and made sure she was comfortable, then stared out at the valley and the flickering lights of Walden City. He and Jolene used to come here.

"The accident was probably a blessing."

He waited as she struggled to explain.

"It made me see that I've been fooling myself. I always thought I'd live my life in Walden City and nothing would change. When I get married that's not going to be possible, is it?"

Jay looked at her face in the moonlight, beautiful even

with the dark bruises, and answered honestly. "No. Married or not, it's life and things change."

She was silent for a long time, and his thoughts drifted to Jolene and the promises made on this spot. Things always changed.

"If you won't accept payment, I want you to do me a favor," she said suddenly.

"Sure, name it," he answered carelessly.

"Will you take me to Chicago?"

It was totally out of left field, and he was thrown at her request. "Chicago?"

"I want to see what it's like. I mean, I want you to go with me, but unless there's a problem I just want you to watch me do things by myself. Things that I'll have to do when I move away from home."

"Why me?" he hedged. "Why not your fiancé?" Curt's phone conversation ran through his mind. Something was wrong with this relationship. Something major.

"I don't want Curt to know how afraid I am."

In the bright moonlight, he saw that the admission was painful for her.

"I want to see if I can be like other women. I want to be more than a rich little blind girl."

He paused at her echo of Parker's remark, looking for an out; flying to Chicago was expensive, and he wasn't about to ride on her money. He heard himself offer a compromise. "How about Wellington instead? Start out a little slower, maybe?"

She considered briefly. "Wellington's a better idea. Can I call this a date?" She gave him a sober grin and offered her hand.

"Absolutely." Maybe she'd change her mind. But his gut and the determined look on her face told him otherwise as she shook his hand to seal the bargain.

11

Traxx promises . . .

In the second booth of the Walden City Soda
Shoppe, Alan Hartford studied the residue from his
third and last refill of coffee. He extracted the realtor's
business card from his wallet. No appetite and unhappy
with the decision he was about to make, he absently
replaced his wallet and heaved himself out of the booth.
Two little girls, one in boys' clothing and absurd purple
hair, the other much younger, came into the shop and
perched on counter stools.

The girl with purple hair ordered two small cherry
Cokes, then counted out a handful of change.
Obviously short of money, she changed the order to
one, large; when it was ready, she grabbed two straws
out of the dispenser. The two moved into his vacated
booth. He smiled at her thrift and admired the indication of strength in her character, so heavily at odds
with his expectation. Character was in short supply in
the youngsters he'd encountered lately, particularly

those members of his sister-in-law's family. He paid his check, added a few quarters for the counter man, and headed toward the real estate office to get it over with.

Charlie positioned the tall soda glass in front of Danielle and moved an empty coffee cup to the counter. She wiggled into the opposite side of the booth and pushed herself up on one foot so she could sit on the other and claim her share of the Coke. There was something soft and squishy under her shoe on the floor. Suspecting a wad of napkin or a dead hamburger, she peeked under the table and saw that it was a wallet, black as the Naugahyde seat of the booth.

She nursed it toward the wall with her toe and reached down to pick it up. It was one of the long, expensive, folding kind that you saw in the movies, and the leather was butter soft under her fingers. The possibility of reward zoomed through her brain. "I'll be right back." She slid out of the booth and dashed to the door to find the man who'd had coffee in the booth.

Outside, the street was empty except for Mrs. Pabst. She ran to the bank, just in case, but he wasn't there, either. The wallet fell open in her hands, and there were layers and layers of the gray-green tops of money on one side. She pushed it up under the tail of Jay's huge wool shirt, then into the back pocket of her blue jeans. Once it was out of sight, she began to breathe again. There was lots of money in there, and she didn't want to think about anything right now.

She waited a few minutes, and when he wasn't visible anywhere she returned to the booth. "I had to go all the way to the bank," she told Danni, her heart pounding a hundred miles an hour.

"I'll bet he was real glad to get it back."

Charlie sat for a few minutes, too distracted to claim her half of the Coke. "You finish it. We gotta catch the bus." Her heart was thumping so hard it hurt.

She bargained with herself furiously. *If the man comes back before we leave, I'll give it to him. I'll tell him I found it and give it back.* Her heart was still hammering when they got on the bus to Wellington Flats. And pounding when she delivered Danni to Aunt Jessie's, and slamming against her rib cage all the way up the ladder to the treehouse.

You stole it, accused the rigidly honest portion of her mind. She stared at the wallet. If she took out the money, it meant really being a thief, but she knew she would die if she didn't at least count it and began another bargain with her guilty conscience. *I just want to see how much it is so I know how much reward I'll get.* It was a razor-thin argument, but the temptation was so great.

She took out the bills—and gasped. They were hundreds. She counted twenty-three of them:fifteen stiffly brand-new ones and eight that were slightly worn, plus three twenties, a ten, and two fives. She'd never seen so much money. Four years of savings suddenly seemed a cruel joke.

There was a neat double row of credit cards opposite the pocket where the money had been and three business cards tucked in their own slot. She turned the wallet sideways to read the name. *ALAN HARTFORD, PRESIDENT, HARTFORD IMPORTS.* She knew whose money it was—she really *was* a thief. Unnerved, she shoved the money back in the wallet; it was too big to fit through the knothole, so she slid it under the mattress in the bunk. Now she had a real secret.

Oh, boy, did she.

°   °   °

Alan Hartford reviewed the two offers for his grand-mother's house. One was an increased but still lowball figure from a prospective buyer he'd already passed on—small down payment, a GI loan, still requesting that he carry the balance of the paper. The buyer was single, twenty-two years old. He shrugged it off. A twenty-two-year-old and a fourteen-room house? It was hard enough selling his grandmother's birthplace without some bucko trying to roll it over for the land value; setting up monthly payments to help the guy was the last thing he'd do. If he had to sell it, he wanted to pro-tect it as best he could from being destroyed.

A second offer had come in from Bowmont Real Estate Properties, a thousand dollars over the increased Sprengsten offer. Lowball as well, but in full, and in cash. He indicated to the broker that he'd like to talk directly with the Bowmont representative.

Parker Bowmont came on the line.

Hartford got right to the point. "I'm considering your offer, Mr. Bowmont, but I'd like to know what your plans are for the property."

"We anticipate no immediate use for the house," Bowmont admitted. "We're purchasing the land value since it's adjacent to my father's property. It is possible that my sister will live there when she's married, but as you know, it's a huge old place, and she'll probably want to remodel pretty extensively."

"I don't mind remodeling, but I would want some assurance that it not be razed. It's been in my family since the turn of the century."

"In that case, I'll see to it that if we find a buyer, we'll move the house. It would have to be dismantled to some degree, but not destroyed. I'm certain we can find a suitable lot among our properties where it can be reconstructed."

"I appreciate your being direct. I'll consider your comments and let you know in the next couple of days." Hartford hung up the phone, annoyed, and reached for his wallet to make a note of the conversation. "Tell Sprengsten it's a pass," he instructed the agent. "Tell him the offer's too low." His grandmother had loved that property. He'd played there as a boy and couldn't stomach the thought of it being pushed over by a bulldozer, but he wasn't getting younger, and there came a time in life when such decisions had to be made.

His wallet was missing. Irritated, he called the Soda Shoppe and waited while the clerk searched the booth and found nothing. The two little girls who'd been in the booth had been gone for . . . oh, thirty minutes or so, the clerk reckoned. He'd been in the back most of the past hour and hadn't noticed anything unusual; he asked another patron if she knew who they were, and the woman had no idea.

Hartford reported the loss to the Walden City Police Department with a very good description of the children. The officer in charge assured him the girls would be spotted pretty quickly if they'd stayed in Walden City, and later that afternoon the officer reached him at the hotel. They'd boarded a local bus and had gotten off in Wellington Flats. The driver had seen the older girl before; he remembered the purple hair but didn't know her name. It was doubtful they'd be found without knowing their identity.

Alan Hartford resigned himself to the loss. He'd already had his office call his credit card providers and was annoyed with the knowledge that he would have the hassle of getting new plastic. He returned to Cincinnati, mulling over his conversation with Parker Bowmont.

That evening at Annie's, Charlie learned that their offer on the Hartford property had failed, and suddenly the name connected to the name in the wallet. *Alan Hartford*. Anger flashed through her body. Because of Alan Hartford, they weren't going to have a house. Because of Alan Hartford, she and Danni were still stuck at Aunt Jessica's, and Tommy and Stephen had to stay in their foster homes. No way she'd give the money back to him. No way.

She watched Jay call Tommy. "Iris says it's over. Any offer we make, Bowmont has a standing order to top," he said into the phone tightly. "We can't outbid Bowmont. We'll have to find something else." He started to dial Stephen's number, and she told him hopefully, "I have some money if it'll help." He looked at her and smiled but didn't respond. "What if it's a lot of money?" she insisted. "A really lot."

Jay put his arm around his earnest little sister and hugged her for all he was worth. "Ten thousand dollars wouldn't help, but I love you for trying," he told her. "Now scoot while it's still daylight. We'll find something else, I promise."

The next morning, Jessica called Jay to tell him Charlie was missing, that she'd come in on her bike around dark and this morning she was nowhere to be found. "She didn't sleep here last night, Jay," she said angrily. "You're home now, and I will no longer have Danni subjected to this kind of behavior." She waited while Stephen searched everywhere he could think of, but there was no trace of her. At noon, over Jay's furious objection, Jessica reported Charlie as a runaway.

The Wellington officer made the connection between the theft report from Walden City and the description of thirteen-year-old Charlene Sprengsten with purple hair. "This is the third time you've reported her as a runaway, ma'am. Looks like she's got stolen money to travel on this time," he said to Jessica. "Over two thousand dollars, according to the owner. Any idea where she might have gone?"

"No." Jessica was suddenly terrified. Two thousand dollars. Had the girl really run away beyond Wellington Flats? "I have no idea," she repeated, and hung up the phone in dismay.

She reported the conversation to Jay. Two hours later an officer showed up to interview Danni, and finally admitting to her niece that Charlie was missing, she and Jay and the officer verified that yesterday Charlie had taken Danni past the old Hartford house and then to the Soda Shoppe for a Coke.

Danni hadn't seen what Charlie found, but insisted that she'd run out of the Soda Shoppe and returned it to a man. If that man said his wallet was gone, he was telling a fib. Charlie had given it back to him.

"Well, she got money from somewhere," Jessica said in frustration, and paced her living room angrily. "This time she's really done it."

The officer made notes and departed. The hands of the clock crawled slowly around its face as they waited. After lunch Danni went to bed with a stomachache; Jessica gave her a Tylenol, and she slept all afternoon. At five o'clock Jay went in to check on her and found her in tears.

"Don't worry, Danni-bug," he said gently. "We'll find her."

The little girl was distraught. Finally she admitted in a choked whisper, "Charlie had lots of money. I wasn't supposed to tell."

Charlie's offer drifted uncomfortably to the top of his mind. "I know, bug, she told me," he answered reassuringly.

"She did?" Teardrops welled in his sister's guilty eyes. "She made me give a Traxx promise."

"It's all right, sweetheart," Jay soothed. "You didn't break your promise. Do you know where she kept it?"

"I promised not to tell," the little girl repeated.

"Okay, was it in the treehouse?"

"I promised not to—"

"Don't tell me where, but will you go look and see if it's still there?"

Danni considered. "Yes."

At Annie's, Jay watched carefully as Danni climbed up to the entrance of the treehouse. After a moment, he heard the scrape of the bunk on the wooden floor. Another scrape, and a few minutes later Danni came down far enough for him to take her off the ladder. "It's not there," she said miserably. "Did Charlie run away for real this time?"

"I don't know, sweetheart." Jay studied the setting sun and fought the dead weight settling in his gut. Obviously she'd taken the money, but where on earth had she gone?

12

No promises . . .

"I take it you shall want to hear this as straight-forwardly as possible?" said the doctor kindly.

Sam settled himself onto the patient's chair in Dr. Edgar's office. "Please."

"We can't be one hundred percent certain without surgery, but we have reason to believe it's cancerous. I fear the survival rate for surgery is somewhat lower than nineteen percent. Normally I would advise the risk, but, as you already know, the cancer has metastasized in your liver and pancreas.

"Were we to be successful in the initial surgeries, there would be additional experimental surgery to replace your liver when it fails. This process is so new that there are no reliable statistics available. At your age . . . It is, of course, your choice." The doctor drew a deep breath. "Without both surgeries and extensive chemotherapy, I'm afraid I have to concur that you have a terminal condition, Mr. Bowmont. I am so sorry."

The rest Sam had heard before. Six months, perhaps; prepare your family. He'd steeled himself not to care, not to hope, but the thin edge of Dr. Edgar's pronouncement wedged its way under that shield, pried it up, and stabbed at his soul, and he knew he had lied to himself.

At the same time, a small weight lifted from his chest. The die was cast. He was now out of choices, out of miracles, and he knew absolutely that he would not spend his last days chasing a fragile, drug- and pain-filled existence at the expense of his family. He cursed himself for insisting on this last opinion and the waste of a week he could have been home.

What was done was done. Regret was a waste of time and energy. He shook the doctor's hand. "Thanks for flying in a day early," he said, and used the phone to call his driver. From here he was going to the airport, and he'd be home tomorrow. At the moment he wanted nothing more than to be with his family and to make sure Leanna had suffered no real injury from that stable incident.

Charlie sat on the bench and tried to decide what to do. The train had taken forever to get to Cincinnati, and now that she was here, she had another eight hours to wait. She'd called the number on Hartford's card, and the recording said business hours started at nine o'clock. If she'd been old enough to buy a plane ticket, she'd have waited until tomorrow to travel. Things were sure going to be different when she got to be a grown-up.

She stared at the station clock, willing the time to go fast. It was after one o'clock in the morning and way too late to call her family; besides, they'd just send someone to come and get her, and that would cost money. She was going to have to find a room or spend the night here. Outside there was a cold wind up, and it sure felt like fall, and the streets in the area were pretty crummy looking, so she shivered and squandered sixty cents on some watery hot chocolate, then sat down on a bench to wait it out. The last time she looked at the clock, it was a little after three.

A rough hand shook her shoulder.

Charlie jerked awake and stared up at a scowling face; hard brown eyes under the shiny bill of a security guard's cap stared back at her. "You can't sleep here, miss."

"I'm awake," she mumbled. She looked around the station. They were alone. Fear shot through her body, and she felt for the wallet. It was right where she'd left it, stuffed down the front of her jeans and covered by her sweater.

"It's all right. I ain't gonna hurt you," said the guard. "But you can't sleep here."

She straightened on the bench, and the guard continued his rounds. The coffee shop was closed. She put another sixty cents in the hot-chocolate machine, and its *clunk* and *plunk* and hissing water echoed in the quiet building.

When the security guard came around again forty minutes later, she stopped him and showed him the business card. "I've got to get to this address for an appointment," she said. "Is it far from here?"

He studied the card. "It's in the business district. That's way 'cross town," he said. "Taxi cost you about twelve dollars."

"What's your name?"

"Alfred."

"Can I keep you company, Alfred?"

"No, miss, you cannot."

When he came around again, she was waiting with a cup of hot chocolate for him. "Thank you." Alfred took a sip and studied her hair.

"I feel safe when you're here," she said honestly. "It's really creepy when I'm by myself."

Alfred nodded agreement. "That's why I'm here. What time's your appointment?"

"Nine o'clock."

"Let me make a call," he said. A few passengers had arrived, and one of the ticket windows had opened by the time he got back. "My son's on his way. He works over that way, and he's going to stop by and give you a ride."

The wallet began to burn a hole in her chest, and Stephen's warning rang in her ears. She'd sworn a Traxx promise never to ride with strangers. No hitching, ever. Accepting a ride with Alfred's son was no different from hitching. "It's okay, I can take a taxi," she said. The clock on the station wall read 5:50. "I don't want to cause . . ." Her voice died away as a policeman entered the train station and looked quickly around the room.

He saw Charlie and Alfred and angled toward them, picking up his pace. Charlie realized he was looking directly at her and tried to decide what to do. "I gotta go," she said to Alfred. She turned toward the nearest exit and escape.

Alfred caught her sleeve. "Now you wait just a second, miss," he said firmly. The officer arrived. "This is the young lady I was telling you about, Eldon. She needs a ride across town."

Charlie looked up at the young officer. The name on his badge read "Eldon Alfred." "You're his son?"

"Sure am. What are you doing in a Cincinnati train station all by yourself? You running away?"

"No," Charlie defended strongly. "I told your father. I have an appointment with this man." She fished Hartford's business card out of her pocket. "I didn't have a hotel room," she improvised. "So I spent the night here."

Eldon studied her hair. "Nice haircut."

Charlie flushed. She'd forgotten about her hair.

"Well, let's go. I gotta get to work."

Eldon stopped the patrol car in front of a twenty-story building; he walked Charlie inside and talked the security guard into allowing her to stay in the lobby until the building opened. At eight fifty-nine, she took the elevator to the Hartford Imports suite. The receptionist spoke to someone on the phone and informed her that Mr. Hartford was attending a breakfast meeting and wouldn't be in until later. She asked Charlie the nature of her business.

"Personal," Charlie told her, and sat down to wait some more.

Alan Hartford arrived at ten-fifteen and immediately recognized the little girl with shaggy purple hair asleep in his reception area. He went into his office, and a few minutes later Charlie, eyes bright from lack of sleep, was ushered in. She quickly came to life and told him her name, that yes, she was related to Jay Sprengsten who was her brother, and that she'd come in by train to see him.

She handed him his wallet. In an hour he knew all about the Sprengsten family and their plans to buy his grandmother's home, about the money she'd saved, and that she'd found his wallet and had tried to find him, but she didn't know where to look for him in Walden City and almost kept it so she could help her brother get a house, but that was stealing so she had brought it to him because it was a lot of money, except she took money for a train ticket instead of a reward, which she figured was fair.

Charlie paused for breath, and Hartford checked his wallet. A receipt for an economy round-trip fare was tucked in with the money. "I think we should call your family."

"Annie," she decreed confidently. "She'll let everybody know I'm okay."

He handed the telephone across his desk, and she dialed the number. A few minutes later she gave him the receiver, and he spoke with Annie Chatfield. It took him longer to convince her that he'd see Charlie safely home than it had taken Charlie to wriggle off the hook for being in Cincinnati in the first place. He consulted his watch. "I was planning to return this afternoon, Mrs. Chatfield, so she'll be there by six." He was returning to take one last walk around his grandmother's house before completing the sale to Bowmont Properties.

He assigned his secretary to take Charlie to lunch and to cash in the return portion of the train ticket. Then he plunged into his backed-up schedule of meetings. At four o'clock, a town car picked them up and drove them to an airfield. Charlie spotted the plane. "You have a private jet," she told him solemnly. "Wow."

On the hour flight to Wellington she wouldn't discuss why her hair was purple, but he learned about Traxx Jobbing, and Annie, and Jay's four years in the army, and their plans for a bed-and-breakfast inn. Clearly the girl was aware that the house her brother had wanted to buy belonged to him, but she treated his decision to sell it elsewhere as his business. Her confidence in her brother was total. They'd find something. It was just a matter of time. Jay had promised.

Charlie's family was gathered at Annie's apartment, even Aunt Jessica, and the round of hugs and tears and scoldings and more hugs became pandemonium for a few minutes. Within the hour Hartford was balancing a plate of fried chicken and lime Jell-O salad on his lap and enjoying the first real homemade baking powder biscuits he'd had since his grandmother had died. And a slice of chocolate cake so rich and smooth that, with a dollop of real whipped cream, it compared favorably with some of the most famous desserts he'd encountered around the world.

He sipped excellent coffee and studied the members of the Sprengsten family until about eight o'clock. One by one they said good night and departed for their various homes. He lingered to talk to Annie. Every one of them knew he'd refused to sell them the one thing they needed, the one thing that would bring them together under the same roof, and not an ounce of resentment had been laid at his feet. It was an extraordinary experience.

"Is there somewhere I can make a private call?" he asked her. Annie handed him the phone and stepped outside while he held a brief conversation. "I'll be getting a return call in a few minutes," he told her, "and then I'll be on my way."

When the phone rang she motioned for him to answer. He listened carefully for a few moments, then hung up, thanked her for dinner, and returned to the airport. By the time the jet touched down in Cincinnati he had the answer, and the next morning he phoned with a novel proposal.

Annie put on her wig and called Jay in from the tree-house, eyes bright with excitement.

"Ten years?" He couldn't believe it.

"He wants a ten-year lease," she repeated, "in my name, with an option to buy at any time, all payments to count toward purchase on the condition that it be kept in repair and improved during the tenancy."

Jay sat, overwhelmed for a moment. In ten years Danni would be eighteen. "God, you told him yes, didn't you?"

"Does the good Lord make green apples, child? Of course I told him yes."

Jay got to his feet and danced her around the living room.

"Iris is drawing up papers today, and they'll be ready tomorrow morning. She says we can go over and open it up whenever we want."

That night in the kitchen of the Hartford house there was a proper Sprengsten celebration. The family members went from floor to floor, choosing rooms. By mutual agreement, Charlie had first choice; fidgety with excitement, she finally claimed the corner nursery bedroom. Stephen chose a large room with a view of the lake, across the hall from Jay. Danielle's choice was opposite Charlie, where two grand windows looked out through the limbs of an ancient maple tree in the front yard; Tommy was next to Stephen. Rooms for prospective patrons were reserved at the head of the stairwell, next to the bathrooms.

Annie took one look at the stairs and insisted on

the ground-floor servants' quarters. With the walls knocked out, the three tiny rooms would make one large, comfy apartment complete with a small fireplace and instant access to the kitchen. As a part of the lease, Alan Hartford had volunteered his grandmother's huge old dining room table and chairs and an original bed that had been in storage. Jay's savings were deemed sufficient to cover the costs of renovation, reroofing, and additional furniture, with enough remaining for insurance premiums for the business.

They were going to be a family again, and in the same house! Even Jessica Sprengsten couldn't find a hole in the solution and reluctantly agreed that Danielle could move in as soon as her room was ready. They partied and danced and planned until they were exhausted, then Jay drove everyone home and hightailed it to Annie's apartment to await delivery of the lease.

"Who is Annie Chatfield?" Alice Faye's furious voice echoed in the Bowmont foyer and she nailed Parker with a deadly glare.

He stared at her. "What are you talking about?" It was noon, and he'd come home to change before meeting his father's flight.

"You said you had the Hartford property all sewn up," she accused.

"I do. We'll probably close tomorrow."

"Well, the real estate office just called, looking for you. Alan Hartford changed his mind and took it off the market. Not only that, the broker says he leased the place to some woman named Annie Chatfield."

"What are you talking about?" Parker refused to acknowledge the icy feeling trying to climb his spine. The deal was done. It was all but delivered. What the hell had happened?

Alice Faye's voice continued through the haze. "Your father wanted that property. He's been waiting years to buy it, and he gave you carte blanche. I want to know what happened."

"I don't know, Mother." He spoke to her sharply for the first time in memory. "I'm not a mind reader. Since you didn't find out, I'll have to call the broker." He went into his father's library and closed the door. Alice Faye was never wrong. The deal had gone sour.

His mind went over the events of last evening, the reality looming larger. The office had tracked him down at Jolene's with an urgent message from a local real estate agent. He'd already waited two interminable hours for Jillian to get out the door to a movie so he could meet Jolene in the pool, and he almost hadn't returned the call at all. The agent had been aware that Bowmont Properties was purchasing the Hartford place, and she had an out-of-town buyer interested in a quick purchase of the house itself, willing to remove it from the property in order to preserve it.

It had been a decent offer with a couple of the usual strings, but Jolene was getting upset that he was making her wait to talk business, so he'd given the offer a perfunctory listen, then blown it off. It had seemed too pat, and after he'd taken possession and inspected the old place himself, he might agree to sell it, but not before.

At that moment his only interest had been waiting naked in the pool. Besides, Hartford need never know there'd been an offer. He told the agent the house was already sold.

Alan Hartford had tested him, and he'd failed. He'd failed himself and failed his father.

He punched the wall in anger.

13

The weather moved toward fall, and while days were still warm and balmy, there was cool in the evening air and heavy dew in the early mornings. After two years in Mideast deserts, the change of season was deliciously welcome, and Jay greeted each day with newly discovered appreciation. He'd almost forgotten how beautiful America could be. He walked among the happy smiles of his brothers and sisters, their shouts and horseplay replacing the discipline of barracks life, Annie's home cooking instead of army chow, and life was wonderful.

There was only one missing element, which he did his damnedest not to think about.

Otherwise, he donned civilian life like a pair of old, comfortable shoes and put in days at Milbrook while his family tackled the outside of the mansion, renamed Chatfield's Bed 'N Breakfast Inn. The name had been granted with Alan Hartford's blessing and attested to by a prim, elegant sign that Tommy had labored over next to the front door.

They unboarded the old house and trimmed away

overgrown hedges interwoven with primroses gone wild, freeing the lower windows to sunlight and unobstructed views of the lake. Annie supervised as the boys crawled onto the roof to sweep out the eaves and scaled ladders to scrape peeling paint from the porches and window ledges with wire brushes.

Inside, Charlie and Danni used vinegar and water to wash the windows while Tommy and Stephen manned ladders and washed the outsides as well, wiping them with old issues of the *Bowmont Herald* until they were squeaky clean.

Midweek they were able to begin repainting the wood portions of the faded exterior a rich, colonial white. Opinions on the color of the window trim had been divided between hunter green and butter yellow; sample splotches on the porch had decided them on the green. Evenings, Jay and the boys reshaped Annie's living area, and when it was finished, they tackled the roof, stripping off layers of old tar paper and shingles, hoisting up lugs of new ones.

Jay called Leanna to see how she was doing and asked her to put her father on so he could apologize in person for the accident; he endured Bowmont's gruff acceptance, unbending disapproval in every word. Eventually Leanna had taken the phone from her father and requested Saturday evening for their trip to Wellington.

While he had mixed feelings about the responsibility of spending another evening with Parker Bowmont's sister, on Saturday Jay knocked off early and had barely dressed when she arrived in a taxi. She was lovely in a short denim jacket, a bright yellow shirt, and a long, swingy western skirt. He'd sorted through his stored clothing and discovered that all his sports jackets were too small across the chest. There was no time to have any of his father's clothing altered, so he'd opted for a navy cable-knit sweater and a pair of chinos.

He escorted her to the pickup truck, and they were off to Wellington. Leanna folded her stick, which she clearly hated, and during the drive he watched her vacillate between apprehension and genuine excitement at the prospect of negotiating unfamiliar streets unaided.

"I'm so used to having things done for me," she confessed. "I'm always with a driver or someone who takes care of me. My father worries all the time that something will happen, Parker worries. Alice Faye reminds me constantly that I can't do things or that I'll get hurt. Practically the only freedom I have is Thumper."

He looked over at her. "Bambi's friend?"

She laughed. "My horse. It was her name when I got her. We used to race down to the lake. I can't do it anymore 'cause she's getting old and it's dangerous for her now. Me too." She smiled a sad smile. "Sometimes I still canter when I know it's flat, but it's not the same. I don't know what I'd do without her."

A short while later they entered the city. She made him promise to give her information only if she became confused or couldn't figure out how to handle whatever situation they encountered. "Just don't let me walk into open manholes," she joked nervously. "I want to practice using paper money, finding my way around on a bus, getting directions and not getting lost."

They agreed on an Italian restaurant in the theater district, and if she found it within an hour, her reward was going anywhere she chose to celebrate. If not, he got to select a booby prize—something disgusting on the menu that she would have to taste. They left the truck in a parking garage, and after giving her basic

orientation information, due north and the name of
the boulevard, he hovered close by as she began her
quest. She found her way to a phone booth, made the
call for reservations, and received instructions con-
cerning the address.

He was amazed that she became confused only once
and then straightened herself out by seeking guidance
from a passerby. He waited with her for a bus, watched
her make arrangements with the driver and find a seat.
She got off at the right cross street, and he allowed her
to bump into a couple of trash cans and a bus bench,
explore them with her stick, and generally make her way
through busy intersections without interference. Not
once did she call out to check if he was close at hand,
which also surprised him. Occasionally pedestrians
would offer assistance but more often than not she was
ignored in the flow of humanity, and he was stunned at
the magnitude of obstacles she was forced to negotiate.
His heart went out to her stubborn determination.

She found the street but passed the small restaurant,
and he couldn't understand how she could miss the
heavy smell of garlic filling the immediate vicinity. Maybe
she'd gotten confused again. He came within an inch of
calling out to her, but she made a smart about-face and
came back to the doorway with a huge smile. "You were
going to let me go on by, weren't you?" she accused
gaily.

"Yeah, I wanted to see you eat squid." Once they
were inside and seated, his congratulations were genuine. "You did terrific. Name your prize."

"Bette Midler's new movie," she demanded snappily,
proud of herself. "I had our cook check it out, and the
theater should be pretty close by."

Dinner was a further test. He read her the menu and

the waiter recited the specials; she settled on fettuccine and an arugula salad.

"Two," he said to the waiter. "And a bottle of Soave."

"Please tell the chef I'm blind and will need the salad leaves quite small," she said to the man. After a short while, their food arrived. She carefully arranged her wine and water glasses at specific angles to her plate and tucked her napkin into the neckline of her shirt, patting it down to make sure it covered the front of her. "I haven't eaten fettuccine in a long time," she warned. "This may be embarrassing."

"Not for me," he told her soberly. He saw the anxious set of her chin and leaned over to drawl obnoxiously in her ear, "I don't give a hoot how you eat your noodles, lady, s'long as you don't git any on my over-halls."

She burst out laughing, and dinner was fine. He offered a final toast with the last of the wine. "You are undoubtedly the bravest lady I know. I salute you." He clinked her glass and drank.

She was slow to drink the toast and suddenly silent. "I'm not that brave," she said after a moment of fighting tears. "Sometimes I'm scared to death." Then she rallied. "But not as scared as I was." She finished the rest of her drink. He felt a distinct pinch at his ego when she paid their bill, insisting that it was part of the agreement. He watched her locate a ten- and a twenty-dollar bill, put payment inside the waiter's folder, then receive and identify change, and leave a tip. Confirming that she had placed the denominations in the correct spaces in her wallet, he was able to convince her to accept two tens and a five of his own, watched her put them in the proper partitions, then took her to the movie.

As they left the theater, he nearly bumped into Jolene Llowell waiting by the ticket booth. He felt himself dropping back in time, into a never-never land of feelings he'd never really suppressed. Slim and gorgeous in a careless white suede jacket, a bright red minidress, and long, long legs ending in sandals, God, she was beautiful, and her image slipped right back into its old haunt in his heart. He couldn't believe it.

Jolene saw him instantly, and he read surprise and recognition in her face. She crossed to the two of them, and he was so astonished at her presence that he barely managed to say hello. Jolene greeted Leanna, but her eyes never left his; he drank in her perfect face and eyes, the joyous golden hair, and a body even more incredible than he remembered. Parker joined them at that moment, his face a glowering study in suspicion and anger.

Leanna reached out to her brother and pulled him away. He was forced to clear a path for them to the other side of the theater. "It's my idea, Park. I asked him to bring me, so please don't get upset."

He was furious. "I do *not* understand, Leanna. Where's Curt? Why the hell are you here with the one person I cannot tolerate?"

She stopped him with unaccustomed strength. "It's a favor to me, and I don't want Curt to find out about it. I'll explain it all later, just promise you won't make trouble. Promise," she demanded.

"This better be good," he grumbled, staring over her shoulder at Jolene talking to Jay. "Why on earth does it have to be Sprengsten!"

Jay and Jolene were caught in a whirlpool of their own feelings, more powerful than either had thought possible. "I didn't know you were home," she said accusingly.

"A few weeks," he admitted, regretting every

instant of that time. Why hadn't he called? Why? His reluctance to see her seemed so stupid now. She punished him by deliberately turning away to watch Parker and Leanna. He deserved it and gave himself the solace that she still cared enough to do it. All was not lost.

Parker's eyes were dull with distrust and territorial imperative. Jay Sprengsten and Jolene. Intolerable. He stalked across the theater entrance, pulling his sister with him; he slid his arm around Jolene's waist, claiming her, but he had to surrender Leanna, and it was a thorn in his side that would fester.

"Let's go somewhere for a drink." Jolene's voice was full of brittle energy as she openly attempted to manipulate the awkward situation. Both Jay and Parker were silent, neither willing to move into proximity and escalate a potentially violent explosion. Nor were they willing to give ground.

Leanna settled the matter. "We have other plans, but thanks."

Jay immediately backed up her decision, every fiber in his body screaming to stay near Jolene, but grateful to Leanna; it would be impossible to witness an evening with Jolene on Parker's arm, her exquisite body next to his. He stood, dreading their leaving together, knowing that she would be in Parker's bed that night despite anything he could do. Parker would see to it.

After tersely awkward good-nights, they rounded the corner. "Thanks for getting us out of there." He searched for something to do. Anything but go home and think. "How about a nightcap to celebrate the evening?" Leanna agreed, and he supervised as she held up her hand to hail a taxi. The driver recommended a new club called Emerald, and a few minutes later they were seated inside. Leanna's cheeks brightened with excitement.

"I've never been to a nightclub," she announced happily. "What's it look like?"

Jay described the small, smoky room with its staging area and the booths along the walls and a cluster of tables surrounding the dance floor. "Sort of a blackish grape green," he told her, "with pin spots onto the tables and booths. It's so dark, it's hard to see." They gave their drink order, and when the cocktail waitress returned, Leanna toasted the success of their evening.

"What's going on with your family?" she questioned, deciding to stay away from the subject of her brother and Jolene. In addition to the standoff between Jay and Parker over her accident, she was certain there was an unresolved situation of some kind between Jay and Jolene. It was written in their voices, and vibes had been bouncing all over the place. It had been impossible to ignore. "Have you located a house yet?"

"Actually, we got the Hartford property." He told her about Annie's lease. "It's almost completely repainted, and we'll be moving in over the next couple of weeks."

She considered for a moment. "My dad's upset," she admitted. "Alice Faye's wanted that place for years. And Parker will be furious when he finds out." Another situation that would add to the animosity between the two.

"Charlie and Annie managed it," he said vaguely, his mind elsewhere. "I had very little to do with it." He picked up her hand and pressed her fingers into his callused palm. "I'm just the roofer." He was unable to continue the charade. The encounter with Jolene had thrown him a major curve, and it was impossible to concentrate; and it was unfair to Leanna to pull her down to his level.

"Do you want to talk about her?"

He realized that dodging the issue was pointless. Even this blind girl had picked up on it. "That obvious, huh?"

"You two are . . ."

"Were. I was going to marry her . . . a few thousand years ago. Give or take four."

"I don't know what to say."

"There's nothing to say. She's with your brother. Has been for two years. End of story."

Leanna, mercifully, didn't pursue the subject. The dance music stopped, and there was a lull while the floor show curtain was lowered. Jay's stomach, already knotted from his confession, curled into a fist when he saw Curt come into the room with a pretty young redhead in tow. She was carrying theater programs. He swore under his breath. The evening was cursed, there was no doubt about it.

The two were shown to a nearby booth, and before he could say anything to Leanna, he was compelled to watch disaster in the making; Curt kissed the girl, then, his voice clearly audible as he left the booth, he called back to her, "Christie, you want to order the usual? I'm going to check my messages."

"Sure, honey," she answered. "Just don't take too long, the show's about to start."

Before Jay could suggest it, Leanna was standing to leave. "If you don't mind, I'm getting a little tired." He breathed a hard sigh of relief and dumped a few dollars onto the table. Guiding her past Christie's table to the exit, he carefully blocked her from her fiancé's view as they passed the public phones. The floor show was beginning, and Curt had elevated his voice above the MC and the overture.

"Just tell Miss Bowmont I called."

Jay felt Leanna stiffen.

"Tell her I'm on my way to the airport and I'll call her tomorrow. Thank you."

Curt hung up briefly, then inserted more coins. As he dialed again, Leanna continued walking. Outside the club, in the chill night air, Jay hailed a taxi. During the ride she seemed to shrink into herself and was silent the few minutes it took to return to the parking garage and retrieve the pickup. He was equally introspective as he worked their way out of the city.

"It was Curt, wasn't it?" Her voice was small and full of pain.

He felt horrible for her hurt and disillusionment, but there was no way to lie to her.

"Did you know he was there?"

"I saw him come in," he admitted.

A thick silence descended.

"I wasn't certain until I heard him on the telephone," she whispered. "Is Christie pretty?" Tears were poised on her lashes, and she searched in her purse for a tissue.

"Look, don't do this to yourself," he told her. "There could be a hundred reasons why he was there." He hated himself as he searched for a way to defend her against Curt's actions. The son of a bitch. He came up dry. At his side, Leanna tried to maintain her dignity as she dabbed at the tears sliding down her face.

His thoughts found their way to Jolene and Parker. It was nearly midnight, and they were probably somewhere in bed together. He tightened his jaw in futility. Another impossible situation. What the hell, they'd been together for a couple of years. What difference did one more night make? He was getting himself nuts for no good reason. "Are we having fun yet?" he joked feebly.

"A fine pair we are." She choked laughter through her tears. "You're in love with my brother's girlfriend, and my fiancé is out with another woman. We ought to make them both crazy and get married."

He had to smile at her courage. Things were a mess. "What, and spoil our fun?" he retorted.

He drove on, and her voice came out of the darkness from her side of the truck. "You know what Bette Midler would do?" she demanded. "She'd order champagne."

"You got it," he said to her, and pulled into an all-night supermarket. She and a clerk selected two bottles of chilled champagne, a couple of packages of deli cheese, a box of soda crackers, and some fruit. He emptied his wallet, and she charged the rest on her father's credit card. He decided Sam Bowmont could afford it, and they returned to the truck. "Now where, madame?"

"I don't want to go home. I'm not in the mood for messages."

"All right." He could certainly understand that.

"How about Annie's? Does she like champagne?"

"I most certainly do, child." Annie disappeared and returned with her wig in place. She examined the icy bottles of Perrier-Jouet. "Ain't never had any of this," she said dubiously. After her first sip she smiled a broad smile, and the first bottle went down; the three of them were ready for more. Annie sliced the last of the fruit and replenished the cheese while Jay popped the cork on the second bottle and poured the expensive wine into Annie's Depression glasses.

"To discovery," said Leanna. "Life would terribly dull without it." There were tears in her eyes as she fingered her watch. It was well after two o'clock in the morning. "If you wouldn't mind, I'd like to spend the night."

"Bed or cot?" Annie answered.

"Cot." For the first time since leaving the nightclub, Leanna felt better, and she knew why. Jay and Annie were treating her like a real person. A sighted person. At the end of the second bottle, it took all their efforts to set up the cot, then Jay retreated to the bunk in the treehouse and Annie provided her with one of her flannel nighties. Leanna was asleep seconds after her head touched the pillow.

14

The next morning, after a quick cup of coffee to override a small hangover, Leanna climbed into the truck and Jay drove her home early enough to be in the house before her family discovered her missing. She did not want to explain being out all night, but as they drove up her father's lane, Jay warned her that Parker was pacing in the courtyard. "Whatever you need, I'm here," he said, and the truck came to a stop.

The passenger door jerked open and Alice Faye's scolding voice emerged from the house. "We've been trying to find you for hours. Your father's out driving around looking for you. Where's she been?"

"Not now. Let's get her inside first." Next to her, Parker's voice held a warning, and she knew she would have some tall explaining to do after all. He helped her down from the cab. "Are you all right?" he asked tersely.

"I should have called. I'm sorry." Her apology was lost in the din.

Alice Faye wouldn't be denied and her voice continued to rail. "Does she know? What's he doing here?"

"Know what?" she asked. Alice Faye was never up this early. Something was obviously wrong. "Tell me what's going on."

The truck door slammed amid a confusion of conversations. Leanna was in a quandary. Questions were coming from every direction, about her, to her, and Parker wasn't answering. "What's going on?" she demanded again. "Somebody tell me."

Alice Faye was merciless. "She may as well know. The vet's been here for hours." Leanna felt the blood drain from her face, and went absolutely blank.

Jay was suddenly at her side. "Do you want me to stay a few minutes?" He covered her hand with his callused palm, and she clung to him tightly, seeking strength.

Parker's voice radiated disapproval that her trust had been given elsewhere. "Thumper's down," he said abruptly.

"Oh, God." Her fingers clutched at Jay's hand, and she was disoriented, lost in blackness. Which way was the stable? There was a thin neigh from the barn, and she got her bearings. She moved instantly toward the sound, pulling Jay along with her.

Alice Faye's irritated voice carried after them. "Why doesn't she come into the house? There's nothing she can do. Maybe her father can talk some sense into her, I certainly can't."

Inside the stall, Leanna let go of Jay's hand and went down in the straw next to her horse. The mare whinnied and tried to rise but was too weak. She put her hands soothingly on Thumper's neck and made small crooning noises into her ear. The horse stopped struggling and dropped her head heavily onto the straw; her sides heaved with her efforts to breathe, great rattling groans each time she drew a breath.

"Can't we get her up? What about the hoist?" Leanna cried. The old mare reacted again to the panic in Leanna's voice and made a valiant attempt to right herself, thrashing weakly about for a few moments. But her exhaustion was too severe. She lay groaning in the straw.

Jay looked to the winch and harness hanging from an overhead beam. What were they waiting for? He didn't know much about horses, but it was apparent that this one was in great distress, and if all of them used their weight . . .

The vet answered Leanna's question. "We've had her up twice, Miss Bowmont. She can't stand on her own."

Already distraught, Leanna was unprepared for this new disaster, and her heart began to break. The man stepped forward and touched her shoulder. "From the looks of things, she's been down most of the night. It's gone to pneumonia. I'm sorry."

He wanted to put Thumper down. He was telling her it was hopeless, that the old mare was dying, and there was nothing to be done. There was no choice. Thumper was suffering, and treatment would only prolong her agony. She nodded tightly, fighting tears. "Do it." She wouldn't cry until it was over. "Do it now."

The vet quickly reached into his bag and retrieved a large syringe. He filled it with chemicals from a glass vial and knelt by Thumper's head. The old mare heaved a strangled sigh, and her great heart stopped even as the vet searched for a vein in her neck for the injection.

Jay's heart broke for Leanna; he saw the fight go out of her the instant the mare died, saw the shattered look and the silent tears. She struggled to her feet and, after a moment, stumbled out of the stall, dazed and disconnected. He made a move to follow her, but Parker blocked his path. "Leave her alone. There's nothing you can do," he said coldly.

Jay pushed past him and walked a few paces away. "She's had a hell of a night, Parker, she's gonna need—"

"Really? Where'd you spend it?" Parker's eyes were full of hatred. "I have Jolene, so you took my sister?"

The questions were so vile, so stupid, and so ill timed that Jay lost it. Not giving a damn that Parker was a Bowmont or Leanna's brother, and rich enough to break him in half for the rest of his life, Jay grabbed Parker's shirt and slammed him against the wall of the barn. A modicum of satisfaction settled in his stomach when the air went out of him. "Not that it's any of your business," he said furiously, "but she stayed with a friend of mine. If you want to know anything else, you ask your sister."

He slammed him again for good measure, then went to find Leanna. She was huddled against the stable partition, racked with her grief. He pulled her to her feet and awkwardly took her in his arms. Crying was absolutely the best remedy he could think of, and he held her until the sobbing eased, daring Parker to do anything about it. "I'm here," he soothed the girl.

Parker waited at the door of the stall. His face was tight with restraint, but he didn't try to interfere. Finally Leanna gave a shuddered sigh and a small hug of thanks, then moved slowly out of Jay's arms. She was a little unsteady, and Parker stepped forward; the two of them walked her toward the house.

Jay said good-bye to her in the courtyard. "If you want to see me, or talk, or anything, call me at Annie's." Parker looked away.

She nodded, exhausted, and Jay watched her brother take her into the house. With the death of the horse, she'd lost an enormous chunk of her freedom, and that would be the next blow to come at her. Her father's Mercedes sped up the driveway and slid to a quick halt in the graveled courtyard. Jay pointed toward the house in answer to Sam Bowmont's unspoken question, and the older man went inside without breaking his stride. Jay wondered how long it would be before she told her family about Curt.

Jolene raged on. Jillian scrunched onto her chair, tucking her knees under her nightgown for warmth, trying not to hear the passion in her sister's voice.

"He's been home for weeks. I know he wants to see me, it was all over his face." She appraised herself in the hall mirror, made a face at her outfit, and pulled off an offending sandal to throw it at the kitchen door.

Jillian sipped at her tea and tried to remain a neutral voice in her sister's tantrum. It had started last night. Mrs. Bowmont had called a little after two in the morning, looking for Leanna and had summarily ordered Parker home to deal with a veterinarian; and Jolene's temper had continued bright and early this morning. It was painfully obvious to Jillian that her sister's interest in Jay had escalated dramatically since the last time they'd talked.

"And why was he with poor, blind Leanna if she's engaged to Curt?" Jolene paced the tiled floor in the kitchen, one copper sandal creating a hollow slap on the floor as she retrieved the other. "Why hasn't he called?" She flopped angrily onto a chair. "No wonder Parker's been such an ass for the last couple of weeks. I'll bet he knew Jay was home. Everybody in town probably knew."

She threw Jillian a grim glance. "Except me. Why didn't he call?" she wailed.

Jillian closed her eyes and cut to the chase. "Is there some law that says you can't call him?"

Jolene sprang out of the chair. "If he wants to see me, he can pick up the damn phone!" She jammed her foot into the sandal and headed for the door. "I'm getting out of here."

"What if someone calls?" She didn't dare say Jay.

"You tell him you don't know where I am!" The front door slammed, and seconds later Jolene's red Jaguar went squealing down the drive.

Jillian sat with her guilt. She'd gained nothing by keeping Jay's presence a secret. After driving by his construction site six different times in the past two weeks, she hadn't had the nerve to stop and say hello, but she'd sustained her hopes when he didn't contact Jolene. Cathy said he was working on the old Hartford house at night. With two jobs, he'd probably been too busy. She placed a sheepish call to Cathy. "I need Jay's number. I've tried information. Can you get it for me?"

"He lives with Annie Chatfield," Cathy told her sleepily. "Wellington Flats."

Annie Chatfield was listed. Gritting her teeth, she made the call. The cheerful voice of an older woman answered, and Jillian asked for Jay.

"He ain't here just now, sweetheart. You want me to have him call?"

Jillian hesitated, then made a decision. "Just tell him . . . Jolene called."

There was a minuscule pause on the other end of the line. "I'd be glad to," said the woman. Jillian gave her the number and hung up.

A few minutes later, Jay came in. Annie's message

prickled his skin. He'd have bet the farm that Jolene would die before giving in to call him. "She say what she wanted?" He tried to keep it casual, but Annie gave him a look. He punched the number and waited. When an answering machine clicked in, he hung up. Damn.

In the Llowell living room, Jillian waited by the ringing phone for the caller to leave a message and knew in her heart that it was Jay. She picked up the phone too late. Disappointed, she almost called him, then resisted. He and Jolene had to work this out before she got further involved. Jolene was interested in Jay and one of the unwritten rules in the lives of sisters was "Hands off the same man." With the bleak satisfaction that she had evened her debt, she went upstairs to get dressed.

Restless and energized and unable to focus on anything but Jolene's call, Jay got in the pickup with every intention of going straight to the Hartford place to check on the roof, but somehow he wound up on the road to the bluff. Jolene's red convertible was parked in the overlook, and he pulled the truck alongside. The body he'd spent all last night dreaming about was standing fifteen feet away, long legs bared in loose, rolled-to-the-thigh green shorts and a T-shirt. She was looking at him. Memories of the nights they'd spent together flooded his mind, and all he could think about was making love to her. Right here. Right now.

Conversation was mundane, awkward, pointless. He wanted to kiss her, to make love to her, but she held him at arm's length, her mouth hard and angry. "Why haven't you called?" she said harshly.

"You know why." Any remaining neutral territory slipped away, and he felt himself losing ground.

Finally she let him kiss her. After a moment she returned his kiss and when she shifted to a hard exploration of his mouth, he was lost. He'd have gone with her anywhere and followed her, kiss for kiss, down a longed-for, desperate path to entry.

"Admit it," she demanded heavily. "You still love me."

Wanting her, knowing no way to deny it, he kissed her until he was breathless. "Yes." She led him to the convertible and moved onto the backseat. He followed, disbelieving she would make love to him after spending the night with Parker. "What about him?" he asked, hands on her everywhere, undressing her, his body driven with need. "What about Parker?"

"What about him?" The question was muffled in his mouth as she kissed him.

He came up for air, uneasy at her casual attitude. "You're sleeping with him."

She kissed him again, urgently, confidently, until all he wanted in the world was to be inside her body, owning her, making her his in one mindless, effortless act. But her voice brought him back to sanity. "What's that got to do with us?"

He realized then that she was serious and felt the moment shift irretrievably. As if she sensed the change, she kissed him with renewed passion, tightening her body against him, but he couldn't buy into it, couldn't get past her words. Suddenly reality was forty feet tall in front of him. This wasn't a renewal of their relationship; it wasn't a commitment, an admission that things were still the same. This was Jolene willing to have sex with him and *not* give up Parker; it was making sure he was still on the hook.

Stung at the knowledge, he pulled away. "You're

sleeping with Parker, and I'm supposed to do what . . . share?" He stared at her, incredulous, his anger building. He got out of the car and walked off his arousal, his mind working furiously. Goddamn, he wanted her and she knew it. Even if it happened, then what? Parker last night, him this afternoon, Parker again tonight? Then who-knows-who next? No way. One or the other. Not both. "No, thanks."

She stared at him, caught, furious. He saw the flush of anger move into her face as she neatened her clothing in short, deliberate mannerisms; not bothering to replace her bra, she tucked in her shirt, buttoning each button of her shorts with prolonged effort, watching his face, gauging the effect of her naked breasts beneath the tight T-shirt, gambling that he'd give in. When the impasse lengthened and she saw it wasn't going to work, she said angrily, "Then do without me."

She climbed out of the car, crossed to him, and put her hands on his shoulders. Standing on tiptoe, she kissed him, rubbing herself slowly back and forth against his chest, her hips against his groin. It sent him spinning over the edge. He kissed her back, hungrily, wanting her absolutely, determined to have her and Parker be damned. But she jerked out of his arms and gave him a stinging slap in the face before she walked back to the driver's side of her car. "You know where you can find me when you change your mind," she taunted.

Aching with want, rigid with need, he watched her drive away and called himself a fool.

Cathy Rice looked at her watch, but the time, as usual, didn't register. It was sometime in the afternoon. She sat in Christie's bedroom, trying to be patient.

"Thanks for the tickets, Cath, me 'n Curt had a real good time the other night. You okay?" Christie was winding her red hair on hot rollers, and she stopped long enough to sit on the bed next to Cathy. "You still messed up over that Nick guy, honey, you been upset over him for weeks."

"You got anything?" Cathy eyed her hopefully. "I need to get up. I could use a little party."

Christie paused. "Yeah, okay, sure. For a friend." She opened a new pack of cigarettes and tapped one out with a long, French-manicured nail, then opened a powder box on her dressing table. Inside was a small plastic eyewash bottle containing a quarter inch of liquid. Unscrewing the top, she carefully squeezed two drops onto the cigarette. "Don't try to drive on it," she cautioned. She handed the cigarette to Cathy, then replaced the bottle in its hiding place. "I been saving it for my first weekend off."

"Is it really good? 'Cause I'm really down."

"I can see that," Christie soothed. "This is very heavy, so remember, whatever you do, don't drive with it, you got enough to get all the way up. The guy I got it from says it's big time, and he knows all about this stuff." She looked at the clock and swore. "Damn, I gotta get going."

Cathy marked a corner of the cigarette with a pen and carefully dropped it into her purse. In the bathroom, Christie was raking curlers out of her hair and talking about her boyfriend. "I think I'm really starting to get serious about him, you know? I mean, we always have a good time together, and he seems like he's really getting ready to settle down and I cain't do this forever, you know."

The powder box was on the dresser. It was so easy to

slide off the top and unscrew the cap to the little bottle. Christie wouldn't care. Cathy liberally dosed three more of her own cigarettes with the liquid before the sound of hairspray came from the bathroom. She replaced the cap and jiggled the plastic bottle. There was still a small amount of the liquid in the bottom. Christie wouldn't know the difference.

"We gotta hurry." She closed her purse. "I gotta get gas."

Inside the bathroom, Christie swore again.

The powder box was in precisely the same place when she came back to the bedroom. Cathy handed her the pack of cigarettes. "Don't forget these," she said happily. "And thanks for the party. I won't forget this." She picked up one of Christie's flight bags and opened the door for her friend.

"That's okay. Sometimes a girl needs a lift, and right now I gotta get to the airport or there won't be no more parties." Christie closed and locked the door.

15

Sam sat heavily on the wrought-iron love seat next to Leanna and studied his daughter's face. This morning he'd found her sitting in the garden again, silent as a shadow, and he chafed at her suffering. She wasn't eating, and he'd seen her avoid two of Curt's calls from Chicago. How on earth was she going to handle her grief when his time came six months from now?

The phone rang, and Alice Faye called out to him that it was his attorney's office. Could they change his appointment to three this afternoon? He nodded in agreement and braced himself to satisfy his wife's curiosity about why he was seeing his lawyer. He put his arm around his daughter and pulled her close.

"Why aren't you talking to Curt, honey? Are you upset with him for some reason?"

Leanna heard the concern in her father's voice, felt the oddly light weight of his arm around her shoulders. She laced her hand with his, and the soft flesh of his fingers gave to the bone. How odd that being away from someone for only three weeks could give her new insight. One of the things about being blind was that it forced a constant awareness of the smallest detail to keep her world defined.

She covered over her ambivalence about Curt. "He wants to set a wedding date," she said, and to avoid discussion about that part of her life, she hurried on to a subject she knew her father would understand. "I'm still upset about Thumper, and it's just too difficult to talk about right now."

"That's what husbands are for, sweetheart. You're not having second thoughts about getting married, are you?"

She was convinced that her father was smaller somehow, and more frail than he'd been before his trip. Even Alice Faye had complimented him on the weight he'd lost recently. And as someone who depended on voice quality, she detected a new, odd note in his speech, something akin to pain, when he talked to her. He moved more slowly, had less energy, less breath.

When Suli had died, she'd been so wrapped up in her own life and her blindness that mortality in general had not occurred to her beyond the death of the beloved collie, but her grief over the loss of Thumper had triggered a much more pervasive fear: the reality of aging and the death of people she loved. It came to her suddenly that her father was not well.

"You're ill, aren't you?" She listened carefully to his response and heard the tiniest beat of hesitation before he replied.

"Good heavens, no." He paused again. "Well, I've got a few medical problems, masculine in nature," he joked lightly. "Perfectly normal at my age. Certainly nothing I care to discuss with my daughter who's about to be married. I'm just worried about you."

Her father had never lied to her, and somewhat reassured by his response, she decided that if her being sad and mourning for Thumper was worrying him, there was no point in distressing him further by a description of Curt's behavior at the nightclub. She resolved to put on a better face.

"I think I'll call Chicago," she ventured, and was pleased at the energy that came into her father's voice when he told her he thought it was a good idea.

Satisfied that things would soon be back to normal, he walked with her into the study and waited while she called Curt's hotel. He had checked out, so Sam kissed his daughter and sent her on her way. A few minutes later an erratic, thundering heartbeat and a resulting dizzy spell from his medication forced him to rest on the couch in the study. After it passed, he found Alice Faye on the patio; he dodged her follow-up questions about Burt Holman by telling her he was seeing the lawyer to tie up a few third-quarter corporate details and would be home for dinner.

At three o'clock he arrived at Holman's office. By three-fifteen he was giving the attorney his decisions regarding his estate. "For the moment, Bowmont Real Estate and Midland Insurance are to stay split between Parker and Alice Faye, sixty–forty, but add a provision that she can't dispose of her portion of either without Parker's consent. Alice Faye keeps her jewelry, of course, and the *Bowmont Herald* goes to Leanna. Make sure it stays her separate property. If her marriage to Curt doesn't work out, I don't want him to have an interest in anything. You'll see to that?"

"I will." Holman made another note.

"Give Leanna a two-acre parcel on the other side of the Hartford place so she can build a house on it if she chooses. Oh, and one last thing. I'll need contracts for the managing directors of all three firms extended for five years."

"I can take care of this in a codicil for the time being," said the lawyer. "If you decide to make more extensive changes, I recommend a new will. What about the trust? Any changes there?"

Sam paused, contemplative, then shook his head. "No, it's fine." No point in opening old wounds.

Curt decided something was up and flew in from Chicago. Sales had gone very well in the Windy City, very well indeed, plus he'd had a couple of promising interviews. He had a great deal of money and a fistful of wedding suggestions guaranteed to take Leanna's mind off her dead horse. Besides, he was tired of her subdued moods and ready to move on.

On the taxi ride from the airport it occurred to him that either Sam or Alice Faye had been working on her and, worst case, he'd have to warm up a mild case of cold feet. Bridal nerves. He broke a few speed laws getting from his apartment to the Bowmont mansion. Thirty seconds in the door, however, Leanna surprised him by suggesting that they go out to dinner. Whatever was on her mind, he wasn't going to have to wait long to hear about it.

After the waiter departed with their order, she got into it, catching him completely off guard.

"Who's Christie?"

"A longtime friend. Someone I've known since, gosh, grade school," he said smoothly. How the hell could she know about Christie? He watched her face and was quiet, waiting her out. Until he knew what information she had, silence was the best defense. She couldn't see, but she could sure as hell hear, and he concentrated on keeping his voice under control.

"You were at the Emerald Club together last Saturday."

"Yes, we were." Obviously they'd been seen, so denying it was the last thing to do. "I ran into her on the street, and we went there for a drink to celebrate her new job." That was safe enough. And it was true, they'd had a drink. Why didn't matter. He waited to see how much information she had so he could figure out where it had come from.

When she didn't elaborate, he took the offensive. "I was on my way to Chicago, and she wanted to go to the Emerald," he repeated. Also true, and he was satisfied that there was honesty in his voice. He took her face in his hands. "You're jealous."

She stood her ground. "I don't know what I am."

"Well, I do. You're jealous. I think it's terrific. It means you really do care about me." He kept her face captive, kissed her, and gauged her response. Cool, but willing to be convinced, he decided. If he tried to discover how much more she knew, his questions might lead to doors that he didn't want opened. He forestalled further discussion by leaping to the obvious and forcing her on the defensive. "You don't . . ." He produced a confused laugh. "You can't think I'd ask you to marry me if I was seeing someone else?"

Before she could respond, he built on a little more truth. "I'll admit that I'm a normal, healthy male, Leanna. If I was seeing another woman, it wouldn't be unreasonable. It has been the better part of a year, and most couples would have a pretty healthy sexual relationship by now. Look at your brother and Jolene.

The fact that you and I don't have sex hasn't been easy."

"I know that, but—"

"But what?" He went on the attack. "You've made it pretty plain that it's what you want and I've toed the line, but it really isn't normal, you know. Couples these days don't remain celibate when they're planning to be married. I mean, I've tried to make allowances, but I'm beginning to wonder if you really want to marry me or you said yes because you're afraid there won't be another chance."

Bingo. From the frozen look on her face, he realized he'd hit a nerve. Totally unforeseen, he'd been right on target, and he was thrilled with his discovery. She was afraid of losing him. Playing her from here would be easy. Confident once again, he relaxed and switched directions to put things back on track.

"Look, this is crazy. I love you and I want us to get married." He pulled her closer and nuzzled her cheek. "We'll invite Christie to the wedding. And if there is some kind of problem, if you're avoiding sex with me for any reason—you can tell me, sweetheart. I'll understand. I really will."

"It's not that at all," she answered finally.

She stayed in his arms, but her voice told him she was utterly confused and nervous, and her body had tightened at the mention of the *s* word. Of course, she was nervous about getting into bed with him. He'd let the incident in the stable cloud his thinking, and he kicked himself for not seeing it sooner. From now on, life with her was going to be a piece of cake. "There's a small hotel about two blocks from here, very private," he whispered modestly. "Very discreet. We could spend the night, and I guarantee you won't have any doubts about the way I feel tomorrow morning."

She stiffened, and he knew instantly that he'd moved things too far; he shifted gears and decided to punish her. "On second thought, I don't think sex is the answer. Maybe sex isn't the problem here." He deliberately moved away from her, sighed out loud, and let the silence build between them again. "It looks like I'm the one who needs to do some thinking. I know how I feel about you, but maybe I shouldn't commit to this marriage until I'm sure how you feel about me." He pushed the napkin into her fingers, and she was startled. "Look at you jump. Clearly you don't trust me."

He signaled the waiter and busied himself ordering wine. He made certain that the rest of the meal was strained. He sent her entrée back to the kitchen as unsatisfactory for a blind person, kept the anxious waiter hovering nearby. By jumping from subject to subject, he spun the illusion of an overt attempt to overcome his growing disappointment in her—all the while being rigidly civil and reasonable—he made her struggle to keep up and watched her fall into every trap he set.

During the drive to her father's estate, he said nothing until he kissed her good night in the courtyard. "I flew in from Chicago because I really wanted to see you," he told her coolly. True. "I have a callback interview tomorrow afternoon." This was also true. He walked her to the door. "When I get back, I really think we should announce our wedding plans or call everything off."

He could see she was shaken as she went in. She'll do it, he told himself. She won't take a chance on starting over. The dragon lady's got her too insecure for that. He kissed his fingers and blew the kiss toward Alice Faye's window, then got in his car to go have a drink and celebrate.

Inside her room, Leanna undressed with fumbling fingers. Curt was angry with her for the first time in their relationship. Somehow things had gotten all turned around. She ran a quick bath and forgot to check the temperature, nearly scalding her foot when she stepped in the tub; she added cold water full force until it was cool enough to bathe in and tried to retrace the ring of logic.

When she'd asked about Christie, Curt hadn't denied being with her, hadn't sounded guilty or caught or deceptive about it. He'd been very forthright that he knew her, that they were friends, and deny as she might, he was right: she'd been jealous.

Looking back, she realized she'd sounded like a possessive, insecure wife quizzing an innocent husband. He had good reason to be upset with her. However she reconstructed their conversation, it came back every time to her being suspicious—because she was blind—and that she was unwilling to make a commitment about sleeping with him or setting a wedding date—because she was blind. It was her fault, not his. Now he was wondering whether or not they should get married at all.

She got into bed fighting tears.

Jillian ran her fingers up and down the middle of her forehead, trying to ease the ache in her temples. From the moment Jolene had slammed into the house after her meeting with Jay and invaded her bedroom,

alternately demanding and pleading for advice, it had
built to what was now a shining crescendo of headaches.
The fact that it was her own doing, that she'd set things
in motion, gave her no relief whatsoever.

She listened a third time to her sister's tale of kissing
Jay, of her confusion about her feelings, mixed with
pleas for sisterly advice.

"Parker's fun and he's got a great future and he's rich
enough to make me secure for life," Jolene repeated.
"And Jay's got this crummy job and all his brothers and
sisters to support. . . . But, oooh, Jill, just kissing him
brought back all these feelings. I'd forgotten! If Parker
finds out . . ." Jolene threw herself on the bed and yelled
at the ceiling in frustration. "I hate this! Help me!"

Her feelings sandpapered raw, her duty exhausted,
Jillian gave her sister the bald truth. "Face it, Jo. You
can't have both."

Jolene rolled off the end of the bed with a stubborn
look on her face. "I think I can." She made a show of
pulling her bra out of her hip pocket.

Jillian felt her face freeze. There'd been more than
kissing going on at the bluff. Her headache catapulted
into a new orbit.

"Jay's not going anywhere." Jolene laughed and dangled the bra from her fingers, then draped it carelessly
across one shoulder. "All I have to do is choose which
one I want." She disappeared down the hall.

After a moment, Jillian followed her and stood in
Jolene's doorway with advice she knew her sister would
ignore. "They're not going to agree to share you. And if
you don't tell them, sooner or later they'll find out, and
then what? They wouldn't trust you again, and you can't
have a relationship without trust." She wandered restlessly around the room while Jolene changed clothes.

"I'm sorry I can't tell you what you want to hear, Jo," she finished miserably. "Listen, I've been thinking, and I've decided to go back to New York."

She hadn't been, really, but Jolene's episode with Jay made it clear she had to get out of Walden City. Jay's continued interest in her sister hurt like hell, but knowing it resolved her dilemma. There was no point in kidding herself further.

"You can't leave now," Jolene argued. "You promised you'd stay for my birthday. The only reason Mom and Dad agreed that I didn't have to go with them was you being here."

"I know, but after that, I'm going back."

"Do what you want. I just have to decide about Parker. Then I'll know what to do about Jay."

Jillian escaped to her room, exhausted by her efforts to remain neutral and battered by the betrayal of her own rules of honesty. Two sisters in love with the same man might work in the movies, but in real life it was a nightmare. She tried her best to drown her feelings with loyalty to her sister, but she wasn't sure she could make it until Jolene's birthday.

For the rest of the day, she avoided answering the telephone for fear it would be Jay trying to reach Jolene. But he didn't call, and Parker stayed that night in her sister's bedroom.

Leanna invited them to the Bowmont estate for a swim the next morning. They all sat in the shade beneath the sun umbrella until Parker and Jolene went for a drive, then Jillian did fifty laps in the pool. It felt good coming out of the water and letting the August sun bake her skin. Standing on the teak decking to let most of the pool water drip from her suit, she let her mind wander to the clamor of the breeze through the drying leaves of the beech trees at the end of the lawn. "It's so peaceful here."

The sun's heat warmed her face. A huge sip of iced tea cooled its way to the pit of her stomach and recoiled nicely as she wiped the butt of the glass across her forehead. She put it aside and stretched out on the lounge to let her muscles sink through to China. "I hate the thought of going back to New York," she said absently.

"I thought you liked New York."

"Nobody likes New York. You either love it or you hate it."

"What about you?"

"I love it and I hate it. And at the end of August, I really hate it."

Leanna laughed. "Why don't you stay here?"

Jillian sighed a deep sigh. "It's complicated. I need to go back." She took another sip and turned over on the lounge, adjusting the back of her suit for an uninterrupted tan line, and allowed herself to doze.

Long moments passed before Leanna directed her question toward the plastic squeak of the lounge chair. "Does Parker talk about me to you and Jolene?" She felt supremely disloyal asking the question, but her brother's "poor little rich girl" comment and her conversation with Curt had been nagging at her like two badly pounded thumbs. If she didn't talk to someone about it soon, she was going to explode.

"He told us you were engaged. . . ."

Jillian's tone wasn't particularly cautious, just carefully honest; having opened the subject, Leanna pushed into it. "You don't have to answer, but does he think I'm marrying Curt because I'm afraid?"

There was another small creak from the lounge.

"Afraid of what? I think he considers you the strongest person he knows. I know I do."

Leanna turned her face away. "That no one else would marry me." It was finally said.

Jillian didn't answer right away. Trust was being given, friendship was now involved, and it had been a painful thing to ask. She gave Leanna's question the serious consideration it deserved. "I don't think your sight has anything to do with it, and I think Parker is convinced that you wouldn't marry anyone you didn't love," she answered. "And, I'm pretty sure you'd know by now if you weren't in love with Curt."

From her thoughtful response, Leanna realized that Jillian assumed that she and Curt were lovers. "That's what Parker says," she continued doggedly. "He says it's something you feel."

The lounge squeaked again, several times, and Jillian's voice now came at her from a sitting height. "He's right."

"Do you love someone?"

Jillian took a deep breath and let it out slowly. God in heaven, how to step out around this one and still be truthful? "I've been in love for a long time," she acknowledged. "He's in love with someone else, and I've never even kissed him. Isn't that stupid?"

There was a light tinkle of ice and the small *thunk* of a glass coming to rest on the deck.

"No, I don't think it's stupid." Leanna sighed tightly and ventured her secret. "Curt and I haven't . . . we don't sleep together, and, well, we had a fight, and I've been worried that maybe we should. That way I'd know if it's going to be okay."

Another painful admission, and a surprising one. Jillian felt helplessness settle over her like a sodden blanket. How on earth could she give intimate advice when her own love life was so nil it was embarrassing? Even before Jolene's meeting with Jay, she hadn't been able to make herself say hello to him, let alone admit to her feelings. She hadn't worked up to even *thinking* about getting into bed with him.

"Oh, God, Leanna, I wish I knew the answers. Right now, I'm not even sure about the questions. I'm sorry."

"That's okay. It's something everyone has to decide for themselves, and it wasn't fair to try to put you in my shoes."

Leanna offered her hand, and Jillian grasped it warmly.

"Between us?"

"Absolutely."

Even though he hadn't been named, Jillian was unsettled at having exposed her feelings about Jay. She excused herself to take a shower and emerged a few minutes later with her hair skinned back, wet curls held firmly in place by an elastic band. Barefoot, dressed carelessly in a baggy orange cotton tank top that came to her knees, she was thrilled and horrified to see Jay Sprengsten open the wrought-iron entry gate and make his way along the side of the pool toward her. He was bloody, screaming gorgeous in an army khaki T-shirt, washed-out denims that hung on his bony hips, and scuffed running shoes. Her heart jumped into a lurching rhythm, and she looked for an escape.

"Is Leanna here?" he asked her politely and without recognition.

Wordless, she pointed to the sunny end of the pool. Finding her voice, she called out, "Leanna. Jay Sprengsten's here to see you."

"How's she doing?" he asked quietly.

"She seems fine," Jillian answered carefully, not certain of the frame of reference. God, he was nine feet high.

He walked the length of the pool with the tall, proud carriage of the military. She joined them and was introduced as Jolene's sister.

"Jillian!" Jay gave her a swift hug and a kiss on the cheek. He didn't let her go immediately and stared down into her face. "My God, I didn't recognize you."

His glance swept down her body, back up, and she was mortified at his open, masculine inspection. No bra, no makeup, no preparation, she was instantly a blushing bundle of nerves, and every imperfection on her body—from her modest breast size to her sunburned, skinny, city-white ankles—ballooned into uglies the size of the Goodyear blimp under his judgment.

Astounded at his greeting, she felt heat flush her face and her body tingle madly at the touch of his arm when he circled her bare shoulder, his hip against hers. She stood on tiptoe and dared to kiss him back; his cheek was smooth with a faint smell of shaving cream. Feelings she couldn't have controlled allowed her to slip an arm around his waist, lean and hard as iron; having him so near, but so out of reach, made her crazy and her ego moaned that she hadn't at least put on lipstick so she'd have a face.

He turned his focus to her status as Jolene's grown-up sister and dropped his arm from around her shoulders; she instantly stepped away from him. Ping-Pong balls were battling for space in her insides.

He gave her a dazzling smile. "So, what are you, nineteen?"

"Twenty, three weeks ago." Crazy electrical forces

rattled and jangled her nerve endings just looking at
him.

"That's right, yours is the first and Jolene's is the last
day of August. Happy birthday, a little late. You owe me
a dance." He grinned, at the end of his interest, and
turned to Leanna. "I got your message. Sorry I couldn't
get here yesterday."

Jillian stayed a few more desperately painful
moments before creating a fictional phone call in order
to let them talk. "And then I'm going to crash for a
while," she lied. She sped into the house and hid in the
shadow of the library window to watch him until they
left the pool area. Seeing him had made things ten times
worse than she'd expected. Running back to New York
no longer seemed an answer. If it had been an adolescent crush before, it was a ten-alarm fire now. Out of
control and unpredictable.

Leanna noticed immediately the changed timbre in
Jillian's voice as she talked with Jay, and when she made
an excuse designed to leave them alone, there was a tension about her speech and manner that Leanna realized
was related specifically to Jay Sprengsten. *In love with
someone who loved someone else. Jay was in love with
Jolene*. If Jillian was attracted to him, and she'd almost
bet the farm on it, her ambivalence about returning to
New York began to make more sense. She'd been there
two years. If she'd come home because Jay was out of
the army, it all fit together.

His voice brought her back. "I have a couple of hours
before I have to go back to work. What's up?"

"Parker and Jolene will be back any minute," she
warned. "Why don't we ride down to the lake?"

He gave immediate agreement, and she changed while he and the stableman saddled a couple of horses. At the lake, sitting on the bench where Curt had proposed, she told Jay about his explanation of the night at the Emerald with Christie, and his deadline to either declare a wedding date or call off the marriage.

"You could see him," she said, hating herself for the question and her doubts but trusting Jay to tell her the truth. "Did you think they were friends, or more?"

After a few moments' thought, Jay conceded that Curt's story could be plausible. He examined his memory of Curt's kissing the girl at the nightclub. It hadn't been particularly possessive, more an offhand gesture. His gut screamed that Curt was lying his ass off, but in fairness, there was no way to know for sure, and he wasn't willing to pass judgment based on a gut feeling.

"I can tell you it wasn't a sexy kiss," he said honestly, ill at ease at dissecting another man's behavior to the woman he was ostensibly going to marry. "It could have been friend to friend, or a man taking a woman for granted." He told her about Curt's call from the hospital, which was equally noncommittal.

She turned away, baffled, unable to take comfort in his words, knowing she was no closer to a decision than before.

"I know this isn't any of my business," he said to her, "but I think this ultimatum business is crap. You two are engaged. If this guy loves you, he'll wait for you to decide what you want and won't be giving you deadlines." He realized suddenly that he could well be talking about his situation with Jolene.

One of the horses had loosed its tether and drifted several yards away. Jay went to catch up the animal, and Leanna moved to the edge of the dock to dangle her

bare feet in the water. *Had* Curt been waiting for her?
Certainly it was possible that he had female friends who
were close enough to call "honey." A drink at a nightclub and an offhand kiss were within his explanation,
but the call from the hospital was puzzling. It might
have been to a friend of a friend or kidding around with
a business associate, even a limousine service. There
were all sorts of explanations if you wanted to allow
them.

Something under the dock brushed lightly against
her calf, interrupting her thoughts; too soft for wood, it
was smoothly firm but inanimate. Probably trash of
some sort, maybe a plastic bottle with just enough air
in it to stay afloat. Puzzled, she put her hand on the
object to try to identify it. The sensations her fingers
sent back were familiar yet alien: a soft, cold thing that
should be warm and living. The object bobbing in the
water was a face. Leanna jerked her hand away and
screamed.

Jay ran onto the dock and helped her to her feet.
He'd seen enough casualties to know that the young
woman in the water was unquestionably dead. Leanna
was heaving deep breaths and trembling as he led her
away from the dock. He made sure she was safe before
returning to be certain; the young girl's arm was cold
and rigid with rigor mortis and confirmed that there was
no point in trying to take her out of the water. He hurriedly secured the body with his T-shirt, then helped a
jittery Leanna mount her horse. Back at the stables, the
stableman went to summon her father while Jay called
the police to report the drowning.

Leanna was near shock, and he kept his arm around
her, hoping to keep her calm. "It's all right," he assured
her. "No one is ever prepared for death—except cops,

maybe." And coroners. While they waited for the police and the coroner's ambulance, Parker and Jillian joined them at the stable and he relinquished Leanna to Jillian's care. Highly aware of Jolene's absence, Jay answered their questions about the dead woman as best he could until Leanna's father arrived. He shook the older man's hand in a brief greeting and after a few questions, Sam Bowmont escorted his daughter back to the house.

Jillian stood by nervously as Jay refused to answer Parker's terse inquiries about why he and Leanna were at the lake in the first place. There was major bad blood between the two, and she surmised that Parker probably had suspicions about Jolene's continued interest in Jay. As time stretched on, her jaw began to ache with tension.

Finally Mr. Bowmont returned to the stable. He was accompanied by the county coroner and two Walden City police officers, plus a reporter and photographer from the *Herald*. There were a ton of questions from the officials, and after what seemed to her like an aeon of time, they were ready to return to the lake. Feeling like a morbid onlooker at a bad accident, Jillian was unable to make herself remain at the stables. Dead people were, unfortunately, a fact of human life, and she was drawn by the dual fascination of seeing what actually happened at a death scene and her desire to support Jay, who was grim-faced and obviously uncomfortable.

Finally they mounted the saddle horses, saying little, and followed the slow path of the coroner's ambulance across the pasture, through the woods, and down to the dock; Parker and his father rode with the coroner, and the police car followed behind with the reporter and photographer.

Jillian stood with Parker and held the horses, unable to look after all. She watched Jay from the corner of her eye as he helped the police and the coroner jockey a giant metal basket into place. The four men strained as they lifted the body onto the dock.

"Anyone know her?"

The coroner's question hung in the air, and there was a stony silence except for the sound of water dripping through the planks of the dock to the surface of the lake and the men's heavy breathing from their exertion. The coroner covered the body with a rubber sheet.

Jillian edged to Jay's side, and it was only when the *Herald*'s photographer pulled back the sheet to take pictures of the girl before they placed her in a body bag that she made herself steal a glimpse of the swollen face of the corpse. Her knees buckled and she collapsed in Jay's arms.

16

The front page story in the *Bowmont Herald* identified the drowned girl as twenty-year-old Cathy Rice, employed at Milbrook Construction and a part-time student at Traxx University. Her car had been located on a private access road on the Bowmont estate, a half mile from the lake. An autopsy revealed an extremely high level of a drug similar to PCP in her system. She'd been in the water a little more than twelve hours and had drowned fully clothed. There was a small high school graduation picture next to the photograph of the body prone on the Bowmont dock; one small hand was visible against the wood. The article went on to describe how Cathy had been discovered.

Curt threw the paper aside and cursed. The girl was a friend of Christie's. He'd met her once or twice and had considered her a possible backup. There was no question it was the same girl. She'd gotten the stuff from Christie.

He paced his apartment with growing unease. Two hundred invested in simple base chemicals had been netting him two thousand dollars' worth of street drugs, just enough to meet expenses. A PCP clone, that's all. A couple of chemicals adjusted, but, Christ, nothing that would kill anyone. Watered down, if anything. Jesus, what a mess. He *never* sold anything locally—the last four batches had all gone to the guy in Chicago. Just the sample to Christie. Maybe a quarter ounce. There was no way they could trace it unless she rolled over on him.

Too bad he wasn't already married to Leanna; cops wouldn't look twice at someone in that family. He would have to move things faster or get the hell out of Dodge. Either way, the first thing to do was deep-six any evidence. He found a pair of gloves and cleaned out his garage, wiped it down for fingerprints, then sealed all leftover chemicals into a box. He drove to the local dump, dug a hole to bury it, and had the box three-quarters out of the car when some jerk chose that moment to park his van next to him. After unloading nine bags of garbage, the guy got chatty and began picking through the trash.

Then the light went on. A dump couldn't be a more logical place to look for it. Even if he poured it out, the glass wouldn't disappear overnight, and chemical residue lasted for years. Putting it into a Dumpster solved nothing; it still ended up in a landfill somewhere, possibly traceable to individual trucks and routes, and the last thing he wanted was evidence of local activity.

He'd have to be a little more creative. Nothing public was safe for a hundred-mile radius. He closed the trunk and drove to Christie's apartment in Wellington. When he confirmed that she wasn't home, he slid the box inside an empty storage bin assigned to her parking space and covered it over with newspapers. If it was gonna get found, let it get found here. Not a great solution, but it would do until he could figure out where to get rid of it. He was in the car and leaving when Christie got in from a four-day run to Houston, red-eyed and weepy about Cathy.

He took her inside, and five minutes later she was admitting she had given the girl a hit. "Two drops on a cigarette," she kept repeating. "Two drops wouldn't hurt anybody."

The cold sweat of fear broke out on his body. "Have you told anyone?"

She denied it.

"Are you sure?" He studied her face intently, willing her not to lie to him.

"I'm not stupid, you know."

"Of course you're not, sweetheart." Just guilty and blabbing about it. "Where's the rest? You have to get rid of it."

She took a container out of a box on her dresser, and he dumped the liquid down the john and rinsed the plastic. She was bouncing off the walls, and he gave her a tranquilizer.

She swallowed the downer with a gulp of water. "I don't understand what happened, Curt."

"Look, babe, the only thing I can figure is someone sold me a bad batch of stuff, or maybe it turned bad. I don't know. It doesn't matter. It's gone and we don't know nothing."

"But what if it killed her?"

Inwardly he cursed her stupidity. She wasn't getting it. And there was no guarantee she'd keep her mouth shut. He tried again. "The paper said Cathy was saturated. High concentration. Two drops don't show up that heavy in anybody's system. She was probably a junkie and was mixing all kinds of stuff that night." He walked her into the bedroom and watched her undress. "You were a friend trying to do her a favor, right?"

"Right."

"And you had no way of knowing she was going to do something stupid, right?" He unhooked her bra and fondled her soft breasts. Suddenly he wanted to get laid, like now. "Right?" he repeated impatiently. He began taking off his clothes.

"Right."

"So there's no reason to ruin your life by telling the cops anything." She was still awake enough for this to sink in, and she looked at him fuzzily. "Right?" he prompted. He dropped his underwear on the floor and slid onto the sheet next to her.

"I guess so."

"You still on the pill, baby?" Her eyes were closing. He pulled her into position and worked himself into her body, getting hard in the process. "I know so. It ain't gonna bring her back, and it ain't gonna solve anything, right?"

"Mmm-hmm." She nodded sleepily, unprotesting.

"Promise you'll keep that beautiful mouth shut."

"Promise."

He satisfied himself, and she dropped into sleep..A few minutes later he let himself out of her apartment.

At the Bowmont estate, a police investigator returned to question the family about Cathy Rice. No one knew her except Parker, who recognized the name from high school.

"There was no personal identification in the car, just the registration. We thought she was a suicide until the autopsy came in. Some kind of PCP wannabe. What we call a designer drug," said the officer. "Drowning's common. Users get stoned, go swimming. The water feels so good they get lost in the high. Unfortunately, the chemicals keep working on their system and they lose the ability to use their muscles. They drown because they're literally unable to use their arms and legs to save themselves. I saw it once in eight inches of water."

Sam watched his daughter absorb this information. She was pale and had dark circles under her eyes from not sleeping. Curt, at her side, was attentive to the police officer.

"The lake's always attracted a certain amount of trespassing, but no one's lost their life in my memory," Sam said sadly.

"The girl was twenty years old and on drugs. Apparently some history of despondency over a breakup with her boyfriend. She wanted to get married, he didn't. Unofficially, it's probably an unintentional but successful suicide. I wouldn't worry, Mr. Bowmont. By the way, we've searched most of the lakefront area, but we didn't find her purse. Could have a note. Who knows how long she walked around before she went in the water. You'll let me know if anything shows up?"

Leanna excused herself to leave the room, and Curt followed her. "I'm sorry I wasn't here, sweetheart. It must have been awful." He took her in his arms. "I'm sorry I ever doubted you love me, and I feel like a first-class fool. All the time I was in Chicago, you were all I could think about. Are you willing to forgive me?"

Leanna leaned into his embrace, longing for safety and security, desperately needing solid ground. The cold, rubbery feeling of the girl's face against her fingers would not leave her mind, and she'd been worried that

Curt would return still angry and tell her he'd decided not to get married.

"Let's run away. Let's do it now," he urged in her ear. He turned her face toward him and kissed her hungrily. "Let's get married and have a dozen kids and live happily ever after. Get the preacher!"

"Okay," she answered. "I'll tell my father, and we'll set a date."

"When?" he demanded.

"A month from today? October first."

"You promise?"

She kissed him back for his answer and shut out the small voice in the back of her head already questioning the decision.

Jillian sat stiffly in the sparsely filled pew and listened to the minister's kind words for Cathy, invisible in the wine-colored coffin flanked with flowers to one side of the pulpit. Since that hideous moment when she'd recognized her friend's body at the lake, she'd cried so many tears that her throat was raw and there was nothing left.

She saw Nick, drawn and dry-eyed, sitting in the front row, his posture rigid and angry. On the opposite side, Cathy's mother appeared frail and defeated in a dark blue suit, her father equally distraught. Their shoulders were shaking in silent grief, and Cathy's sister and brother were numbly doing their best to comfort their parents.

Two rows back, Leanna was sitting between Parker and her father. Across the aisle a redheaded woman was crying. A small sound at the back of the church caught her attention; she turned to see Jay enter with his brothers and an older woman who fit Annie Chatfield's voice. Jay, too, looked drawn but handsome in a somber charcoal suit, blue shirt, and navy tie, and despite her pain, her pulse quickened at the sight of him.

Jay saw her; as the other three seated themselves quietly, he came down the aisle and she made room for him on the hard wooden bench. He reached over to briefly squeeze her hand, and tears she would have sworn were impossible began to spill down her cheeks. She forced her splintered concentration on the minister's words.

Cathy's interment was to be private at the family's request, and at the completion of services Jillian managed to dry her tears long enough to be introduced to Annie and the boys. Annie gave her a hug. "I'm so sorry," she said sympathetically.

"If it hadn't been for Jay, I don't think I could have held it together." Jillian looked at him with gratitude.

Jay seemed ill at ease at her side. "How long are you home?"

"The police detective said he might want to talk to me again," she responded. "I'll be here until Jolene's birthday. Then, I'm not sure." He nodded and seemed to see her for a few moments, then she felt him shift to the information. Jolene. Always Jolene.

"So, Tuesday's gonna be the big annual birthday bash?"

She smiled, determined to hold on to her feelings. "Not this year. Mom and Dad are in Europe. Small private party, last I heard, but you know Jolene."

"Yeah." His focus drifted a moment, then he came back. "You owe me a dance before you leave town," he said, and kissed her cheek. Then he moved away, and she watched him approach Cathy's parents, her heart leaping with hope that he'd meant it, that he wanted to see her.

After a few painful words to the Rice family, Jay braved Parker's wrath by saying a brief hello and good-bye to Leanna and her father before he and Annie left for home with the boys. Jolene's birthday on his mind, he threw himself into yard work. If nothing else, the drowning of Cathy Rice had brought home to him that there were no guarantees that tomorrow would show up. If he wanted Jolene Llowell, he was going to have to get off the dime and do something about it.

A quiet man in his early thirties, medium height, slender, conservatively dressed, took care to blend with the mourners. He moved smoothly through the gathering and stood for a moment outside an alcove where Christie Scott was tearfully identifying herself to the minister and relating how Cathy's death had come as a terrible shock. He moved on, meeting no one's eyes, and paused next to a gangly teenager who was proudly informing a pretty young woman that Chatfield's Bed 'N Breakfast Inn had its license, that he and his brother had already moved in, and the rest of the rooms would be ready next week.

The following morning he showed up at Chatfield's. "Saw your sign," he said pleasantly. "I'm a writer, and I plan to be in town about three months. I need privacy, a reasonable rent, and I'd be willing to pay in advance if I like your coffee." He gave her a small grin and offered his hand. "Matt Halston."

"We ain't exactly open yet," Annie said slowly.

Before she could take a firm position, he motioned toward his car. "I have a suitcase and a typewriter. I don't snore and I don't hog the bathroom." He widened the grin into an open smile.

Annie was unconvinced, but she invited him in for the coffee and threw in a couple of oatmeal cookies as she chatted him up. Her sixth sense told her he was complicated and probably not entirely truthful, and the pain lines in his thin face gave her pause, but three months' rent in advance was a great temptation toward restoring their sorely depleted funds. Stephen called her aside.

"Give him my room, Annie," he said quietly. "It'll take the county weeks to place another kid with the Ellises. They'll keep me another month."

Annie was in a quandary. "I just don't know, child. You've waited so long—"

"We need the money." He took his key off the board and handed it to her. "It's the only other room that's ready. I won't move in, so you may as well rent it to him." He left the house.

Annie returned to the kitchen, not her usual self. The cost to Stephen was exceedingly high, and the opportunity was not to be wasted. "So, how's the coffee?" she prompted.

"Delicious. Would you want a check or cash?"

"Cash." She turned Stephen's key over in her hand, debating. "I'll show you the room while I make up my mind."

Matt followed Annie to a pale blue room on the second floor, with a view of the lake, a desk that locked and a chair, a large closet, and a patriotic red-white-and-blue-braided cotton rug on the floor. Naked pillows, a blue chenille bedspread, and folded, washed-soft sheets were stacked on the chair, and a mattress leaned against the wall next to the box springs. Inexpensively framed posters of Eric Clapton were propped against the far wall, ready to be hung.

The bath was across the hall with old-fashioned floor-to-ceiling tile, cream with black detailing, and boasted a tub as well as a shower; thick, line-dried terry-cloth towels, green as raw celery, were draped over the racks. He paused a split instant at the lies he'd told this obviously good woman, then upped the amount of money he'd intended to offer if she'd throw in laundry privileges, which she accepted immediately.

"Breakfast ends at eight o'clock, after that you fix your own. There'll be a pay phone in the hall next week—in the meantime, you can make local calls on the house." She handed him the key.

He held one end of the mattress as she flopped it onto the springs and, after the bed was made, helped hang the posters. After lunch, he positioned a typewriter on the desk and hung a meager wardrobe in the closet. He locked a batch of paperwork in the desk and went out to have a look at the lake that Cathy Rice had drowned in.

17

Sam slowly paced the length of the library in an attempt to ignore the headache, reached the light switch, and darkened the room. The pain in his eye socket eased a barely discernible moment, then settled into a dull throb; it would be his constant companion for the next six months, so he might as well get used to it.

Alice Faye hadn't said anything, but he knew she was upset at his inability to perform last night—and again this morning. It was happening frequently now, and he was sure as hell more upset about it than she was. She'd gone into Wellington to do some shopping, and if he knew his wife, she wouldn't be home for dinner.

The pounding in his head settled into a bone-jarring rhythm that paced his heartbeat, and his face in the library mirror was a pasty gray; he'd have to tell her soon, and he quailed at the thought. He'd have to tell them all, but first he'd have to tell Alice Faye. It wouldn't do to have her learn it elsewhere.

His thoughts turned to his daughter. Her behavior since her engagement to Curt had bordered on bizarre; first, the accident in the stable that had put her into the hospital. She'd suffered no apparent injury, but she had gone to great lengths to convince him that it had not been Jay Sprengsten's fault. Within the month she'd been out all night with this same boy. Other than apologizing for worrying him, she had offered no explanation except they were friends and it had been an innocent evening. Then the loss of Thumper and the discovery of that poor girl in the lake, again both times with Sprengsten. He'd met the young man, who seemed straightforward and likable, but Parker clearly hated the fellow; he'd had some concern until he made the connection to the loss of the Hartford property and Leanna had explained that Sprengsten was one of Jolene's former boyfriends.

Just as he was beginning to wonder if she might break her engagement over Sprengsten, Leanna had informed him that she and Curt had set a definite date; she'd seemed genuinely happy again and was busily planning her wedding with Alice Faye.

A sudden shooting pain in his good eye pushed him onto the chair at his desk. His mortality had been weighing heavily on his mind lately, and the knowledge that he would die soon had triggered his memories of Louise and her death, which inevitably led to his second marriage. Perhaps he should try somehow to make up the damage. If he couldn't manage it before his death, it could be a part of his will, but would easing his conscience be worth the pain to his wife and children? Nothing would be legally binding until he'd agreed to it in writing, so he grabbed a pad of yellow paper to make some notes. For the next several hours he labored over the wording of a document. At four o'clock, exhausted, still unable to decide whether or not to give it to Holman, he locked the notes in his desk and went upstairs to bed.

Jillian slowed in front of the driveway to Chatfield's. It had taken her half the night to decide what to wear, and she'd finally settled on black stretch pants, knee-high boots, and a clingy, white, thigh-length sweater—and another two hours to get her hair just casual enough to look, well, casual, and she'd applied four shades of lipstick before she was satisfied. But she looked terrific. Three different guys had checked her out when she looked at apartments in a new building on Main Street. Finally she allowed herself to drive into the parking area.

The fragrantly sweet smell of baking pies came rolling through the open front door of the inn. She checked the area behind the house; the Traxx Jobbing truck was missing. Jay wasn't here. Before she could leave, Annie Chatfield stepped onto the front porch and waved her on to the west end of the house. "They're going to be here any minute," she called.

Indeed, the Traxx pickup, with Jay driving and Tommy and Stephen in the back steadying a precarious assortment of headboards, box springs, dressers, and mattresses loosely wrapped in bedding, pulled carefully into the drive and wound its way to the front of the walk. Jillian drove on to the indicated spot and stopped the engine. The three brothers began taking the furniture out of the back of the truck, and Annie came chugging down the steps to pass judgment.

"These'll do just fine," she said approvingly. "Let's

get 'em in the house. I got pies bakin'." She charged back into the inn.

Jay saw Jillian and said hello, but his focus was primarily on unloading the furniture. Tommy gave her a big chesty grin and Stephen flashed a small smile before they turned their attention to handling the heavy pieces with their brother. Eventually she was allowed to pitch in and help carry dresser drawers. When everything was set up in its designated room under Annie's critical eye, they were all deemed to have earned a wedge of pie and something to drink. Tommy and Stephen adjourned to the front porch while she and Jay and Annie sat around a small table in the glassed-in breakfast alcove.

The room had been recently painted white with a pale lemon trim, and the vague smell of enamel was mixed with the oven's wealth of pie and the aroma from a pot of fresh coffee. Jillian gazed at the intricate black-and-white tile design on the floor, her thoughts twisting and curling with the mosaic pattern. She'd been supremely conscious of Jay's tall, wiry presence all afternoon, and here, rubbing elbows with him in the breakfast room, was electric contact that sent shivers straight through her skin to the base of her brain.

She declined Annie's offer of more coffee and settled back as much as she dared to enjoy the light pressure of his knee when his long legs occasionally brushed against hers under the table. "It's a beautiful house. I've been curious about it for years," she told them. "The lease is up on my apartment, and I've been thinking about coming back to Walden City. Maybe I'll be your first customer."

"Second. Already got me a writer," Annie informed her.

"Really? That's what I was trying to do in New York."

"Well, I'll just have to introduce you, honeybun." Annie grinned and gave her a giant wink. "He's about your size—cute, too."

Jillian felt herself blush and refused to look at Jay.

"Weren't you working for a newspaper?" he asked. "I thought you wanted to be a reporter."

She looked into his eyes, as clear and blue as the summer sky shining through the curtained windows at his back, trying desperately not to let her feelings show. "Actually, I did the grunge work. Never got beyond part-time. I did finish a novel, but I haven't been able to sell it. Most of the time I was a waitress at the Hard Rock Cafe."

"Nothin' wrong with waitressin'. I did it for years," said Annie. "Don't pay nothin', but it's honest work."

They each rinsed their dishes, and Annie shooed them out of the kitchen so she could start preparations for supper. Jay excused himself and disappeared; she hung around for half an hour on the back porch swing, staring at the water, unsure how to make herself leave. The breeze of the warm Indian summer afternoon came drifting in off the lake, and Tommy and Stephen pushed old-fashioned rotary mowers back and forth across the yard, adding a rich, cut-grass smell to the afternoon; the lawn sloped gradually downward past a delicate white gazebo surrounded by a low hedge of English lavender, then took a sudden drop to the shoreline.

She wandered down to a small wooden dock built between what looked like an old section of canal and a spillway for the lake and sat on a log bench for a while, watching a rowboat nudge against its mooring on one of the pilings. Feeling she'd stretched her welcome past a "visit," she returned to the porch swing and had made up her mind to go, when, to her absolute joy, Jay came out and joined her. His sandy brown hair was sun-bleached nearly blond on top from working outdoors and damp from a shower; he'd changed to fresh jeans and a loose dark blue sweatshirt. His huge, bony feet were encased in worn running shoes, and he was gor-geous, gorgeous, gorgeous, and she didn't have a chance in the world against Jolene.

He looked at her and gave a small laugh. "You grew up on me."

A flush began working its way up the back of her neck. "It sure took long enough," she ventured, speak-ing past the lump of pleasure that was threatening to choke her speech.

"You were a scrawny twerp when I left," he agreed, and settled sideways into the swing to examine her more closely. "With your hair that color, you look a lot like Jolene." He fixed her with a bone-tingling attention that helped her past the glutinous thud that Jolene's name provoked in her stomach. "So, are you married, engaged, what?"

She was thrown at the question. Why on earth would he want to know? "None of the above," she managed quickly. "What about you?"

"Single as they come." He glanced backward toward the CHATFIELD'S sign next to the front door. "With a family to support." He paused for a moment, then blasted her with those blue, blue eyes once again. "Is she going to marry him?"

"I have no idea," she answered soberly. "I don't think he's asked her," she added for no logical reason.

Then the magic happened.

"You want to go out for pizza?"

She didn't pause an instant. "Yes."

He got off the swing and held out his hand for her to grasp. It was too good to be true, but she didn't care. She was able to hold on long enough to be pulled to her feet, and he poked his head in the door to tell Annie that they were driving into Wellington and he wouldn't be home for supper.

At the Wellington Pizza Place a gaggle of teenage girls had a table in the corner; two of them took turns sidling by their booth in order to drop quarters into the jukebox, then return, giggling, to endure teasing remarks from their friends. Jay laughed and tried to pass it off: "Kids." The young girls' attention brought a mild sexual charge to the air that built in the space between them. At least from her end.

"Yeah, right." She'd been their age when she'd fallen in love with him, and at the moment all sorts of feelings were zinging their way through her middle, predominantly various types of envy; oh, to be so young and have the freedom to flirt with him.

During the drive to the restaurant, she had confined herself to questions about the inn and his plans for his family. He was driven to reunite his brothers and sisters, and she realized that his goal would work against him where Jolene was concerned. Her sister was not accustomed to competing for attention. But it was miles too soon to allow the thought of him having an interest in anyone other than Jolene, so she opted for a topic that might restore the comfort zone between them. "Have the police asked you anything more about Cathy?"

He was watching her carefully as he responded. "No. They think it was suicide. What do you think?"

"I hope not. I don't know. I know you can't make people love you." A sudden, unexpected riptide of emotion threatened to take her under, and she looked down at the checkered tablecloth a long time before she was able to go on, tears close. "It's just that I'll never get a chance to say good-bye. It's so permanent."

He patted the back of her hand and spoke in a voice that knew the experience of heartbreak. "It hurts either way," he said, and barriers to friendship were safely crossed.

The young girls made a noisy exit, and by the time their pizza arrived and had cooled enough to eat, it was obvious that Jay wanted to talk, and she was content to listen.

"I used to wait for your letters," he told her. "I know I never wrote enough, but it was so good getting mail and yours were always funny and full of interesting stuff. I still have them." He paused, introspective. "You take a lot of things for granted in life. When I went into the service I had no idea how lonely it would get. There I was, stuck with three or four thousand guys and every one of us homesick as hell. But I was the only one who could count on getting something at mail call."

She basked in his appreciation, forgetting to eat. His eyes got far away. "I was going to be a lawyer and I was going to marry your sister." He looked down at the calluses on his palms. "Now I'm raising four kids and working construction." He lifted his eyes to her face. "You look just like she did when I left. The same hair." His eyes dropped briefly to her chest, and he smiled, caught in an obviously masculine preoccupation. "Well, she wasn't quite so, uh . . ."

"Yeah, well, she is now," she said, hating the truth of it and fighting mixed feelings that he'd finally gotten around to Jolene, who had filled out quite a bit in the past two years. She wondered fleetingly if sex on a regular basis had anything to do with it. If that were the case, no wonder she was still undersize compared with her sister.

He shifted on his chair and abruptly changed the subject. "So you're on the fence about going back to New York. Why is that?"

"Actually, I was thinking about moving into Chatfield's," she dodged.

"Hey, we'd be roommates. I recommend it very highly." He smiled at her with curiosity. "You don't want to live at home?"

"My dad thinks being a writer is a waste of time. He wants me to go to medical school. He says I can spend fifteen years trying to write or the same amount of time and become a doctor." She couldn't help a sigh. "He's relentless."

"No guarantees either way," Jay pointed out.

"He is right about the fifteen years. It'll probably take that long to find out whether or not I have anything to say as a writer. If being a doctor gives me the same lifestyle he has, I'm not interested. I don't want to deal with illness twenty hours a day. I'd either get too caught up in the pain or become so deadened to it that I'd be like he is. Either way, it's not what I want."

"You don't always get what you want," he said shortly. "Sometimes you settle for what you need. C'mon." He pulled her out of the booth. "You promised me a dance. You even get to pick out the song."

They walked together to the jukebox. Three coins plunked into the slot, and she pushed the codes for "Thing Called Love" and "Constant Craving"; he punched Whitney Houston's "I Will Always Love You." She went into the strong circle of his arms with great longing. Unlike men who were stiff and uncomfortable on a dance floor, Jay enjoyed music and was a considerate, confident partner. The first song was upbeat, and she could have been an extension of him, so smoothly did he guide their motion and communicate with his body.

Then came the ballads, back to back, and she was able to give herself over to the music and her emotion, to feel the full rush of pleasure at being so close to him. She circled his neck with her arms, and it was so natural, so right, to rest her head against his shoulder and lose herself in the warmth of his body pressing against her.

It was better than she'd imagined, better than she'd hoped. It was Iowa.

He sat on a stool in Nicholson's bar and watched the woman finish her fourth drink. She took inventory of the remaining patrons and moved confidently to his side. "You look out of place here." She placed her glass with deliberation next to his half-empty beer on the wooden bar.

He looked at her in pleasant surprise. If she was a hooker, she was sure as hell overdressed for the clientele, all of whom were dying to make a move on her, including the bartender. She'd been slugging down Glenfiddich Scotch since he'd arrived an hour ago and making a career out of placing calls from the bar telephone. All signs pointed to her having been stood up. He was waiting for Dino to call him on the pay phone. Nicholson's was the first place he'd come to in the outskirts of Wellington, and the scruffy little bar offered the nondescript, anonymous existence he required.

She balanced herself gracefully on the stool next to him and crossed long, shapely legs accented by the dull shine of pale gray stockings. He smiled appreciatively and signaled the bartender for another beer and tapped her glass as well. "I'd guess this isn't your regular stomping grounds," he answered carefully.

"What I am is bored," she said pointedly. Their drinks arrived. She clinked her glass against his and took a strong sip of the Scotch. "What about you, are you bored?"

"Not with you sitting here." In point of fact he'd been without a woman's company for nearly two months, and after watching her for an hour, if she was willing, he was in the mood to do something besides report in. She was great looking, somewhere between forty and fifty, and definitely in a mood of her own.

She stood next to him, her body too close for polite conversation and her voice just loud enough for him alone to hear. "My name's Alice Faye," she said, "and I have a small apartment about fifteen minutes from here with a full bottle of Scotch in it. No strings, no fuss, no bother."

The pay phone jingled, and he slid off the stool. "I've been waiting for a call," he explained. "Hold the thought."

"I'm through holding in two minutes," she said succinctly.

He nodded and slid into the booth, closed the door. She moved back onto the stool, and he watched the tight swing of her leg under the wine knit dress and assessed the expensive pumps as he talked. Ferragamo's or he was losing his touch. "It's the same stuff," he confirmed to Dino. "He must have a bathtub operation somewhere in this area." By the time he made the usual arrangements for reporting in and hung up, some guy had joined her and he came out of the booth in time to watch them leave together. Some days it just went that way.

He shrugged for the benefit of the other patrons and girded himself to hang in the local bars for the next four hours, hoping to scare up a connection.

Suddenly it was Tuesday, and Jolene's twenty-first birthday had arrived at last. Jillian tried her best to stay happy and upbeat through dinner as she watched her sister bask in the combined attention of Curt, Leanna, and Parker. It was odd that their parents hadn't called since that morning, and she glanced at her watch with vague concern. This was too big a day in Jolene's life to go uncelebrated, particularly by her father.

Everyone was full of champagne and rich food from dinner, and Jolene was opening her gifts; they were taking a break before her birthday cake made its entrance. She'd already opened her present from Curt and Leanna, a butterscotch cashmere sweater she'd pronounced "fabulous," and had even professed to love the hand-painted gambler's hat Jillian had brought for her from New York. Parker's gift was last, and Jillian's heart sank when she saw its size; the beautifully wrapped box was big enough to contain a basketball. Inside was another gift, also exquisitely wrapped, and Jolene opened three more, each one gift-wrapped inside the other.

As the boxes became smaller and smaller, her hopes began to revive, and Jillian crossed her fingers as Jolene reached one that contained a striking emerald ring—a single row of slender baguettes totaling at least two full carats of deep, rich, and expensive green in a delicate gold mounting.

She was delighted to help Curt describe it for Leanna as Jolene slid the ring onto her finger; her sister's kisses of gratitude were real and passionate, and Jillian prayed fervently that the ring had more significance than friendship. She'd never seen Jolene so happy; her smile was radiant, and her eyes never left Parker's face.

The moment came for him to make an announcement, and passed, and Jillian retreated to the kitchen to regroup. Surely Jolene would forget Jay now. Surely. So far, she'd kept their date a secret from Jolene, preferring to hold it private and warm in her memory and not have it picked to death by Jolene's scrutiny and questions and opinions. Calling it a date would be stretching the truth anyway. All told, they'd been alone together a little more than three hours, and he certainly hadn't kissed her good night. But he'd pulled her close while they danced to half a dozen more songs, and he had hugged her a long time at the door of her car when they'd gotten back to Chatfield's. Three hours that had spun her head around, that had added to her feelings for him, thrown her emotions into turmoil about what she should do.

As if she didn't know. What she *should* do was go back to New York and get on with her life. What she was doing was making herself crazy. It took five matches to light the twenty-one candles; she picked up the cake and put on a smile.

Everyone sang. Emeralds winked and twinkled in the candlelight until Jolene smiled at Parker and made her wish, after which they made short work of mutilating the cake; half an hour later, there was a mutual decision to go swimming. While Curt and Parker changed in the pool house, the doorbell rang; Jillian answered to a deliveryman, accepted the slender carton created for long-stemmed roses, and took it upstairs to Jolene.

Jolene eyed the box and wrinkled her nose in disdain. "Roses?" Everyone knew she hated roses. She took the carton from Jillian's fingers, tossed it carelessly onto the bed, and returned her attention to Parker's gift. She pulled the glittering ring off her right hand and moved it onto the left. "Which do you like best?"

Left. Definitely, left.

Leanna came in from the dressing room and sat on the bed, her one-piece swimsuit as bright and green as the emeralds. "Mmmmm, I smell daisies."

Jillian stared at her, unable to smell anything over the mix of perfumes in the room. The emerald ring flashed gaily on her engagement finger as Jolene paused abruptly to shake open the carton. A spicy fragrance from at least three dozen huge yellow-petaled flowers filled the room. A look of understanding crossed Jolene's face, and she grinned with delight as she reached for the card. She read it quickly, then pushed it into Jillian's jacket pocket and skipped out the door to go down to the kitchen for a vase.

"They are daisies, aren't they?" asked Leanna.

"Black-eyed Susans." She could hear the misery in her own voice. Jay had always sent her sister black-eyed Susans. Jolene's jubilant expression at this simple gesture and her turnaround from the excitement over Curt's expensive ring and attention at dinner—it was suddenly too much. Being home was too much. She retrieved the card from her pocket and read the simple message. "Happy 21st. All my love. J." Too much.

She was coming apart. Once she was tipped over she

knew she was rotten at hiding her feelings, and this was out-of-control jealousy; Jolene had two men in her life—one Jillian wanted desperately. Painfully aware that she had no one, she fled down the hall into her own bath to splash cold water in her face. She had to pull herself together before Jolene returned. What could she say, that flowers made her weepy?

Leanna sat quietly next to the florist's carton and gently fingered the delicate blossoms. One of the things she missed most was the incredible beauty of flowers, so intricate, so elegant and fragile. Their fragrance was enticing, but not to see them ever again somehow played into her concern that something about these particular flowers had upset Jillian very much.

Jolene returned, and the occasional crisp snap of shears began as she cut the bottoms off the stems; Leanna enjoyed the pungent smells and imagined the high golden yellow of the petals, the burnt-coffee black of the centers. "Did your parents send them?" she asked, curious. Just then Curt called up the stairs, demanding she come for a swim, so she made her way to the door and down the stairs.

Jillian forced herself to return to Jolene's bedroom and admire the flowers. "They are beautiful." She held out the card. Jolene looked past her; Parker was standing in the doorway.

"You ladies coming down or are we going to have to come and get you?" he joked. He crossed to the box. "Who sent these?" he asked curiously.

"Jillian," Jolene answered casually; she took the card from Jillian's fingers and gave it to him. "Aren't they great?"

Jillian slipped out the door. Downstairs, she paced

the living room in agitation before finally throwing herself onto the corner of the sofa. Hell would freeze over before she supported Jolene this time. She wouldn't turn her in, but she wouldn't confirm it; if Parker asked about the flowers, Jolene would just have to own up. She and Parker were coming down the stairs when the front door burst open.

"Surprise!" Their parents came rushing into the foyer. "Surprise! Happy birthday!"

Jillian looked up, astonished. Jolene screamed and flew into her father's arms. "I don't believe it! Oh, I'm so glad to see you. This makes things perfect." She danced her father around the foyer while Jillian struggled to her feet. After a few moments she was able to hug her mother.

"I'm so glad you're here. We never worried at all." Her mother sailed seamlessly through the bustle of introductions and shedding of coats while Curt and the taxi driver brought in luggage and bundles and parcels with airline tags dangling. "I do wish you'd stay on, dear," she urged.

"I know, Mom. Let's not go into it tonight, okay?"

"If you promise to think about it."

"You know it would make your mother very happy." This from her father as he hugged her a few moments later.

"Don't use Mother against me," she warned him gently. "You know it won't work."

"I'm sure when you and I sit down and discuss it, you'll change your mind." Her father turned to her mother. "Talk to her, Madeline."

"Please say you'll think about it," her mother entreated.

"No promises. I'll think about it," she conceded

finally. Anything to end the conversation. "I thought you came home to celebrate a birthday."

Her father took up the ball. "That's right, we did. We were sitting in this cold little castle in Scotland yesterday and I said to Madeline, 'You know, your older daughter is only going to turn twenty-one once. We ought to go home.' And here we are." He kissed Jolene. "Now, three or four of these packages are yours and three or four belong to Jillian, and the rest belong to your mother. What say we start sorting them out? Is there any cake left?"

Jillian watched her father take charge of the evening. Her sister proudly exhibited the emerald ring, newly returned to her right hand, and he smiled broadly and pronounced it worthy of his daughter, while her mother praised its beauty. "It's going to make the little gold bracelet I bought in Glasgow look anemic," he joked, "but then it looks like I'm no longer the central man in my daughter's life."

Jillian didn't miss her father's pointed look in Parker's direction and prayed with all her might that he was right.

18

Traxx promises. . .

Charlie edged her way around the staircase
and scoped out the hallway full of kids. Jack Myers was
nowhere in sight, so she worked her way to study hall.
School had started three days ago, and she'd managed
to avoid him so far, but her luck was bound to change.
She checked the room and didn't see him in there,
either. This was her last class, and if she could make a
clean exit, she'd be home free.

She stepped inside the doorway. He was in the room
after all, far back in a corner with one of his buddies. He
saw her looking at him, and she could tell from the way
he tried to stare her down that he was going to make
trouble.

She watched the clock for thirty-three minutes, and
when the bell rang she was out the door in a flash and
down three flights of stairs, in and out of her locker like
lightning. Out a side entrance of the building, she
looked again and didn't see him, so she took her usual

shortcut and was halfway across the ball diamond when she saw him coming.

Running was useless; he was twice as fast as she was. A few feet in front of her at the pitcher's mound was a sack of softballs and against the wire fencing behind home plate she saw half a dozen wooden bats. She chose her ground next to the bats and dropped her books at her feet. A couple of guys from the track team jogged away from her on the clay track that circled the field. By the time Jack got to the pitcher's mound, nobody else was coming around and they were all by themselves.

She picked up one of the bats and held it at the ready, just in case.

"Hey, nubs." He was his usual insulting self. "Whatcha gonna do, hit me with that?"

"Leave me alone, Jack."

"Why, am I *botherin'* you?" He had a big jock attitude that made her jumpy because she knew it had to do with sex. He grabbed the ball sack; a few of the softballs spilled out onto the ground and rolled toward her. "I'm not *botherin'* you," he jibed.

"Yeah, why'd you follow me out here?"

"I got practice." He picked up one of the softballs and tossed it at her. "You wanna *play?*"

The ball missed her shoulder, but she backed up a few paces. He took a couple of steps forward and picked up more of the balls. "Cut it out, Jack." She was going to have to hit him, she just knew it.

"Cut what out?"

He started tossing them at her and advanced again. The first one made her move aside or be hit in the knee. The next ball backed her up against the wire fence. He picked up two more and came toward her.

"Don't think I won't hit you with this," she warned. She waved the bat at him.

"You're still one hot little blonde. What happened to your hair?"

"Hey, Charlie. . ."

Stephen stepped around the wire fencing, his eyes on a startled Jack Myers, who was a full head taller than he was. Stephen walked to her side, and she allowed him to take the bat from her hands, but she was worried at the look on his face and the strained tone of his voice.

"Who's this?"

"This is Jack," she said quickly, trying to head off trouble.

"Is he a friend of yours?"

"No!"

"Has he got a problem?"

This was a Stephen she'd never seen before. She looked around for reinforcements, but there was no one. He nodded toward the Traxx pickup parked in the school lot at the other end of the ball field. "Charlene, why don't you wait in the truck."

Charlie started to argue, but Stephen shut her down with a look. He moved to one side so he could see her pick up her books and drag reluctant feet toward the truck. Two members of the track team came around again, and one of them nodded; he nodded back briefly, then fixed his gaze on Myers. "Friends of mine say you got a problem with my sister."

"Yeah, what are you gonna do about it, asshole?" Jack hefted one of the softballs and threatened to throw it.

Stephen moved forward suddenly and whacked the bat against Jack's elbow; Jack dropped the ball and grabbed at his arm, and Stephen hit him in the shoulder muscle. This time he yelled in pain. Stephen whacked him again on the outside of one of his knees hard enough to really hurt.

"Jesus! Stop it!" Jack crouched, trying to protect himself with his arms, and backed away; he hit the fencing.

"The 'hot little blonde' is my sister, pal." Stephen pushed the cowering junior into the wire and held him in place with the bat. "If I were you, I'd find somebody my size to bully." He pressed the taller athlete against the fence for emphasis. "You hassle my sister one more time . . . one time, and I'll shove this where the sun don't shine." He placed the fat end of the bat against Jack's gaping mouth. "You got it?"

Jack nodded and looked at him uncertainly.

"Good." He tossed the bat away and started toward the truck; when he looked over his shoulder, Jack had picked up the bat and was ready to throw it at him.

"Don't even think about it." Tommy's voice came at both of them as he charged out from behind the dugout in his track uniform. He grabbed Jack by the hair, and Jack froze in place and dropped the bat.

Stephen retraced his steps, and he and Tommy sandwiched the defeated bully between them. "So far this is private," he said angrily. "What I said before now goes double. I hear about you hassling anybody—*anybody*— it goes public, and your ass is grass, you got it?"

Jack nodded miserably, and the brothers stepped aside to let him walk away.

"What the hell was that about?" Tommy fumed under his breath. "I'm in the locker room and two guys come hustling in to tell me you're in a shootout with Myers. He could've beat the crap out of you. Out of both of us." He rolled his eyes and blew out his breath in relief.

Stephen was back to his customary reticence, but

there was a definite gleam in his eye. He tapped his brother lightly on the shoulder with a fist. "Thanks for the backup."

Tommy looked at him in surprise. Stephen hadn't made a personal gesture like that since they were kids. And to challenge Jack Myers? Whatever had happened had been well worth it. He hit Stephen back in kind and sprinted to practice as the track coach blew his whistle.

Charlie waited for Stephen in the truck and looked at him with new, wide-eyed respect; during the drive home, she admitted that Jack had been tormenting her all summer and told him why. Stephen was tight with silence by the time she finished.

"I want a Traxx promise," he told her, "that if he or anybody else bothers you again, you'll let me know."

"Traxx promise," she said uneasily. From the quality of her brother's voice, she understood that from now on Jack Myers had better be somebody else's problem.

Leanna recognized that she and her stepmother had never been close, but in addition to her openly displayed resignation that the wedding was indeed about to take place and mumblings about things being unnecessarily "rushed," Alice Faye's disdain for her decision to marry Curt began to take on the consistent sting of raw lemon juice in a fresh cut.

A well-known hairstylist from Chicago was summoned to supervise a "proper" cut; skin and cosmetic specialists were called in to correct her makeup for the wedding portrait. Then more improvements and a second sitting, because neither Curt nor Alice Faye had been happy with any of the choices from the first.

To keep her sanity, she decided to visualize in water-colors and assigned a pale shade of vanilla ice cream to the wedding dress they had helped select, described to her as "cream" by Alice Faye, "eggshell" by the store clerk, and "white" by Curt. She did the same with her shoes and veil. Her garter was "light blue," "pale blue," and "blue." She wanted to scream at them that there were dozens of families of blues: flower colors, sky colors, sea colors, gems, birds, fruits, the list went on, plus a range of hues, then shades of light and dark.

Her stepmother's concern about what kind of target Leanna presented to would-be thieves was cited repeatedly, and she was discouraged from wearing Curt's engagement ring in public. Curt poo-poohed the danger argument but echoed negative opinions in near continuous support of Alice Faye's positions; he'd abandoned her in both the hair and makeup arguments and agreed with her stepmother's opinion that a certain dress was less than flattering and she shouldn't wear it again. He assured her all the while that he was trying very hard to make peace with his soon-to-be mother-in-law and not to take his opinions to heart; that he was simply walking a middle line about things that were, after all, opinions and certainly much less important than building a good family relationship.

Unable to argue with his logic, and since the decisions were inevitably about matters that she couldn't judge without sight, she began to feel like a Ping-Pong ball being smacked back and forth between two disapproving paddles. Nothing she did pleased anyone, including herself, to the point where she began to question her own ability to know if it was because she couldn't see, a case of prewedding nerves, or that she was just hopelessly inept.

Parker had remained withdrawn and abrupt since her evening with Jay, which he insisted on calling a date in spite of her careful explanation, apparently still angry that she wouldn't give up her friendship with the "handyman," as he referred to him. That, and his "rich little blind girl" remark still stung enough to keep her from seeking his counsel and support. For the first time since her accident, she began to feel isolated.

Curt's statements about their sexual relationship not being normal, coupled with his continuing implication that she was avoiding sex with him, worried her to sleep at night. Questions about marrying him because there might not be another chance for a blind girl wouldn't be put to rest. Her father's health nagged at her as well; he admitted to taking new and, she suspected, more serious medications and was dealing with constant headache pain. He rested in the middle of each afternoon these days, something he'd never done before. As she stood for fittings in a bridal gown she couldn't see, his cheerful questions about the progress of her wedding ran diametrically opposite to her fears that somehow she was making a giant mistake.

Since Curt's explanation regarding Christie, his behavior had altered in a subtle, almost indiscreet way, and he was treating her in a more sensual manner. Kisses were becoming longer, deeper, and more intimate; his arm around her had a new, more possessive manner, a lingering touch, and contrary to her expectations her own feelings did not rise up to meet his. The more familiar he became, the more she found herself withdrawing.

After three sleepless nights of wrestling with her growing anxiety, she called Jillian. "What if I can't make him happy? What if I don't know how to do things that I'm supposed to know how to do?" she whispered, desperate and embarrassed.

"Whoa. Hey!" Jillian stopped her. "You're treating this like it's some sort of trial and you're going to fail. It doesn't work that way. When you love someone, there aren't very many things either of you can do wrong. People in love have a pretty good time when they get married. That's why they call it a honeymoon."

"I just wish I could be sure. I just keep having this feeling that he'll be disappointed."

"Why are you assuming he's going to be terrific and you're going to be awful? Tell him what you've just told me. See what he says. If he's going to be your husband, you have to talk about these things sooner or later. Don't wait until after the wedding. Do it now."

Leanna hung up the phone in a quandary. Jillian was right. She'd simply taken it on faith that Curt would be a good lover; why hadn't she done the same for herself? And her mind came back with the answer. Because she was blind. It always came back to being blind. The lack of sight of an attractive man to cue her physical response. Of being dependent on colognes and nuance of voice and that insubstantial something called chemistry that she knew so little about.

"If I'm this uncertain of the sexual side of marriage with Curt," she reasoned, "how am I going to turn it around overnight because someone says we're married?" She fingered her watch. It was nearly noon. Curt was going to pick her up for lunch at one o'clock. She decided suddenly what she wanted to do for lunch, and she went to get dressed.

◦   ◦   ◦

Christie was pounding on the door of his apartment, clearly unwelded. Curt hustled her inside and calmed her down long enough to learn that she'd been questioned by another police detective investigating Cathy Rice's death.

"He wanted to know if we ever did drugs!" Christie paced around his living room, too worked up to sit. "I'm a suspect, I know I am, he'll find out and I'll go to jail and I'll lose my career and—"

She was babbling her way into full-blown panic and pushing him to the brink of losing it himself. Drugs were one thing—plead first offense and pay the fine, do probation or short time—but he wasn't about to take the rap for contributing to Cathy Rice's death. With the wrong judge, that one could put him away for a long time in a mean place. Frustrated, he looked at his watch. He was due at the Bowmonts' in an hour to take Leanna to lunch, and here he was, still in his underwear, with Christie in his face.

"What did you tell him?" he shouted at her. Christ, it was the fourth time he'd asked. Finally he lost it and slapped her.

"Nothing! I didn't tell him anything," she whimpered. "He knows, I tell you. He knows and it's all over." She was rubbing her cheek where he'd hit her, agitated and on the edge of breaking down, but at least she was listening.

Cognizant of the thin apartment walls, he lowered his voice and went over it again. "There's no evidence. There's no way anyone can discover where she got it. If she'd told anyone before she died, you'd be arrested by now."

She began to cry, but she was calming down. "But she's dead because of me."

"You didn't take her to the lake and hold her under-water," he whispered savagely. What did it take to make her understand? "She was a grown-up, for Christ's sake. If she was stupid enough to get that high and go swimming, there's nothing anyone can do about it! It's nobody's fault. Get that through your head. It's nobody's fault."

Christie dissolved into sobs, and he selected a shirt and tie while she cried it out. Eventually she pulled herself together. "I'm sorry. It's just that there's no one else to talk to, and sometimes I get so scared that you're gonna leave me. . . ."

He kissed her and rubbed himself against the front of her uniform. "Never. I gotta finish getting dressed, I have a business meeting in a few minutes, baby. Can you hold it together?"

"I got time to go to bed if you want. I don't have to be at the airport until one."

He checked his watch again. So he'd be a few minutes late; Leanna could wait. It wasn't like she was going anywhere. He kissed Christie again and pulled her toward the bedroom. "We gotta make it fast."

Twenty minutes later he was dressed and pushing her out the front door. She hugged him good-bye and kissed his neck, smearing perfume all over his shirt collar. Damn, he'd have to change, but he'd still be on time if he hurried. He gave her a pat on the ass. "I forgot something. You go on. I'll call you later." He charged back up the stairs.

He grabbed a new shirt and changed his tie, slapped on a fresh layer of after-shave, and checked the mirror, satisfied he'd pass the dragon lady's inspection. There was a light tap at his door. "Curt?"

He opened the door to Leanna carrying a picnic

basket and wearing a short yellow sundress that showed off a deep summer tan on long legs and bare shoulders. A wonderful, light perfume drifted in the door with the breeze, ruffling her skirt delightfully higher. If he hadn't just had Christie, she'd be one terrific entrée. "Hi, sweetheart, what are you doing here?" He brought her inside and looked quickly around the apartment for evidence, then relaxed. What was she gonna see?

"I thought I'd surprise you."

"You surprised me all right. How'd you get here?"

"The taxi driver brought me up. He said your car was downstairs, so I knew you were still here."

"It's a good thing I was running late." He kissed her, and she kissed him back.

"I had the cook make up sandwiches and lemonade. I thought we could talk without waiters and everyone. . . sort of a picnic."

"Great idea. Where do you want to go?"

"I thought we'd do it here. If you want to."

She was blushing furiously, and it was written all over her. She intended to seduce him. This ought to be really interesting. He kissed her again, slowly this time. "I'd love to do it here."

He settled her carefully on one of the bar chairs and pulled plates and glasses out of the cupboard. "I think this is terrific," he said, and watched her closely. To his knowledge, he'd never had a virgin. There'd been a couple who'd claimed they were, but this was a sure thing, maybe a once-in-a-lifetime opportunity, and he intended to make the most of it.

It was too quiet in the apartment; he could hear "All My Children" seeping through the walls from the apartment next door.

"How about some music? Country and western okay?"

"Fine."

He picked out a CD and pushed it into the player, then hit the repeat play button. Garth Brooks filled up the silence. She was picking at her lunch and getting more and more nervous by the minute. He'd have to move things along or she might get too spooked to go through with it, and the idea of a virgin had definitely put him in the mood.

"Let me show you the apartment." She nodded and slid off the stool. He took her hand. "We're standing in the living room." He led her down the hallway. "That's the bath, and this is the bedroom. This is the bed." He pulled aside the covers. "Here, touch." She patted the bed obediently, but when he took her in his arms to kiss her again, her body tightened under his touch. "Hey, we both want to do this," he said soothingly.

"I know," she answered. "But we need to talk."

"We need to do a whole lot more than talk." He kissed her, and she kissed him back. Progress. "You go ahead and talk while I show you what I want you to do, okay? This is gonna solve a whole lot of problems."

He kicked off his shoes. "I like to be undressed by a woman, so why don't you start with taking off my tie?" He loosened it, and she slipped it through the knot, pulled it from around his neck, and dropped it onto the bed. He kissed her shoulder. "See, now that's not so hard, is it?" he encouraged. "Now the shirt. I'll do the cuffs."

She began unbuttoning the front of his shirt, and he felt himself getting ready for her, right on schedule. It was a perfect world. He wondered if it would feel any different for him; it was supposed to hurt them if it was truly their first time. Well, he was about to find out. "That's right," he praised her, "just pull it up out of my pants and take it off. No, don't put it on the bed because we're gonna use the bed. Now the belt, and then unzip me." He took the shirt from her fingers and tossed it onto the dresser. "You never did this before, did you?" he verified.

She shook her head and felt down his chest to his waist. She was trembling and taking forever to figure out the buckle; he fought the impulse to do it for her and forced himself to wait. He was already hard as a rock. By the time she figured it out, he'd be solid steel. He unzipped the back of her sundress. Her skin was moist and soft under his touch. "That's nice, baby. That's great." God, she was slow.

He stopped her efforts to unbuckle his belt long enough to pull the straps away from her shoulders and drop the sundress to the floor. She was wearing a lacy pink bra and cotton bikini underwear with a pink rose pattern. As he'd suspected, her breasts were way too small, but so what? She was Sam Bowmont's little girl. He chuckled. What kind of woman wore underwear to a seduction?

Impatient, he pushed her hands below his beltline. She felt him for an instant, long enough to send "ready" signals rocketing through his body. When she pulled away, trying to avoid touching him, he realized she was starting to change her mind, and he ignored her. Not now. No way. This was going to happen. "No, baby, do it like this," he encouraged. If he waited much longer, he was going to go off like a missile.

He moved away from her long enough to unzip his pants, kick them off, and drop his underwear. One thing for sure, he hadn't been this hard since high school. He moved next to her on the bed and rubbed himself against her thigh. "Put your hands on me," he coaxed. "Come on, touch it for me, honey. Make it feel good, baby. It's for you."

"Curt, I don't think this is—"

"Sure it is, you're just not used to it." He kissed her into silence when the phone began to ring. He ignored it and reached for her panties.

"Curt, I don't want to do this," she said.

He tried to kiss her again. "Sure you do, honey, we both do, you said so."

"I know, but I—"

The phone rang again. Oh, Christ. He'd either have to answer it or let her hear the message when the machine picked up. It could be anybody. Damn it to hell and gone. He got off the bed, awkward and aching. "I'll be right back."

He picked up the phone in the living room. "Yes!"

It was Christie, and he'd made the right decision—if she'd babbled on the answering machine, it would have been over. "Hi, honey, I'm here at the airport and I didn't think you'd be home but I was just going to leave a message about how much I love you and tell you thanks for . . ."

The minute she heard him leave the room, Leanna began to search for her clothing. This was all wrong. This wasn't supposed to be frightening, and she was scared to death, scared of Curt and scared of the situation. She listened to him on the phone and fought panic. This was suddenly a man she didn't know, and things were out of control. He wasn't listening to her. He was giving her orders and being insistent, and surely it wasn't supposed to be like this.

Something in this room was wrong, too, disturbing and upsetting her equilibrium. Unable to focus, she located the sundress and slipped it over her shoulders. When she had it zipped, she retraced her path toward his voice in the living room, aware she was trembling.

"I understand," he was saying impatiently. "Yeah, right." The phone banged into its cradle. "Where are you going?"

His voice was different, under control, contrite. The Curt she knew had returned, but it didn't matter. "I'm leaving. I don't want to do this. I've changed my mind."

"Oh, sweetheart, I'm sorry." Bare arms came around her shoulders, restraining her gently. His erection pushed insistently at her stomach. "Hey, I promise it's okay. I'd never do anything you didn't want me to do, I swear."

She was unable to relax, not sure how to handle things. "It's just wrong, Curt," she murmured. "I can't do it. I don't know why."

"Is it because we're not married?"

His voice was gentle, probing for understanding. She seized the notion. "I think so. Probably. Maybe things are happening a little too fast."

"You're right. It's my fault." He kissed her. "It's just that I know how terrific it's going to be for you once it happens. You're so beautiful, and I just wanted you so bad that I forgot it's your first time. I'm sorry, honey, I really am." He began to kiss her fingers. "I love you and I would never, ever hurt you. Just let me show you. Let me make love to you. I'll go slow, I promise." He was pulling her toward the bedroom.

"No, I need to think about this, Curt. I need to—"

He stopped her with another kiss, slow and gentle. "I don't need to think about it," he told her. "I love you and I want to make love to you. Let me prove it."

"No." She began to panic. "I want to go home."

It was too late. He'd blown it. Damn her, damn Christie, damn the whole goddamn world! His balls were aching as he tried to pick up the pieces. "Will you let me drive you?"

After a few moments, she agreed. He dressed in record time, and while she allowed him to pull her close and keep his arm around her during the trip, even kissed him good-bye, the wall was there and he was back to square one. He cursed to high heaven. He raged at Christie and her stupid phone call that had interrupted the moment. He'd have brought her around. He'd never had any complaints about his bedroom technique. If the bitch hadn't called, he'd have brought her around. The stupidity of the situation made him crazy.

It wasn't fair. For the first time in his adult life he felt as though he'd made a mistake; he realized that he wasn't coming up with a plan, wasn't figuring a way out of the box. He found a liquor store and bought a bottle of gin to put himself to sleep.

There was a way out of this. All he had to do was find it.

Rattled to her core, trembling with feelings she wasn't sure she could handle, Leanna escaped to her bedroom the minute Curt drove away. She needed to talk with Parker. This wasn't something she could talk about with her father, but if she could talk to Parker, maybe she could make some sense of things. She called Jolene's. Jillian told her that Parker and her sister had driven into Wellington to a baseball game; he'd told her that morning, and she'd forgotten about it. She burst into tears. She'd gone to Curt's with such high hopes, such romantic notions of slow kisses and gentle passion, and it had gone so wrong. So wrong.

"I'll be right over," Jillian told her.

The minute Jillian walked into her bedroom, Leanna lost control and everything came out in a torrent: the evening at the nightclub, Curt's explanation, Jay's advice, her fears about getting married, all mixed up together. Eventually she was calm enough to talk about the debacle of that afternoon. "I saw Curt," she confessed. "I went to his apartment to go to bed with him."

"I said talk to him, not seduce him. What happened?"

As she remembered, Leanna realized what about the room had been wrong, and bitter tears began to flow once again. "There was perfume all over his pillow." It had surrounded her senses like a cloud, but she'd been too upset to identify it at the time. A bold, exotic fragrance. Heavily floral. The same perfume as the woman in the nightclub. Christie. It had been in the hallway, too.

"Oh, God, are you sure?"

She nodded miserably. A tissue was suddenly at her fingertips, and she used it to blot her tears.

Jillian went immediately practical. "If you weren't engaged, I'd tell you that guys sleep with women all the time and it doesn't mean anything. But he shouldn't be sleeping with anyone but you." She paused. "Are you in love with him?"

"I don't know if I love him or I need him." It hurt like

hell to admit the truth at last. The tears became a river.

"Why on earth do you need him? Don't tell me about being blind. You don't marry someone just because you're blind."

"I don't know."

"Well, you better find out. Marry in haste, repent at leisure," Jillian quoted. "It's a tired old maxim, but oh, boy, is it true. If there are children involved, leisure can be twenty years. I think you ought to take some time and think it over. This is pretty serious."

Leanna felt her friend move off the bed, and her next question came from across the room. "I know this is none of my business, but is there any reason this wedding can't go on hold?"

Jillian's voice held the slightest hint of embarrassment, and Leanna didn't get the drift. "I don't know what you mean."

"I mean, is there any chance you could be pregnant?"

Leanna caught a wavery breath and laughed out loud. Her tears stopped at last. "Absolutely none," she responded, pleased with herself for the first time in weeks. That much, at least, she'd done right. Besides, she'd been on birth control since she'd gotten engaged—just in case. She began to feel centered and renewed. Jillian was correct; this had turned into a wedding in haste. More than that, it was time she took herself in hand and decided on charting her own future. Not to appease Curt or please her father. Not to placate Alice Faye. Not to prove anything to anyone, including herself.

By the time Jillian left, there was no reason to discuss the matter further. To avoid talking to Curt, she told her family she had a splitting headache, which was true, and wasn't taking calls, then went to bed early.

The following morning she walked over to see Annie Chatfield. Within an hour she'd arranged to rent the room at the bottom of the stairs for the next three months. That accomplished, she called Jillian to tell her where she was planning to live, and her friend ecstatically agreed to help her move. Then she called Curt. There was no answer, so she left word on his answering machine that the wedding was off and she planned to return his ring.

19

Sam pressed a cold compress to his eye. He'd been fine until Curt had called to admit that he and Leanna had had a major misunderstanding and she'd called off the wedding. The young man hadn't elaborated, only assured him that it would all be straightened out, but Sam was greatly perturbed. First, that Leanna hadn't confided a decision of this magnitude, and second, that Curt was hiding something, which usually translated to another woman.

When he called Leanna into his study, she confirmed that she had postponed her wedding and confessed to having had grave doubts about getting married for weeks. He was thoroughly stunned, however, when she informed him she'd already arranged a room and planned to live on her own at least three months before making a new commitment to Curt, one way or the other.

That she would be virtually next door did little to ease his anxiety until he realized it was probably the best solution all the way around. She could embark on an independent life-style and learn whether or not she could handle it well before his life was over; he would make suitable arrangements in either instance. He assured her of his support and was rewarded with her smile and a kiss and a lilt to her voice that had been missing for weeks. After she left, he called Burt Holman and asked him to check into Annie Chatfield, and aware that it was something he should have done months ago, he added Curtis Baylor to the list of people to be investigated.

Then he considered his situation with his wife. Alice Faye was beginning to be suspicious about his health. His "temporary" move into an adjacent bedroom was becoming permanent, and sex was no longer a driving force between them. Leanna's engagement had been a source of strength. Now it was questionable that she'd marry at all, but to tell his family of his illness might destroy the far more important spark of independence that was suddenly alight in her. To have it die an early death with information that could wait wasn't worth it. Best to let sleeping dogs go undisturbed.

After a couple of hours of walking on hot coals with her father and Alice Faye, Curt was able to talk with Leanna. "I don't understand why you're doing this," he pleaded. "Is it because of yesterday? What on earth happened that was so bad?"

She listened with a determined expression but refused to let him sit next to her or hold her hand.

"I realized that it's part of a larger problem, Curt. I'm just not ready to be married, and yesterday made that very clear. It wasn't anything you did, it's me. I'm not ready."

He tried every argument he could think of, but he was only able to persuade her to continue wearing his ring in friendship. The wedding date went by the boards. Her moving out was a major break, however, and he succeeded in obtaining her promise that she would continue to see him.

In three months, I can turn her around thirteen times, he assured himself, driving back to his apartment. "She finds out that living away from Daddy isn't what it's cracked up to be, she'll be thrilled to get married." Satisfied that the damage was reparable, he breathed a hell of a lot easier.

Leanna found Parker by the pool, told him she was having second thoughts about getting married and was planning to move into Chatfield's. As she expected, he was less than pleased the minute he found out that Jay Sprengsten lived there.

"I'm moving there because I know Annie," she explained impatiently, ticking off the reasons on her fingers. "She's not uncomfortable with my blindness, and it's close by. Would it make you happier if I moved into Wellington?"

"No," he said grudgingly. "I just wish I understood this thing with Sprengsten."

"There is no thing with Sprengsten," she insisted. "I can't dislike him just because you do, and I don't know what I have to do to convince you that he's not remotely interested in me."

"Then what's going on with Curt?"

She explained her suspicions about his friendship with Christie, and he joined with her father in giving his support. While she was at it, she decided to clear the air.

"By the way, don't ever refer to me as a 'poor little rich girl.' I'm not poor just because I'm blind, and I'm certainly not little."

After his stunned and genuinely repentant apology, she hugged her brother tightly and heaved a huge sigh of relief.

Having put her world right, she was ready to leave within the week, and in the midst of her family's mixture of concern and pride, she, Jillian, and Traxx Jobbing in the persons of Stephen and Tommy managed to have her moved within three hours, lock, stock, and clothing labels.

Jillian sat in front of the fireplace in Annie's den. The last of Leanna's boxes had been unpacked and put away, and she'd been studying the old mansion and the various members of the Sprengsten family most of the day; Annie was a jewel, and the house was a marvelous find. Aside from her feelings for Jay, the price was right, she could manage the rent if she used the income from her grandfather's trust, and the pale yellow bedroom with a huge balcony overlooking the lake, with its own private stairway exit, would be ideal for a writer.

Running back to New York would only prolong her problem. If she didn't ride this out, at least try to resolve the conflicted emotions where Jay and her sister were concerned, she'd wonder about it for the rest of her life. Leanna tapped her way into the room and stood in front of the fire.

Jillian came to a decision. "What would you say if I moved in, too?"

Leanna's face broke into a luminous smile. "Are you serious?" she answered. "I'd love it."

Jillian went to find Annie and came back a few minutes later to broadcast the news. "I'm in," she crowed happily. "I have the room directly above you. I'll close the apartment in New York and move next week."

Predictably, her parents were thrilled that she was staying in Walden City. Her father was set to call in favors to gain her a late acceptance to Traxx as a premed student, but she pleaded a semester off. Undeterred, he began lobbying efforts to shoe-horn her into January's schedule.

Jolene's response had been a mild, "Oh, yeah? Fine."

Her own excitement created a momentum that carried her through the hundred and one details of packing up her New York apartment and storing her belongings in the family garage; it took nearly a week to move, and, in at last, she was exhilarated at the thought of seeing Jay daily, not to mention that his bedroom was right down the hall. His balcony connected to hers, not that she had fantasies or anything.

She hadn't been settled two hours when Jolene showed up to visit, the glitzy band of emeralds no longer on her finger. After a cursory tour of Jillian's bedroom and the rest of the house, she and Jay were off in the music room before Jillian knew what was happening, and a few minutes later they were driving away in her sister's car. "Move in haste, repent within hours," she flayed herself wearily, refusing the relief of tears.

She watched the clock as punishment to herself for not thinking through the consequences of moving in here from Jolene's point of view. Under the guise of visiting, her sister would now come and go as she wished, seeing Jay without Parker's knowledge.

Why did she never see these things coming?

It was nearly midnight before she heard a car slow to

a halt on the drive. Jay climbed out, and Jolene slid onto the driver's seat. Her heart contracted painfully as they kissed a long time before Jolene finally drove away. There were strawberry marks on his throat the next morning at breakfast.

Jolene was back the following afternoon to return the teal sweater she'd "borrowed and forgotten to return." This time she was wearing the ring. And this time Jay was waiting for her. This time it was after midnight before Jillian heard the Traxx pickup drive into the parking area and, a few minutes later, her sister's car went gliding down the driveway. And this time the tears came unbidden, and her throat hurt keeping the sobs silent.

Days passed with incredible slowness until it was finally October, with early morning corners of frost etched on her bedroom window and leaves on the trees surrounding the lake going overnight from a hundred hues of green to a paintbox of russet fall colors.

She adored Danielle and Charlie, Tommy was cute and funny, and she watched silent Stephen become Leanna's shadow. He rarely engaged in conversation of any length with anyone else and spent hours guiding her through the rooms of the house, walking with her in the yard, answering her questions, and making certain no obstacles entangled her progress until she had learned the house and grounds by heart.

"People don't have to love you back," he said to her suddenly one morning. He'd shrugged with a wisdom entirely too old for his sixteen years. "Sometimes it's better if they don't."

Jillian fought tears, knowing he was perceptive and aware of her feelings for his brother, and she loved him for his honesty.

Despite her preoccupation with Jay and Jolene, she looked forward to fall evenings that were warm and wonderful among the sprawling couches and pillows in front of the huge brick fireplace in the music room. Tommy had been designated as the master popper of corn, and kitchen duty was posted for everyone except the mysterious boarder to whom she'd been introduced for a brief instant, who seemed very nice but was generally sleeping or "out doing research."

Stephen was released from the foster program and moved in at last. Jay was tight-lipped in anger as he walked out his rage in the backyard of the inn, describing to her and Annie the appalling conditions in which his brother had been living. "It's a factory! She had five kids there. The state pays her five hundred dollars a head, and she feeds them watered-down macaroni and cheese. I called the county on her. They're going to investigate."

Annie was furious as well, but Stephen had been surprised at their reactions. It hadn't mattered to him where he lived. He'd been waiting for Jay's return and the promise of living together as a family. He was thrilled to have a home at last. That night Jay hadn't gone out, and they'd celebrated long into the evening.

Everyone had an assigned seat at the huge dining room table, with place cards to be turned over if you weren't going to be home for dinner so Annie could plan meals. The place card for Matt Halston was always turned over, as he was inevitably out for the evening.

Every morning for breakfast and every evening for dinner when Jay was home afforded Jillian the misery of conversation and proximity and the pain-filled joy of his occasional attention. Those nights she knew he was with Jolene brought the grinding ache of his absence. Those nights, she no longer watched out the window for his return. By day she stared at her computer, seeking inspiration, and during the evenings she sought distraction. Occasionally she talked with Leanna about her situation with Curt; more often she left the house and spent hours by the lake, trying to come to terms with the reality that Jay was out of reach. And she hurt every minute of her existence with the knowledge that the man she was falling more and more in love with was sleeping with her sister whenever Jolene would allow it.

Jay had reached seventh heaven. The one missing piece of his life was within his grasp. Withdrawing his ultimatum about Parker had given him the past ten days with Jolene, and from the afternoon on the bluff where he'd finally made love to her to exhaustion, to the lunch hours at Lockerby's fishing cabin, his passion for her body dimmed at last the four years of anger and frustration at losing her.

Each time they were together, he became more determined to have her to himself and make her forget that Parker Bowmont existed on the face of the earth; however, no matter what he did, she wouldn't agree to give Parker up. Discussion of the subject inevitably ended up with her refusing to make love at all, and he'd come away from their meeting in agony.

He worked long hours for his family to earn the time to be with her, to be driven crazy with the perfection of her body. On those occasions when she would sleep with him, he trembled under the heat of her hands as she slid her fingers inside his jeans and between his legs when she was in a hurry, getting him so hot there was no room to unzip the zipper.

Sometimes, exhausted, he longed to talk to her about planning their future, sharing his dreams for their life together, but she inevitably stopped him and either convinced him to make love to her again or, if he couldn't, got dressed and left. He'd be forced to wait for the time when he could see her again. She was like no liquor or drug he'd ever tried, an addiction, pure and simple.

It was inevitable that he and Parker would collide. He spent hours looking forward to it. The sooner they had a confrontation, the sooner Jolene would be forced to choose, and he was confident that Parker would lose.

Sure enough, Bowmont stopped by one afternoon to visit Leanna while he and Jolene were in the music room; not three seconds before Parker walked in, they had broken from a breathless kiss and she still had her hand below his belt. Parker stalked out without a word.

Jolene told him to wait and followed Parker outside. He decided it was best to let them have it out, to let her tell Parker he was history and get it over with. But after a major shouting match, she got in Bowmont's car and they drove away before he could stop them. Her convertible stayed the next two days in the drive and was gone the following night.

He couldn't believe it at first. She wouldn't see him, and she wouldn't answer his calls for two more days. By then he was furious. Furious with Jolene, furious with himself, and furious with the world. Everyone in the family gave him a wide berth, and for the first time since entering the army he did something stupid: he began to drink to get through the nights.

When she did call, she admitted that the emerald ring she'd been wearing was a gift from Parker and not her father. He realized he'd gained no ground at all, and his fury increased until the afternoon she agreed to see

him and they went to Lockerby's. She was wearing the
hated ring, and despite his determination not to badger
her about it, he lost his temper.

"Are you engaged or was it payment for services rendered?" he demanded, out of his mind with jealousy.
Her answer was to get out of bed and begin dressing.
Then nothing mattered except getting her back into bed
with him and taking possession of her body. This time
he didn't go back to work, and she didn't go home.

When he called and Jolene wasn't there, Parker
knew she was with Jay. He drove to her father's house
and when she showed up, he blocked the entrance to
the driveway until she agreed to talk to him. She got
into his car, openly unrepentant, her swollen mouth and
tangled hair making no secret of the afternoon's activities, her eyes challenging him to do something about it.
They went for a drive. Conversation granted no solu-
tions; she wasn't willing to stop seeing Sprengsten. They
wound up spending the night in a Wellington hotel
room, where they made love for hours. He was turned
on in spite of himself at the thought of wiping out traces
of another man in her body, and their lovemaking was
better than it had ever been.

When he came out of the shower the next morning,
she was lying on her stomach on the bed, nude as he'd
left her, ankles crossed, with the emerald ring on her
right hand. She glanced up at him brightly. "Are you
really serious about getting married?"

Determined to punish her for seeing Sprengsten, he
said, "I was." He crossed to a chair and began to dress.
"But I don't think so now." He was gratified to see her
jerk to attention.

"What do you mean?"

He deliberately let her wait a full three beats before he answered. "I mean you still have a thing for the old boyfriend." He pushed his legs into his trousers and stood up to close his zipper. "This boyfriend no longer sees a reason to buy the cow." He pulled on his shirt.

She was incensed at his callous attitude, and he felt terrific. He put on his socks and stepped into his shoes.

"How dare you call me a cow!" She was off the bed in a flash and dressing furiously.

"Right now the milk appears to be free—all over town." It was a proper slap in the face she hadn't expected, and the enjoyment was supreme. It served her right for sleeping with the son of a bitch.

"He'd marry me tomorrow," she flung at him.

"Sure, right." He stared elaborately at her left hand. "Gee, I don't see a cheap engagement ring."

She tore off the emerald band and threw it at him. It bounced off the headboard and fell onto the carpet. "Your *cow* just jumped the fence." She grabbed her shoes and purse and stormed out.

He left the ring on the floor and calmly finished dressing. She didn't come back, so he retrieved it and slipped it into his pocket. When he got to his car, she was waiting. "You'll cool off," he said reasonably. "You'll take a look at him and a look at me, and when it comes to marriage, I win, hands down. The ring is yours anytime you ask." She rode home in stony silence.

20

Leanna was waiting for Curt to arrive. It was the first time she'd agreed to go to dinner since the infamous afternoon she'd tried to seduce him, and her knee jumped up and down, rapping a steady rhythm on the sofa cushion until she became aware of the outward sign of her nervousness. He'd called her every day, cajoling and entreating and apologizing until she'd given in. The whole incident continued to confuse her.

Part of her was fascinated at the sexual side of what had happened, at the discovery of this new, mysterious, physiological phenomenon that was the male half of sex. But every instinct she had warned her that, despite his explanations, there was more to Curt's behavior than passion and not to permit a similar situation to develop until she was ready.

She and Jillian had decided that seeing him tonight came under the heading of an examination of her feelings, not his. She checked her watch; he was due any minute. Thanks to Stephen's tutelage, she was now largely familiar with the old house, and the presence of her friends and the low crackle in the fireplace helped ease her anxiety.

To distract herself, she ran her hand across the velvet plush of the squishy old couch, assessing the worn spots with the tips of her fingers and imagining the rich, royal gold it once had been. Sort of like life, she decided: worn spots and damage were the price of participation. She resigned herself to the knowledge that it was impossible to gain a sense of independence without the pain of experience.

Her goal redefined, she centered and listened to light banter as Tommy sat down with Annie to work on a puzzle that lived on top of the card table at the other end of the room; they'd been working on it for the past five days.

Jay had been a bear since Jolene had chosen Parker over him, and she knew Jillian was hurting as well, but tonight things seemed mellow. They were sharing kitchen duty and had reached the pots and pans; the removed sound of their conversation mingled with mild clanks and clatters of metal cookware. She heard the slam and rattle of stainless tableware as individual pieces hit their slots in the wooden drawer.

Stephen fingered his guitar to let her know he was seated to her right on one of the easy chairs. Footsteps came toward her across the wooden flooring, then were muffled on the rug; she was not surprised when she felt a light tap on her hand and her cardigan appeared. "Here's your sweater."

She'd forgotten it. "Thanks, Charlie."

Someone settled to her left on the couch, and after a few moments of silence, Danni asked innocently, "What's it like being blind?"

"Close your eyes and I'll see if I can give you an

idea." Glad to have something to do besides anticipate the evening with Curt, she reached over to Danni's face. The little girl gave a slight startled reaction, then sat quietly as Leanna lightly ran her fingers over her closed eyelids.

"Charlie just brought me my sweater. Until I felt it with my fingers I had no concept of its existence—just like you didn't expect me to touch your face. Other than hearing someone walk across the room toward me, I had no way of knowing it was going to arrive in my hand. And until she said something, I didn't know it was Charlie."

She folded the cardigan over her lap before continuing. "It's like being surrounded with sound but not having any advance knowledge of what relates to you. I don't have visual anticipation." She realized her words were pretty sophisticated for an eight-year-old and tried to simplify.

"When Stephen plays his guitar I know he's in the room and where, but most things don't exist for me unless I can hear them, feel them, or identify their taste or smell." She renewed her efforts to make it clear to a sighted person. "It's the same in a car. Without seeing the scenery go by, I have no awareness that I'm traveling anywhere. I feel bumps and motions right and left, and I hear the sounds just like you do, but otherwise I get in at one place, wait a while, and get out somewhere else. There's no sensation of distance or change."

"What else?"

The front door eased quietly open, and Curt stepped undetected into the foyer.

"It's always dark for me. I have to check my watch to know what time it is." Leanna tried to identify ordinary things that only blind people had to consider. "I have to remember to smile and to open my eyes and look at someone who's talking to me, otherwise they don't think I hear them. There's no reason except that it's polite, so I do it."

She heard new understanding in Danni's voice. "Does it ever get any easier?"

"If you've been sighted, you never quite get used to it. You do learn a new way of interpreting the world—for instance, I hear differently than you do. I listen for sounds bouncing off solid objects. They used to call it facial vision, but it's echo location, actually. Usually I can tell when I'm approaching a wall because there's like a dead space in the middle of air that's in motion and you know there's something there."

Charlie took over the questions. "What do you see? Is it black or just nothing?"

"I have the sensation of black. I don't know that I'm 'seeing' it, but the impression is black."

"That's enough, kids. Give her a break." Leanna turned her face toward Jay's voice, from a high place next to the fire. The soft clink of glass hit the mantel. He'd been drinking beer at dinner, and he had Scotch now. She had smelled it when he'd passed behind her.

Jillian discovered Curt in the foyer. He feigned innocence at her meaningful look at the open front door and offered to shake hands. She took his outstretched hand with limp fingers and announced, "Leanna, Curt's here," and closed the door with a thump.

Leanna rose to her feet; she'd almost forgotten Curt was coming.

"Hi, sweetheart," he said, moving to her side and taking her hand. "I didn't want to interrupt." He gave her a small kiss on the cheek. "You look terrific."

She introduced him all around.

"You ready to go?" he asked pleasantly. "I have reservations at six-thirty, and we'll just make it if we leave now."

Jillian stopped her in the foyer. *"Citius, altius, fortius,"* she said gaily. Leanna translated from her rusty memory of Latin and laughed. Faster, higher, stronger.

"Carpe diem," she replied.

"What was that about?" Curt asked.

She told him, and he laughed. It turned out that her anxiety over the evening was misplaced, and she needn't have worried. Curt was on his absolute best behavior. He was bright and funny, protective and considerate, and assured her at every opportunity that he had no intention of pressuring her in any way. He seemed so happy that she had agreed to see him, she felt guilty.

He brought her home at nine-thirty, gave her a sweet kiss at the door, and reminded her gently that he was in love with her and willing to wait as long as she needed to know her own mind. He told her that he'd turned down the position in Chicago in order to stay close by, and he was, step by step, going to bring her back into his life.

She agreed to see him again the following week.

Carpe diem. Seize the day. Jillian wandered to the gazebo to watch the fall sunset across the lake and smiled at her friend's response to her comment. Leanna hadn't been specific, but she suspected that in addition to the incident with the perfumed pillow, Curt had gotten pretty insistent about sex. Personally, she couldn't help feeling that the guy was a little too "on" when he'd shook hands all around the room. Borderline smarmy. Hopefully, Leanna was on to him, and he'd have his hands full getting her anywhere she didn't want to go.

She crushed a handful of lavender and rubbed it between her palms to let the spicy fragrance surround her as the pleasant notes of a folk song came drifting from the front porch; Stephen was waiting for Leanna's return. It had been a fluky day, warm and balmy, creating a perfect Indian summer evening. A couple of nights ago, a light frost had begun the work of fall, and the maples and elms bordering the yard were on fire with thousands of shades of red and gold and beginning to drop their leaves.

She abandoned the boat dock and was walking along the shoreline when Jay sauntered down to join her. The bottom rim of the sun was transforming a stand of spruce on the far side of the lake to slender black spires edged with gold. He offered his glass, and she made a face at the harsh taste. She knew enough about drinks to recognize that any club soda in the mixture had been recently overloaded with fresh Scotch.

Unsettled by his presence, uncomfortable that he was drinking, she held out hope that this time it would stay over between him and her sister. However it stood, she didn't want to risk discussion about Jolene. She moved restlessly along the lakefront and he followed in companionable silence. Ripples of water slid and eddied endlessly around worn rocks scattered along the shoreline, and mellowed sunlight danced on the oily surface of the water; she gave up searching for reasons to abandon his company. Being here was his choice, and she decided to accept it.

Gnatcatchers flitted above the skyline at the top of the grassy bank, catching insects, while she and Jay worked their way along the edge of the water. By the time the sun had burned its way to the base of the trees to spread fingers of light across the lake, they had reached a small cove. Their presence silenced bullfrogs noisily setting up territorial stations along the shore, as well as katydids and crickets tuning up their suites in the last warmth of the year.

There was half an inch of liquid remaining in the highball glass when he passed it to her. She lifted it toward him in wry salutation, and in the incredible still of the air, she saw the last of the sunset shine through the liquor, lighting it to a magic glowing amber. She swallowed it like Alice and turned away, wanting no change from this moment in her life.

"Hey," he said quietly, and put down the glass.

Shafts of sunlight breaking through the pines layered his face and hair with gold; she stopped, suspended on filament. He came close enough to take a strand of her hair, pulled it away from her face, and tucked it deliberately behind her ear. Then his thumb lightly explored the line of her cheek, his eyes a clear, crystalline blue in the honeyed light; he slid his hand to the back of her neck, winding his fingers deep in her hair, and suddenly he was kissing her, wetly, insistently, his tongue seeking entry.

Despite the Scotch, his taste was enticingly good. Her hands caught his face and held his open mouth hard against her own. Discovery and delight entangled together into one giant surge of joy, and, oh, she kissed him back, refusing for one moment to be honorable and loyal, willing herself to drown in every aching moment of his attention, determined to have all he would give. He ground his body against her own, holding her fast until her brain caught fire, incandescent with the knowledge that being in his arms, kissing him,

was a hundred times better than she'd dared imagine—
and so incredibly possible.

His kisses continued, demanding, possessive; no
negotiation, no quarter. He wanted her, and she welcomed the hunger in him, felt his need, embraced his
fever. Kissing him, oh, God, kissing him and savoring
the feel of his mouth, the strength in his body, she
strained to make it equal, sent every signal she knew
that she, too, wanted something mystical to happen
between them. Here. Now.

Their passion carried them to the grass, and his
hands roamed her body, pulling her tighter against him,
willing her compliance; his fingers under her sweater
unfastened her bra, pushed it away to caress her breasts
and pleasure her nipples. She unfastened his jeans and
helped slide them away from lean, hollowed hips, off
strong, slender legs. At last she was able to open her
body to him, match his need, feed her own emotion
with the strength of him until she couldn't think anymore and damn tomorrow.

21

Jay's mind was in turmoil, and the last time he remembered looking at the clock, it was three A.M. Dozing at last, he became aware of someone trying to open his balcony door. Before he could get out of bed to investigate, a partially opened window of his bedroom slid upward and a woman's body eeled into the room without a sound.

She undressed in silence, and when he held the covers aside to welcome her naked body, he was already hard. She held one hand over his mouth as she stroked him with knowing, subtle fingers, teasing him with pleasure; within moments he joined in her soundless lovemaking, returning frantic, eager kisses, raking his fingers through her hair as he crushed her mouth and made love to her once again—wonderfully exciting, forbidden, quiet love.

She made her way soundlessly to the kitchen. Reliving the wonder of the night's incredible events,

Jillian retrieved a cup from the china cabinet and froze at the unmistakable sound of her sister's laughter, muffled, and the low rumble of Jay's voice coming from the upstairs hallway. Seconds later they stole quietly down the stairs; his arms wrapped possessively around her body, he walked Jolene through the living room and out the front door.

Destroyed beyond words, she was unable to move. Her mind refused to function, her heart a cold stone in her body. Before she could recover, Annie came rustling into the kitchen in her robe and slippers to set about preparations for morning coffee and breakfast. Under her questioning gaze, Jillian rinsed the dry cup under the faucet. "Couldn't sleep," she mumbled, and padded numbly out of the room and up the stairs even as the sound of her sister's car receded down the drive.

She stood still as a mouse as Jay came through the front door and she heard him walk into the kitchen. In the quiet of the sleeping household, his solemn declaration came echoing up the stairs. "I'm going to ask Jolene to marry me, Annie, and if she says yes, we'll do it as soon as I can buy a ring."

Annie's response was inaudible.

Jillian flew down the hallway to her room and quietly shut the door on the world. He hadn't said a word. That had probably been the most hurtful part. After he'd taken her to her climax and had reached his own, while she'd sailed on, totally and gloriously euphoric, he'd been gradually, terribly, still. He'd raised himself on his arms and looked into her face, and in the milky twilight she'd been forced to see the shocked dawning of disbelief, watch the expression in his eyes change from languid confusion to an astonished comprehension. He'd dropped his head onto her naked breast and his whole body had sagged into a dead weight. But he hadn't said a word.

She'd heard it in the soft groan of acceptance as he became aware that it was too late, that there was no way to rectify the damage. It had hit her then, like a blow, that it hadn't been his intention to make love to her, that he'd been making love to Jolene. She'd been the stand-in.

They'd gotten dressed in embarrassed silence and he'd stared at the ground, unable to look at her. She'd taken his face in her hands and he'd closed his eyes to her. "I know," she'd assured him, "and it's all right." Then she'd kissed him, probably for the last time, and he'd clutched at her shoulders to kiss her back with something between gratitude and desolation in his touch. "Just don't say you're sorry," she'd demanded. "I couldn't stand it if you said you were sorry."

His face had been wretched in the growing darkness, steeped in an inability to accept what had happened; he'd spread his hands in a helpless gesture that indicated he indeed did not know what to say. She'd left him there and walked back to the inn, caught between elation and sorrow, discovery and loss, her body soaring with joy, her soul mired in sadness. It wasn't that it was over. It had never happened.

Except that it had, and for the time they'd spent together it had been ecstasy. She'd tossed for hours, unable to sleep, unable to deny the thrill of making love to him at last, while her mind had built shining castles. Surely he would remember. Surely he and Jolene couldn't be better together than their experience tonight by the lake.

She relived the warm, sweet taste of his mouth, the

intimate salty smells and the smooth skin of his body, the hard feel of him—sensations that wore at her senses, ground down her defenses. Aftershocks of emotion spiked through her body. It hadn't been having sex; they'd made love as equals. They'd shared the same time and space, taking turns as lovers, exploring and delighting each other—surely he'd want more. If she was patient, if she could wait things out, surely he'd forget Jolene and come back to her.

Reality brought her castles crashing to earth, and she broke down in tears at last. He wanted Jolene. He'd always wanted Jolene. He'd taken her to his bed within hours of their union at the lake, and he wanted to marry Jolene.

When she was certain he'd left the house, she took a shower in water as cool as she could stand, soaked her puffy eyes with cold cloths, then came down to face the day. She found Annie and informed her that she would be leaving, that she had decided to move back to New York after all. Annie nodded knowingly and said, "Whatever you want, honey."

Trying to hide her devastation, Jillian told Leanna that she'd given notice. Burning her bridges, she admitted to being in love with Jay.

"I know." Leanna was sympathetic. "Actually, I didn't know, but I've suspected it for some time."

"He's never going to love anyone but Jolene. He's planning to ask her to marry him," Jillian said miserably.

"Aren't you forgetting my brother? He and Jolene are practically engaged. If she marries anyone, she'll marry Parker."

Jillian sucked in her breath in quiet realization. "Whether or not they get married, he loves her," she amended with difficulty. "He loves her even if we, I . . ."

She stopped, afraid that she'd said too much already. She'd made love with the man who was going to propose to her sister. A wild ray of hope leaped through her mind. If Jolene said no, he'd come back and it would all work out. Eventually he'd forget Jolene and follow her to New York. . . .

She abandoned her hope as quickly as it had sprung to life. Jay would never leave his family.

After Sam had signed copies of the codicil, Burt Holman handed him folders containing the status of his requested investigations of Curt and Annie. He ignored the papers. "What did you find on Baylor?"

"Nothing unusual. Blue-collar family in Texas, mother was a schoolteacher, deceased. Father's a retired welder. Decent student, no record of any kind. We're still looking. Did you want to add local surveillance?"

Sam thought a moment. "No. Not yet."

His eye ached as he glanced through the report on Annie; he hit the high spots: widow, well thought of in the community, pristine past.

On his way back from the lawyer's office, he stopped by Chatfield's for the first time to see Leanna and introduced himself to Annie. After a preliminary shuffle, and only after a subtle but effective determination on her part that he was in fact who he said he was, did Annie Chatfield seem willing to discuss his daughter; she was concise and to the point and left him with the distinct impression that Leanna was in good, caring hands and making progress.

Before he left, Leanna arrived with Jillian Llowell and insisted he meet several of the Sprengsten clan that made up the balance of the inn's residents. When he allowed her to tow him down to the lakefront, he sensed a new strength of purpose, particularly when he asked about Curt.

"I'm still wearing his ring, but I'm not sure I'm going to keep it," she told him. "I don't want to be as dependent on a husband as I have been on my family."

"I know I've overprotected you," he admitted reluctantly, "and you're doing the right thing by learning to live on your own. But, just know that you can come home whenever you're ready. You don't have to prove anything to Curt or anyone else."

Leanna stopped him. "I'm not trying to prove anything to anyone but myself, Dad. Just me."

Sam brightened at her confidence, and she returned his hug with fervor. It did him good to know that she was happy in her surroundings, and they made a date for lunch the following day. He left with a lightened heart.

Annie's sixth sense told her something was dreadfully wrong with Sam Bowmont's life—something money could not cure. Something in his sadness and sallow complexion, the loose skin of recent weight loss. The man was ill. She'd bet all the tea in China that he hadn't told Leanna.

She sighed at Jillian's decision to leave; the girl was desperately in love with Jay, a hundred times worse than Stephen's infatuation with Leanna and written all over her since the day she'd moved in, but in view of his intentions toward her sister it was probably best. She heaved herself to her feet and retrieved a small white envelope from the bottom drawer of the television cabinet. The instructions were explicit: she was to tell Jay before he married. If he was going to marry Jolene, it was time to give him the letter. She put it in her apron pocket so she wouldn't change her mind.

Jay sat on the monumental boulder that defined the bluff, his emotions doing the dance of the damned. Things had gotten so far out of hand that he wasn't sure he hadn't lost his mind. For a while this morning, he'd been so wrapped up in Jolene, in being so shocked at her coming into his bed in the middle of the night and being able to make love to her again, that he'd actually forgotten what had happened with Jillian.

He rebelled every time he thought about it. It wasn't possible that anyone could turn him on like Jolene; he'd been in love with her since high school! For a while in the army, he hadn't been able to have sex at all unless he thought about her while he was doing it. She'd been on his mind practically every day of his life for nearly five years. What had happened with Jillian at the lake was a mistake, pure and simple, and he was determined to deny it.

It had started out with him a little drunk, and he'd tried to make her Jolene. He'd kissed her like Jolene, he'd held her like Jolene, but he hadn't been able to get past it. When she'd kissed him back, held him, made love to him, there'd been no confusion. He knew it in his heart, he knew it in his soul, and he knew it in his head. When he'd entered her body, he'd known it was Jillian. There'd been a difference that he couldn't yet define, but there had most definitely been a difference.

He told himself it was ridiculous. You don't change years of wanting someone overnight. He was living a nightmare. A living, breathing, hellhole of a nightmare—Jolene had come back to him, and if her sister told her what had happened last night. . . He twisted in agony. Now, when it was over between Jolene and Parker—now, when she'd returned Parker's goddamn emerald ring and was finally admitting they were through, and that she loved him, when it was possible for him to have the only woman he'd ever wanted in his life—he'd managed to make love with her sister!

The whole thing was crazy. And what was crazier was that until he'd come fully awake and seen her face, the body he'd watched come through his window had been part of some weird, exotic dream; he'd been convinced it was Jillian until he'd kissed Jolene in his bed last night.

An hour ago, Annie had told him Jillian was moving back to New York, and he knew there was no getting around it: he had to see her and he had to stop her from telling Jolene. He returned to the inn and found her in the gazebo, staring at the lake. She wouldn't look at him, and he was embarrassed at what he was about to do. "Annie says you're leaving," he began awkwardly. "If it's because of last night . . ." He felt miserable and wrong, and the pain in her face nearly stopped him. "I don't know what to say, Jillie."

She turned to him at last, and he read the disillusion in her eyes. "You made love to me and my sister on the same night."

"Oh, God, Jillian, please don't." Feeling lower than low, he veered to the edge of the lake and picked up several flat stones to give his hands something to do besides hang too large and useless at his sides. He began his explanation. "I didn't mean for it to happen, I swear it. I just saw your body and your hair all gold in the sunset, and I wanted you to be her." He shuffled uncomfortably. "I wouldn't hurt you for the world."

She was dead silent and he tried to make her understand. "Jillie, when I lost my mom, I learned a hard lesson. Don't put off life. Live it, get on with it. There's no such thing as safe, and there may not be a tomorrow." He tossed the stones into the water and stooped to select more. "When I got home, Jolene was with Parker, and I got caught up in getting my family back together. I've loved your sister since I'm seventeen. And last night I was drinking. . . . I wanted her, and she wasn't here. I had no idea you would . . ."

Jillian flushed. It hadn't been entirely his fault. Yes, he'd made the first move, he'd kissed her, but if she had said no, nothing else would have happened. He'd been insistent, but not out of control. She'd wanted it to happen between them, helped make it happen, and he was owning up to his end of it. But he was also asking her to take responsibility for her part. She nodded in acceptance, tears sliding down her face.

She saw his body ease in relief. "She and Parker are quits, and if she agrees to marry me, you and I will be family. If you tell her, which is your right, it'll never happen. Maybe I deserve that. Maybe it would be best all the way around, and it would be over. Either way, I don't want this to cost me your friendship. I care too much about you."

But you want my sister.

"It won't," she managed, and he opened his arms to her. She moved inside and laid her head against his chest, listening to his rapid heartbeat as she clasped her arms around him and held him near; he held her tightly in return. "I won't tell her," she whispered, "I promise." She felt the pressure of his kiss on the top of her head, before he released her and stepped away.

"Thank you," he said fervently.

They walked together back to the inn and she waited nearby, refusing to yield to her feelings while he called Jolene and arranged to meet her at the bluff. The knowledge of what he was about to do was tearing her apart, but she stood on the steps as he started toward the truck. "I hope you get what you want," she told him quietly.

"Thanks for making it possible," he answered, and came back to kiss her softly on the lips. Softly.

She watched him drive away.

Jolene stood watching him, incredulous.

"They're part of the package," he said slowly, studying her face, determined to ignore the part of him that wanted to lie, to tell her they were going to run away and leave everything behind. Everything.

If you marry me, you marry my family. It's no secret that I don't have money, but someday I will, and you know I'll take care of you," he vowed. "But I have to take care of them, too. At least for a couple more years until Tommy and Stephen can help."

He could see she was flustered, which was reasonable, but her silence told him much he didn't want to know—that despite what she'd told him last night in his arms, in his bed, her decision would ultimately rest with Parker. Quits or not, it was only when Bowmont didn't come up with the right answer that he would have a shot. She walked a few paces away from him before answering.

"I know what I said, but there's a lot to think about, and I want us to be sure," she said.

"Fine. I understand. How much time?"

"I don't know. A week."

"Will you tell me sooner if you decide?"

"I'll come to your room and tell you, just like last night."

He kissed her, walking a tightrope between restraint and an overwhelming desire to make love to her with an impulsive, possessive act of sex that would somehow convince her to give him the response that was going to change their lives forever. She kissed him in return, but reserve was there, enough to tip the balance in favor of holding back, so he buried his urges and put her in her car, watched until she'd pulled safely onto the roadway and disappeared down the hill.

When he told Annie he was waiting on an answer from Jolene, she looked at him soberly. "We need to talk, darlin'."

She had on her serious face. Annie, who never missed a thing, probably knew about him and Jillian—definitely something he did not want to deal with at the moment. The phone rang, saving him.

It rang a second time as she moved to answer it, and he restrained himself from pushing past her to pick it up. Not possible that it was Jolene; still, he couldn't entirely stifle his hope and listened shamelessly to Annie's end of the conversation. After a few minutes, she asked the caller to hold and put her hand over the phone. She was pale and looked as if someone had kicked the wind out of her. "It's County General in Los Angeles about your father," she said. "I was listed as a contact on the missing persons report, but I think you should talk to them."

He took the phone while a flat wall of dread toppled onto his life, crushing his brain into little pieces. "This is Jay Sprengsten." A woman's tiny, birdlike voice identified herself as a social service representative and told him that his father was a patient in their hospital, gravely ill. The voice chirped on, giving him an address and urging him to make arrangements to fly to California. Suddenly he shut it out, refused to hear, and handed the receiver to Annie. "You'll have to do this." She took the phone, and he walked on rubber legs to the couch.

Transient. Dog tags identifying him as James Sprengsten. Not expected to live. He reeled in denial and tried to pin it down, stop the spin. Not five minutes ago the most important person in the world had been Jolene Llowell. Suddenly his father was back in his life, and he was drowning in ice water. His mind clawed its way to the surface, and he felt the beginning of rage.

This was some kind of monumental joke. He couldn't leave town now. He'd just made one of the most critical decisions life had to offer; he was planning to get married. Jolene would give him an answer soon. He'd lost her once because of this man and had managed to put things back together only to have it happen again? No way. His future was riding on the line, and no way his father was taking precedence again. Not this time.

Annie hung up the phone and came to sit next to him on the sofa.

"I'm not going," he told her roughly. "Let him die."

"You can't do that, honeybun."

"The hell I can't." His anger built to the ceiling, blew through the roof. "He walked out, we didn't. Well, he can just bloody well stay gone." He got to his feet and saw Stephen's stricken face staring at him from the entrance to the hallway. "What are you doing here?" he shouted at him.

"Where is he?"

"He's dead," he said savagely. "They want me to come pick up the body."

Annie looked at him askance, and he swore. He wanted to beat the hell out of something, hurt someone. He wanted to scream. But he pulled himself under control and forced his anger back into its box. "He's not dead, but he's dying, and I guess I have to go to Los Angeles to see what I can do."

"I'm going, too."

Stephen's expression told him it was pointless to argue. The kid would go if he had to hitch. "On one condition," he bargained cruelly. "I don't want the rest of the family to get their hopes up until we know what's going on. Tommy, okay, but not Charlie or Danielle."

Stephen agreed with reluctance.

"And when he dies . . ." He sighed heavily. "He's already dead where they're concerned, so we'll bury him and forget about it."

"What about Jessica?" Annie's voice of reason penetrated his conscience.

He cursed again and forced himself to call his aunt. The hope in her voice strained at his determination. "Jim will explain," she said to him excitedly. "He'll explain everything, I know he will."

He ground his teeth to maintain his silence and waited out her anxiety and need to believe. Who cared what his father's reasons had been? Any man who walked out on five kids wasn't a real man. Real men stayed and took care of business. They paid rent and bought food and held their families together. If life and the army had taught him nothing else, he'd gotten that one cold, hard fact down pretty good.

Annie uttered a prayer and pushed Jim Sprengsten's letter to the bottom of her apron pocket before setting about preparing food and clothing for their trip as the boys checked airline flights to Los Angeles. The cheapest fare was a red-eye milk run through Las Vegas, and at that the cost of two round-trip tickets was staggering.

On a hunch, she called Alan Hartford, explained the situation, and asked if he could help. He made a few inquiries and called her back to let her know that all his cargo planes had gone out for the day, but he gave her a list of people to contact in Los Angeles who would allow them to board return flights.

The rest of the evening was a barrage of preparation; Aunt Jessica was thrilled to suddenly have Danielle for the night and promised not to say anything to the little girl about her father until Jay had called from Los Angeles. Annie drove Stephen and Jay to the airport in her station wagon, the envelope still in her pocket.

Charlie hitched her bra, uncomfortable in its constriction, checked her makeup one more time; satisfied she looked at least fifteen, she walked back into the party, wishing she were a little more mature and sophisticated. Hanging out with juniors and seniors was very enlightening. The boys all looked at the girls and drank beer until they were stupid, and the girls all looked at the boys being stupid drinking beer.

The whole thing was really dumb. Not worth getting benched for, that's for sure. She didn't have to worry about Jay. He and Stephen were on some wild, secret mission that nobody would talk about, and that whole thing was probably pretty dumb, too. They'd all gone racing to the airport right after dinner, and she'd left a note for Annie that she and Sally Ridgeway were going to the movies and would be home at eleven. It was ten-thirty now and she was looking for Sally. No way she wanted Annie on her case.

Sally was in the kitchen drinking something brown that looked like root beer and lighting a limp cigarette with a blue ink mark on the filter. "Oh, please. When did you start smoking?" Charlie challenged.

Sally took a puff, the cigarette elegantly poised between two of her fingers, and blew smoke toward the ceiling. "I've been smoking for months. Don't knock it."

"I'm not knocking it, I just don't get it. They taste awful and they cause cancer."

"You use a drink to kill the taste, dummo."

Charlie decided to try it. Waving it around did feel pretty cool. Sally showed her how to inhale, but two puffs later, and two mouthfuls of cola, it still tasted awful, and she was getting dizzy.

Jack Myers invaded the room. He grabbed the cigarette out of her fingers, looked at both of them like they were dirt, and walked out of the kitchen. Charlie was shaken. "When'd he get here?"

"Couple minutes ago. I thought you saw him. It fell out of his pocket and I took it." She giggled and sat down abruptly.

When Sally giggled, her face began to squeeze together and the room got very bright. Her skin started to run off her body. Charlie shut her eyes in terror. "Something's wrong," she gasped.

Sally was blinking rapidly. "Yeah."

Charlie staggered toward a glowing wall. "I gotta get outta here."

Sally sank slowly onto the kitchen floor. "Yeah."

Annie picked up the phone on the third ring and heard nothing for a few moments. She checked her watch. It was too soon for the boys to be in Las Vegas. "Hello?" Finally there was an incoherent sob, and a voice said her name. She jerked to attention. "Charlie? Where are you? Talk to me."

"Annie. . . ?"

Her heart rolled over in her chest. Something was desperately wrong with Charlie. Another person came on the line. "Charlene's sick," he said thickly.

"Give me the address right now," Annie commanded, leaving no room for argument. She grabbed a pencil and began writing.

Leanna came in from her bedroom and sat on the easy chair, listening intently.

Annie finished writing. Thank you, God, it wasn't forty miles. She told the boy to put Charlie back on the phone. When she could hear breathing, her heart began to beat again. "Charlie, I'm coming to get you. You talk on this phone and you don't hang up," she ordered. "Do you understand?"

There was a vague "Uh-huh."

She handed the receiver to Leanna and told her the address. "Can you remember it?" At Leanna's nod, she grabbed her purse. "If you lose her, you call nine-one-one and tell them where to go."

Leanna nodded again and began speaking into the phone.

Ten minutes later Annie's station wagon caused skid

marks in front of a small apartment building. She left the car in the street and charged up the walkway. Inside she beat on doors until she came to an open apartment. High school kids scattered in all directions. It took her about thirty seconds to locate Charlie in the kitchen, nodding off but still on the phone. She told Leanna to call the hospital and commandeered three suddenly sober teenagers to help her put Charlie and another little girl into the backseat of her station wagon.

She collared one of the boys. "You spread the word, son. I find out who's giving drugs to kids, I'll kill him. You got that? I'll kill him."

"Yes, ma'am."

"Now get in the car and help me get these kids to the hospital."

Jay was tired of flying and wired with frustration. It was one o'clock in the morning in Ohio, and he'd tried to reach Jolene from three different airports. Dr. Llowell had understandably lost patience with taking messages. Either she really wasn't home or she wasn't willing to talk to him. The last call had been a few minutes ago from the lobby of the Vegas airport with the mindless ding-ding-ding of slot machines and coins clattering into metal trays in the background. That had probably gone over real big.

They'd been on board the last leg of their flight for about five minutes. Midweek, the plane was less than half-full and most of the passengers were either sleeping or resigned to wait out the hour flight with a drink of some kind. When they arrived in Los Angeles, he still had to arrange a cheap place to stay, and he wouldn't be able to reach Jolene until tomorrow. Irritated, he turned to his silent brother, who was staring out his window into blackness. "I need this trip like I need cancer."

Stephen, as usual, didn't answer; the kid hadn't said anything for the last two hours, and his silence was beginning to get on Jay's nerves. "Last of the great conversationalists, you are." It was mean, but he didn't care. He didn't want to be on this plane with all these people who looked as wrung out as he felt; he didn't want to land in a city thousands of miles from home to see a dying man he couldn't tolerate; he didn't want anything except for his life to settle down . . . and marriage to Jolene.

More than anything, he wanted Jillian off his mind. He stopped the stewardess and bought a drink. He'd thought about Jolene for eleven hundred miles, and Jillian's face kept crossing over and confusing his thinking—her face, soft and beautiful, after they'd made love by the lake. Why on earth had she let him? More than let him, welcomed him, blown him away. Jolene's little sister. Amazing.

And not so little anymore, his body reminded him, and he twisted uncomfortably at the memory. He'd known it was Jillian. Somehow he could never climb past that one. He'd known. And it hadn't stopped him. Hell, it hadn't even slowed him down. She'd been incredible, exciting to touch, and kissing her had been different from Jolene, slower, more sensual, more carefully aware. Locked together, totally his, her cries had driven him crazy. And his climax had been different from times with Jolene, deeper, more shattering. . . .

Stephen's voice fractured his concentration. "Dad almost died because of me."

The statement shocked him into forgetting about Jillian for the first time in hours. There were white lines around his brother's mouth. "What the hell are you talking about?"

"When he broke his back."

Jay stared at his brother, speechless, unable to comprehend.

Stephen's words were labored in his determination. "He was trying to tell me something. I didn't listen, and he finally got upset. He was yelling at me when he fell."

Jay tried to compute the information into his own memory of the accident. To his knowledge, this was the first time Stephen had ever discussed it with anyone.

"We lost everything. The house, the business. Probably why Mom had the stroke. That's why he went away—after she died." The terrible indictments uttered, Stephen's voice faded into silence.

Jay was at a loss. He remembered his father's accident all too well; he'd been taken from the construction site in an emergency ambulance and had spent weeks in the hospital. Mom had been gone for hours, sometimes days, at a time, and Annie had taken over the family. Stephen had changed overnight from an outgoing, yakety-yak, pain-in-the-ass kid brother to a silent shadow slipping around the house.

They'd all assumed he'd been traumatized when he saw his dad fall off the scaffolding; he'd gotten better when their father had started walking again, but after his disappearance, Stephen had stopped talking altogether for nearly a year. To discover that he considered himself at fault was an astounding revelation. It explained so many things. No wonder he didn't care what happened to him.

Jay had insight for the first time in his life of the silent hell his brother had built for himself. "It's not true," he countered angrily. "You had nothing to do with it." He grabbed Stephen's shoulder and forced him to look around. "He tripped on a welding cord. I heard him talking about it with the foreman."

A fleeting glimpse of hope passed through his brother's eyes, then it was gone. He wasn't buying it. "Wouldn't have happened if I hadn't been there. Tom Johnson said—"

"Tom Johnson's an idiot. We were always hanging around Dad's construction sites. All us kids. I'm telling you the welder started working without letting him know. It was a black cord on black scaffolding."

"He didn't see it because he was looking at me."

"He didn't see it because he didn't know it was there. You were eight years old, for Christ's sake. You were a kid and he was an adult. You weren't responsible for him, he was responsible for you."

It was a losing battle. His brother looked away, unwilling to continue, and Jay knew that Stephen would have to hear it from their father. He gripped the arms of his seat, furious. Why was nothing goddamn simple anymore? Was that the way it worked, the older you got the more complicated everything became? Suddenly he wanted to be in Los Angeles more than anything on earth. *If you do nothing else, old man, you tell my brother the truth before you kick off.* He willed the plane toward California. *Just don't die before we get there.*

22

There was no rush to get back to the inn. Annie had gone to the hospital to pick up Charlie, and Danielle was still with her Aunt Jessica. Leanna asked the taxi driver to stop at Apple Lane, then waited until he drove on. She and Stephen had counted out the distance from this corner to the inn two different times last week, and since it was a glorious fall morning, she was determined walk the three blocks and try to sort out her feelings.

Last night the situation with Charlie had been terrifying, and keeping her on the phone until Annie had reached the boy's apartment had been all she could handle. Still, she had managed it, and she'd called to alert the hospital, and she'd stayed up until Annie let her know that Charlie was going to be okay. Lack of sight hadn't interfered one iota with her ability to function, and she allowed herself to feel proud of her actions.

She shifted a canvas sack of groceries to her left hand and unfolded her stick. It was a straight two-lane road with no sidewalk until the next corner; there was about a two-foot strip of wildflowers and clover between a wide sandy berm and a tight growth of young trees and blackberry briars that acted as a fence row. Thanks to Stephen's description, she could see it in her mind. The count was a hundred and seventy-eight to the next corner.

She thought about her friend's decision to go back to New York and wondered if Jillian would be strong enough to walk away from her love for Jay, comparing it to her own inability to walk away from Curt and her struggle to come to a conclusion where he was concerned. Clearly there was a difference. Jillian was in pain every time she saw Jay because she was in love with him and her decision to end her pain was logical. On the other hand, she had a date with Curt tomorrow night, and while she had no anticipation toward seeing him, she hadn't been able to break off their relationship despite her knowledge of Christie. What was it that Curt provided that she couldn't let go of? The knowledge that he wanted her?

She had progressed to forty-two when there was a sudden rush of footsteps behind her on the macadam. She made a quick note of the number and paused to gauge the position of the runner. At the change from dull slaps on the pavement to the crunch of sand, she realized he had moved off the road and was running along the berm directly behind her. She moved onto the clover to let him pass.

Her stick caught on something as the runner reached her side, and suddenly it was jerked from her grasp. She staggered, trying to keep her balance. Nearby saplings struck her full in the face, and she threw out her arm to catch herself. The bag of groceries flew out of her hand to land on the roadway with the exploding plop of breaking glass that rolled swiftly away to her left, tinkling merrily as it bounced along the pavement.

Something, an arm, threw her to the ground, and she was pinned into sandy gravel with the runner's weight heavy against her body. Panicked, she tried to rise. A force landed hard inside her elbow, hurting her and grinding her arm into the ground. She was helpless to stop damp fingers from covering her mouth and smashing her lips against her teeth; the moist, ugly smell of old sweat bled into her nostrils, gagging her. She couldn't breathe, couldn't get air. Rasping sounds came into her ears and a male voice, foul and threatening. "Don't move or I'll hurt you."

Terrified, she struggled to hit out with her free hand. He twisted her hair into his fist and pounded her head onto the hard ground; the thud of dizzying impacts rebounded through her skull, and fear filled up her mind. "Want some more?" He smashed her head again and she went limp. Dazed, she fought being sick. He gripped her wrist until her hand was numb; ragged nails scraped along her fingers to tear away Curt's ring. It hurt, and inside her head Alice Faye was scolding, "I told you so."

Something clawed at her throat, and she cried out in pain. A moment later his weight left her body and he was gone. For a few seconds there were rapid footsteps running on the pavement, then silence. An engine revved into the nightmare, and a squeal of tires. She was abruptly alone as terror closed in around her.

Dog tired, Matt was alert enough to notice a man in sweats hurrying to the passenger side of a stopped vehicle but lacked the energy to be curious; he'd had enough for one day. He scanned the license out of habit, then dismissed the Ohio plates and braked to a stop for the turn.

Three-quarters of the night had been invested in soaking up the local bar action; he had stayed up to make the morning flight to Chicago and had just gotten in from the second half of a round trip. However, he had Christie Scott's address and phone number in his pocket—his strongest potential lead to date, so it was a pretty good night's work at that.

Some cops got off on it, but hustling female junkies was the part of his job that he hated most. Ninety percent of them were already victims of some asshole or other, and he'd ten times rather work the assholes. Still, it came with the territory, and he'd gone by the book; the requisite department permission to be involved with a suspect had been obtained, and he'd hit on her during the flight. They had a date for dinner that evening.

The blue sedan's tires squalled onto the highway, and it sped away in the rearview mirror. Aware of his fatigue, he was careful to signal a proper left turn and tapped into a diminishing supply of patience to wait for an oncoming vehicle. Finally he was able to pull onto Apple Lane and freed his mind to look forward to a cup of Annie's coffee and anything he could find in her refrigerator; then he was headed for a hot shower, a bed, and at least six hours of sleep.

A few yards ahead of him on the right, a young woman was struggling to free herself from what looked like a blackberry vine suspended through the lower limbs of a couple of small trees. As he watched, she fell, pulling the vine to the ground with her. He stopped the

Camaro just short of broken glass scattered along the roadway and took in the battered groceries with a glance; from the corner of his eye he spotted a thin white cane some thirty feet away that told him the girl was probably the blind boarder Annie had mentioned, and she was clearly in trouble.

He hurried to help her, evaluating automatically. No question she was blind; there were tears in her eyes but no indication of sight. Several scratches on her throat were unmistakable. A mugging. Son-of-a-bitch bastards. No wonder she was frantic. He ignored his dulled amazement that society inevitably produced scum low enough to prey on the blind.

"My name's Matt." He spoke calmly and put his hand under her arm to steady her balance while she jerked at her hair, caught in the bramble. Her efforts caused the vine to whip around the both of them until he was able to grab it and break its spine away from her face. Wicked barbs bit into his thumb, and he cursed in irritation. The instant he swore, she panicked again and succeeded in freeing her hair; she turned to flail at him, trying to get away from his grasp. He pulled her out of the briars before letting go of her, avoiding most of her bewildered attempts to defend herself.

Leaving her briefly to retrieve her stick, he approached to push the handle into her fingers. "I'm Matt Halston," he repeated cautiously. "I live at Chatfield's. Don't hit me with this 'cause it'll hurt." With the familiar instrument in her hand, she calmed down and began to hear him. When she confirmed she'd been attacked, he experienced a weary stab of rage. Christ, she couldn't weigh more than a hundred fifteen pounds. The guy he'd seen getting into the car would top two hundred easy. If he'd turned the corner two minutes earlier, he'd have caught the macho bastard.

He looked her over for additional injuries and found bruises forming on her forearm. Her purse was missing. If the thieves were true to form, it would probably show up somewhere along the highway in the next mile or so. If they were sloppy, there'd be fingerprints.

He retrieved what remained of the groceries, automatically kicking most of the glass off the road as he walked her to the car. She adamantly refused to go to a hospital, and by the time they arrived at the inn, shock had settled in and she was trembling so badly that he had to help her walk. A look of pain crossed her face as he steadied her up the walkway, and she told him she had a headache.

He sat the girl on a kitchen chair. A quick inspection of the back of her skull located a goose egg but no broken skin. He couldn't order her to talk to her parents or take her for help without her permission, so he dialed 911 for a patrol car and medical personnel. A note from Annie stuck to the phone indicated that she wouldn't be back until three o'clock.

Leanna asked for a cup of tea, which he was able to provide. The fingers on her right hand were turning black and blue where the mugger had torn off a ring so violently that half her nails were broken. She was trembling too heavily to hold the cup anyway, so he held it to her lips and observed her carefully while she drank. If she came too unwelded, he'd call an ambulance, permission or no permission.

There was an open cut on the back of her neck where the bastard had ripped off her necklace. He used one of Annie's big mixing bowls for a basin, filled it with warm, soapy water, located a washcloth from a downstairs bath, and found a first-aid kit in the kitchen. As he prepared to treat her injuries, he realized that she was older than the nineteen or twenty he'd first estimated, certainly prettier now that she wasn't terrified of him. Given the circumstances, she exhibited a surprising ability to suppress her anger to make way for intelligence. Being blind had probably given her a hell of a lot of practice.

Bending down on one knee in front of her, he pulled the lapels of her blouse away from her throat and began to cleanse the fingernail scratches as gently as he could.

"He wasn't tall," she said shakily. "Kind of heavy around the middle, not an athlete."

"Would you know him if you saw him again? I mean heard . . ." Felt. Smelled. Damn. Where the hell was the patrol car so somebody else could ask these questions before the details left her memory?

"I think so, I'm pretty good at voices." She smiled directly at him for a brief moment as she answered, and he was struck by the beauty that poured into her face.

Swabbing iodine along the scrapes on her throat turned them into thick, bloodred streaks as he proceeded. When he was finished, he blew on her skin to dry it, forgetting that she couldn't see. She was startled at the sudden sensation and jumped, then shivered. "When I was little, my father used to do that," she told him after a moment, unable to steady her voice. "Do you have kids?"

"Not married." He got off his knee and stretched out the stiffness that had settled into his back before moving behind her. "If you'll undo a couple of buttons, I'll be able to dress that cut on the back of your neck." Best to keep her occupied.

She nodded and opened the top of her blouse with shaky fingers, holding one hand to keep the garment flat against her breasts before moving the rest of the material.

Supremely conscious of her modesty, he loosened the fabric only as much as necessary. Without warning, she began to weep, great racking sobs that shook her body. He steadied her shoulder and reached for her good hand; she held on for dear life.

"I couldn't stop him," she moaned brokenly. "I couldn't see to do anything." The tears flowed and she was clearly undone. "I can't even help you—"

Her grief took over, and he soothed her distress as he would a little girl. "It's all over. No one's going to hurt you."

A few minutes later she cried out furiously, "I can't do this. I can't . . . I will not be helpless."

Her anger passed, and she let go of his hand to search her skirt pocket for a tissue and began to pull herself together. "I'm sorry," she apologized shakily. "I'm okay now." She heaved a shivery sigh and tried to express her feelings. "It's just that I haven't been so terrified . . ." She paused to take a deep breath. "Since the day I knew I was never going to see again," she finished quietly.

He didn't know how to respond as he studied her tearful face, aware that her eyes were clear and beautiful in color but held no recognition or animation. He wasn't up on injuries to the blind, but the huge gray pupils didn't appear to be dilated; they didn't drift, stared straight ahead, which confirmed to him that she'd once had sight.

"What a loss that must have been," he said, unaware that he'd spoken aloud until she nodded her head. The movement caused her to utter a small groan of pain; he looked again at the cut on her neck. It was seeping blood and needed treatment. Mindful of being alone with her, he was careful to touch only the bloodied linen of her blouse. He gathered her hair up off her neck and gently twisted it out of the way.

"Hold this." She reached back, covered his hand with hers to hold her hair in place, able to assist at last; as his fingers slid out from under her grasp, he had a sudden awareness of her touch—something he'd never experienced in all his years of treating victims on the street. He wrote it off as pure exhaustion and continued to examine the cut. First aid to wounded civilians, male and female, had been standard procedure in his life forever. His thoughts went spinning over the years, isolating himself from what was happening. He'd dealt with blind people before. Genuine and fake, young and old. Straights and junkies. *Protective,* he decided. His mind clung to its logical explanation. *Perfectly natural. You're dog-ass tired, and the fact that she's helpless—couldn't stop you if you wanted to look at her—is playing with your mind.*

Using the utmost discretion, he moved the expensive fabric aside to clean her injury. Half an inch below her hairline, where the rich tan of her skin faded to unexposed, pale cream, the cut was mean and ragged and probably hurt like hell. She was going to have a scar. Her whole body winced with pain each time he doused the raw wound with alcohol, and he had to force himself to continue; the skin on the back of his own neck prickled with discomfort.

Before he was through, a few strands of her hair had escaped, and she used her damaged hand to sweep them aside and hold them in place; after warning her, he blew on the alcohol to hurry the drying process. This time she gave a violent shiver and a shaky laugh. He hurriedly applied a couple of Band-Aids, crisscrossing them from tan to cream, cream to tan, so she could lower her arms.

"That'll have to do until the medic gets here."

"Thank you." She lowered her arms into her lap with obvious relief. "And thanks for taking care of me. I'm very lucky you came along."

"I just wish I'd been a few minutes earlier."

She laughed again and it ended in a sob. "So do I."

Her hair was a dark cornsilk brown with reddish highlights in the afternoon sunshine. "Hold still," he told her, and she sat immobile as a rock while he removed a stubborn leaf still tangled in it and placed it in her fingers.

Out of iodine, he stood at her side to apply a wide swath of alcohol to the abrasions inside her forearms. They ran all the way to her elbow. Her face tightened in resignation, and other than a small intake of breath, she made no sound.

She was spirited; he'd seen grown men collapse under similar circumstances. And fragile. And blind. And he was on special assignment on a short-term basis. He pushed away his thoughts.

A faint police siren was audible at last; he saw her body become alert to the sound. It would be here within two minutes, he gauged, and a fleeting streak of regret merged with a larger sense of relief. The cavalry was on its way.

He fought the guilt that he hadn't noted the license or the driver or the make of the suspect blue car to give his fellow officers. Later he'd reconstruct the scene in his mind and details would come back to him. They always did. He'd seen the guy, and his subconscious would give him a better picture. If the bastard knew what was good for him, he'd leave the country.

Outside, the siren chirruped to a stop; he opened the front door and stepped aside to let professionals take over. Their response to the fact that she was Sam Bowmont's daughter told him that both she and her father were VIPs of some sort in the community, and both men were visibly nervous when she vigorously declined being taken to a hospital once again. As he watched her submit to the police paperwork and the medic's unusually careful examination, he settled his mind into its evaluation routine, determined to return things to normal.

The theft was logical: easy victim, expensive engagement ring, gold necklace, cash. But why so rough with a person the mugger outweighed by ninety pounds and obviously knew was blind and helpless to run? He worried it like a pup with a sock.

Unless the guy was a pervert—or a rank amateur who had panicked—it didn't compute. She said the whole thing hadn't lasted more than two minutes, and he believed her. The lack of an attempt at molestation appeared to rule out a sexual deviate, and an amateur usually copped a feel, at least. But this guy had been fast and thorough. He'd gotten everything of value and managed to work her over pretty good in that two minutes.

Matt could tell she was giving in to exhaustion when he had to help her remember details she'd mentioned earlier. He confirmed her impressions with his recall of the mugger's description. All the while, the cop mentality that he worked very hard to maintain was telling him something he didn't like. Leanna's injuries had most likely been deliberate; they'd been designed to intimidate and to hurt.

Although she was hesitant and embarrassed at some

of the more graphic details, he was impressed at her skill in remembering very important facts that most victims missed. She gave a perfect description of the dough-faced man he'd seen getting into the car, no question about it. A short, fat slimeball—with a bad body odor.

By the time the officer was finished taking the report and the medic had given her a couple of Tylenol for pain, she was starting to fade. As soon as they left, Matt walked her to her room and put her to bed fully clothed; he left the door ajar and pulled up a kitchen chair to sit watch and be sure she didn't wake up alone.

His own adrenaline faded to empty, and he felt tiredness descend like a load of bricks. A steel band that wouldn't ease had wired itself across his shoulders, signaling repressed rage at the girl's attacker, and for no reason he could think of, he began building his defenses. It was no time to permit distractions. *You've been around pretty women before and kept your head. You're tired, that's all. You've never gotten involved with a victim, and you're not going to start here.*

The stern lecture to his psyche was interrupted by Annie's return with one of the little girls who lived there, who looked as if she had the flu; he waited until she'd shepherded Charlie up to her room and, when she returned, gave her a brief rundown of what had happened.

"What's this world coming to?" Annie said angrily. "A body can't walk the streets in broad daylight?"

He passed on the instructions about rest and pain medication; she clucked in maternal irritation that terrible things were happening to people and took over watch duty, leaving him free to drag himself up the stairs for a shower and a few hours of sleep.

At seven o'clock his alarm went off, and he was immediately awake and back in synch. The license was an Ohio plate beginning with 006 or 005, on a blue Ford Taurus. The driver had brown hair and was under thirty.

Psyched, he got dressed and went downstairs. Annie was coming out of Leanna's room with a tray and told him she'd eaten a small meal and had gone back to sleep.

"You call her family?"

"No. She doesn't want her father to worry. He's not well," she confided. "She's fine. I'm watchin' her real close."

Satisfied everything was under control, he readied himself to drive into Wellington to take Christie Scott to dinner.

23

"*Proposed?*" *Parker leaned* forward to refill Jolene's glass with the last of the white wine and laughed. She was using Sprengsten to bluff him? He reached for his American Express card, signaled for the check, and waited until their dishes were cleared before he looked at her.

"As in he wants to marry me," she needled.

Damn the guy. Maybe she wasn't bluffing. She was too sure of herself, playing it to the hilt and enjoying it. "I'm sure he does," he said nonchalantly, and succeeded in rattling her cage.

"Just what does that mean?"

He was relieved to see her confidence slip a little; he hadn't lived with his mother twenty-odd years for nothing. If Alice Faye had done nothing else, she'd given him a degree in how to survive high-maintenance women. First, however, it was time to take Jolene down a couple of pegs with a major dose of reality. "We are talking about the guy who's supporting five or six brothers and sisters?"

"Four," she retorted airily. "So?"

The waiter returned with the check. He signed the charge receipt and returned the credit card to his wallet, making her wait again purely to annoy her. Then he began pressing her buttons in a manner that would have made his mother proud.

"Forgive me, but somehow I don't see you as mommy of the week." He gave her a tolerant smile. "Den mother to an instant family . . . interesting. And the youngest is how old?"

"You're deliberately missing the point. *Jay* loves me." She watched him over her glass as she took a sip of wine. "*Jay* not only loves me, but he's willing to do something about it."

He matched her emphasis with glee. "*Jay* has four kids that need to be taken care of, and apparently the best way to accomplish that is for *Jay* to get married."

She abandoned the "Jay" duel. "It's not like that—and I know it if you don't. He has a housekeeper."

"Housekeepers leave," he said stonily. "My family's had dozens."

She lowered the glass and stared him down. "He's willing to make a commitment to me and you're not."

He suddenly realized she was serious and that playing games was pushing her farther out on the cliff. "You're thinking of doing it, aren't you?"

"Yes, I am."

Parker elected not to gamble. He reached across the table and carefully positioned his fingers under the tip of her pretty chin. "I genuinely care about you, Jolene. If you want to marry someone, marry me." He saw immediate triumph in her eyes and cursed Jay Sprengsten's existence. He changed tack. "Tell me, did you enjoy the wine?"

"The wine?" She gave him a blank look. "It's okay. It's white wine."

"It's okay, or it's okay for forty dollars a bottle?" She tried to look away, but he held her face toward him. "I know you. You're not used to doing without. You marry some guy who's scraping by, and that's your future—scraping. No more hundred-dollar lunches. Take a real good look at that, and then take a look at me."

She was properly cornered, and it was his opening. He took the emerald ring out of his pocket and exhibited it end for end before offering it to her. "This cost a little less than five thousand dollars because I bought it at cost from a jeweler who's a friend of my father's."

She took the ring, and he enclosed her hand in his before she could put it on her finger. "You want me to say I love you? I love you. I love every greedy little inch of you." She tried to muster anger, but to his relief she couldn't manage it.

"I gave you some shit to get even for Sprengsten, but I do love you. I'm not going to let you marry him just to get back at me."

She smiled confidently. "I want to think about it."

"Don't play with me," he warned. "If you really wanted to marry him, you'd have accepted already—and you wouldn't be sitting here with a better offer."

She couldn't field that one, and he knew instinctively that it was make or break time. "You want to use this to get engaged or do you want to pick out a diamond?"

She laughed and gave in with delight in her eyes, the old Jolene. "A diamond," she demanded saucily. "A big one."

He grinned, triumphant. Suddenly he couldn't wait

to get her into bed. "You want a big one?" Every passing second added to his need; he wanted her so totally, so immediately, that he didn't care if she wanted forty carats.

She looked at him with knowing eyes. "Very big," she said slowly; she slid her right hand under the table and convinced him absolutely. Circling the tip of her tongue wetly inside his ear, she whispered, "Let's go somewhere." He came close, very close, to losing it.

Rigid, he took the ring from her palm and slipped it onto her left hand, and they made a quick exit from the restaurant. She kept him hard all the way to a motel.

Jay looked around the small, efficient room at the peach walls and peach carpet and the pink woman with pale blond hair wound into a bun, seated behind the desk and talking to him; he didn't want to hear any of it. Neither he nor Stephen had slept, and it was too early in the morning to concentrate.

"Can we see him?" he interrupted, barely containing his impatience.

"I know you're anxious, but we've found that it's best if you have some preparation." County General's patient representative consulted his father's file and shuffled a few papers before she continued. "He's been receiving treatment for alcoholism and drug addiction. He's in and out of delirium. . . ." She looked up, resigned to her job. "I don't know how long since you've seen your father, but he's in the final stages of liver failure."

He tried to hurry it along. "Yes, and?"

"His appearance will be pretty shocking, Mr. Sprengsten." Her use of "Mr." shocked him more than any of the information she'd given them to date, and it occurred to him that when his father died for real, his own status would irreversibly shift to that of older generation in his family.

"How?" Stephen's voice filled the sudden gap in their conversation.

"His skin color will be quite green. His weight is only about ninety pounds."

"Green?" Surely she wasn't serious, but she nodded and looked at them with sympathy. Jay wanted off the subject. People didn't turn green. "How long is he expected to live?"

"Not long. It's good you were able to get here so quickly." She closed the file and rose to her feet. "If you'll come with me."

They followed her to a bank of elevators and got out on a floor marked Oncology. She led them to room 411 and opened the door.

Nothing she'd said prepared him for the sight of the man in the bed—none of the deaths he'd witnessed in the army, Cathy Rice in the lake, nothing in his life experience. Less a man than a skeleton draped in papery skin, and he was green—a living cadaver covered in dead, crepey gray-green skin, whose body was wired to machinery with tubes and catheters; two IVs fed into his arms, and the sound of his pain-filled breathing soaked up all the air space in the room.

Mouth suddenly and desperately dry, Jay swallowed and was profoundly aware of his ability to do so normally and without pain. A terrible, surreal voice came at them, thick with phlegm, belligerent, devoid of recognition. "Whatcha doing here? Wha—" The question dissolved into a prolonged, hacking spell of coughing and emerged a querulous, "Want?"

Jay's reaction was immediate and overwhelming. There would be no relief for his brother's pain, not from this man. This man could not be a father to him or his family. There was no possibility that the living dead man on the bed was James Sprengsten.

For one brief, lucid moment, the patient made eye contact; Jay quickly identified himself as Jim Sprengsten's son and asked the man his name. "We need to find my father," he told him soberly. "You have his dog tags from Vietnam."

"Gave 'em to me so I could get in a VA."

Stephen spoke at last in a gentle voice. "When?"

The man rambled into inner space. "Me and Jim're friends. Coupla years back."

Jay tried to clarify. "He gave them to you two years ago?"

The old man moved his head back and forth on his pillow with a ghastly smile. "Jim's kids," he said, as if he actually knew who they were.

"What's your name?" Stephen asked.

It took forever for the old man to focus. "Mac." This was followed by another coughing fit, and the light of reason began to fade from his eyes; he tried to hold on to the conversation. "Three . . . maybe mo . . ." The light was gone. The crepy green body went lax.

A nurse moved past them and took the old man's pulse. He was still living. They left the room and called the patient representative, who made arrangements to release their father's dog tags.

Calls to Annie and Aunt Jessica were an exchange of bad news: Leanna had been mugged. Charlie was recovering from a bout with drugs she'd gotten at a party; he and Stephen talked with her briefly, but she was lightly sedated to sleep through the occasional hallucinations and too groggy to make much sense.

The new problems, while painful, gave him a place to vent some of his frustration and helped pass the afternoon. There was no answer at the Llowell residence the entire day, and the answering machine wasn't on to receive messages. Finally he called Jillian to see what he could find out. It was a strained conversation, and she told him that according to her father, Jolene had flown to Orlando to spend a few days with their grandmother. She confirmed that Leanna and Charlie were okay. There was a long, terrible pause, and he listened to the silence from her end of the line while he tried to find something more to say to her. Failing, he simply said good-bye.

He and Stephen waited, torn between hope that the old man would regain consciousness and give them more information and their need to be home to investigate what had happened to Charlie. In the end, assured by Annie that the doctor felt she was stable and that the drug would simply have to work its way out of her system, they stayed overnight; but it was hopeless. The old man died the following morning without regaining consciousness. There would be no answers.

Jay gave in to anger and wished with all his might it had been his father. At least something might have been accomplished. Some closure. He paced the lobby of the cargo office, waiting for the plane. He needed to be home. He needed to know what was going on with Jolene. Why was she suddenly in Florida? Had Jillian's voice sounded flat, guarded—or was it his imagination? Had she said anything to Jolene?

Blahhh!

The whole thing with Charlie was from left field. He'd have bet his life that she didn't use drugs and had no explanation for how she'd gotten involved with people who did.

Finally the cargo manager signaled it was time to board, and a few minutes after takeoff, he found a place to sleep. Each time he woke, Stephen was awake and staring at nothing. Damn the old man, anyway.

Annie's patience had worn pretty thin, and against her better judgment, she opened the door to Curt Baylor. He'd called ten different times that day, giving her heart an attack each time and tying up the phone as he tried to convince her to let him speak with Leanna.

After he'd ignored two of her warnings, she'd finally hung up on him to keep the line clear for calls from California. Now here he was at the front door at six o'clock in the evening, and the poor girl was sleeping.

"I want to see her." Curt moved past her into the foyer. "Did you tell her I've called?"

"Yes." Annie bit off her words. "And the answer's the same as it was the last time I told you. She's not feeling good and doesn't want to talk to anyone."

"Well, I decided to come anyway. We had a date and I want to see if she's all right."

Annie stared him down. "She lives here, you don't. She says no visitors, you ain't gonna visit."

Matt came to the top of the stairs to check on the verbal confrontation. Annie seemed equal to the situation, so he returned to the bathroom to finish shaving. He left the door open in case things escalated.

"Just tell her I'm here. If she doesn't want to see me, I'll leave."

Leanna's voice entered the fray. "It's okay, Annie. I'll talk to him." Standing barefoot in the hallway outside her bedroom door, she had pulled a thin robe over her nightgown and was trying to tie it, but the sprained fingers on her hand made it too difficult.

Curt moved into the living room and caught sight of her. "Oh, my God."

Before he could cross to her, Annie motioned him toward the music room. "You go on and sit down. I'll take care of her." She helped Leanna with her robe, insisted on slippers, and made sure she was warm enough.

Curt was still standing in the middle of the room. "What the hell happened?" he demanded, and hovered as Annie led Leanna to the easy chair and settled her.

"You just sit right here, honeycakes. I'll bring you a nice cup of tea."

"I knew something was wrong. I've been trying to reach you for hours. I even called your father, and he said he hadn't heard from you."

"He doesn't know. I haven't told anyone, and you have to promise not to tell them." Leanna's voice rose with concern. "There's nothing they can do, and I don't want them to wor—"

"Shhhhhh. Okay. What did the doctor say? Have you been to a hospital?"

"I don't need a hospital, I need rest."

"And quiet." Annie deliberately intruded with cookies and an empty cup balanced on a tray. She placed it on the coffee table in front of Leanna's chair, scowled at Curt, and stomped out again.

"You look terrible. When did it happen?"

Matt came down the stairs in time to hear Leanna deliver a decidedly mild version of the attack. To his knowledge, it was the first time she'd been out of bed since yesterday afternoon, and a good sign. He entered the living room and introduced himself to her fiancé. "How're you feeling?" he asked, and watched her adjust the angle of her face toward his voice.

"Pretty good. How do I look compared to yesterday?"

"Well, let's see." He stepped back to give her an elaborate appraisal he knew full well she couldn't see. "Hmmmmmm." When she smiled at his actions, he walked around the back of her chair and appraised some more. "Um-hmmmmm." When he came around the front of the chair, she had an open grin on her face, double dimples, and looked adorable in her little-girl robe. "Looks terminal to me," he kidded. "Better pick out the coffin, Curt."

Curt's face held no humor.

"Matt found me," she explained. "He brought me home and patched me—"

"You didn't take her to a doctor?"

Hackles on the back of Matt's neck rippled to attention. The guy had a bad case of controlling attitude.

"She didn't want a doctor," he said easily. "The police medic looked her over. He seemed to think she'd live." He decided to stay in the living room and took a seat opposite Leanna.

"She should have seen a doctor. She might have been badly injured."

"Curt, I'm fine. I'm scratched up and bruised, but otherwise I'm fine."

"You look like you lost a fight with a wildcat," Matt teased. "You have monstrous red iodine stripes all over your throat and big white bandages on both arms. Who dresses you?"

She dimpled again.

Curt cleared his throat to declare solemnly, "I was afraid something like this would happen."

"You know who you sound like?" Leanna countered.

"Well, she was right. I don't understand why you, of all people, were walking on a deserted road. As soon as we get married . . . either I'm going to drive you or we'll hire someone."

Matt noted the dramatic pause that he was certain had been planted for his benefit, and Leanna's sudden silence. It occurred to him that the injuries she'd sustained were on her right hand. Engagement rings were customarily worn on the left. She'd never actually said she was engaged—he'd simply assumed. Something was wrong with this picture, and he'd missed it the first time around. He sharpened his focus on their manner with each other.

Annie came charging in with a pot of tea, a small bowl of ice cubes, and three more cups. After fussing with Leanna's robe and tucking it tightly around her ankles, she poured tea all around. Milk and a dollop of honey went into Leanna's, followed by an ice cube to cool it.

Leanna reached out to receive her cup, and Curt reacted to her damaged hand. "Oh, poor baby. Look at your fingers." He shook his head at Annie's offered tea and moved to Leanna's side. "I can't believe this happened. Sweetheart, I'm so sorry." He put her cup aside so he could examine her injuries. "I insist you let me take you home."

Leanna started to object, but he was determined. "Shhhhh, now, hear me out." He stroked her hand and kissed her bruises as he overrode her objection. "You can stay here until you feel a little better, and I promise I won't tell your parents if that's really what you want, but I'd feel a whole lot better if we moved you back home. I'm sure these people are very nice, but what you need is your family around to make sure nothing like this happens again."

Matt could see Leanna was embarrassed, and if Curt shushed her one more time, fiancé or no fiancé, he was going to deck the guy. Christ, she'd been beaten to the ground and mugged. She needed applause for surviving the attack, not a lecture tearing her down. He brought himself up short. *What she decides with this guy is absolutely none of your business. Out of your jurisdiction. End of story.*

Charlie called down the stairs, and Annie excused herself. "Comin', honey." She highballed out of the room to go upstairs, and Matt used the interruption as an excuse to take his leave. He deliberately kissed Leanna's cheek before saying good night to the both of them. "Hang in there," he said, giving double meaning to the words. He deliberately spoke loud enough for Curt to hear, which made him feel better, and called a good-night up the stairwell to Annie and Charlie before he left the inn.

Leanna waited until the front door had closed before she let her irritation show. "Curt, really. 'These people'? Annie and Matt have taken very good care of me, and there was no reason to be rude." She felt for her tea and was annoyed again when he stilled her hand, then gave her the cup.

"I'm sorry. I was so concerned about you that it just slipped out." He sat at her elbow, hovering again. "I really insist that you see a doctor. Your father's already mad at me, and he'll hang me by my thumbs if I don't let him know what's going on."

"Curt, I'll tell you right now that if we're ever going to work this out, you have to let me make decisions about my own life," she said stiffly. "My father's ill. I'll tell him when I'm ready. Besides, I hate hospitals. You know that. There was no reason." Her energy was suddenly exhausted, and she slid forward to get to her feet. He took her tea and helped her rise. "I'm enough of a burden on my family, and I don't want them to see me looking like I've been fighting wildcats, thank you."

"I'll help you back to your room." He walked with her to the hallway and opened her bedroom door. Unwilling to have him accompany her inside, she paused; he dropped his arm and gave her a little boy's voice. "Will you let me kiss you, grumpy face?"

"Of course."

His arms wound around her body and brought her too close; every bruise on her body ached in protest as he kissed her soundly. "Good night. Think about what I said," he told her, and released his hold.

His footsteps echoed down the hall and through the foyer; the front door opened and closed. The hall clock chimed the quarter hour, and she had no idea what time it was. She paced the seven steps to her bed, too tired to look for her watch. Her arms were aching as she took off her robe and placed it across the quilt before crawling gratefully into a soothing down mattress from Annie's own bed. It had magically appeared yesterday, sometime between getting undressed, a quick soak in a steaming hot tub of water, and donning a nightgown.

The bed was warm and soft and welcome, and her sore body sank gratefully into sleep.

◦   ◦   ◦

Upstairs, Annie heard Curt's car move down the driveway and sighed in relief. Now that he was gone she could concentrate on one problem at a time. Charlie's hallucinations were coming less and less frequently, but they still scared the little girl to death. She'd been repeating the story time and again for Annie's assurance as they swayed back and forth on an ancient rocking chair.

"I didn't mean to do it, Annie."

"I know, honeybun."

"I thought it was just a cigarette."

"It's all right, sweetheart."

"You tell Jay I didn't do it."

"Yes, I will, sweetheart."

"Am I going to be okay?"

"Yes, you are, darlin'."

She'd almost make it to sleep, then it would start again.

"I didn't mean to do it, Annie."

"I know, honeybun."

"I thought it was just a cigarette."

"It's all right, sweetheart. . . ."

Christie's apartment was a model of efficiency for her life-style, Matt decided. A stewardess, never home, she kept no dog, cat, bird, or fish to feed or otherwise care for; her kitchen counter held a coffee maker, a cookie jar, and a dish drainer holding two dry plates and a batch of knives, forks, and spoons.

"I'll be right out," she called. "Make yourself at home."

He heard her rummaging through her bedroom dresser for a photograph of herself as Miss Midnight Run. She'd told him about it for seven minutes on the way home, and it would probably take another five to find—assuming that's what she was looking for. He took the opportunity to check out the bath.

An assortment of makeup that rivaled the contents of half a dozen cosmetic counters littered the vanity. He dismissed the multitude of plastic cases to pop the medicine cabinet and scan the usual bottles of Midol, alcohol, Tylenol, and a few other "ols," including Clairol, Burnt Auburn, and a half-empty wheel of birth control. There was no evidence of uppers, downers, or anything suspicious. Wherever she kept it, he knew she was a user because this was their third date, and the third evening she'd started out as chatty Cathy, only to wind down like a clockwork monkey, jerky and spastic.

Tonight, he'd sat through half a pack of cigarettes at dinner before taking her to a movie, and at the moment, right on schedule, she was nervous as a cat and looking for something to get her smoothed out again. He pushed open the door to the bedroom. She was sitting on the bed, hungrily sucking in a lungful of smoke from another cigarette. The acrid odor of burning marijuana hung in the air. She saw him in the doorway and motioned him in.

"I didn't find it, but I found something else." Smoke came out with her words. In the half-lit room she looked old and tired. She patted the bed. "You want some?"

He decided to go for it and sat next to her. She passed him the joint, and he drew in ninety percent air and a small mouthful of smoke before he inhaled, gambling that it was only grass. It was reasonably high grade and apparently untampered with. The last thing he needed was an unscheduled trip—one of the hazards of his profession.

She took another drag and leaned over to kiss him. He ducked the kiss and nuzzled her neck. "I'd like to make some big-time moves on your body," he told her, "but it's not fair unless I tell you."

She pulled away and looked at him. "Tell me what? You married?"

"Supposed to be, six months ago. She dumped me."

"You serious? Gee, that's awful." She breathed in the smoke trail from the burning end of the cigarette, turned it around to inhale deeply from the other end, then held her breath.

He ran the story. "No, what's awful is she was messing around with a friend of mine—turns out he's HIV. I had another test yesterday, but the lab screwed up and I won't get the results for a couple of days. So unless you're willing to risk it, there's not much going to happen with us."

Still holding her breath, her eyes widened as she processed the story. Then she shook her head and offered him the last of the joint.

He waved it away. "I understand and I don't blame you. You got anything besides grass? Doesn't do it for me. I need to seriously party." He saw temptation streak through her face and pursued it. "Nothing with needles," he cautioned. "That's how this guy got it."

Her breath released in a thin rush of smoke. "No, I don't have anything." She stretched out on the bed and finished the roach with a hair clip pinched at the edge of the paper, and held her breath again until he looked at her with concern. At last she let it out and smiled at him, relaxed. "Nobody ever worried about me before," she said. "I can ask around for you."

"You're really a sweetheart, did anybody ever tell you that?"

She looked at him sadly and smiled. "They all do."

24

Broken promise . . .

"*She knows you've called,* she knows you got back from California yesterday, and she knows you want to talk to her. Is there anything else?"

"No, sir." Jay thanked the impatient Dr. Llowell and hung up the phone. He eyed Annie's somber face and decided as long as life had gone to hell, he might as well take the next load, whatever that turned out to be. They'd already covered Charlene's bout with drugs and the relatively good news that she'd only had one flashback in the last twenty-four hours. They'd discussed Danni's nightmares in the wake of Charlie's hallucinations and Leanna's mugging, plus a couple of inconsequential pain-in-the-butt matters, but there was still something on her mind. Jillian was waiting outside somewhere, and he suspected she wanted to warn him that she'd told Jolene. That would be the next item on the agenda. One nightmare at a time.

"Okay, let's have it," he challenged. "Let's get it over with."

Annie took an envelope out of her apron pocket and handed it to him; it was addressed to her, and it was old.

"You need to read this," she said quietly.

His gut began to shrink. "Be careful what you wish for" came barreling through his brain, but it was too late to stop his fingers from taking out the letter.

Dear Annie,

I'm heading into the sun across the lake in Mac's Explorer this morning. I was never a coward for pain but this hurts too much. I can't stop feeling it. When I see the kids I see her and it hurts that much more. They're too young to understand, so I won't even try to make

You know how much I love them. Mailing this on my way to the airport, so understand I didn't change my mind.

There are things for Jay in the Bible. Dot wanted him to know before he got married. Hate like hell to do this to you. I love you like my own mother, but there's nobody else to

Kiss the kids for me

The unfinished letter was not signed. He sat in stunned silence and turned the envelope over in his hands; it was postmarked Cleveland. The world filtered back in bits and pieces. The old man in Los Angeles had said his name was Mac. An Explorer was a plane—a Piper Explorer; his dad had a pilot's license, and they'd looked at one once . . . before the accident.

Finally he met Annie's eyes.

"I didn't know how to tell you," she said brokenly. "I don't know if he did it or he didn't." She broke down in tears, and he felt as if he'd hit her. "I bought the Cleveland paper for weeks but there was nothing that said . . ."

She was talking about suicide. He read the letter again. "Heading into the sun across the lake." That meant early morning, long-ways across Lake Erie. His father had committed suicide four years ago, and she hadn't told him.

There was heartbreak in her eyes, and he tried to make himself tell her it was okay, but nothing came out. How could she not let him know? He walked numbly to the big old family Bible that had been his grandmother's. Page after page of tissue-thin paper turned from one side to the other. Soon he was fanning whole sections through his hands. Three-quarters of the way through, he found it, compressed from the weight of the heavy book and sealed, an envelope with his name in his mother's handwriting precisely across the middle, straight as a ruler. Something icy crawled into his stomach, lay down in an endless hole, and died.

Carefully positioning the envelope back into its indentation, he closed the book. "Not on top of Dad." He walked out.

Annie watched him go and knew there was no way she could help. She'd cried endless tears when she'd first received the letter. She'd kissed his kids over and over, praying in her heart that Jim had changed his mind and one of these days he'd come ambling up the walk. But he hadn't. Her old heart had nearly stopped the day of the phone call from Los Angeles, and after the boys were on the plane, she'd gone down on her knees that it was him. Jay's call to let her know the man wasn't their father had not surprised her. Jim Sprengsten had flown into the sun.

Jillian arrived at her father's house with the usual knot in her stomach. Jolene was back and had insisted she come to dinner, indicating there was a big surprise involved. A surprise could be anything where Jolene was concerned; whatever it was, it was certain to be something her sister wanted. She parked her white Mustang in a getaway position and opened the car door. A gust of wind hit her, wet with fall moisture and chilling, skittering a rain of leaves from the sugar maples along the driveway.

Jay had come home tired and discouraged from Los Angeles and had gone into a closed-door meeting with Annie, probably about Charlie. He'd left suddenly, before she could tell him she was going to New York tomorrow to look for an apartment. Sometime this evening she would also have to tell her family—not conversations she looked forward to having. She took a deep breath and let herself into the house.

Jolene met her in the foyer. "Oh, good. You're here. Daddy's upstairs."

Jillian slipped out of her parka, and her father descended the staircase to give her a hug. "I haven't given up on medical school for you. You can start after the first of the year—"

For the first time in Jillian's memory her sister came to her rescue. "Daddy, not tonight."

"Now, Jo—" Her father stopped abruptly and released his hold on her; Jillian turned to see Jolene poised on the bottom stair step with her hand dangling over the newel; a beautiful diamond solitaire glittered on her ring finger.

"Surprise! I'm engaged." Jolene looked at them joyously. "Two whole days."

After a gigantic silence, her father exhaled slowly to ask, "Just when did this happen, and why am I the last to know?"

The question was addressed to both of them, and Jillian was the first to respond. "It's a surprise to me, too, Dad." She'd had no idea Jay had given Jolene a ring. Tears were blurring her vision, and she was already much too numb to do anything except see her sister's enjoyment of one-upping their poor, poleaxed father.

"We didn't tell anyone." Jolene was in the center ring and thrilled with the spotlight.

Jillian watched her take-charge father stumble for the proper response. "I believe this calls for a celebration," he managed finally. "Where's the lucky guy?"

Jolene nodded toward the living room. "He wanted me to tell you first. Are you surprised?"

Jay was here? Jillian realized that it was going to take every ounce of willpower she owned to get through the next twenty minutes. "We should call Mom." She struggled for normality and a sense of order. "She'll want to know." Hugging her sister, she gave in to tears. "Congratulations, Jo. I'll see if we have champagne."

In the kitchen, frantically seeking refuge from the sinking feeling, she tried to center. "What'd you expect?" she mumbled to herself. "You knew it was going to hurt. You'll get through it. You always do."

She found a couple of bottles of sparkling wine in the refrigerator, her mother's crystal flutes from the third shelf. Four? Jolene, their father . . . him. Four. Mechanically peeling the metal wrapper off one of the bottles, she heard her father's voice and Jolene shushing him as they placed a call to Florida.

The doorbell rang, and grateful for any legitimate excuse to continue avoiding the living room, she opened the front door and was doubly thrown. It was Jay. Oh, God, of course, Jay. Why on earth hadn't Jolene waited for him? But, hey, that's Jolene, she thought crazily.

"I'm very h-happy for you," she stammered, unable to think of anything else. "She's just told Dad."

Jay looked at her oddly as she gestured with the half-opened bottle of wine toward her sister. Jolene was standing inside the living room with the phone in her hand. "They're calling Mom right now," she explained wildly, trying to get a handle on the roller coaster coursing through her brain. "Congratulations. We're going to have a toast. Why don't you go on in."

He stepped into the foyer with another quizzical look and kissed her cheek. "Jillie, what's—"

At that moment Jolene's excited voice rang like a bell through the foyer. "Parker, come talk to your future mother-in-law. She wants to say hello."

Parker came into view to take the phone from her sister; Jolene looked past him, saw Jay next to Jillian in the foyer, and quickly turned her back.

Jillian struggled with confusion as Jay burst out the door. Then she raced after him, trying to explain.

"Your idea of getting even, or hers?" he threw at her. He jerked open the door to his truck and swung inside. "You win dirty, lady!"

He drove hell-bent out of the driveway, and Jillian stood immobilized. How could she have been so totally, destructively wrong? Caught up in her own feelings, she'd simply assumed Jolene had accepted Jay's proposal. Suddenly it was Jolene and Parker.

She swiveled weakly onto the lawn and tried to think what to do. He couldn't possibly think she'd break her promise. He couldn't believe she'd told Jolene. But her rational side knew it was exactly what he thought—and what he would say to Jolene the next time he saw her. It would all come out for no reason, and then he'd really never forgive her. Nor would Jolene. She collapsed inside. A few minutes later she pulled herself to her feet, shivering. Maybe he'd listen after he calmed down. All she could do was try. She had to get back inside.

The wind riffled an envelope down the walk along with half a dozen leaves. It was addressed to Annie. As she rescued it, its letter fell out. The first few lines jumped at her, and she read through the rest before she realized what she was doing. The erratic writing and the meaning of the words slowly sank into her soul with a chilling insight.

Jolene came outside and picked up the forgotten bottle of wine. "What did he say to you?" she demanded.

Jillian struggled to answer. "He was pretty upset, Jolene. He thought I knew about you and Parker."

Jolene shrugged and eyed the letter still clutched in her fingers. "Is that from him? Did he leave it for me?"

"No." Jillian refolded the letter and stared hard at her sister. "Do you love Parker, Jo?"

Jolene looked at her. "Of course. I'm marrying him." She walked back into the house.

The next hour was an agony. Jillian drank her father's toasts and made up a brief one of her own somehow, that Parker and Jolene would have a great life together, and ached to get away so she could find Jay and make sure he was okay. All three tried to get her to accompany them out for a celebration dinner, but she begged off, unable to stand any more, and swore to make it up when their mother got home. She drove to the inn the minute they left.

Annie met her at the door. "He's not here, honeybun," she said wearily. Jillian told her what had happened. Annie sat heavily on the sofa and sighed, deeply troubled. "I probably shouldn't do this, but I'm gonna interfere where I got no business," she said.

He knew it was cold because he could see his breath, but he couldn't feel it. He couldn't feel much of anything except anger. He tipped back the bottle of Jack Daniel's and stared out at the lights of Walden City, trying to list the people who'd betrayed him in order of importance.

Annie, he understood. She'd made the best choice she could at the time—his father was dead; he was already in basic training and nothing would have changed. Missing or dead, the kids would have been wards of the state or orphans. Same difference.

As far as his father was concerned, there was nothing to reach out and smash. He'd gone down in a plane and hadn't even left a grave; killed himself because he couldn't face life without Mom. The only thing left of him was a piece of paper that didn't even have his name on it.

Then there was Jolene. Betrayed again. He took another bitter mouthful of whiskey.

He'd gone to see her to do battle. He was entitled to an answer. She'd promised that much. Even if it was no, he was entitled to hear it. His life had been hell for three days, he had a letter in his pocket that said his father was a suicide, and Jillian had met him at the door full of phony congratulations. He tried to blame her for the whole fiasco, but he couldn't make it stick. Blood was thicker than water, and in spite of her promise, she'd had every right to tell Jolene about their night together.

If anyone was at fault here, it was him. And Jolene.

He'd never made a secret of how he felt about her, that he'd wanted to marry her. She'd let him hang in the wind long enough to put his life out there and ask her to marry him, then she'd gone running to Parker. After two years of sleeping with her, Parker had suddenly decided to propose? Not a chance. She'd used him to get Bowmont off the dime and hadn't had the balls to let him know—didn't have the goddamned gonads to get on the phone and tell him it wasn't going to happen.

Every fiber in his body wanted to hurt her, cause equal pain. The whiskey killed his throat and brought tears to his eyes. Half the bottle hadn't helped. He reached for the letter to baptize it with Uncle Jack, but it was gone. As gone as his old man. He poured the rest of the liquor onto one of the rocks and watched it splash onto his good slacks and shoes.

When it was empty he threw it away, narrowly missing Jillian coming up the path toward him. He stared her down, having no desire whatsoever to talk to anyone. He was mean and ugly and dangerous. Damn, she didn't look anything like Jolene, and he'd almost hit her.

"I found this in our driveway," she was saying. "I shouldn't have, but I read it. I'm sorry."

He grabbed the letter. "We shouldn'ta done lotsa things, Jillie."

"I didn't tell her, Jay. She doesn't know."

"Yeah, right."

"I found out when you did."

"You're just all kinds of sorry, aren't you?" The liquor was meandering around in his head, and his attention span was as stable as a three-year-old's. "I'm drunk," he warned.

"I can see that."

He jammed the letter into his jacket pocket. "Anybody know about this?"

She shook her head.

"Good. My family's got enough t'deal with right now." He stood up, and the whiskey sent him spinning. "I am drunk." He realized he was weaving. "Stupid drunk. I gotta go home. Will you drive me?"

She walked him down the path toward the parking area. They approached his truck, and she started to help him inside. "Wait a minute," he demanded. "Where's your car?"

"Stephen gave me a ride. He went to pick up Danni and dropped me off."

Satisfied, he climbed into the passenger side of the cab; she shut the door and crossed in front of the truck. God, she looked good. Right at the moment, however, he'd had enough of the Llowell sisters to last a lifetime. "Can you drive a stick?" he challenged.

Jillian eased onto the driver's seat and looked at the unfamiliar array of a floor-shift vehicle. There were three foot pedals instead of two, and the gearshift was a lever protruding out of the floorboards into the middle of the cab, topped with a large, round black rubber handle. "Oooohh, boy," she breathed, unnerved.

"It'seasy. Here's whatcha do." Jay slid next to her, and there was a violent smell of whiskey about him. He hiked her skirt well above her knees, eased his left foot inelegantly between her legs to reach the clutch. He took her right hand, put it on the knob of the gearshift now positioned between his legs, and covered it with his own.

"When y'shiff, push this in. Lettet out, you're in gear. It'seasy." He demonstrated; his long, hard-muscled leg moved heavily across her thigh each time he pushed the clutch to the floor. "In, shiftout. In, shiftout. You do it." He held his foot out of the way, giving her room to work the pedals.

Her wrist and the heel of her hand, wrapped around the knob, came within millimeters of his crotch every time she "shiffed,"making them highly intimate gestures.

"I'll probably pass out," he warned, "so you'll hafta drive."

She nodded and held tight to the gearshift as he reached to switch on the ignition. The engine groaned abruptly; the old truck lurched violently, bucked forward, then shuddered to a halt as the motor died. They began rolling backward, and she stomped on the brake. "You didn't have it in neutral," he scolded. He moved closer, held the clutch to the floor with his foot, and helped her jiggle the gearshift. "Now try."

This time she was successful, and by the time she'd "shiffed" into reverse, then first, and reverse again, she'd gotten the hang of it pretty good and his private life had become more than familiar with her right hand. He made no effort to avoid her touch, and she tried to keep the heat in her own body from interfering with her driving. Finally she ventured onto the road in first gear.

"That's pretty good," he praised. "Very good."

His body pressed close as he helped her find second, and a few hundred yards down the road from the bluff she was forced to brake as he blocked her vision, giving her an open mouthed, thoroughly whiskeyed kiss. She nearly killed the motor.

"You're terrific. You are. I remember . . ." He sagged against the upholstery, and she took the next couple of turns a little too fast, her heart even faster, until she managed to slow their speed.

"You were not Jolene," he said solemnly.

Her sister's name hit her like a dirty punch, unexpected and unfair, and tears blurred her vision. She blinked rapidly and held burning emotion inside in order to concentrate on the road, determined to bring this nightmare of an evening to an end without killing the both of them.

A jerky mile later, Jay abruptly came to life and motioned for her to pull over. She stopped the truck in time for him to go staggering into a small ravine to dump Jack Daniel's all over the goldenrod. Settling herself, she searched her purse for tissues and then took them to him in the brush.

"I'm sorry," he said. "I've been a real bastard, and you don't deserve it. I'm really sorry."

She handed him the tissues, too empty to care.

A patrol car pulled behind the truck, lights flashing. She steadied him as they walked to meet the officer. The truck had rolled a few feet, and the back of it was hanging out in the roadway.

Smelling the whiskey, the patrolman adopted a mood. "You broken down?" he demanded.

"No, sir, just drunk," Jay responded.

"You responsible for this vehicle being stopped in the middle of the highway?"

"I most certainly am, Your Honor." Jay had gotten to the silly stage.

"Jay, he's serious." Jillian moved to intervene. "I was driving, Officer. I forgot to set the brake."

"Hey, I was handling the clutch and the gearshiff . . . and a coupla other things."

"Really, I was driving, Officer," she repeated.

"Can I see your license, miss?"

Jay reached for his wallet. "Here's my license, Officer. Thisis my truck and thisis my license and thisis . . ." He paused and looked at her. "Thisis Jillie, who is taking care of me."

"Have you been drinking, too, miss?"

"No, sir. He's too drunk to drive, Officer. I was driving. Jay, tell him I was driving."

"She was driving," he parroted infuriatingly.

The officer was skeptical. "Is that true, miss?"

"Don't you call her a liar, Jack!"

"Just step over here, sir."

Matt felt the pinch in his stomach as his liaison with the local police filled him in. This time it was a couple of teenage girls, and one of them was Charlie. She'd taken a pretty good hit, apparently, and had experienced heavy hallucinations and subsequent flashbacks, which explained Annie's close attention of late. So far, according to the investigating officer, she had no recall of the party.

It was good news and bad news; apparently the cooker was still in the area and hadn't moved on, thus his time under cover hadn't been wasted, and he was close. Very close. He'd have to be patient and bide his time. In the meantime, poor Charlie was going through a wringer. She was a sharp kid and he liked her and it made his gut hurt to think some scum was wasting decent kids like her for a buck. Bastard probably had himself convinced he was just supplying a demand.

When he asked Annie, she was closemouthed about the incident, understandably refusing to discuss Charlie's condition with anyone outside the family, but he gleaned enough around the edges to figure out the little girl was having a pretty rough time. Sooner or later she'd remember about the party, and sooner or later he'd move one step closer to catching the son of a bitch. All he had to do was be patient.

25

Leanna held her face under the shower and gingerly added shampoo to the back of her head. The swelling had receded, but a persistent, generalized ache remained, ten times worse than from what had happened in the stable, and she decided to call Dr. Peachtree to see if he could fit her in for an examination soon. He'd been quite clear for years that any time headaches persisted she was to consider it an unusual sign; it was always possible that an injury could activate damage from the original accident, and she'd had two incidents within weeks of each other.

Before she could work the shampoo into a lather, the spray of water slowed to a dribble, then trickled to a halt. Turning the shower handles produced nothing. She stepped wetly onto the cotton mat and found the faucets at the sink. After an initial teaspoon or two, no water sprang forth, hot or cold. She dried her body and pulled on her terry robe; pushing her feet into her slippers, she scuffed her way down the hall to the kitchen to find Annie.

Matt, nursing a mild hangover with a cup of Annie's cure-all coffee, looked up from the kitchen table to see Leanna come into the room, a soapy wet kitten, seeking help. He greeted her with the news that Annie had taken a quick trip to the market.

"Is the water off everywhere?"

He confirmed it while she found a chair and sat down to decide her next option. "Do you know if she keeps bottled water?"

He made a quick search of the pantry. "Sorry," he called out. "I can run over to the market and—" Returning to the table, he saw the teakettle on Annie's stove. "Wait a minute." He tapped the kettle. Full. "Think we might have an answer here," he said to her. He put a low fire under it for a few moments, then scooted one of the kitchen chairs to the sink and eye-balled its height. Too low.

"What are you doing?"

"Working on it. Working on it," he stalled. A couple of pillows from the music room made up the difference; he realized Leanna was unable to decipher the sounds and reasons for his movements, so he described his solution. She smiled and allowed him to guide her to the improvised shampoo chair. The injury on the back of her neck hadn't required stitches and was healing nicely, and when he was satisfied the water had warmed sufficiently, he laid her towel on the counter and helped her tip her head so her soapy hair fell into the sink.

"Welcome to Halston's Salon," he deadpanned. "Straight Out of Africa." Pouring enough of the warmed water through her hair to wet the shampoo, he moved in closer to work his fingers gently in the lather. He'd washed a couple of kids, but never a woman's hair. He found himself enjoying it.

Both tails of his opened shirt trailed in her face. She brushed them away and laughed. "What's this got to do with Africa?"

"It's a movie." He tucked the bottoms of his shirt-front into his Levi's, then continued soaping her hair.

"Oh, the hairwashing scene. Robert Redford." She paused a beat. "I didn't see that one."

He got instantly that she was teasing him and laughed with her. Studying her happy face, he was unable to escape the remarkable contrast between her and the drugged-out Christie. Without veneer, without pretense, Leanna was openly enjoying his efforts, safe in his care, her arms limp and relaxed in her lap. As he worked the shampoo through her hair, the heavy robe loosened—just enough to afford him a less-than-discreet view past the tan line on her breasts, and he damned himself for being interested. She'd been in the shower and was clearly naked beneath the robe. And trusting. *Sam Bowmont's daughter? Blind? What are you, crazy?* He felt suddenly younger than his thirty-four years and forced his eyes away from soft, disturbingly pale curves before his body started thinking about something else entirely.

Proceeding slowly, he deliberately conserved the water as long as possible, using the kettle's spout to guide the warm stream delicately along her forehead and around moist pink ears, pouring it carefully through her hair. He concentrated on seeing nothing else, but the heat of her upper arm warmed the length of his thigh and despite his best intentions, his body grew in awareness.

Eyes closed, completely relaxed with the process, enjoying the light pressure of his hands, Leanna had an odd sensation of light. Opening her eyes, she

experienced a burst of dim motion and the shadowy outline of a face—a good face, thoughtful and open, with a
rapt expression of concentration. Black lashes, light
brown eyes, rich and clear as clover honey with steel
gray rims, under dark hair as rich and dense as wet pine
bark. She'd have sworn it. Then he was gone, and only
familiar blackness remained. She was so astonished that
she refused to believe it had happened.

She heard him put the kettle aside and felt his hands
squeeze excess water from her hair before wrapping a
towel around her head; he tugged the lapels of her robe
together as she sat upright. Life was as devoid of vision
as before. It hadn't happened. She'd just wished to see
him so hard, so totally, that her mind had supplied a
face. The burst of light was new, but she'd had a similar
experience years ago. She let go of it. "That was terrific,"
she bantered gaily. "I'll recommend Halston's to all my
friends."

The emptied kettle gave a hollow clank against the
stove top. "I'd be careful," he said gruffly. "We're pretty
fly-by-night."

"Can't beat the price." Aware that the special rap-
port they'd shared seconds ago had vanished, she
realized he had retreated from her somehow.
"Rescued again. Thank you, Matt," she said cautiously, confused at the change and uncomfortably
aware suddenly of the scantiness of her clothing. She
really didn't know all that much about him, after all.
Tightening the belt to her robe, she made certain she
was properly covered.

"Any time." She got to her feet, and he watched her
orient herself toward her room. He tossed the pillows
back into the music room, changed into sweats, and got
the hell out of the house.

He spent the next couple of hours jogging the highway off Apple Lane and finally found what he'd been
looking for since her mugging. The purse was empty
except for a packet of tissues. Her wallet was nearby;
identification and a few of her father's credit cards had
survived. He put everything in a plastic bag, and that
afternoon he shipped it to Chicago for prints. Maybe
they'd get lucky.

A distress call to the water company identified the
source of the trouble: a local main was under repair, and
there hadn't been time to notify affected residents.
Service was restored by the time Annie began lunch for
Charlie and Stephen. Word about the drugs had gotten
around school, and Charlie was having a difficult time
being "onstage," as she called it, with everyone staring at
her and waiting for her to throw a fit or something.
Stephen rarely left her side.

The phone rang. Annie was putting the finishing
touches on an apple pie, and her hands were covered
with flour; she asked Leanna to answer it. The woman
caller asked for Matt. "Tell him it's Christie," she said
with breezy confidence. "Tell him I'm going to Chicago,
but I'll have what he's looking for sometime next week,
okay?" The line went dead.

Leanna wrote the message with shaky fingers, printing in capitals with a pencil and carefully bringing the
ends of each letter to the edge of the stiff cardboard she
used as a guide. She never forgot voices. Never. It was
the same Christie who'd been with Curt at the nightclub. And in his bed. Matt was a friend of hers?
Probably more than a friend, she chided herself.

Stephen and Charlie came in from school, and

Leanna tucked the thought away in her mind. Charlie volunteered to slip Matt's message under his door, and when the phone rang again it was her father, asking that she come to see him at three o'clock. After lunch, she decided not to wait and, uncomfortable walking alone since the attack, asked the kids to accompany her to her father's house on their way to school.

She crept quietly up the familiar stairs. The housekeeper was pretty sure he was resting, and as she approached his doorway there was silence. She decided not to disturb him and had turned to leave when he spoke, low and insistent, to someone in the room. "Because I'm not going to be around to do it. You understand?"

"Yes, sir." Parker's voice was strained.

"I don't think she's going to marry Curt, so it's going to be up to you to take care of her."

"Yes, sir."

There was silence again, and Leanna's heart nearly halted; they were talking about her. Her father's tired voice went on. "It's a great deal of responsibility. You think Jolene will be up to this?"

"I'm sure she'll understand."

"I don't want her farmed out."

"No, sir." Parker's voice was emphatic.

"If you have to choose between your wife and your sister—"

"It won't come to that, Dad. I promise."

"Make sure before you marry her."

"Yes, sir. I will."

"She's not to be dependent on Alice Faye, you hear?"

Leanna stood frozen in the hallway. Her father was speaking as if he were dying. She stepped into the room. "Hello, Dad."

Parker came immediately to greet her and gave her a kiss. "Hey, Sissie," he said slowly. "I'm glad you're here." There was enormous relief in his voice, and fear.

She seated herself on her father's bed and reached out her hand to him. She could feel herself trembling. His frail fingers slipped slowly into hers and squeezed gently. "You heard us talking?"

"Yes." Understanding began to pour in at her from all sides. Her father was gravely ill. "What's going on?"

Her father sighed deeply. "I didn't think I'd have to tell you so soon." She heard him pause for strength. "My doctors don't give me much hope, and in case it comes to that, I want you and Parker to be prepared. I've already told Alice Faye." His voice trailed off.

Her mind filled with denial. How could this be happening? He couldn't be dying. Couldn't be. Inside herself she knew it was real, and she could feel tears gathering to slide down her face. She had to be strong and not worry him. Stiffening her back, she listened as Parker gave her the medical details, and her brain filtered out all but the three dreaded words. Cancer. Inoperable. Terminal.

"I'll be leaving you too soon," said her father, agitated and fretful. "It could be any time now, and I want to make sure everything's taken care of."

She nodded miserably, unable to think of anything to say that would ease his fears, lessen his burden. Just the ever-widening hole of her own pain. He wanted her "taken care of." It was to be Parker's job. Somehow she made herself function even as her thoughts turned in on themselves and refused to make sense. "I don't want you two to worry about me. I've been giving a lot of thought to marrying Curt, and there's no reason to continue delaying things. If you still want to give away the

bride, we can certainly have a wedding," she said
brightly.

There was a long silence in the room, then, "Let me
talk to your sister."

"Yes, sir." Parker left them alone and closed the door.

"I don't want to hear talk about your getting married.
Certainly not because of this," she was admonished. "I
know all about getting married for the wrong—" Her
father stopped short, and she wished with all her might
that she could see his face. His hands grasped hers
painfully, and every instinct told her that he had not
intended to say those words and would give a great deal
to take them back. "Just don't marry him unless you love
him," he demanded urgently. "Promise me."

"I won't, Dad. I swear."

His fingers relaxed in hers, and his breathing eased.
Her mind raced to find something to hold on to through
the ordeal of his illness. A starburst filled her head, and
she saw a vague outline of his face for a brief instant—a
painfully old version of the man she'd known as a child;
the same eyes, one a pale, milky blue, in a gaunt face,
but his hair was nearly white. She blinked and the vision
was gone, inked over once again. "Dad? Is your hair
gray?"

"Oh, yes, honey. Several years now."

"Salt-and-pepper or full gray?"

"Alice Faye says it's 'silver.'"

She decided she had to tell him, not knowing if it was
real or imagined. But twice in one day? "You remember
when Dr. Peachtree told me that the optic nerves hadn't
atrophied? Not completely, anyway."

"I'd always hoped that some new medical procedure
would come along." Her father sighed.

"If I tell you something, will you promise not to let

anyone know until I can make sure it's really happening?"

"You can tell me anything."

"I think . . ." She plunged ahead. "I think I just saw you. Are you wearing something blue?"

Her father's fingers jerked in her hand, and she heard him take a deep breath. His voice was filled with wonder and disbelief. "Yes."

"Light blue and shiny like raw silk?" Her own excitement began to build. She hadn't imagined it.

"They're my old blue pajamas. You gave them to me years ago for Father's Day." His hands were wringing hers.

"I can't see a thing right now," she explained breathlessly, "but a moment ago there was a flash of light and I saw your face, I know I did. It's the second time it's happened." She admitted to being attacked and, mindful of his concern, carefully minimized her injuries. "Maybe something came loose," she said jokingly, giving in to her own excitement. "But if I can see, no one will have to worry about me. Not you, not Parker. . . ."

Her excitement passed into the beginnings of a violent headache, and she struggled to keep her equilibrium. "Promise you won't say anything," she entreated. "I couldn't stand it if it's not real."

"I won't, but I want you to—" He picked up the phone.

"See Dr. Peachtree. I'll see him as soon as he's available." She waited on tenterhooks while he called Chicago and bullied the doctor's office into giving her an appointment the following morning. He sounded exhausted by the time he'd gotten off the telephone. When she kissed him, his cheeks were wet; she leaned down so he could hug her good-bye. "Get some rest," she whispered.

"You see him tomorrow and let me know," he demanded weakly.

"You know I will," she promised. "Now get some rest."

After Leanna left, Sam was rigid with excitement, and his mind skipped past his physical exhaustion to enjoy hope. After all these years, was it possible? He was too old to believe in miracles but willing to be convinced. He'd held on to his dream so long it was impossible not to consider her returned vision the next best thing, an incredible fluke, an accident of fate. Dr. Peachtree had always been surprised at the slow deterioration of her optic nerves, consistently less than her condition had warranted. He'd attributed it to the exercises he'd given her: imagining actual events and picturing them in her mind—keeping the system healthy just in case, and Leanna had practiced faithfully.

Sam prayed for a chance for her. If there was a system of checks and balances that governed life, he would make an offer here and now to give up everything in order that she regain her sight. That she would suffer the attack of a thief and deal with it privately frightened him but supported his pride in her as well. She was strong and capable, and she'd be all right, with or without sight. Still, if there were a bargain to be made . . .

His mind drifted to Alice Faye. His wife had been totally unprepared for the depth of his illness. Frightened, then angry as their conversation inevitably progressed to his plans for disposal of his estate, she'd taken offense at his unwillingness to leave it to her in its entirety. He made a mental note to check with Burt Holman on the status of contract extensions for the managing directors. He'd have to sign his new will soon.

Leanna had reacted better than he'd expected, but he was certain there would be repercussions to his disclosure that she would deal with privately. Sending her to see Dr. Peachtree would serve more than one purpose. Keep her distracted and focused on herself instead of him, as it should be.

One good result of admitting his illness had been his son's reaction. Parker's innate strength had emerged; he had vowed to buckle down to his studies at Traxx and was talking about crash courses in real estate and insurance matters, as well as undergoing a sobering assessment of marriage. His engagement to the Llowell girl had come as something of a surprise, certainly, and Sam privately questioned whether or not Parker was equal to adding marriage to his other responsibilities. Time alone would decide that for him.

For the moment, his family's life was as much under control as it was possible for him to make it, and he closed his eyes at last, in order that tomorrow's events would come that much sooner.

Annie answered the doorbell. "Oh, my stars in heaven," she cried, and opened the screen. Matt came in from the music room to see what had happened. Nursing a swollen fist, Tommy limped into the kitchen, followed by a bloodied Stephen.

A young police officer stepped into the foyer. "These boys live here, ma'am?"

Annie nodded wordlessly.

"They're in some trouble. We hauled them out of a fight with another boy named Jack Myers. They were taking turns beating him pretty good. You know anything about it?"

She explained, and the officer took notes. She'd been concerned that something like this would happen. This morning, Charlie had remembered the party and told her brothers. Jay had gone to the police station with the information; Tommy and Stephen had disappeared, obviously looking for Jack.

"I'm going to release them into your custody, but they better be here if I want to talk to them, you understand?"

"They'll be here, Officer. They ain't going nowhere."

Matt made a note of the officer's name and walked into the kitchen. One look at the battered faces on the Sprengsten boys, and he wondered what Myers looked like. Neither boy would discuss what had happened in front of him, but he had the information he wanted: Jack Myers had supplied the drugs that Charlie had ingested, and her brothers had enacted sibling justice. He left to make a call. Myers had a broken nose and jaw and was unwilling to press charges.

He went to the hospital.

After identifying himself to the officer in charge, he was given leave to question Jack, who looked as if he'd barely survived a train wreck. He cut to the chase. "Either way, you're screwed for giving drugs to a minor," he said to the boy. "Cooperation will go a hell of a lot farther with a judge than giving me bullshit, so where'd you get it?"

After a few minutes of dancing around, Jack admitted he'd found Cathy Rice's purse near the Bowmont lake a couple of weeks prior to the party. There'd been cigarettes inside, and he'd smoked a few of them, but he denied knowing whether they were laced with a hallucinogen. The purse was hidden in a closet in his room.

After his initial disappointment that he didn't have a

buyer and a witness, Matt believed him, but he let the arrest for endangering a minor stand, added withholding evidence, and drove to the Myerses' home to get the purse. He'd lower the charges if the kid told the truth. No point in making his folks hock their house to pay a defense lawyer for the same result. Let him sweat a while.

Cathy Rice's purse was in the boy's closet, and in the bottom, among chewing gum wrappers and used tissues, coins, candies, loose tobacco, and theater stubs, he discovered another cigarette and a receipt for gasoline purchased the day of her death. Charged on Christine Scott's MasterCard, signed by Christie. Another chink in the wall.

26

"It's not good news, Dad." Leanna deliberately kept her voice cheerful and upbeat. "Dr. Peachtree says he's unable to determine any change in my condition." Having to say those words hurt more than she had imagined. All during the flight to Chicago, she'd cautioned herself not to be too optimistic, not to give in to hope, and she'd sensed her doctor's reservations ten minutes into his examination.

He'd been enthusiastic at first that she'd been having light bursts, then scolded her for not coming to see him sooner; after personally supervising the CAT scans and sonograms and various other ocular testing, he had come to the conclusion that she was simply having flashes of memory triggered by her recent head injuries. And most likely the injuries were the cause of her headache activity. There was no physical evidence of returned sight.

"Dad wants to speak to you," she said, and waited until the doctor picked up the line before replacing the receiver. Her own expectations had long since sunk into a quagmire of guilt. Her father was too ill to be receiving this kind of news. She should never have given him reason to hope. The doctor's phrases receded into the background; everything she'd heard from him this morning was being repeated to her father, almost verbatim.

Her mind was leaden with disappointment, and she dreaded going home with Curt. When he'd learned she was coming to Chicago, he'd insisted on accompanying her on the flight instead of Parker. She'd agreed only because her brother was so immersed in their father's illness that she hadn't wanted to add a "routine trip for a check-up" to his burden.

Curt had arranged a limousine. After the first hour of her examinations, he'd taken the car and gone about his business. He'd called a few minutes ago to insist they go to an early dinner and catch a later flight. Since he'd already made the arrangements, perhaps it was best; she'd need all the time she could manage to steel herself to face her father's letdown.

The portable buzzed next to his bed at a little after four in the afternoon. Matt pulled the antenna and held the phone next to his face. "Yeah."

"We got a fat guy down here, trying to pawn a gold necklace. Fits the description. You want us to hang on to him?"

Matt rolled out of sleep. There were no days off. "Yeah," he muttered. "I'll be down." He shut off the phone and pulled on a pair of Levi's to make the trip to the bathroom. A quick shower and shave later, he blinked his way into Annie's kitchen for coffee. "How's Charlie?" He spooned in three teaspoons of sugar for energy and layered on rich cream.

Annie looked at him. "She's okay," she answered cautiously.

"I couldn't help overhearing," he said, savoring the rich, warm caffeine circling its way to his stomach. "I know she got into some drugs by accident. Has it happened around here before?"

"You interested as a person or as a writer? 'Cause I don't want that child showing up in no book."

He sized her up and decided to trust her. "I think you know I'm not a writer, Annie."

"Well, I ain't heard that typewriter going, so I sort of figured you weren't." She sucked in her lower lip and tilted her head at him, speculating openly. Apparently he passed the test. "We ain't had anything around here before that I know of," she answered. "And I been living here sixty years. I seen pot and diet pills, alcohol, but I ain't never seen anything like this."

He nodded. It fit with his own assessment. If there were drugs in Walden City, they were so far underground that he hadn't been able to find them. Every inquiry, every feeler, had been met with blank incomprehension or wry disdain. Whoever was cooking hadn't been supplying locally—except to Cathy Rice. Her family and every one of her friends, other than Christie Scott, was clean, including the ex-boyfriend.

Christie was on twenty-four-hour surveillance starting this afternoon.

"Where is everybody?"

Annie gave him a brief glance. "Jay's working, kids're in school except Danni, and she's taking a nap. Jillian went to New York to look for an apartment." She paused.

He kept silent, knowing he would ask if she didn't tell him.

"Flew to Chicago this morning," she said evenly, eyes missing nothing, face mobile as stone. "With Curt. Got an appointment with her eye doctor."

He nodded and moved to get more coffee. Something about that guy really grated on him, and the idea of the two of them . . . That she'd settle for so little. *Christ, I hope it doesn't take forty years to wrap things up. I gotta move on before this gets serious.*

"She's supposed to be back this afternoon." Annie's voice was so neutral, he could read her disapproval across the room. She didn't like Curt, either. He gave her an impromptu hug; she laughed out loud and straightened her wig. "You gonna be home for dinner?" Her eyes were twinkling.

Damn, she didn't miss a thing. "Yes, ma'am." He gave her a wink and hustled out the door.

The fat guy was the man he'd seen running down the road; his name was Johnny. Johnny Nabors. Johnny Napson. Johnny Nyborg. Johnny had a rap sheet six pages long. Johnny lived in a fantasy world of his own making that had him at the center of the universe. And Johnny was a junkie snitch.

Matt dangled Leanna's gold necklace from his fingers and eyed the repaired clasp that had alerted the pawnbroker.

"You stole this from a very rich little girl." There was no need to manufacture threat; it was very real. He wanted to put marks on the bastard's throat. "Her family has more connections in this county than the phone company. We got your ass trying to sell this and me as a witness, because I saw you that day. You're gonna hang high and dry on this one, unless you want to make yourself a deal."

Johnny's eyes darted around the room and closed in stubborn denial of reality.

"I don't want you, I want him," Matt said coldly. "I get him, you walk on a battery." *Until the next time, and then I'll fry your ass.*

Johnny's eyes glittered, and he started supplying his end of the deal. "He said I could have anything I took off her except the ring. I had to give him the ring, everything else was mine."

"And?"

"And, I gave him the ring."

Matt circled the room impatiently. "You want to tell me his name?"

"Get real, like he gave me his name. He said rough her up, don't hurt her bad, and disappear. He got what he paid for."

Matt gripped the back of a chair and held on. "How'd you know where to find her?"

"He had her cased, and we followed her. Supposed to be in front of her house, but she got out of the cab and started walking. We couldn't believe it. A blind chick walking down this road. It was like she was asking for it."

"Whose car?"

"His. My Ferrari's in the shop."

Matt ignored the sarcasm. "Make? Model?"

"Hell, I don't know. Blue."

"How do you know it was his?"

"We hadda throw everything out the window. He didn't want anything in the car."

"Everything from the purse?"

"Yeah, Dick Tracy. 'Everything from the purse.'"

Matt let go of the chair and forced himself to walk toward the door before he lost it. "Who went through it, you or him?"

"I got the money. He threw all the plastic out."

"I'm going to call in an artist, and I want you to give me a picture."

"Sure, whatever you want."

"Johnny?" He let his anger show at last. "I saw the guy. I don't get him, you don't walk. Don't waste my time."

"Yeah, okay."

A follow-up call to Chicago confirmed that in addition to Leanna's, there were two sets of prints from the contents of the purse, one matching Johnny-last-name-du-jour and another they were still tracing. If the driver had a record, if he had a valid license, sooner or later he'd come out of the system and Matt would be there to nail him.

He got in the car and drove back to the inn to wait for dinner.

When she didn't show, he was antsy as a parent on a school night. Finally he shrugged in resignation and spent the evening studying Charlie, who seemed to be pretty much her old self and excited about seeing a Ninja Turtle movie with Danni and her brothers. After the kids scrambled out the door, he was at loose ends until he heard Baylor's car come up the drive. It was nearly eight o'clock and about goddamn time.

Their relationship was cordial enough when Curt brought her inside, but Leanna seemed subdued; the guy, as usual, was all over her, overbearing and possessive. Matt joined them in the music room long enough to say hello. As soon as Annie planted herself on the easy chair, he went outside to cool his heels, pretty certain that Curt wouldn't make much headway with Annie staring him down. Sure enough, the control king bailed out after ten minutes.

Matt came back in, hung up his jacket, and joined the women next to the fire. Leanna didn't respond to casual comments about jack-o'-lanterns on the lawns and Halloween being around the corner, so he poked at the embers while Annie brewed a pot of tea. She brought it into the room on a tray with two cups only, made an excuse about not wanting to miss her honey on "Quantum Leap," and disappeared. He smiled. *Subtlety, thy name is Annie.*

"She mentioned you were seeing your doctor." He watched from the corner of his eye and waited. It was, after all, none of his business. The statement hung in the air quite a while before Leanna responded.

"He says there's no change, but I'm not—" She stopped speaking, and when she positioned her teacup back on the tray, it rattled in the saucer. Something in her body language spoke volumes. "There's no window in this room," she said tightly.

The shift in her conversation threw him for a moment. Then he understood absolutely and moved to her side. There were no windows for her anywhere. She was more than angry, she was coming unglued. Probably a delayed reaction to the mugging. The best remedy he could think of was motion. Unless she moved, she'd try to control it. "Come on," he said. "Let's go outside."

When she didn't object, he grabbed his suede jacket from the hall closet, helped her into it, then pulled on one of the boys' school jackets. Outside in the crisp fall air, he tucked her arm in his and walked past the kids' pumpkin lanterns to the gazebo, glowing white under a harvest moon she couldn't see. The night air tossed her hair, and she seemed impervious to the chill. Seated side by side inside the little shelter, he zipped up the front of the jacket, turned up its collar around her neck, then took her hand. "Tell me what it's like," he said firmly. "I want to know, exactly."

She took her hand away to feel along the wall of the enclosure and grab a fistful of lavender growing through the latticework. She offered it to him. "What it's like?" she echoed bleakly. "It's so black I could pick it up and give it to you." She crushed the leaves between her fingers. "Every day I wake up and I'm optimistic, and every night when I go to bed I feel defeated because I accomplish so little." Opening her hand, she spilled the leaves onto the gazebo floor. "I spend hours making movies in my head, terrified to stop. If that part of my brain atrophies, the pictures will disappear and they're all I have left. My father . . ."

She moved her head from side to side in distress, and he ached for her. The lavender's spicy fragrance swirled up from the floor and danced away with a gust of wind, into the night.

"I want to see people's faces," she continued tautly after a few breaths. "I'm tired of the dark. I'm not sure light exists anymore. I think I see things. . . ." She started to shake. "Something's going wrong, and I don't know what it is."

She turned away from him on the bench to shut him out. He pushed his shoulder lightly against her rigid back to make contact once again and closed his eyes against her hair to share her darkness; after a moment she pulled her knees up onto the bench and allowed him to cradle her against his chest as he would a child. She was wired with tension.

"What else?" he prompted softly. "Tell me."

She sighed with a yearning that he knew must weigh a ton. "I'm tired of being led and helped, and coped with." Her hand moved across her chest to finger his jacket. "I want to know what color it is. Not just this, everything. I want to see what I'm eating—just *see* it, so I can decide if I want it and know it has a . . . an appearance, not just a taste and a texture at six o'clock on my plate!"

She shifted impatiently in his arms, and he almost opened his eyes to see her but did not. "I want to know what I look like," she confided with feminine concern. "Sometimes I wonder if I still have a face. People see me whenever they want, whether I want them to or not, and I can't see them, ever, and it's not fair. It's not fair!" Her control broke at last, and she began to moan against his throat.

He held her tightly and let her cry it out. He'd never thought about life from a blind person's perspective, and she was right. It wasn't fair. Nothing about it. She must use a ton of energy adapting to that single aspect, let alone everything else. He cursed the deal he'd made with Johnny that afternoon but knew he'd do it again to find out who the instigator had been. The driver. God help the guy when he found him.

Eventually her sobbing eased, and he was surprised when she stayed nestled in his arms. She rested her forehead lightly against his chin. Fighting the urge to seek light and knowledge, he began to understand more strongly the limitations of the world she was forced to live in. Surrounded by the spicy fragrance of lavender, unaware he was going to do it, he dropped his head forward to find her lips and discovered that kissing Leanna was the most natural thing in the world.

The next sixty seconds became an intensely sensual experience. Fascinated, he touched her face, found tears on her cheeks, and kissed her again, gently coursing his fingers through her hair. Her mouth was soft and innocent, and he sensed her uncertainty whether to continue at first, then she joined him in a slow acceptance that evolved into growing exploration and merged into breathless wonder as she spilled her tension into his mouth and body.

Each kiss held a longing that jolted him with irresistible pleasure; he was knowingly, joyously blowing the rules of conduct right out the window and could not have stopped had his life depended on it. Not as long as she wished to let him. Whatever was happening between them was too rare in a lifetime, too good to be real, and much too good to resist.

Sexually he had himself well under control and was very much aware from her reactions that this was all pretty new to her; emotionally, however, he entered a wondrous place—somewhere he could have gone on for hours, enjoying the sweet taste of her, exploring enticingly slick textures inside her mouth and the smooth precision of her teeth. She let him inside little by little, meeting him gently, widening her mouth to examine him in return, slowly, thoroughly, with the tip of her tongue, and awareness invaded the very skin on his body.

Everywhere she was next to him created airy sensations that crested through him; her fingers lingering on the skin of his hands, on his shoulders through the jacket, were less touch than caress. He fought his body's growing urge to take things further, carefully maintaining his balance, keeping it equal, aware that something extraordinary was happening.

When she pulled away at last, he felt her rapid breathing against his chest in the dark. It was increasingly difficult not to see, not to seek light, however faint, but he refused his brain's demand to open his eyes and look at her, determined to be as she was, to listen and learn with his senses, with his body and his heart. When her fingers covered his lips he felt their trembling; her whole body was trembling. He kissed her palms, ran his tongue lightly over the skin between her fingers, unable to stop himself. It put him over the edge, and he knew he could not continue without putting his hands on her, taking possession, owning her.

When she copied his actions, he knew that her brain and her body were making the same demands. More. The right to stay in this incredible place where feelings dominated the universe and nothing else was real. More! The right to go forward. Somehow, when they kissed again, they became the same person. It was unbelievable. He wanted to take her to his bed, become her body, expand his feelings to the limit of their endurance. He wanted to drown in her, pull her under with him, never come back.

She shuddered with a sudden sigh; he broke away and lifted his chin to let it rest lightly on the top of her head, pulled her body tightly against his chest. His skin had a pleasant ache where her fingers passed as she explored his jaw; he was alive only where she made him happen. Her hand, sliding down his throat to rest lightly against the base of his neck, not merely touched him but exploded feelings in him. He was aware of the difference and glad for it. The warmth of her was a searing glow against his chest, an aura, as his breathing slowed with hers; they sat in silent darkness for a long time.

"The jacket's an old hunter green," he said finally. "I've had it for years, it's worn. . . ." He felt her cheek move into a smile against his chest. "And you have a great face, dimples, pretty eyes with long dark eye-

lashes . . . and I can personally attest to the fact that you
have an extremely kissable mouth."

She made a sound, somewhere between a sob and a
laugh.

"I want you to know that I . . ." he began, unsure of
what he was going to tell her but needing to convey
some portion of what he was feeling. "That was beautiful," he finished simply. There was nothing else to say.

Leanna heard him speak her thoughts. Beautiful.
Absolutely beautiful. His heartbeat was a steadying
rhythm, and she nodded against his chest, holding tight
to the magic she'd discovered in this night, in this man.
She wanted more—to be held forever, safe in his arms,
while she explored this wholly new awareness. Every
moment she stayed next to him created a need that
ached to take them further. Her body demanded more.
To kiss him was to enter a realm of existence she hadn't
known to be possible—warm and soaring, unimaginable
until a few minutes ago. This, surely, was how it should
be between two people.

She knew nothing whatever about him except that he
seemed to be there whenever she needed someone.
And in her life, she had never needed anyone more than
she had this evening. He'd provided safe passage, somehow, and she would never be the same; something
magic and mysterious and . . . chemical had emerged
between them. Kissing him was the closest thing to
climbing inside his body and disappearing.

When the magic came to an end, melting away under
the weight of real events, she was saddened and resent-
ful. The sound of Jay's truck came up the driveway.
Angry voices carried in the night; doors opened,
slammed shut. Another vehicle started, drove away. She
didn't want her old world back. She wanted never to

move out of Matt's embrace, never to release his body from her grasp. He held the key to a new and better place she did not want to give up. It was that powerful and vital and wonderful.

At the intruding voices, Matt loosened his arms, and she reluctantly placed her feet on the floor. The lavender fragrance sprang up once more as her boots disturbed the leaves. She broke off another sprig and held it in her fist; she would never smell lavender again without knowledge of this moment. What would happen now?

Matt opened his eyes, and reality flooded in. He blinked in the moonlight as his sight adjusted to the dim night. *This is nuts. This has to stop. What are you planning to offer Sam Bowmont's daughter, Officer Halston? Sex? I don't think so. What happens when you wrap this case and go home?*

"I live in Chicago, and I'm not going to be in town much longer," he said quietly.

She sat stone still.

"I don't want you to think I didn't mean it," he hurried on uncomfortably. "I did. It was wonderful, but . . . It's just that when I have to leave, I want you to know it won't have anything to do with . . . this. You." He felt like an idiot. Babbling about leaving when she was still here, still next to him, still in need. Not to mention his own need for her.

Leanna shrank inside herself. He was saying this was all very nice while he was here but was warning her that when he left town, he was not interested. "My father's dying," she said to him, carefully having traveled a million miles away.

"God, I'm sorry," he said quickly.

"I found out yesterday. He wanted me to see if there

was anything they could do. About my sight." She stood, shivering as the wind robbed the warmth and safety that his body had generated, and moved into the doorway of the gazebo. "There's nothing. It's cold. I'm going inside."

Her father was dying, and she was blind. No wonder she'd been a mess. Her emotional state a hell of a lot clearer, he got to his feet and put his hand on her sleeve. She was in no condition to make decisions, but he didn't want her to leave; and he didn't want her to stay because if she let him kiss her like that again, things had the potential to get complicated in a big way. "Don't. Please, just for a minute. I didn't mean to say that the way it came out. What just happened kind of—"

She eased away from him. "I really want to go in," she told him. "I don't need help. I do it all the time."

He watched her walk in measured steps to the back porch and go inside the house. *Damn.* He left the gazebo and, avoiding the house, paced angrily down the drive and along the roadway, trying to understand how in the hell he'd let it happen. *You broke rule number one, asshole, you kissed the girl. You got involved with a local, and you know better. She's already a basket case, and you just dumped all over her, damn you. Damn you!*

27

Jay said good-bye to his aunt, closed the door, and sagged against the door frame. The scene with Jessica had been destructive and was going to have a lasting impact; he was tired beyond tired, and fear kept creeping under his rib cage that she'd act before he could prevent it.

She'd arrived a few minutes after dinner, and they'd taken a drive to talk in private. He'd known from the look on her face that it was going to be another plea for Danielle, and he was dead set on not giving in. Until this drug thing with Charlie had come along, Danni had been happy as a little clam, doing well in school and a joy to come home to at night. She'd gotten a little taller and was beginning to fill out on Annie's pies and cookies.

Admittedly, this past week had been a little rocky. Charlie's behavior during a flashback, coupled with the attack on Leanna, had frightened her; she'd been having nightmares, calling out for her mother and grinding her teeth in restless sleep. She'd moved into Annie's room last night and had fared much better, but this morning her little face was still drawn from stress and lack of sleep. Annie had kept her in all day, and he'd had about five minutes with her before Jessica had arrived.

He'd driven as long as he'd dared to forestall their confrontation, finally stopping at a local park, and the minute he'd killed the engine his aunt had skipped the preliminaries and gone to the main bout right on cue. "It's not going to come as any surprise that this is about Danni. I want you to let me have her."

He had adamantly refused; she'd insisted on spelling out her reasons.

"Whether or not it was harmless, Charlene's running away to Cincinnati was unnecessary and frightened the daylights out of Danielle. Charlene was very lucky, that's all."

"You're right," he agreed. "She shouldn't have gone. But if she hadn't, we'd still be looking for a house."

"She had no way of knowing it would turn out all right," she insisted, "and now she's sneaking out to wild parties. She's had a terrible experience with drugs that might affect her for years. Tommy and Stephen are both in trouble for fighting with the Myers boy because of her, you've been cited for drunk driving—"

"I was drunk, but it wasn't because of her. I admit it was stupid, and I wasn't driving."

"That's not what it said in the paper, and my attorney says—"

"Attorney?" He fought being angry with her and tried to listen.

"Yes, attorney. He says I have a good case for custody and to try to talk to you before taking it to court. I'm her blood relation. I had her with me four years, and nothing like this happened. Jay, she's only eight years old. She's entirely too young to be exposed to these kinds of things. It's not good for her. Let me have her. I love her, I'll take care of her."

He refused to discuss it and started the engine. Jessica built her agitation, increased her pleas all the way back to the inn. "Suppose it had been my brother in Los Angeles. It could have been. You wouldn't even have told Danni he was alive. He'd have died, and she'd have missed her only opportunity to see her father."

He hadn't bothered to respond. She had no idea what kind of nightmare that had been, and there was no reason to tell her how wrong she was. It had taken all the willpower he possessed not to throw his father's suicide into the equation, knowing full well that one thing had nothing to do with the other. He caught up with her arguments as they arrived in the driveway to the inn.

". . . she lies awake every night. What if something serious happens? You're not going to be able to get work in construction until spring. She's already missed two more ballet classes, she's worried to death about what's happened to Charlene. Jay, it's wrong. She should be with me."

Finally he lost his temper. "What was wrong was leaving town to see my 'father.' If I'd been here where I belong, I wouldn't have missed a week's work, I wouldn't have paid a fortune in airfare, Charlene wouldn't have gone to that party, and the drug thing wouldn't have happened!"

"You don't know that! You're determined to keep making it Jim's fault so you can duck your own responsibility here. Danni needs a mother, not someone your age trying to be a parent. No judge in his right mind—"

Then he really lost it and yelled at her. "I promised my mother! Not my father, my *mother!*" he reminded her severely. "She knew my old man was losing it. She asked me on her deathbed to take care of her kids. She didn't ask him, she asked me. Me! No judge in the world is going to make me change my mind, and I don't care what he says!"

He'd slammed the door of the truck, and they'd parted in anger.

He closed his eyes and sighed. He'd promised his mother, absolutely, but if he was honest, he was also doing it for himself. He couldn't stand the thought of Danni looking out Aunt Jessie's window the way she had when he'd left for the army. Charlie had hidden in her room and refused to say good-bye, but four year-old Danni had watched him bravely out the window, followed him with her eyes until he'd turned the corner. Four years it had haunted him, and he could still see her, heartbroken, fighting tears. His sister was home and she was staying home. End of story.

He sighed again, tired. Tired of fighting Aunt Jess over Danni, tired of worrying about Charlie, tired of trying to see everything coming; tired of losing out to Parker, tired of worrying about Jillian. Tired of opening the Bible and being afraid of what was inside. He'd opened it forty times since reading his father's letter, and each time something prevented him from breaking the seal, warned him that once the envelope was opened Pandora's nightmare might well descend—whatever it was—and never go back in the box.

With Jessica's threat in his face, it wasn't a good time to find out what was waiting, but tonight he was determined to get whatever it was behind him; he pushed himself away from the wall and removed the envelope. In his room, he closed his eyes and ripped a metal opener through the end of it, willing himself that whatever it contained, it would not matter.

For some reason, he wasn't surprised that the contents were legal papers, several of them. The first and largest was a multipaged document entitled "Judgment and Certificate of Annulment." Unprepared, he skimmed the wording in shock. Dorothy Stevens had been granted an annulment of her marriage to Samuel Parker, and her maiden name had been restored. He read through several paragraphs setting forth the terms of the settlement. She'd been given title to a house, a car, a financial settlement. . . .

Unable to focus, he backtracked to decipher the contents in simple terms. He had no idea that his mother had been married twice. Could it have had something to do with his father's decision to leave? He knew enough about law to understand that certain conditions in a marriage permitted annulments. But, why an annulment and not a divorce? He skipped through the language to discover the basis and found it.

Bigamy. He read it again, disbelieving.

Samuel Parker had conceded bigamy, and there was a child involved, born July 4, 1970. A burning sensation crept up the back of his neck as he recognized his birth date. There were several paragraphs setting forth the terms of a trust and an initialed paragraph stating that Samuel Parker was to have no further legal standing where the child was concerned. His mother's initials were written in the space next to Parker's.

Numb, he laid the judgment aside and unfolded the next document. Adoption papers. He read through the legalese, knowing in his heart what they were going to say. James Jay Sprengsten had adopted his mother's child, Jeremy Jason Parker, changed his name, and he was now Jeremy Jay Sprengsten.

He was adopted. He was Samuel Parker's son, adopted by James Jay Sprengsten. *And the merry-go-round went round and round, the merry-go-round went . . .*

His hands were trembling so violently by the time he unfolded the last piece of paper that he had to smooth it out on the dresser in order to read it. An old-fashioned birth certificate with his baby footprints; the information swam on the paper. Chicago Municipal Hospital. Dorothy Parker, housewife; Samuel Parker, insurance representative. His throat constricted, and he couldn't breathe fast enough.

He didn't want to know any of this. It had nothing to do with him. None of this had anything to do with him. He gathered the papers and stuffed them back into the envelope. None of this had anything to do with anything. He shoved it all in a drawer, walked woodenly out onto the balcony and down the stairs to the lake, too upset to have a clue what he was going to do next. He untied the rowboat and jumped inside, shoving it away from the dock; he began to row, striking the water viciously, refusing to feel anything except the pull of the oars and the chill of the night air off the lake.

My father's not my father.

It took him a full hour to reach the opposite shore, and his hands were punished with blisters. At each stroke, the phrase became a litany in his head as the oars cut through the black surface of the water and until he had dragged the rowboat past them: *My father's not my father.* He sat, sides heaving from the effort, and allowed reason to reenter his life. His mother had been married to a bigamist. He was a product of that union. Christ, did this kind of thing happen in real life? He tried to tell himself it didn't change anything, but that wasn't true. The entire world as he knew it had slipped sideways a notch and was out of his control. Solid ground was no longer available. Everything he'd accepted about his life had been built on a lie. *My father's not my father.*

He tried to construct the facts into a plausible explanation. Samuel Parker—the *biological* father—had made a settlement for his child and walked back to a wife somewhere, or, the *biological* father had been discovered and bought his way out of his child's life. Either way, he'd gotten out. His mind refused to identify with being the child involved.

He began the return trip across the lake, welcoming the exhaustion in his body and the pain in his hands, piercing and constant enough to keep him from pursuing the information racketing around his brain. When he got to his room at last, he fell across the bed, too tired to undress, and sought the safety of sleep.

Alone, lost, without horizon, no lee in sight, he was wading in shifting sand and swamped with wave after wave of dull, ominous weight that threatened to drag him under, each swelling larger and more overwhelming than the last, impossible to survive.

He awoke in a sweat, his heart beating wildly, hands aching; he let himself out onto the windy balcony for air. The black sky threw a blanket of stars across the night. No pattern, no order. No purpose. Just cold and

unreachable in their distance. Never in his life had he
been so alone with himself.

Suddenly he was no longer certain of anything.

Maybe Aunt Jessica was right. Maybe he had no
business trying to make it all come out right. Maybe
Danni would be better off in her care. Maybe they had
all been better off before he'd come home with all his
plans that pulled their lives into his own orbit. He stood
at the railing, his breath freezing into brief puffs of
white in the frigid air, and stared at the black of the
lake until he was in pain from the cold. *My father's not
my father.*

He went back inside, kicked off his boots, and
crawled under the covers, chilled to his soul. A few minutes later the door opened and a woman came into his
room with a rush of freezing air, and into his bed; she
lay down next to his icy body and put her arms around
him. Wordless, he curled into her embrace and the
warmth of her, and was able to sleep.

When he woke the next morning he was alone and
not sure it had happened at all.

At breakfast, after everyone had gone, he showed
Annie the documents. "Do you know what's in these?"

She looked at his hands and pursed her lips in disapproval, shook her head. "No, darlin', I never
looked." She left the table and returned with a bottle
of witch hazel and a box of cotton, then set about
treating his broken blisters. "Wasn't my business," she
said grimly. After she was satisfied, she got out her
glasses and began to read. Her astonished reaction
nearly matched his own. "I had no idea, Jay. I swear
on my life."

He sat slumped against the table and dragged the
documents across in front of him to search for the date

of annulment. August 30, 1971. "I was a little over a year old." He scanned the "Father Information" lines on the birth certificate. Place of Business: Midland Insurance. Age: 38. He'd be 61 now, this stranger who was suddenly his father. The handwriting at the bottom of the page was spindly.

The man who had walked out of his life and caused so much heartache in his family, the man he'd held a five year rage against, was no longer his father; the man who'd fathered him had spindly handwriting and had paid money to walk out of his life. He looked at the price. One hundred thousand dollars. First National Bank of Wellington.

He grabbed the phone and got the number from Information. Several transfers and explanations later, he was informed that the trust had been dissolved some seven years ago. About the time his mother and fath— about the time Jim and Dorothy Sprengsten were declaring bankruptcy. He laughed in derision and began to pace the kitchen. The doorbell rang, and he marched through to the foyer and opened the door. A middle-aged man in a brown overcoat stared at him through the screen. "Jay Sprengsten?"

"Yes."

"Are you Jay Sprengsten?"

He snorted a laugh. "Well, I was. I guess I still am to some people." He set aside his brittle humor. "What do you want?"

"I have something for you."

Jay opened the door to accept a slender envelope and watched the man walk away. He returned to the kitchen and tossed it onto the table in front of Annie. The envelope was blank. "You wanna bet this isn't good news?" he challenged.

Annie was silent.

He threw himself onto a chair and stared at the twelve or so pieces of paper that had cracked open his life, and poked at the newly arrived envelope. "Sure as hell ain't the lottery."

She pushed it in his direction without her usual smile. He tapped one end and tore off the other to find another legal document. "Notice of Motion for a Hearing in the Matter of Custody of Danielle Marie Sprengsten" was typed on one side, and his aunt's name appeared in the space for the complaining party on the other. His name was listed below hers as the party being served. He slammed the notice onto the table and stood angrily; the kitchen chair went skidding on its back across the room. He was too incensed to care. She'd already filed. The whole goddamned discussion last night had been a waste of his time and energy. He had thirty days to respond.

He started shouting, unable to stop himself. "Who the hell am I, Annie? Who the hell's my father? How can I defend myself in a hearing for Danni? My sister who's suddenly my half sister? My mother's child, but not my father's. Not my 'biological' father's. Let's get the terms straight! Hell, Jessica's not even my aunt. Not by blood. She's probably got as much right to Danni as I have!"

The ripples widened.

"She's known about this all along. She had to. I was at least two when Mom married her brother, probably older. That's not something you tuck under the rug. She's just been waiting for me to screw up. She said it last night—she's Danni's 'blood' relation. She's known for years! It's like a sick comedy of some kind. She has no idea that her brother committed suicide, but she knows I'm not his kid. . . ." He raked the papers onto the floor. "I guess it'll all come out even. I don't know what's right, I don't know what's wrong. I don't know what the hell's going on anymore."

Annie finally spoke to him. "What's going on is, you were the same guy who got up last week as you are this morning, the same guy who loves his brothers and sisters—half or otherwise," she said firmly. "And somewhere, a man cheated himself out of having you for a son. Someday, who knows, maybe he'll be sorry enough to find you and try to make up for it."

He began to hear the voice he had trusted for years and the common sense in her words, and slowly regained control.

"In the meantime, you have to decide what you're going to do about this where your family's concerned."

He picked up the papers, separated the hearing notice from the rest of the documents, and put them away. "There's nothing to do," he said tiredly. "It doesn't change the way I feel about them, and it doesn't change the promise to my mother."

"Good. Now what about the hearing?"

"I'll find an attorney and put up the best fight I can."

The next day at noon, Annie called him home to eat. She slid a copy of the *Wellington Express*, folded to an inside page, on top of his plate at the kitchen table and laid out lunch. He looked at one of the articles in surprise. LLOWELL/BOWMONT NUPTIALS ANNOUNCED.

"You wanted me to come home to read this?" He couldn't believe it. This wasn't like Annie at all. Jolene's picture next to Parker's was beautiful, and he read through the announcement. His gut rolled over. They were planning to be married three weeks from now. Just what he needed to ice the cake.

Annie slapped across the kitchen, refolded the paper to the opposite side, and pointed to an article at the bottom of the page. PUBLISHER OF *BOWMONT HERALD* ILL WITH RARE CANCER. The piece went on to describe Samuel Parker Bowmont's standing in the community and various of his charitable and philanthropic activities. The last line caught Jay's attention: "Executive Directors at the *Herald*, Midland Insurance, and Bowmont Real Estate Investments indicate that business matters at their respective firms will not be affected by their owner's illness."

"Did you know Bowmont owned Midland Insurance?" Jay looked at Annie, something undefined rolling around in his head. Parker's father was dying, and Jolene was getting married. It was in cement. She wouldn't change her mind after making a public announcement.

"No, but accordin' to this, he does," she agreed expectantly. "Anything else strike you as odd?"

He looked at the article again and refused to see it until she put her thumb over *Bowmont* in the column and *Samuel Parker* leaped out at him. He felt the blood drain from his face, and he looked at her in disbelief. "Aw, come on, Annie." But there it was in black and white. Samuel Parker. Not possible.

"I been thinkin' about it all morning," she said starchily, and poked him on the shoulder with her finger for emphasis. "In order to get married, you got to prove who you are. Your mother wasn't no fool. If somebody told her he was Samuel Parker, he had to have something to back it up with. He'd have to have a false identity, and he'd have to be in a position to create one. If he owned a big company like this one, he could make up a hundred names for himself."

"What makes you think his name wasn't Samuel Parker?" It was just a freaky coincidence, that's all.

Her slippers slapped around the kitchen, and she poured herself an umpteenth cup of coffee. "Because Martha Ridgeway just happens to work at Midland Insurance, and she says Midland never had an employee named Samuel Parker, before or after 1971. She's been there fifteen years and looked it up on their computer just to be sure." She plunked herself at the table. "And Sam Bowmont's owned Midland since 1969," she added judiciously. "He used to be an employee for years, then he came into a whole pile of money and bought the place."

"Wait a minute." He left the table to pace the kitchen, too jacked up to believe what he was hearing. "This is . . . I mean, I appreciate what you're saying, but . . . This is nuts, Annie. So he lied to the hospital—if he could lie about a wife, he could lie about a job. Maybe it's that simple."

She looked at him, considering. "True, but it assumes your mom either believed it, or deliberately put wrong information on your birth certificate, and I know better'n that."

Rich guys didn't do stuff like that. "If this guy worked at Midland and made up the name until he had identification, it could be almost anyone, or a friend of someone."

"Maybe." Her conviction faltered, and she sat down, deflated. "I hadn't thought about that. I'm sorry I got all worked up, but I did think it was something you should know about."

"It's okay." He looked at the clock. "I needed a break. I didn't need to know about Jolene," he kidded her bleakly, "but I needed a break. I have to go to work." He got heavily to his feet. "Too bad it's not real. I could sure use some of his money."

He kissed her and drove back to the site with the bizarre information nagging the back of his head. An eerie coincidence any way you sliced it, but there was no way old man Bowmont would risk an empire by being married to two women at the same time.

28

"Here he is, bigger'n life." The stakeout cop, whose name was Sheets, handed Matt a batch of pictures. "Looks like he got laid with your girlfriend."

The top photograph was a man coming out of Christie's front door, and Matt's jaw dropped in surprise. Curt Baylor!? Leanna's boyfriend was jumping Christie? Sure enough, Christie's face was visible in the background, hair disheveled and a shortie robe barely wrapped around her body. Astonished, he shuffled the pictures: Curt kissing her, one arm around her waist, Curt fondling her breast and Christie slapping at his hand. He looked through the rest. Equally classy until he got to the last of the group.

"Where'd you take these two?"

Sheets glanced at the pictures. "Her garage. He was picking up a box of some kind. Had it under some newspapers. That's him putting it in his trunk. Want me to blow 'em up?"

"Yeah. Can't hurt." Why would Curt keep something hidden at Christie's? And how did she relate to

Curt and Leanna? A new situation since their broken engagement?

"And this is the only guy she's seeing? Nobody else?"

"Not so far."

Out of answers, he pushed the photos aside and sent for the artist's sketch of the mugger's partner. When it came, he did a slow take and tossed one of the photographs of Curt and Christie next to it on the desk. Son of a bitch if this made sense. None of it. "What do you think?"

"Same guy," said Sheets.

"Or twins. Let's run him." Something was way out of kilter here. Guys hustling rich girls sleep around on them, okay, but they don't have them mugged. Or do they? What the hell was going on with this guy?

Thirty minutes later he had Baylor's thumbprint from the DMV and Chicago had faxed blowups of the prints on Leanna's purse. A match. Matt spent the waiting time racking his brain to remember more about the driver of the blue Ford sedan: brown hair and under thirty. It killed him, but he couldn't be sure it had been Curt. By this time he no longer trusted his own judgment. After seeing Curt in the photo with Christie, his dislike for the guy had escalated three or four notches above normal and he wanted it too badly. He kicked himself for the personal involvement. Always a bad move.

Besides, so far he had nothing. He had Curt in Christie's apartment screwing around on Leanna. *You had an hour of kissing Leanna in the gazebo last night.* His body reacted to the thought of her, and he forced himself to concentrate.

He had a mugger as a witness who was a junkie trying to make a deal on his arrest and a sketch of a guy who looked like her boyfriend—a relationship that any jury in town would logically accept as a reason for Curt's prints to be on her purse. *What about your own relationship with the victim, Officer Halston?* He put the thought out of his mind. It was still one asshole's word against another's, and after last night he was one of the assholes.

Then he got what he needed: a positive ID from Johnny the junkie on the photographs, and more important, according to the state of Ohio, Baylor was the registered owner of a 1991 blue Ford Taurus, Ohio license OO6-GNT. Formerly registered in Texas. For some crazy reason, Baylor had paid Johnny to mug the innocent, gentle blind girl he supposedly wanted to marry. He requested a twenty-four-hour tail on Baylor and put in another call to Chicago. According to Dino, the street rat had checked in—said he'd heard from the cooker yesterday afternoon and had arranged a buy next week.

It was going to go down pretty quick now, and after that he'd be going back to Chicago. Not before he took Curt down for hurting Leanna. *Not your territory.* Screw the territory. The son of a bitch had set out to marry Leanna and her old man's money, was getting horizontal with Christie on the sly, and his gut was screaming at him that Baylor was going to get away with it unless he dropped him. What didn't fit was the mugging. Sam Bowmont was rich as all get-out—what was the point of having his daughter mugged? "Rough her up, don't hurt her bad." If Johnny was telling truth, Curt had set up the whole thing in order to get back his engagement ring. What the hell could be that important about a ring?

Whatever he was, Curt Baylor was unpredictable, and

as any cop could tell you, unpredictable was dangerous.

Unable to resolve it, he called Christie and got her answering machine. He left word to get in touch with him as soon as she got the message. The information on Curt churned in his head all the way to the inn, and he came in the door just as Leanna was leaving.

"Hey, need a lift?" he offered. He hoped to hell she wasn't going anywhere near Baylor.

"No. I'm going to see my father," she answered, polite and understandably remote after the way he'd botched things last night. "He's better today. I'm going to spend the afternoon." She pulled on a blue-and-gold-plaid cape that made her look terrific; he repressed the urge to close it for her and watched her manage the button at her throat with ease. He wanted to touch her.

"What are you doing later?" he pressed. "I'd like to talk to you."

"It's Halloween. We get lots of trick-or-treaters."

Hell, he'd forgotten it was Halloween. Not like him. "How about dinner tomorrow . . . ? Night? Uh, a few things have changed, and, well, I'd really like to see you." Christ, he was tongue-tied as a teenager.

He breathed a sigh of relief when she reluctantly agreed and immediately lost it when Curt's car pulled into the drive. Blue Ford Taurus, 006-GNT. Why the hell hadn't he seen it sooner?

Baylor gave him a casual salute and opened the passenger door for Leanna. He clenched his jaws and watched the arrogant asshole help her into the same car he'd used to track her down and have her beaten. He turned on his heel and slammed the front door in anger.

He'd broken the first rule of police work. Never get

personally involved. Well, it was sure as hell too late now. Now he was worried about her. The son of a bitch had arranged to have her mugged. What else was he willing to do? He stopped with a chilling thought. Curt Baylor had been in Chicago yesterday. With Leanna. The buy had been arranged yesterday. There was an achy feeling in his mind that this was all a little too convenient. Was he putting it together because he wanted it to fit?

There was a note under his door in Annie's messy handwriting. "Got your message. Trick-or-treat me tonight. Christie." The last thing in the world he wanted to do was work. *Come on, shape up. She's safe at her father's. Get your act together and get this asshole arrested. Then figure out where you are with Leanna.*

Business first. He called Christie to make sure she was home for the evening, then asked a puzzled and suspicious Annie to come up with an excuse to call Leanna at her father's. When he was sure she was there, he relaxed a little. "You got to help me keep a real close eye on her, Annie," he said, unable to explain further. When she got it and nodded with the determined air of an ally, he burned up the highway to Christie's apartment.

She was waiting, tricked out in a cat costume and stoned on something heavy. "Hey, honey," she crooned. "You wanna party, hardy?"

"Yeah, baby, what you got?"

"What I got is the weekend off." She handed him a couple of megadose downers. "Trick-or-treat . . ."

"You only have two left?"

"That's okay. Curt's bringing me something later."

She'd never used his name before, so she must be really stonesville. Curt supplying? He hoped to hell it wasn't grass. A grass bust wouldn't put him away for five minutes. *Cut it out. You want this too bad, and you'll blow it.* Slipping his arm around her, he twitched the tail of her costume. "You got anything to drink with these, kitty?"

"There's some vodka left."

He dallied fixing himself a drink. "Is Curt your boyfriend?" He casually palmed the pills for evidence. "Should I be jealous?"

"Oh, Curt and I go way back," she said dreamily. "We knew each other in high school in Mississippi but we didn't date or nothin' until he moved up from Texas last year. Said it took him two years to track me down."

"What's he gonna bring you?"

"I don't know. Whatever he's got. I hope it's that stuff he gets in Chicago. It's great." She rolled her eyes.

"Oh, yeah?" *Chicago again. And too good to be true.*

"Yeah, gotta be careful with it, though. It's dangerous, but it's a great high. I only do it when I got a couple days off."

"Sounds like what I'm looking for," he hinted broadly. *Too goddamned good to be true. Curt? Oh, please make it Curt.* "You gonna have enough for me?" He nuzzled her neck.

"Gee, I don't know, honey."

"Maybe you could call him?" He rubbed his hand along her back. "Please, baby? For me?"

"Nnnn, I dunno."

"C'mon, kitty. If I can't get you in bed, at least help me get high."

Her resistance folded. "Yeah, sure."

He stood next to her and wrote the number down in his head as she dialed. A faint male voice came through the phone next to her ear, and he knew she was waiting to leave a message after the recording. "Curt, honey, it's me. If you don't mind, could you bring me a little extra of that really good stuff tonight, okay? I got a whole three days off and I'd really, really appreciate it, honey, see ya later."

"You're a sweetheart," he told her. For the next two hours he helped her answer the door and sort out candies for groups of trick-or-treaters under the eyes of watchful parents. And ate his feet with anticipation. It had to be Baylor. The phone rang a few minutes after eight. From the conversation, he could tell it was Curt and that he was giving her hell.

"No, I didn't, honey. Just me. . . . Nobody, I swear it." She walked back and forth, carrying the phone, denying as she went, the cat tail on her costume trailing between her legs. "It was dumb, I'm sorry. Can't you erase it? I just want a little extra, that's all." She took the receiver away from her ear long enough to grin at him conspiratorially. "Curt, there is nobody here."

The doorbell rang, and Matt pushed a handful of candy out the door to a couple of teenagers too old to be beggars. Christie smiled at him and continued her conversation. "Aw, come on, I got a little buzz on earlier, but I need something better, that's all, honey, really.

"Okay . . . Okay . . . Okay!" She hung up the phone. "He's on his way over. Uhh, I don't think it's a good idea for you to be here."

"Right." He looked at his watch. If Curt was coming here, he was leaving Leanna. "You sure he's cool? I don't want to get you in trouble."

"Nah, he's a good guy." She grinned. "We'll probably get married one of these days."

He looked at her in the ridiculous cat costume and heard the hope in her voice, unable to feel anything but pity for this lost, once pretty girl. She was hooked on a bad news guy and the drugs he supplied; a one-way elevator. Down. "I'll call you tomorrow," he said. "Make sure everything's okay."

He located the surveillance team and told them Baylor was on his way, possibly delivering drugs. If Curt brought Christie the Chicago acid, he'd bust her as soon as Curt was out the door, then go through the bastard's apartment with a fine-tooth comb for the rest of it and ship his ass on a fast flight to Chicago.

He used the van phone to call the inn. When Leanna answered he relaxed and asked her to give Annie the message that he wouldn't be home until very late. Satisfied Annie would understand, he spent the next ten hours trading watches with the stakeout team, waiting for Curt to leave Christie's apartment. But the blue Ford Taurus stayed on the street.

Drug deliveries usually lasted less than five minutes; overnighters were getting laid. When Curt made a quick exit around nine o'clock the next morning, Matt decided to hold on the bust and talk to Christie to see what he could learn. When he got her out of bed, she was pretty ragged. "Jeez, honey, you just missed him. He brought me a few more downers," she told him. "I only got one left. He says I use too much and I'm tired all the time. Do you think I look terrible?"

She looked like hell. "Yeah, but what about me, baby? What about the stuff from Chicago? I thought you were gonna take care of me."

"He said he'd bring all I want from Chicago next week."

"How much you need?" He flashed the money in his wallet and took out three hundred-dollar bills.

She waved them aside. "Nah, he gives it to me. I don't pay for it."

He looked at her. She might not pay with money, but she paid. "Well, I want all I can get if it's as good as you say it is. When's it going to be, do you know?"

"Monday or Tuesday, he's not sure. I'll give you a call."

It occurred to him again that it was pretty cozy that the street rat was expecting a delivery next week and Curt was making a large buy. A little too convenient? Was he manufacturing again?

He pumped her for as much information as he dared. If Curt was bringing in drugs next week, it was worth the wait to nail him with evidence in hand. The second stakeout team came in, and he stayed for the briefing, then headed back to the inn and Leanna.

Annie told him she'd driven her to her father's to spend the day, but she'd mentioned having dinner with him that evening. He told her what he could about Curt, without blowing his case. "I don't trust the guy, Annie. I happen to know he's a liar and he's seeing at least one other woman. He's not a good guy, and Leanna shouldn't be alone with him if we can help it. I just got a feeling."

"I'll do what I can," she answered.

"I gotta get some sleep," he added. "If Christie calls, let me know, okay? It's important."

She looked at him sharply, and he was compelled to explain. "It's business, Annie. I promise."

"She better be. I don't want two liars in this child's life."

"It's business," he repeated, and hit the shower and the bed, in that order, and slept all afternoon. That evening he shaved at the last minute to remove any trace of beard, used the expensive after-shave, and changed his mind twice before settling on a blue corduroy shirt tucked into clean, pressed Levi's; he added a pale gold wool tie and pulled on a tan Polo jacket, wishing he'd brought more clothes. "You're taking her to dinner, not the prom," he said to the mirror.

Leanna turned one last time for Jillian's inspection.

"I like the gold belt better," Jillian pronounced. "You're going to knock his socks off in that dress."

Leanna adjusted the belt and nervously pushed up a sleeve to fasten her watch. It was seven-thirty. "You're sure the color's okay?"

"It's perfect. Where's he taking you?"

"Haven't the faintest idea."

"I'm going to want details," Jillian warned, and escorted her to the music room. "Now just sit there and look gorgeous," she prompted. The sound of hurried footsteps disappeared up the stairs.

Leanna settled into the sofa cushions that had plumped up her impromptu shampoo chair, determined to be casual and make things work, but her heart was skipping to another rhythm entirely. She laughed, and the echo came back to her in the empty room. Who was she kidding? She was more excited about the upcoming evening with Matt than anything in recent memory—except being able to see again. That short-lived joy had turned out to be devastatingly painful but had led to her discovery of him and their wonderful emotional sleigh ride—and his asking her out this evening. She was sure of it.

He really wanted to talk to her because he hadn't taken no for an answer. Anticipation was giving her butterflies. What could have changed? Him staying in Walden City was too much to hope for. She knew he was dating Christie, and he'd been honest enough to make it clear he wasn't interested in a long-term relationship. After thinking about it a long time, she'd come to the conclusion that before he left town, she wanted at least one more chance to kiss him. Another chance to get lost in that delicious new place that had opened up in her life. Maybe more.

"More" wouldn't precisely define itself, but admitting the thought made her blush and get twitchy inside. Most definitely not the kinds of feelings she was used to having where Curt was concerned. With Curt, what she'd always identified as excitement was closer to being on edge, a mix of nervous apprehension and concern that she wouldn't measure up. Her feelings about Matt Halston, she realized suddenly, were closer to anticipation, full of expectation.

In a very real way, they were much more dangerous.

With Curt, she'd expected little more than what she'd already experienced of him; she'd allowed him to be in charge, to make emotional decisions for her, had remained the dependent person in the relationship— assuming his knowledge and expertise as an absolute. It was clear to her now that she'd gotten engaged to him because she was afraid of losing that safety. And because she'd never shared any other feelings.

With Matt, it wasn't safe, but she expected everything. The thrill of a repeat performance. Another wildly giddy flight on sensation and emotion—as an equal. A partner. To lose this, to never find it again, was riding for a much bigger fall. A disastrous one. And the alternative, with Curt or any of the other boys she'd kissed, she now knew with certainty, was to experience less, to feel less, to settle for less than was possible.

Less was already in her life. Not to see was less. Losing her father was less. Yesterday, when she'd tentatively admitted to him what had happened with Matt and some of the emotions she'd discovered, she'd been shocked and astonished at her father's change in attitude. "You only live once," he'd commanded. "Don't you dare waste it on someone who doesn't deserve it." Clearly he'd been referring to Curt.

Her dear, conservative father had urged her to explore her feelings and to stay strong and not dwell on him. She knew that to return to feeling less was "waste" and no longer possible. "Carpe diem" was her new motto. Matt had warned her that he would soon leave for Chicago; it was more than likely she'd never see him again. Maybe this evening could change that, but if it had to happen, she had every intention of carpe-ing the diem and to have part of his leaving, at least, on her terms.

When Matt came downstairs, she was waiting in the music room in a beautiful, loose cashmere sweater dress, a deep orange-gold color like apricot jam, cinched with a wide gold belt, and wearing slender brown walking boots. He helped her into a matching brown leather coat and white silk muffler and felt like a million dollars when he looked at her next to him in the Camaro.

"I talked to a friend of mine who owns a restaurant," he told her, stretching the truth a little. "Maine lobster okay with you?" He'd racked his brain all the time he'd watched Christie's apartment, determined to come up with something she'd enjoy. Lobster was messy, but it was finger food, and they'd be equals.

"I had a whole lobster once, before I was blind," she said slowly. "That's where they put a bib on you, right?"

"Yep." He thought she was going to balk, then saw her reconsider. "Okay," she said flatly.

Conversation became awkward, and she was wound pretty tight by the time they arrived at the restaurant. He'd reserved a small round booth at the far end of the room for them. Sliding in opposite at first, he moved around to sit close to her right hand, in case she needed help. Plus, he wanted to be next to her.

She hadn't settled by the time the waiter took their order. "You can change your mind," he said, not quite sure where it was going wrong.

"Lobster is fine," she said with determination.

He ordered a bottle of Chardonnay and tried to relax. The waiter poured the wine, and they had a few minutes alone. "The other night was very special to me," he said awkwardly, "and I feel like I've made a mess of a very delicate situation."

She took a sip of wine and carefully replaced the glass. "You were being honest." Her voice was dry.

"Yes, I was," he countered, "but there's more to it than that." He mentally crossed his fingers and went to work, unsure already how much was going to be professional and how much would be purely personal. "You have this guy Curt in your life who wants to marry you. He's already given you a ring and you were serious enough to accept it. That says you were thinking about it."

"I was." She took another sip of wine. "But if it hadn't been stolen, I'd have given it back to him."

"You're still seeing him. I mean, you went to Chicago with him. Not something someone like you does casually," he continued, thrilled that she was dumping the dangerous bastard. Unless things got out of hand, he'd be able to keep Curt away from her until he was nailed. The waiter returned to tie bibs around their necks and refilled the wine.

"My brother couldn't make the trip. Curt and I are friends," she insisted.

"I don't think he sees it that way."

"You're right. He probably doesn't. I haven't exactly been honest with him. What about you and Christie?"

He'd forgotten totally about Christie. "She's a little hard to explain," he said defensively.

"Oh."

"What does 'oh' mean?"

"It means you're still seeing her."

Inadvertent or not, she'd cornered him, and he was glad to see the waiter arrive with their lobsters, each a bright angry red and too hot to handle. A match for the situation. He had to laugh. She had him tied in a neat little bow. "I'll make you a deal," he offered. "Let's leave Curt and Christie out of the conversation."

"No deal," she said stubbornly, and picked up the metal cracking tool. "Where's my lobster?"

An unspoken truce descended during dinner. He had to admit she did almost as well without sight as he could manage with twenty-twenty vision. Other than having to check on the position of her melted butter once in a while, she was unerring in her ability to locate claw meat, both with her fingers and the lobster fork, after he'd helped her break open the shells.

An hour later, his former wet kitten was well fed and purring through the last of her Chardonnay. She declined coffee or dessert, and he signaled for their check.

"We haven't settled this, you know," she reminded him.

"No, we sure haven't," he admitted. "You want to do it here or in the car?"

"Not here."

He knew when he started the engine that there was no way in the world the evening was going to end without him kissing her. Something in his chest was guiding and demanding it. It was in the car between them like a living thing. He turned on the radio and forced himself to drive to the inn and park in the lot. Anywhere else was absolutely unsafe, and he knew it.

"Where are we, Annie's?"

"You're pretty perceptive."

"It was the same amount of time as going. I think we stopped at 'oh.'" She waited expectantly.

"I'm doing some work with Christie," he hedged. "It's not what you'd call a relationship. It comes under the heading of business."

"Are you sleeping with her, too? Honest answer, please."

Where the hell was she going with this? "Why are you asking me?" he countered.

"Is that my answer?" she asked carefully.

"Your answer is, no, I'm not sleeping with her. I'm not sleeping with anyone." The admission shot through him like the hot end of a poker. Not the admission, he acknowledged, but the fact that she wanted to know. "What's the answer to my question?" he demanded in return.

"Curt is," she answered bluntly. "Sleeping with her."

His breath stopped and he looked at her, astonished. "How on earth do you know that?"

"We broke up over her. I went to his apartment a few weeks ago and she'd been there. I know her perfume. It was in his bed."

Every inch of his body became aggressively territorial. *Were you in his bed, too, goddammit?*

"They were in a nightclub together a couple of months ago. Being blind has certain peculiar advantages." She smiled brightly. "I'll admit not very many, but I do remember voices—and I remember perfumes."

He digested this very carefully. "If you hadn't found out, would you have married him?"

"Probably. I wanted to please my father, I think, but my father's dying and he says I have to please myself. He doesn't want the responsibility," she joked lightly, then sobered.

She had tears in her eyes, and he couldn't help it. He kissed her. He cursed the Camaro's configuration that prevented him from moving to her side, that kept his body away from hers, and kissed her again. She was there, open and inviting, and he had a steering wheel in his lap. He groaned in frustration. "What are we going to do about this?"

She kissed him softly. "I don't know, but I don't want to stop."

"I can't do this all night," he warned after kissing her longer and slower. "Not again. At some point, bucket seats aren't gonna get it."

She nodded and led him farther down the path with a kiss that left no room for doubt that she had her own plans for the evening, and he had a central role. His body began to slip out of his control, and he glanced longingly at the inn, so close, so impossible.

"Not here," he said tightly. "Annie'd skin me alive." He couldn't think, and he couldn't not kiss her. "I want someplace warm and safe and special," he told her between kisses; self-control had long since jumped out the window, and desire was now burning in its place, a bonfire in his body. A hotel room. A great, huge one with an excess of privacy. Months of it.

"No, let me." In the darkened room his hands slid inside her coat, caressed her back, and pulled her to his side; the cashmere was enticingly soft under his fingers, and her body was warm and welcoming beneath the fabric. He hung the coat over the back of a chair and unbuckled her belt. He placed it on top of the coat, then ran his hands along the planes of her, learning the curves and soft places with his mind and fingers.

This is crazy. This is so out of the rule book, they're going to invent a new chapter.

He didn't care. He didn't care. He didn't care. And it no longer mattered that she was Sam Bowmont's daughter. This was important, for her as well as himself. Not making love with her would be tantamount to rejecting her because she was blind. He'd caught himself making excuses not to take her to a hotel, and that had cinched it. He wouldn't have thought twice about it if she were sighted, and she'd have figured him out in a second.

He'd arranged the room and told himself that the instant she wasn't sure, no matter how far along things had progressed, he'd call a halt and take her home. Part of his functioning intellect hoped like hell she'd simplify his life and change her mind, but the overwhelming majority of his body was praying she'd kiss him for a couple of weeks, at least.

The bellman had switched on the lights, but he'd turned them off again and the hotel room was dark as night.

The dress slid easily over her head, and his fingers

told him that a silk slip had molded itself to her body. He sat her on the bed and removed her boots, slid his hands up under the silk to the waist of her panty hose, and coaxed the soft covering down long, smooth legs and away from slender feet. She stood and kissed him as he unfastened her bra, allowed him to tease the straps from her shoulders and along her arms until thin silk was the only thing between his hands and her breasts.

Then he encircled her in his arms, melted into her body, and was lost in kissing her. Soon her fingers worked at the buttons of his shirt while he kissed her shoulders, memorized her perfume, the contours of her throat, the texture of the creamy skin next to her hairline, along her ears. He drifted, senses ever-increasing, as she found and unbuttoned his cuffs and gently pulled his shirt out of his Levi's and off his body.

He'd been hard forever when her fingers moved to his belt, unfastened it, and searched for a nonexistent zipper. He felt her pause, then the tentative exploration as she identified more buttons and worked each one free. Fly open at last, she deliberately touched him and he felt himself grow even harder, slipping close to the edge of mindless pleasure.

She pushed his jeans past his knees to the floor, then, with his eager help, removed his T-shirt. Finally she stooped to hold his jockeys as he stepped aside, and whisper-soft hair slid over him. He couldn't believe he could want her so totally. When she deliberately brushed him with her cheek, he knew she was enjoying her power over his body.

"I can't wait much longer," he pleaded, and pulled her under the covers.

But he did. He waited for her to sit up to remove her slip, and until she put her hands on him again and explored his contours with both the front and back of her hands and fingers. He learned her in the same way and when her mouth was open and kissing him urgently, nothing held back, and her breasts were crushed against his body and her fingers were digging into his back and shoulders, he waited until he was inside and drowning, and until she was with him and their rhythm was in place, and until she stopped kissing him to gasp in pleasure. Then he lost himself somewhere over Denver for a couple of hours.

29

Curt tossed the maroon velvet ring box in the air and caught it confidently with one hand. A full two carats and emerald cut, point seven clarity. Leanna might not be able to see it, but the dragon lady was going to drop her teeth. If Leanna didn't accept it, he'd know it was time to hit the road.

He wasn't too sure it wasn't time to split anyway. Either he was imagining things or something was a little too slick in the Windy City. The street dealer was French-kissing him for more product. The same jerk who'd been a consistent asshole until this last deal was suddenly Mr. Nice Guy, accommodating as all hell, money no object. He'd hate to be wrong, because he had a lot riding on the deal, but on the other hand . . .

He'd set up a buy but blew it off at the last minute just to jerk the guy around on the outside chance that things weren't kosher. There was no percentage in gambling this far down the line. He was too close to major money to get busted for a few thousand dollars' worth of acid. Not with millions on the plate. He'd called a friend of the late Mickey Scolari and laid the tabs off on him for three-quarters cash and a few grams of high-grade blow. Ordinarily he didn't allow himself to do coke because he had a real weakness for it, but the guy had bitched at the short-notice buy—and done him a favor, so he'd gone for it.

The cash had been enough to cover the ring, and if he'd rolled over the coke, he'd have had all he needed for the moment. Penny-ante wasn't his style. If he couldn't bring off the Bowmont marriage and set himself up for life, he'd stick with meeting expenses until he lined up something else. Nickel-dime greed had busted every hustler he knew, buying cars and clothes and women, and lack of it had kept him with a clean record. So far, it had been a pretty good credo. There was nothing out there for cops to find, and once he was married to Bowmont money, he'd kiss all this crap good-bye.

Doing the coke had been stupid. He'd started late last night and blown the last of it an hour ago. This time he'd handled it, but never again. He could name a dozen heavyweight honchos who'd put thousands of zeros up their nose and wound up like the junkie he'd picked up two weeks ago. For a few dollars and the contents of Leanna's purse, presto, he'd had one mugger to order. The guy had gotten away with her gold necklace, but, true to some sort of street code, he had roughed her up as promised and hadn't really hurt her.

It had shocked the hell out of him when he'd seen her all scratched up and bruised, and it was a damned good thing he hadn't given the guy free rein. The idea had been to scare her into giving up the independence crusade. His and the junkie's idea of "scaring her" differed greatly, but it was done and she was okay.

He hadn't counted on some samaritan cowboy picking her up and taking her home. The original plan had been to visit her in the hospital, wait a couple of days, then work on her to move back home and make points with old man Bowmont; somewhere in the process, he'd have gotten her into bed and set a new wedding date. But she hadn't called her father, and he had gone barging in too soon. No real harm done. All things considered, it had still worked out to his advantage. She'd been seeing him for dinner, was kissing him good night, and had let him take her to Chicago—all major steps forward.

Since the fiasco in his apartment, it was clear that getting her pregnant was going to require marriage, not the other way around, so it was time to get the show back on the road. He tossed the box onto his bed and called her. The old battle-ax who ran the place told him she was sleeping. Lying old witch. "Okay, I'll leave a message," he said politely. "Tell her I have something to give her and I'll be coming by this evening." He hung up before she could argue about it. He was coming sooner, but no point in letting her know that.

He checked his wallet. Two hundred would get him through a couple of days, but he was going to need some more supplies and plane fare back to Chicago soon. He called Christie and got her out of bed. "You said you knew someone looking to party? . . . Yeah? Well, I scored pretty good last night. A lot more than I need. Is he interested in quantity?"

"Yeah, I think so, he was gonna give me three hundred, but he might go more."

"Tell him it's five and call me back."

"Curt, honey? You got anything for me?"

He buried the urge to tell her to shove it. Lucky for

her it was a little too soon to burn bridges. "Sure, baby. I always got something for you." He hung up the phone and retrieved the brown bottle from its hiding place under the sink. It checked out three-quarters full against the light. It was worth at least seven, but he could let it go at five.

He could always tell when they had another man in their bed. They always needed a little something extra. He slipped the bottle back in its hiding place. Hell, take as much as you want. You and whoever you're screwing can work that out. A going-away present, so long as I get the five. If he did the tabs, he'd get a thou, but it took a couple of hours to space the dosage with the eye dropper, plus drying time. So he'd take five and stay with the plan.

Matt lowered his eyes to keep Annie from reading him like a book; he and Leanna had gotten in very early this morning, and he was pretty sure she knew it. He'd only been up about twenty minutes, but he'd gotten five hours of marvelous sleep that felt like a week and was feeling seriously terrific.

The only sour note was Dino's call from Chicago that the deal hadn't gone down for some reason and the rat had no explanation. Philosophic from long experience, Matt chalked it up to the percentages. Dope dealers were notoriously paranoid, and it could have gone south for a hundred reasons. If the cooker needed money, he'd be back. Sooner or later they always came back.

Annie was treating him to a late breakfast when the phone rang again.

"It's Christie." Her voice was neutral. Storm warning. He swallowed the last of his coffee to avoid moving toward the phone. "I told you, Annie, she's purely business."

"Anybody else 'business'?"

He didn't pause. "No. She's special. Very."

"I find out she ain't . . ." Having delivered her warning, she left the kitchen. He moved to the telephone in the hallway. "Hi, honey, what's up?"

Christie told him the deal. He forced himself to stay calm. "Hell, yes, I want it, baby, all you got," he told her. "How about this morning?" he said with a user's impatience.

"I'm going over there now," she told him. "I'll pick it up for you. You got five hundred cash?"

"Absolutely," he pushed. "Can I meet you there?"

"Nah, I'll get it for you. He wouldn't like me telling anyone where he lives."

No way he was going to talk her past that one. "Okay, I'll see you later, sweetheart. Don't change your mind." He'd have to hustle, but he could beat her to Curt's and claim he'd followed her. One way or another, the bastard was going down.

He hung up the phone, grabbed his jacket, and turned to see Leanna in the hallway; her face was pale, and he had no idea how long she'd been there, but she'd overheard most if not all of his end of the conversation with Christie, that was certain.

Before he could stop her, she retreated quickly down the hall to the door of her room and disappeared. There was no time to explain, so he did what he had to do. He grabbed his portable, jumped in his car, and hit the highway so he couldn't change his mind. He called Curt's stakeout unit and alerted them to watch for Christie.

This is no time to let yourself be distracted.

Distractions get cops killed. She'll be upset for a couple of hours. You nail Curt and you can explain the whole damn screwball situation. You mess this up, the son of a bitch skips and you have to start over.

He was six blocks from Curt's and hung up behind a stalled freight at a railroad crossing when the phone buzzed. "Yeah!"

It was Sheets. "She's here. Now what?"

"Shit. Let her go in. I'll figure it out when I get there."

He threw the phone into its cradle, furious to his socks, and watched snow spit down from the heavens onto the immobile boxcars.

Christie was getting undressed, and Curt watched her closely. He wasn't in the mood, but he didn't stop her. She did have great tits, soft and white; maybe he'd get inspired. One for the road.

"He's definitely interested, honey, I wouldn't tell you wrong."

"So who is 'he'?"

"Just a guy I met on the plane."

He didn't believe her. "You screwing him, too?"

"No, I'm not."

She was defensive. Now he really didn't believe her. "Oh, yeah?" He moved around the room, impatient to be rid of her. He'd been up and flying this morning, now the whole thing seemed like a bad idea. She was a bad idea, the sale was a bad idea. He'd been stupid to trust her. Had his head up his ass from the coke. "Why not?"

"Because I love you and he's just a friend, that's why."

She had tears in her eyes. He decided to let it go. The

last thing he needed was a crying woman in his face. "So where's the money?"

"He's bringing it to me later. What's wrong with you?"

"You're fronting the money for this 'friend'?" he accused.

"What do you think I'm going to do, keep it? Forget it. Forget the whole thing." She started putting her clothes back on, whining, "You brought it up to me. You made the offer. I don't care if he buys it or not. I thought I was doing you a favor."

"Okay, I'm sorry. I'm just a little jumpy, that's all. I blew the job in Chicago. They're not going to hire me, and I was counting on it." He got the brown bottle out of the bathroom. What he really needed was a cold shower and another hit to clear his head.

"Here, help yourself." He tossed her the bottle. "Just make sure you get five hundred. Don't let him stiff me."

"I won't."

She put the bottle on the dresser and took an eye-wash container out of her purse. She had it filled by the time he came back into the room.

"Hey, whoa! That's enough to keep you high for six months. You dealing on me?"

He took the plastic bottle out of her hand and emptied most of it back, then screwed on the cap and threw it at her. She was getting her back up, and he ignored her. What the hell did he care how much she used? She was history.

Annoyed, he grabbed a clothing brush and worked on his sports jacket hanging on the valet, then put it on a wooden hanger and hung it in the closet. One of the things he was going to do when he married Leanna was fill his closets with every expensive jacket he hadn't allowed himself to buy and hang them all on cedar hangers, starting with black cashmere and ending up with white silk. He checked the inside pocket and satisfied himself that the ring box was safely out of Christie's sight.

The coke had been a mistake. Big high, bigger drop. He was squirrely for no reason unless it had been stepped on with something cheap. "Come here," he told her. "I just want you to be careful, that's all. No more accidents. I don't want those tits to wind up in a morgue." He gave her a kiss and had no reaction. Christ, he didn't even want to get laid.

"Yeah, thanks, honey. You wanna go to bed?"

"No." Out of here, that's what he wanted. Tomorrow he was either going to be engaged to Leanna Bowmont or pack everything he owned and leave for Boston. He'd had it with this pop stand. Leanna had been jerking him around for two months, and at some point he had to draw a line; there were lots of rich little girls in Boston. "I'm gonna take a shower and try to find a job," he lied. "I gotta meet some guy in an hour for another interview." He shut the bathroom door in Christie's face and jumped in the stall.

After a few minutes he turned off the water, and her voice came through the door, harsh and annoying. "You got anything else for me, baby?"

He gave it back to her in kind. "No. Which reminds me, I may have to go out of town for a couple of days, so I'll stop by later for the money. Make sure you get it. I'll call you when I get back." He stepped out of the shower and heard the door slam as she left. Good riddance. Now he could think.

∗   ∗   ∗

Matt let her drive another three blocks, then flagged her down. He waited until she pulled to the curb, jerked the emergency, and walked to her car, shield in his pocket. Christie looked up at him, glazed and uncomprehending. He signaled the backup officer to stay put, opened the door to slide next to her, and cracked the window.

"You got anything for me?"

She nodded and opened her purse, then handed him an eyewash bottle. It was a little less than half-full and not five hundred dollars' worth by any stretch of the imagination. "Is this all?"

She nodded dully.

"I can't give you five hundred for this, honey. Where's the rest?"

"I don't have it." She laid her head against the steering wheel and started crying.

He tried to calm her down. "Why not? What's going on?"

The phone in his car buzzed. "I'll be right back," he told her, and went to answer it.

It was Sheets. "He's leaving, I'm going to stay on him. My partner still with you?"

"Yeah, she's here. Whatever you do, don't lose him."

By the time he returned to Christie, she was incoherent. He rolled the windows all the way down to let in the freezing air, and finally she calmed down enough to talk to him.

"Where is it, baby? You promised me."

"I didn't get it. I left it there," she told him, shivering in the chilly wind. "I don't want to see him again."

"Why not? What happened?"

"It doesn't matter. It's over and I hate him."

He sighed, knowing he would have to decide, and

fast. *Not enough evidence versus a bird in the hand.*
Make the right decision, Halston. Don't blow it now.
Screw it. His gut told him this was as good as it was
going to get. He reached out the window and waved his
hand to summon the backup.

"I'm going to have to arrest you, honey."

She looked at him, stricken.

He showed her his badge. The backup officer pulled
her car behind Christie's vehicle and came to the driver
window with her shield. "This is Officer Arnold," he told
her. "She'll read you your rights. Please step outside."

Christie's tears turned to hysterical laughter as she
got out of the car. Officer Arnold's voice droned
through the Miranda warning given to every arrestee.

"What's going to happen to me?"

Christie submitted to a preliminary search by the
woman officer while he ran it down. "We're going to
charge you with a whole string of things, starting with
possession. I think we can prove you helped transport
drugs across state lines for the purpose of illegal sale."
He picked up the plastic bottle. "Supplying illegal drugs
to an undercover officer. If this matches the stuff that's
been showing up in Chicago, the charge could go to
manslaughter, maybe murder."

She nodded miserably. "I knew it. I knew the minute
she died. I said so, and he wouldn't believe me. This is
about Cathy, isn't it?" She collapsed suddenly and sank
to the sidewalk. "I didn't mean to do it. I didn't know
what she was going to do with it."

"Is this what you gave her?"

She was spilling it all. "I told her to be careful. I told her
it was dangerous. Curt said no one would know. He said it
was all taken care of, but I knew this would happen."

None of this was admissible. She hadn't waived her

right to an attorney. He had to either shut her up or go for Curt.

"You got this from Curt?"

She nodded again. He and the officer helped her stand.

"Listen to me, Christie. Four months ago in Chicago, five kids got hold of a batch of drugs and had a swimming pool party. Three of them drowned, and two disappeared into the twilight zone. They're still in comas. For all intents, they're dead. One of them is the police commissioner's niece, so we're talking big-time problems here."

She tried to look away, and he caught her face, forced her to hear him. "We know the street supplier who sold it to them, we know another batch came in two months later and junkies wound up in intensive care all over town. I think we can prove the stuff came in on your flights, and we know someone on board the plane was using a phony name on his ticket. We know it's a man. We have pictures of Curt at your place, you just gave me a sample of the drugs he's selling. About twenty minutes ago, the supplier picked Curt's face out of forty guys, and the girl at the ticket counter is pretty sure it's him, too.

"If he gets out of this, he'll do it again, Christie. You gotta help me stop him from killing these kids. You and I are the only ones who can do it. Will you testify against him?"

She stared at him, horrified.

"Make it right for Cathy. Make it right for these kids. Get this son of a bitch off the street. He's dangerous and he's killing people. We gotta put him away and you gotta help me. Will you do it?"

She nodded slowly.

"Everything you know?"

"Everything," she choked, tears running down her face.

"Good girl."

He turned to the backup officer. "I'll wait for another female officer to make sure it's clean. I don't want any screwups on this arrest." The officer moved to her vehicle and picked up her mike. "I got bad news," she shouted to him. "He made Sheets."

His stomach dropped. "When?"

"Just now. Stopped in a mom-and-pop, disappeared out the back, and came around. Wanted to know why he was being followed. Sheets told him he was crazy and drove away—says he circled around, tried to pick him up again, but he was gone." She gave him the location. About seventeen miles out on Interstate 1. What the hell was he doing out there?

He confronted Christie. "Do you know where he's going?"

"He told me he had a job interview."

"Interview, my ass." He was furious. Baylor had blown the tail. One more officer would have made the difference. Deliver him from small towns with inadequate manpower. He tried to calm down and think. Right now, he had no choice. He'd have to put Curt away without the sale, and he'd have to stay close to Christie until they had her statement on paper. "Forget the backup. Let's get her booked." He looked at Christie. "Anything else you can tell me?"

"I hate him."

"Yeah, well, get in line." He turned to the officer. "I'll follow you." He walked to the Camaro, and it began to snow in earnest.

Ten minutes later they arrived at the police station.

Officer Arnold got out of her car and handed him a maroon ring box. "Had it in her bra," she said sheepishly.

He broke it open and stared at a beautiful emerald-cut diamond ring. "What the hell?"

"She says it's his."

"Whose, Curt's?" He looked over his shoulder at Christie, in tears again, sitting in the back of Arnold's car.

"She says she switched it for the acid she was supposed to get for you, and he's got it on him right now."

"What do you mean, switched it?"

"She says she was leaving him a note, found the ring in the pocket of his jacket. She took it, put the bottle in his pocket, and split."

"Which means the first time he looks in his pocket, he's going to beeline for her apartment. Who's covering?"

"Blake. I already called him."

He began to breathe a little easier. Maybe it would straighten out after all.

An hour later, Christie had been booked; she'd called an attorney, and he had a complete statement on its way to Chicago. The symbol on the ring box had been traced to a wholesale jeweler in Chicago, who said the ring had been sold to a man fitting Baylor's description; he'd accepted a previously purchased stone as down payment and received the four-thousand-dollar balance in cash yesterday afternoon. His description of the earlier ring matched the engagement ring stolen from Leanna.

Matt stared out the window at the early snow. *Now all I have to do is find you, you cheap, vicious son of a bitch.*

Then it hit him. Yesterday. Curt had been in Chicago two days ago with Leanna; the street rat had been contacted and a buy set up. Curt had gone back yesterday and paid four thousand cash to buy an engagement ring—money he apparently didn't have one day earlier. Made a special trip to do it. He'd blown off his dealer and sold the drugs elsewhere.

He hadn't shown up yet at Christie's. Had he converted the money into a ring, easy to transport, easily salable? For all intents Curt had dumped her. If he hadn't come back for the ring or the money, was he already gone?

Or was it just possible that he was still going to try to get married to Leanna? He called the inn. No answer. After seventeen rings, he slid through the snow to his car and hauled ass.

30

No promises . . .

 Leanna pulled the woolen muffler closer
around her chin and scraped a boot against the dock.
She was wearing Matt's hunter green suede jacket and
drew strength from the scent of him and its warmth.
The air hung cold and damp around her body, still as
cotton batting; every sound was dulled, and the occasional creak of the boats nudging each other against
the dock was faint. She couldn't hear the lap of the
water against the pilings, but she could feel snowflakes
hitting her face and eyelashes on a pretty regular basis
and knew it was snowing. A gray, fall day that didn't
usually show up until well after Thanksgiving.

She bruised the sprig of lavender between her fingers and tipped her head to enjoy its fragrance. It wasn't
as if she hadn't known about Matt and Christie. It
wasn't as if he hadn't warned her he'd be leaving town.
After her initial upset this morning, she'd identified her
reaction to his phone conversation as the jealousy that it

was. Parker and Jillian had been right. No one had had to tell her she'd fallen in love. She'd figured it out all by herself, and this afternoon she'd faced up to two more things: telling herself it didn't matter that he was leaving was a lie, and the fact that it mattered greatly was going to be her first genuine test of emotion over someone she had fallen in love with.

Making love with him had been everything she'd dreamed it could be, and more. He'd been incredibly gentle and caring, and their passion had soared beyond anything she'd ever imagined.

Absolutely the last person she wanted to see was Curt, but he and Annie had joined her a few minutes ago, interrupting her sweet memories and introspection; she decided it was time to be honest and straightforward with him. Despite Matt's leaving, despite his seeing Christie this morning, last night had been nothing short of wondrous, and anything Curt would say to her couldn't possibly change her feelings. Matt Halston hadn't gone away from her yet, and until he did, she intended to spend every possible moment with him.

Curt listened impatiently as the old bird cackled on about the weather being so odd for this time of year. She was trying to build a nest between himself and Leanna, fumbling at her coat and tying a scarf around her head. He confidently patted the lump in his jacket pocket under his raincoat. She was wasting her time. And his.

Ignoring his attempts at subtlety, she'd been blabbing for at least ten minutes about one thing or another, and he'd been polite to her as long as he could stand it. "I have something private to say to Leanna," he interrupted. "I don't want to be rude, but would you mind leaving us alone?"

She blinked at him and then looked at Leanna. "Out here? In this weather?" she objected. "It's snowing."

"I'm aware that it's snowing," he said impatiently. "Are you aware your phone's ringing again?" He hadn't thought to wear boots and his feet were getting cold; he didn't want her buzzing around and disturbing his conversation, here or in the house.

"They'll call back if they want me."

She'd said something to that effect three times already. It was crystal clear that she didn't want to leave him alone with Leanna, and he was getting irritated. Finally Leanna solved the stalemate. "Curt and I have a few things to talk out, Annie. I'll see you in a few minutes."

"See that you do. Don't catch your death out here." The old biddy got to her feet with maddening slowness and made her way up the yard toward the ringing phone. She glanced back at him over her shoulder at every other step. Nosy old bird. She didn't like it at all that the two of them were out of earshot.

By the time Annie reached the phone, it had stopped ringing, and she looked out the front door to the parking area. The only car was Curt's, with a light covering of snow across its windshield. Where was Matt? He'd as good as said Leanna wasn't safe alone with Curt. Every other day of the week he was sleeping upstairs this time of day, but today, of all days, he was gone. She returned to the kitchen window to keep watch on the two figures by the lake.

"Look, it's time we were honest with each other," Curt said quickly.

"Yes. I agree with you absolutely."

"Okay, here's what I want to say." He realized he was rushing things and tried to slow down. He moved closer to her on the log bench and reached into his pocket. "I made a special trip to Chicago yesterday to get this for you."

"Curt, please, let me—"

"Shhhh, I want to finish," he insisted. "Now I want us to get married, and I want you to wear this."

Leanna gave up trying. Jamming her fists into Matt's jacket pockets for courage to tackle the conversation she'd been avoiding, she heard the rustle of Curt's clothing. It would be over today; she'd tell him no and he would be out of her life. Something in her stomach was buoyant at the thought, and she smiled; closing her eyes to feel the snowflakes drifting onto her cheeks, she held on to the sprig of lavender and burrowed into the warmth of Matt's jacket around her shoulders.

"It's a replacement—"

His fingers closed around the cold glass of a bottle wrapped in a piece of paper. He drew them out of his pocket in disbelief. "Go to hell you bastard!!" was printed on the note. The ring was gone. Christie! God damn her! He eased the bottle back in his pocket before crumpling the paper and throwing it into the water.

"Well, I'm real embarrassed," he said smoothly. "I can't believe I picked up the wrong box. What I was going to give you was a replacement for the engagement ring that was stolen, but it looks like I was so nervous I left it in my apartment. I'm sorry."

She was smiling, and it annoyed him even further that she didn't bother to give him the courtesy of facing his direction. "But I still want an answer. I think I've been real patient, Leanna. I made a wrong move, and

I've paid for it a hundred ways. I had a normal man's reaction to a desirable woman who's, unfortunately, afraid of sex. I don't know what else to do, so I'm gonna ask you one more time. If you still don't have an answer, I'll respect it, but I'll have to move on," he threatened.

"I have an answer," she said to him, eyes still closed. "I can't marry you."

He lost hold of his temper. It wasn't supposed to work this way. "Can't or won't?"

"I don't think there's a way to say it that wouldn't hurt your feelings, I'm sorry."

"Sorry, hell." He grabbed her by the jacket, pissed at her condescension. "I just want to know why not, that's all. Just why the hell not? Who are you to say no to me?"

From the corner of his eye he saw old busybody Chatfield open the back door and start down the lawn. She was carrying a frying pan. He laughed and tightened his hold on Leanna, determined to get an answer. He jerked her to her feet and pulled her out onto the dock. It was blanketed with snow and the going was slippery.

"First you're willing, then you're not, then you are. When you came to my apartment you were. Changed your mind when I got a hard-on, didn't you, honey? You left me hurting for two hours." He jerked her again. "You don't do that to a man. Your problem is you don't know what you want. You don't want a man, that's for sure. You keep me dangling for months and finally say no. I just want to know who you think you are."

She'd clammed up like a rock, and he was losing it. "Answer me!"

"Take your hands off me, Curt," she said to him, shaken. "I don't have to tell you anything."

Annie's voice came crackling through the still air. "You let go of her, you hear? You leave her alone right now!"

"Back off, old lady. You come out here, I'll dump her in the lake." She didn't pause and he warned her again. "I mean it."

"You do and you'll go in after her."

Leanna was twisting in his grasp. The footing was treacherous, but he held her with both hands and edged closer to the water. The old woman kept coming and he realized she wasn't going to stop. He waited until she'd reached the dock, then pushed the girl as hard as he could and watched with satisfaction as she sailed into the lake. Served her right. He heard her gasp as she hit the water, then turned to face the old woman. "You want to go in, too, you old hen?"

"Annie!" Leanna was yelling from the water. "Annie?"

The old woman slipped on the snowy dock, going down on one knee. The frying pan clanged against the wood as she used it to break her fall. "You get out of here!" she screamed at him. Both women were making too much noise hollering back and forth, and the whole situation was botched. It was way past time to get the hell out.

"Annie, you be careful!" cried Leanna. "He's crazy!"

"Don't you worry about me," Annie yelled back. "You just grab on to something!"

Curt dodged around the fallen woman and started up the lawn toward the parking lot. The yard was slick with snow, and he was careful. About twenty feet up, he heard a car arrive and five seconds later the cowboy came charging around the corner of the house. He had a badge in his hand and a gun out. A cop. A son-of-a-bitchin' cop! He *had* been followed. He *knew* it! He *wasn't* paranoid! Oh, Christ, and he was dead meat unless he got rid of the acid. The lake. All he had to do was throw it in the lake.

He switched back, his mind working furiously. The bottle would float. He'd have to empty it. He grabbed it out of his pocket, unscrewed the top, then sent the plastic cap spinning into the lake. Before he could throw the bottle, the old lady was on him with the frying pan; the bottle flew out of his fingers and dropped over the edge of the dock. It was too heavy to float without the cap. All they'd find was water in it. He was home free. Unless it had gone into one of the boats. He'd have to make sure.

Matt sprinted down the yard toward the dock and fired a warning shot in the air. Curt didn't seem to hear it. Annie was going at him with a skillet of some kind, and Curt had knocked her down. They were too close together for a clean shot. He fired again. Curt was scrambling toward the boats, and Annie had him by the ankle. She let go of him as Matt reached the dock, and he hit Curt broadside hard enough to knock him into the lake. Annie scrambled to her feet. "Leanna's in the water," she yelled at him. "She's in the water!"

He dropped to the edge of the dock and saw Leanna clinging to one of the pilings, shivering with cold. "We'll get you out," he shouted. She held up one arm, and he and Annie both tried to catch hold of her hand, but they were frustrating inches too short. "We can't reach you," he called to her. "Hold on to the dock and don't let go." Steps of an old rotten ladder to the water level were broken or missing, and the lake was so low that without a boat there was no way to get to her.

Leanna went weak with relief. Matt was here and somehow it would be okay. It had taken her moments after hitting the water to orient herself by listening to sounds from the dock. She'd tried to warn Annie to stay away and was terrified that Curt was going to hurt her for interfering. About the time she'd located the pilings, there had been what could only be gunshots, and she'd been frantic until she heard Annie shout to someone that she was in the water.

She was so cold that it was an effort to breathe, and then Matt's voice had come through the blackness like a lifeline, telling her what to do, giving her strength. She'd reached as high as she could, but each time she let go of the piling to reach toward him, her body sank deeper into the water. She wrapped both arms around the wood and used one foot to pry her boot off the other, then managed to kick off the second one to get rid of the weight, and waited for Matt's voice.

At the other end of the dock, Curt hauled himself into a wooden rowboat, untied it, and deliberately tipped over a small metal dinghy; he pushed away from the dock.

Matt let him go. The bastard probably knew that without a boat, it would take him longer to get Leanna out of the water, and was buying time. How far could he get in a rowboat? Unless he managed to get it off this planet, it wouldn't be far enough. Stripping down to his T-shirt and kicking off his shoes, he grimly gauged the distance to the nearest shoreline. He hated cold and he hated water. "I'm coming in after you," he called to Leanna. In the rapidly falling snow, a heavy mist was springing off the top of the water, graying things out and making it difficult to judge, but it looked to be about thirty feet. He handed Annie his weapon. "He can't get away," he told her. "Don't shoot him unless you have to."

The last thing he heard was a grim, "What if I want to?" before the water hit him like a fist, took his breath away for a full ten seconds. If he'd known it was so cold, he'd have had second thoughts about shooting Curt for the rowboat. He reached Leanna and released her fingers from the piling, unzipped the jacket, and pulled it away from her body. "Kick your shoes off," he instructed.

"I already did."

"Good girl!" He kissed her icy mouth, and her whole body was shivering. The water was less than fifty degrees, and hypothermia wasn't too far in the distance. "You with me?" She nodded. "We're gonna go straight out about fifteen feet and then to the left, just out around this bank," he said quickly. "Can you swim that far?"

She nodded again, scared but game. "Don't leave me."

"I'll be right next to you."

She allowed him to pull her away from the dock, and he gave her a push. He heard her start counting her strokes. She was already too cold, and he knew she wasn't going to make it without his help.

"Look out!!" It was Annie's voice. He rolled over in the water as she yelled his name; Curt was rowing toward them through the mist. Matt thrashed the water to get to Leanna's side, then sank down to feel for bottom. Nothing. It was still too deep. He came up again, put one arm around her waist, and kicked for all he was worth. She'd already been in the water for quite a while, and he knew he was only good for another few minutes. Curt was ten feet away and still coming. He took his bearings and pushed Leanna as hard as he could before turning to position himself between her and the rowboat. He heard the sound of a shot a split second before a heavy oar came crashing down across his neck and shoulders with the force of a pile driver.

His muscles refused to function, and he felt himself sinking under the water. Little by little, sensation came back into his body, and he fought his way to the surface. Still underwater, he heard the muffled report of a second shot, and when his head broke the surface again, the echo was dying away. Curt was no longer visible in the boat, but the mist had thickened and he couldn't find Leanna. One of the oars was floating nearby. Useless.

He used the edge of the rowboat to pull himself up and search the water. When he spotted her, she was still swimming but off course and thrashing toward the middle of the lake. Annie's voice was shouting at her to turn around. Deadened echoes were bouncing off the rocks and all over the place. He could barely understand Annie's words; he doubted if Leanna could hear her at all; he forced himself not to shout but to follow her. He pushed off against the boat, and it seemed a century of time, but eventually he reached her side and turned her in the water. The minute she stopped swimming, exhaustion moved into her body; he cradled her chin with his elbow and held her against his chest, began treading water for the both of them.

When he thought he couldn't last another minute, a dinghy materialized out of the mist, and he recognized

Sheets. Backup had arrived. He'd never been so glad to see anyone in his life. It took his last bit of energy to help lift Leanna out of the water; he was too cold and sore to do more than cling to the little metal boat until they reached shallow water.

Annie had gone to the house and was waiting with several blankets wrapped around her teakettle, which had half a dozen teabags inside; as soon as Matt carried Leanna safely to the dock, Annie and Officer Arnold immediately surrounded her with a couple of warmed quilts. They sat her on the log bench, poured her a cup of tea, and covered the kettle with another blanket before placing it in her lap for warmth.

A woolen blanket around his shoulders, Matt began to function. With Leanna safely in Annie's care, he turned his attention to Curt. Sheets had gone back to retrieve the drifting rowboat with Curt huddled inside, bleeding profusely from a shoulder wound and cursing a steady stream of invective at the world in general and Annie in particular. By the time they arrived at the dock, his body was jerking in shock.

Paramedics arrived, and two of them moved into the boat to assist Curt while a third began tending Leanna. Annie left Leanna's side long enough to station herself at the edge of the dock. "There's a pharmaceutical bottle in there," she said to Matt. "I saw him go after it." She spied it next to Curt's feet and pointed it out.

Curt lunged abruptly to the side of the boat and succeeded in grabbing the evidence that would destroy him; the paramedics scrambled to hold on as the boat lurched in the water. Victorious, Curt held the bottle over the side; Matt leaned down to seize his hand and prevent him from pouring it out, but Curt's added weight tilted the rowboat violently and, one arm useless,

Curt toppled backward into the bottom of the boat, shrieking in pain. The brown bottle went spinning over his head, the arc of its contents spilling before it smashed neatly in two against a metal oarlock and disappeared over the side into the murky water.

Curt tried to spit it out, tried to force the bitter taste out of his mouth and nose, out of his eyes, but the concentrated narcotic seized his breath and destroyed his strength. The medics grabbed his arms and shoulders, lifting him up, and Matt pulled Curt's convulsing body onto the dock; moments later he was on a stretcher, being rushed into one of the ambulances and on his way to Traxx Hospital.

Matt found his way to Leanna's side, and Annie wrapped another blanket around his shoulders. "How're you doing?" he asked gently. The same paramedic who'd treated her for the mugging was taking her blood pressure.

"No h-h-hospitals," she said, her jaw set stubbornly. "I h-h-hate hospitals."

Matt laughed and leaned down to kiss her. "No promises."

The paramedic shrugged and shook his head. "Seems fine to me," he said wonderingly. "She ever do anything normal?"

Matt kissed Leanna again. "She kisses great," he reported.

Suddenly the whole world began to arrive. Sheets and Arnold hurried to tape off the area as photographers and reporters came skidding down the lawn with questions and flashing strobes.

Before it built to chaos, Matt and Annie helped Leanna into the house; Annie shooed everyone out of the kitchen and shut the door while Leanna called her father to let him know she was safe. Sam insisted on seeing her and told her he was sending Parker to pick her up. She'd changed clothes by the time her brother arrived, and while a local television crew from Wellington had Sheets and Arnold on camera near the dock, Matt escorted her and Parker quietly out the front door. When Leanna called half an hour later, he had gone.

31

Promises . . .

Leanna's father had taken a bad turn. She'd stayed at his home since the night of Curt's arrest, and Matt had mixed feelings as he drove up the winding lane of the Bowmont estate. He'd spent the last three days wrapping up the investigation: doing paperwork, tracking down phone records to locate Curt's last deal, arranging the arrest of yet another street rat in Chicago. Working with Christie on details. More paperwork. Trying and failing to arrange a couple of days off to unwind before returning to Chicago.

The diver he'd hired had taken three hours to locate the bottle cap and glass fragments at Annie's dock. Also rescued were Leanna's boots and his green suede jacket, which were drying in Annie's basement; the sprig of lavender he'd found in its pocket had taken up residence in his wallet.

He'd managed a couple of conversations with her, mostly about Curt and what had happened with the mugger. He'd talked separately with her father and, with his agreement, had deliberately eliminated the connection between the two events. There was no point in letting her know that she'd been stalked and targeted for an entire year; being blind was enough of a burden in life without worrying about nut cases.

She'd accepted his explanation of Christie without comment. He'd spent three sleepless nights trying to fit her into his life in Chicago, and so far he hadn't come up with a solution. His current salary meant sharing a moderate apartment without live-in help or someone to drive for her. It wasn't much of an offer for Sam Bowmont's daughter. He'd only known her a month, and he didn't see Sam Bowmont agreeing to subsidize an affair with his daughter.

Inside the mansion, he was unable to shut out the overt wealth that constituted the Bowmont home. Marble staircasing, Austrian crystal lamps and chandeliers, an intricately parqueted hallway that led to richly carpeted rooms, sprays of fresh flowers in huge, designer vases on an antique lacquered table in the foyer and again on a monstrous white grand piano in the living room—expensive paintings, or he missed his guess, on most of the walls. For a nickel-dime cooker, Curt had had grand aspirations.

He saw Leanna first. She was seated at the end of a massive yellow suede sofa, holding the hand of an obviously ill man in a wheelchair. The sight of her in a fawn silk dress that matched her eyes, half a dozen ropes of pearls, and looking positively wonderful got something inside him going a little faster. An attractive couple, the young man obviously her brother, sat next to her on the couch and stood as he entered.

He addressed the older man. "Mr. Bowmont?" He

saw Leanna respond to the sound of his voice and come alive. What the sight of her had been to him, he realized, his voice had been to her. The frail man nodded and reached out; Matt hurried across an expanse of white carpet to take his hand. He leaned down and brushed Leanna's lips as he kissed her cheek, not at all the kiss he wanted to give her. "You look beautiful." She held on to his sleeve long enough to introduce him. Jolene Llowell, her brother's saucy fiancée, gave him a frankly appreciative stare. He didn't envy Bowmont, Jr.; she was going to be a handful as a wife.

"Well, Detective Halston, I owe you a great many things, starting with my daughter's life." Parker Bowmont echoed a similar statement and shook his hand. Jolene gave him a smile.

"Well, I'm not sure about that, sir," he answered. "She was doing pretty well by herself, but I thank you. My backup team was on its way when Annie called for help, so it would have worked out either way." He turned to Leanna. "Here's your necklace." He placed the small box he was carrying in her hands, then sat on a nearby chair, declined an offer of something to drink, and watched her face. She didn't open the box, nor did she look away from his direction.

"We've had it for a while," he continued, trying to keep it simple. "Your mugger was apprehended trying to pawn it. He's in jail and pleading guilty, so you won't have to make an appearance. Your purse and wallet should arrive within the next few days."

He cleared his throat, determined to get through it all. "As I explained to your daughter, Mr. Bowmont, I'm on loan from Chicago's twelfth district. We had a bad drug situation a few months ago, and when the same formula showed up in Cathy Rice's system, I was sent in to follow up on it. Kind of a long shot, but it paid off."

"I see." The old man's good eye didn't waver. "So you're leaving. I was kind of hoping you'd be in town for a while."

"Well, we have things pretty well wrapped up. I'll be going back shortly."

"I understand Curt died yesterday," said her brother.

"Heart failure. He never regained consciousness. They took him off the respirator at his father's request."

"Are you sure he's the one you were looking for?"

He nodded. "We have evidence that he was keeping chemicals at his girlfriend's apartment. We found empty bottles and the boxes at his place. It was his own formula, highly toxic, amateur, really. Pretty deadly when it's new. Fortunately, it breaks down rapidly, and we're satisfied we have it all."

"My daughter thinks very highly of you," Sam said to him roughly.

He flushed. Leanna was blushing as well. "Well, Mr. Bowmont, I'm glad to hear it. You have a very fine daughter."

"Yes, I do. And I still have her, thanks to you."

At that moment, an impeccably dressed woman with auburn hair made an entrance and was introduced as Sam's wife. Matt contained his shock but broke a cold sweat. He'd been inches from leaving Nicholson's with her that night. A private apartment? Sweet Jesus! "Mrs. Bowmont."

"Alice Faye," she directed. "I wanted to express my appreciation for everything you've done for my step-daughter, Officer Halston. I feel particularly vindicated since it certainly looked as if she would marry him despite my opinion. Thank you for rescuing her."

When Leanna seemed tolerant of her stepmother's high-handed attitude, he relaxed half an inch. "Not at all, Mrs. Bowmont." He was conscious of softening his voice, and distinctly uncomfortable.

She looked at him.

"Alice Faye," he amended. Stepmother or not, this was not one of the meetings he was interested in repeating. The longer he stayed, the more time she'd have to remember. He looked at his watch. "Unfortunately, I do have to go," he said awkwardly. "I have a flight to catch. I appreciate your taking the time to meet with me." He rose to his feet, eyes on Leanna. "Whenever you're in Chicago, just let me know."

He shook hands all around and took his last opportunity to kiss Leanna, on the cheek, squeezed her hand, then got out. Parker and Alice Faye walked him to the door; Leanna did not, electing to stay with her father, and there was a giant empty feeling in his gut as he addressed her brother. "Take care of her," he mumbled, and left. As he neared the end of the drive, he passed Annie's station wagon, waved, then headed for the inn to pack.

Annie wiped her feet and stepped into the foyer to look around. "Boy, this is some palace," she said to the housekeeper, and handed her a still warm pie covered with a linen towel. "Feels like the Taj Mahal." The housekeeper juggled the pie to take her coat. "Can I peek in the kitchen before I go?"

The woman laughed and nodded. "I have the feeling you could do just about anything you want," she confided.

Annie patted her wig into place and double-checked her Sunday dress in the six-foot mirror. "Well, okay, I guess I'm ready." She stepped gingerly onto the white carpet in the living room without checking behind to see if she was leaving tracks. Anybody with a white carpet ought to know how to keep it clean, she reasoned.

"Hey, cutie," she greeted Leanna. "Gosh, it's good to see you. Brought you folks a cherry pie. They're frozen cherries, but hell, they was fresh when I picked 'em."

Sam Bowmont made up his mind at that moment that he was going to have a piece of cherry pie and his doctors could go hang. What was it going to do, kill him? He laughed and offered Annie Chatfield his hand. This woman had gone after someone threatening his daughter, armed with nothing more than a skillet. He watched her smiling face as she checked out his home with an unabashed and refreshingly honest curiosity, and he wished mightily that he'd made friends with her years ago.

After half an hour of her company, he sent the rest of his family away and had himself wheeled into his library so he could talk to her. "You and young Sprengsten have done some fine work on the old Hartford place." She nodded and gave him her full attention. "I'd really be interested in your opinion of a couple of people living there, starting with Matt Halston," he began. "I'd like to know everything you can tell me about him."

Jay handed Jeannette Stone the court order to open her records and settled onto his chair while she read through it. "This seems in order," she acknowledged. "I remember your mother very well. I was the first woman attorney to hang my shingle in Wellington, and she was my third case, bless her little feminist heart. My mother and father were the first two. They each came in to have

their wills prepared, so I counted them as separate
clients. But she was my first court appearance."

"My mom was a pretty special woman."

"She was indeed. I've pulled all my files on the annulment as well as your adoption. What is it you want to
know?"

She studied him carefully while he told her as
unemotionally as possible about Jim Sprengsten's disappearance, the recent discovery of his probable suicide,
and his mother's directive at the time of her death.
Finally he cited his aunt's decision to move for custody
of Danielle. "I don't look too good on paper, so I need
you to represent me. And I want to know who I am, I
guess."

"You seem to be handling this pretty well."

"I'm not sleeping too good," he admitted.

She nodded. "I've thought a lot about this since you
called, and just so you know, I don't think I've ever met
any two people more in love than your parents, and I
mean Jim Sprengsten worshiped the ground your
mother walked on. And I also remember he almost postponed their wedding because I couldn't get a hearing
date for your adoption less than two weeks later. He
wanted it the next day."

Jay drank in the meaning of her words, his anger
gone, replaced by something more important. Peace.

"They met here in Wellington when he bought the
house she received as part of the settlement. He tore it
down, made it a playground, and gave it to the city. I'll
bet you didn't know that."

He shook his head. "No. I didn't."

"She adored him, I know that much for a fact. She
told me that when she met him, she'd 'found heaven.'
I remember very well, because I was jealous." The

attorney smiled at him. "Probably still am. Now what else can I tell you?"

"Did you ever see Samuel Parker?"

"Once. In court. For about twenty minutes. Is that what all this is about? You want to find him?"

"I don't think his name was Samuel Parker." He began the list of reasons he'd spent the last several days compiling. "They were married in December, and I was born in July the following year. I was full term, so they had to get married."

She eyed him carefully. "It happens."

"He wouldn't have changed his name, so she was under the impression he was Samuel Parker at the time they met. He listed his business as Midland Insurance here in Wellington. According to Midland, no one named Samuel Parker ever worked there. Social Security won't tell me who the number on my birth certificate belongs to, but they will confirm that it is not Samuel Parker's.

"I've met with the people in the legal office he used for the annulment. His attorney's dead, but his records indicate the guy was a walk-in client, always paid in cash, used a post office box for correspondence, and didn't have a phone—always called him. According to his notes, the guy demanded that the annulment be completed by August 30, 1971. He was fanatic about it; he instituted the action, insisted on an annulment and not a divorce, and volunteered bigamy as the reason to make it happen."

She looked at him. "Assuming all this is accurate, and he wasn't Samuel Parker, what are you getting at?"

"I think my father is Samuel Parker Bowmont. He owned Midland at the time, he could have created a false identity very easily, particularly one so close to his own name. According to county records, his first wife died about a year after he married my mother, which would have made him a bigamist, and he married his current wife one day after the annulment."

"Okay. We'll assume for purposes of this discussion that Sam Bowmont is your father. Now what?" She sat back on her chair. "I thought very highly of your mother, and in honor of that, I'm going to give this to you pretty straight. If you're after an inheritance, it's not likely to happen. If he's gone to this much trouble, he doesn't want you in his life, and believe me, he can keep you out. Biological children get disinherited all the time, and particularly since there's a clause eliminating him from further responsibility where you're concerned.

"The best that could happen is he'd agree to give you some money to keep you quiet, which amounts to extortion and is called a nuisance suit. I think you're grasping at straws, and I don't see what any of this has to do with custody of your sister." She sat forward again. "A judge won't give a tinker's damn if Sam Bowmont's your father, and going after him for money is not something I'd be comfortable representing you in."

Jay stared at her. "I don't care about an inheritance. You think I'd show up at his house? Wreck his family? Make his kids feel the way I feel?" He got to his feet in irritation. "His daughter is one of the best friends I have. I wouldn't do that to her, let alone to him."

He began pacing the room. "I just want to know if he's my father. I don't want money. What I want is for Danni to stay home with her family. If I go into court knowing who I am, I think I can be ten times better at convincing a judge that I can take care of her. I just need to get my head on straight, so let me finish this, okay?"

She nodded, clearly relieved.

"Bowmont owns three companies, and spokesmen for all three claim they have a policy of no photographs. It doesn't make sense. He's the owner, why wouldn't he want photographs?"

"He's eccentric, he's careful, he's afraid of being easily identified, kidnapped . . ."

"Okay, he's all of the above. Nothing was published at the time of either of his weddings except a picture of his wife, and there isn't anything available from any of the charities he supports. But I managed to find a photograph, and I'd like you to look at it and tell me if you think it's Samuel Parker."

He gave her the Xerox of a photograph and waited while she gave it close examination.

"He was much older," she responded slowly. "He was probably forty when I saw him, and that was twenty years ago."

"Sam Bowmont's sixty-one."

She glanced over the top of the paper. "This boy is what, sixteen, seventeen?"

"Seventeen."

She looked back at the picture. "I couldn't be sure that this person grew up to be the same man I saw in court. Where did you get this?"

"From the newspaper. Bowmont was involved in an automobile accident his last year in high school. They published that picture from the year before. He was pretty badly hurt, and as far as I can find out, nothing exists after this was taken."

He handed her another photograph. "This is a high school photo of me at seventeen."

Jeannette compared the two. "I'll grant you there's a very strong resemblance, but it still proves nothing."

"But what do you think?"

"I don't 'think,' I'm a lawyer. I deal in fact."

He sat back, defeated. "Well, it was a shot."

She returned the pictures to him. "As a part of the settlement," she said pensively, "Samuel Parker agreed to pay your mother's legal fees. They were paid in cash, and arrived by messenger. Struggling new attorneys notice things like that." She smiled and paused a moment before she continued. "The man I saw in court was blind in one of his eyes—left, I think."

"Sam Bowmont's blind in his left eye," he said slowly. "It's milky white." He waited, but she said nothing further. "And?" he prompted. "How many facts do I need?"

"I'd say it was strongly circumstantial, but I still wouldn't take it to court."

"Can he do that?" Danni looked up at Stephen with distrust in her eyes. "Can a judge give me to Aunt Jess? He can't do that, can he?"

Stephen looked her, uncomprehending. "A judge?"

"She said a judge was gonna decide. She said Jay should have told me by now."

He moved to the phone. "I don't have a clue what she's talking about." There was no answer at Jessica's number. "She's probably on her way over here," he said worriedly. "Did you tell her you were leaving?"

Danni didn't answer, just slammed up the stairs to her room. Stephen stared after his normally happy sister and wished for Annie's strength. Sure enough, a few seconds later his aunt's car came skidding up the drive at twice its normally cautious speed. He opened the door as she parked and got out of her vintage Chevrolet. "Danni's here," he called out.

Hatless, an indication of her distress, his aunt slowed her pace to a fast walk and came into the house as Jay pulled into the drive in the Traxx pickup, with Annie's station wagon right behind him.

"She's here, she's fine," Stephen repeated calmly.

Jay and Annie came through the door with a draft of cold air and a barrage of questions.

"What's wrong, Aunt Jess?"

"What's going on? Is everything all right?"

Jessica promptly burst into tears and hid her face. "I just love her. I miss her. I can't stand the thought of the holidays without her. Christmas . . . I can't work . . ." She was unable to continue.

Annie took Jessica's arm and firmly guided the crying woman into the music room. "Now you come on in here," she commanded, "and let's us talk about this. Stephen, you make some tea. Where's Danni?"

"I'm up here," came a sullen voice.

"Well, come down here. We got some things to settle."

"I'm not going to live with Aunt Jess."

Jay raised his voice. "Danni, get down here."

"You promised. It was a Traxx promise. You said we'd be a family again." Her voice was frightened and threatening tears.

"Please come down. I don't want to argue about it." His voice was final, so she edged down the stairs and sat on the bottom step. "In here," he insisted. "We are a family and we're going to deal with this like a family. Where's Tommy and Charlie?"

"Upstairs." Danni's face was thunderous but she stepped inside the room.

Jay called Tommy and Charlie down as well and waited while they came silently into the room to sit by the fireplace, trying to figure out what was going on.

"Now." He surveyed the faces in the room. "Aunt Jess has asked for a hearing about Danni," he announced, and turned to face his aunt. "I haven't said anything to anyone in the family, Aunt Jess, because I was going to try to work it out with you first. I saw an attorney today. She assures me that I am in no danger of losing my sister."

Jessica, distraught, pressed her handkerchief against her mouth and made a move to get off the couch.

"Please, hear me out." Jay approached his aunt. "I owe you an apology. I think we all do, but I will speak for myself. It did not occur to me that you'd be so upset when the girls moved out."

Jessica's shoulders heaved with sobs, and he sat next to her on the sofa until she'd pulled herself together, while the others waited in silence. "I was focused solely on the promise to my mother, and I'm sorry. My mother's dead and you're very much alive. I forgot that. And I'm sorry. I'm sorry I didn't make it clear that I was not removing my sisters from your care. Four years of loving and caring creates a family, even if you fight—" He eyed Charlie, who ducked her head.

"It was never my intention to take away your family. I simply assumed you'd want your life to go back the way it used to be, and I didn't hear you when you said otherwise."

Jessica broke down again, and Annie poured her a wobbly cup of tea.

"And," he continued, "when I thought about the possibility of losing Danni, it nearly killed me. Then I realized that five years ago when we lost a father, you lost a brother. Now you feel like you're losing a child."

"Two," sobbed Jessica, and Charlie teared up, chewing her lip in distress.

"Aunt Jess, I am so sorry that I haven't told you that you're an important part of this family, and I promise you it would make me very happy if you'd be willing to live here with us. And that's a Traxx promise."

Jessica's wails started them all crying. Tears and hugs and assurances were shared all around and it became pandemonium for a few minutes. Danni crawled into Aunt Jessica's lap. Annie wiped her glasses and confronted their aunt. "Well, Jessie?"

Too emotional to speak, Jessica could only nod her head. "I don't care if it's in the basement," she managed finally. Even Charlie cheered her decision before everybody's tears started flowing again.

"Hot damn," cried Annie. "We got us another Sprengsten. You can have Matt's room, or Jillian's as soon as she moves out, or any room you want, for that matter. 'Ceptin' mine." She winked, and Jessica's face brightened with a teary smile before Annie crunched her in a hug and the Sprengstens smothered the both of them.

32

Promises . . .

By common consent, Curt's death was not generally a topic of discussion; however, for a time, things at Chatfield's were measured against the night of his arrest. Leanna had been gone since the night of, and Sam Bowmont had been taken to the hospital the day after, Matt had gone back to Chicago and Jillian had begun removal of her things to her father's house three days after, and Jessica started moving her life into Chatfield's two days after that.

With the custody hearing relegated to history, Jay became conscious of the ache caused by Jillian's absence. He called her parents' home and left word on four occasions, missing her each time for one reason or another, aggravating her father into calling him "one of the most persistent young souls he'd ever met." She'd avoided him at the inn pretty consistently since the night he'd gotten arrested for drinking, which hadn't been difficult because he'd been buried in searching out information for the attorney.

At the time, he'd convinced himself that as soon as Jolene married Parker he'd be able to get a better idea of how he felt about her sister, but the moment Jillian moved out he'd discovered that the lack of her presence was jarring. As if a light had gone out in his life.

He quizzed Leanna until she told him that Jillian planned to spend Thanksgiving with her grandparents, and he was finally able to get her on the phone a tight two hours before her flight to Orlando; she'd been vague and distracted, unsure when she intended to return. Aware that the Wellington airport was an hour away, he quickly drove to her father's house to see her and say good-bye.

He spent a stilted five minutes with Mrs. Llowell in the foyer before helping Dr. Llowell with the luggage; Jillian made a last minute call to make sure the flight hadn't been delayed. Her father mumbled and paced around the entry, looking at his watch while her mother eyed him and Jolene circumspectly.

"I think it's sweet that you came to see her off," Jolene said to him, hanging over the banister. "After they're gone, we'll have a few minutes to catch up before Parker gets here."

He gazed past her at Jillian on the phone in the living room and listened for her voice. "Is she spending Christmas with your grandparents, too?"

"She's coming back for my wedding. I don't know about Christmas," Jolene answered lazily. "I think she's planning to move to New York in January."

The Llowells nodded good-bye to him, and Dr. Llowell pointedly shepherded his wife out the door and into the family car.

"I heard your aunt's moving in. Do you still have your same room?" Jolene teased.

He tried to change the subject. "Where are you and Parker planning to live?" Jillian was writing something on a pad of paper, her hair falling down to cover her face.

Jolene brightened at his question and fiddled with the engagement ring that had to have cost Parker a bundle. "Oh, we haven't decided. Probably at his folks' for the moment. With his father being so ill, it's hard to make decisions about anything. We might get an apartment." She came down the stairs to wind her arm around his and looked up at him. "We're not having a big wedding because they don't expect him to make it until Christmas even," she confided. "There's just not enough time. I've been trying to get Parker to fly to Acapulco, but he wants his father there, which I understand, so that's out, too." She smiled knowingly. "So, are you lonely in that old bed by yourself?"

He looked at her in surprise, but before he could move away or respond, Jillian came in from the living room, carrying her coat. Jay opened the door for her, and Jolene moved with him, still arm in arm. Outside, their father started the engine.

Jillian acknowledged the two of them. "You both have a good Thanksgiving. I'll see you when I get back." A quick kiss for Jolene and a sealed-in smile in his direction, and she was gone.

He eased away from Jolene as Dr. Llowell carefully backed his Cadillac around the truck, down the snowy driveway, and then screeched its tires onto the street. He saw Jillian glance back for a moment and was highly aware of how it had looked to her. "I owe you a dance," he said quietly, and got in the truck.

"A dance?" Jolene looked at him, annoyed. "Why don't you stay a few minutes? You didn't answer me about your room."

"Are you and Parker planning to invite me to the wedding?" he asked pointedly.

"Would you come?" she taunted.

"Absolutely," he assured her. "I wouldn't miss it."

"Then I'll see that you're invited," she said tartly.

He looked at her for a long moment, then drove away.

Thanksgiving, the Sprengsten family held hands at the dining room table, and Jay's voice was filled with strength as he expressed for them all a genuine thanks for their good fortune. "I know Mom and Dad would be proud," he concluded quietly; hands clasped tighter all around, and it was an extra long time before the circle was broken. Amen.

Annie's turkey was rich and brown and golden, and there were generous helpings of traditional trimmings and dozens of homemade baking powder biscuits. Aunt Jessica's pumpkin pies and real whipped cream held center stage for dessert. It was about the most perfect day any one of them could remember.

When the phone rang a little after seven, Charlie leaped to answer it.

"Stephen," she teased. "It's Stephanieeeee . . . agaaaain," she singsonged.

Stephen colored and sauntered to the phone.

"It's the fourth time this week," she announced with the accuracy of sisterly scorekeeping.

"Charlie." It was Aunt Jessica's warning voice, and Charlie scooted back to the table for another sliver of pumpkin pie. Aunt Jess might be a pain, but she made pies as good as Annie's.

Friday after Thanksgiving, Jay went to see Leanna at her father's house. When she'd called to invite him over, the temptation to confront Sam had ballooned in his mind, but logic won out. For what purpose? The old man was dying, and there was enough hell in her life. He entered the Bowmont foyer with misgiving and handed over his parka to their housekeeper.

He looked around with detachment; his life would have been so vastly different that it was unimaginable. Leanna would have been his sister, Parker his brother. When she joined him and he kissed her cheek, he realized that much of his life wouldn't have been so different after all.

She took him into her father's library.

"Tell me about everyone," she demanded. He brought her up to date on Aunt Jess moving in, and Annie's new wig and the truce between Charlie and Stephen over Stephen's new girlfriend, then gave her the package that contained a giant piece of Annie's apple cobbler and a slice of Aunt Jessica's pumpkin pie. Leanna placed it on the desk and listened with relish, her face following his every motion. When he'd finished, she explained that her father had defied his doctors and, while he was in a great deal of pain, was still very much alive.

"Something wonderful's happened," she confided happily. "And I think it's part of why he's still here."

He looked at her, aware of something unusual but not quite certain what it was.

"I can see," she announced joyously. "Well, actually

not see, but I have light and dark instead of black, and the doctors say there's hope that I'll have some sight."

He was speechless. That was what was different. Her eyes were following his movements, not just his voice.

"It started with the headaches I got when you clobbered me with that board. Then after the guy robbed me and hit my head again, I started getting light bursts. They have absolutely no explanation for it other than sometimes things that have been knocked out of alignment get knocked back in. The nerve cells have atrophied somewhat, but it's possible . . ." She was speechless with joy.

He hugged her. "God, that's wonderful! When?"

"Gradually since that night in the water. I woke up to black the next morning, but it wasn't as black—more like charcoal, and every day it's gotten lighter and it doesn't go away. At least, not yet. Right now it's like shadows in muddy water."

"That's fantastic!"

She was bubbling with happiness. "Yes, it is, isn't it? I'm not counting on anything yet. Just one day at a time, but my father is thrilled." She took a deep breath. "Listen, the reason I called you—my dad wants to see you. To thank you, I think. That's okay with you, isn't it?"

He stumbled over his tongue. "Thank me for hitting you? Yeah . . . well, sure, I guess so."

She was equally flustered. "Before you go up, you have to help me. I don't know what to do."

"Anything," he told her. "Name it. What?"

"It's, um, about Matt."

"Halston? The police officer?"

She blushed. "I think it's serious, at least for me it is, but he went back to Chicago. I don't know what to do."

He contained his surprise. "Did you tell him about your sight?" She shook her head, and he was confused again. "Why not?"

"Just because I can see light and dark doesn't make me self-sufficient."

"I'm not getting it," he confessed. "You seem pretty self-sufficient to me."

"Since I lost my sight, I've never cooked, cleaned, shopped for groceries, I haven't the faintest idea of how to do laundry. I'm useless at the most basic level of caring for myself. I can learn it all, of course, and I will, but he might find someone else in the meantime, and . . ."

"You want me to take you to Chicago?"

"No, I can go to Chicago. I just need to know if you think I should. I'm rich, and according to my father, I'm about to inherit a great deal of property. Is he going to feel pressured? How would you feel?"

"I'd probably feel pretty terrific. To have someone who looks like you follow me to Chicago? I'd feel terrific."

She nodded. "Are you sure? I mean, he hasn't called or anything, and I don't want to put him in an awkward position."

"He's gone, right? What do you have to lose?"

She considered. "Pride?"

"Pride's expensive. Are you ready to pay the price of not going?"

She shook her head emphatically. "No."

"I'll take you to Chicago. You pick out the date."

"Uh, not for a while. I want to see if this gets better." She sobered. "Maybe after my father . . ."

"Whenever you want."

She walked him through the house and up the stairs

to her father's room. Samuel Parker Bowmont was bedridden and clearly in pain.

"I'll see you later," Leanna whispered, and left them alone.

He stared at the man who might have fathered him and waited.

Sam Bowmont looked back at him with one blood-shot eye a good long time, appraising; the other, the left, milky white and sightless, seemed to stare at him also. Her father gestured toward a nearby chair and continued his gaze. "I owe you," he said with difficulty. "A great deal . . . as it turns out. I'm glad I lived long enough . . . to say so."

Jay nodded, unsure how to respond. "Leanna's a terrific person. I like her a lot. I hope it's real. Whether or not she regains her sight, you can be sure that there'll be a lot of us watching out for her," he said slowly.

"It's real," Sam said urgently. "Son, I'm a rich man. Things might have been different . . . if I wasn't. I can't make it up to you but I'm going to try." He shifted painfully on the bed. "Is there anything you want?"

Jay had the distinct impression they were having two entirely different conversations, and temptation beat madly against his brain, gorged his throat. *What do you want to make up to me? Did you marry Dorothy Stevens? Did you get her pregnant and lie to her and buy your way out of it? Tell me you're my father. Tell me.* Then it was gone. Over.

"No, sir. Nothing."

The dying man watched him carefully, as if he were weighing something in his mind. Finally, slowly, he offered his hand, and Jay clasped it in his own, and the old man fought tears as he held on for a full two minutes before allowing him to leave the room.

* * *

"Halston. It's for you. Old guy, says he's a friend."

The usual chaos of precinct conversation cluttered the air, so Matt pushed his paperwork aside and walked to Dino's office so he could hear. He punched the blinking light and was surprised to be talking to Sam Bowmont. "Yes, sir, what can I do for you?"

"This is an awkward call for me," the ill man responded with difficulty, "so please appreciate that I'm doing it because I can no longer travel."

"Yes, sir." Matt stopped his mind from bouncing through the possibilities: Leanna was ill, Leanna was upset, Leanna was—holy hell—not pregnant! There'd been no precautions that night. He kicked the door shut and concentrated on the conversation.

"In view of my daughter's interest in you . . . I've taken liberties I might not otherwise. It seems you're a pretty good officer . . . two commendations in three years, fast-track promotions. Thirty-four, eligible for retirement in twelve years."

An eerie feeling crept up his hairline. This wasn't the kind of information that was readily available, and however Bowmont had obtained it, it was jarring to hear his pedigree read to him over the phone.

"I run a newspaper business here in Wellington, Matt. And I was wondering . . . if you'd be interested in looking into a career along that line. Now I'm sure this is coming at you a little fast. . . ."

"I'm not sure I understand," he hedged. "You're offering me a job?"

"Well, that's where the awkward part comes in," the older man admitted. "Can I just say I've made a judgment about you where my daughter's concerned? . . . As you know, I'm not going to be here much longer to look out for her welfare, and since you seem to do a pretty good job of it, I'm seeing if you'd be interested."

"I don't know what to say. I've always been a cop, and I hadn't thought much beyond that. How does Leanna fit into this picture?"

"She's going to inherit the *Bowmont Herald*. The current management is in place for five years, and I'm willing to give you a two-year contract . . . with a guarantee that it'll be picked up in the event you were to . . . come to an understanding with my daughter."

"I'm not sure I'm real comfortable with this conversation, Mr. Bowmont."

"I can understand that, and frankly, it comes as good news. I don't think I'd be comfortable if I were you, either, and as you know . . . circumstances being what they are, I don't have time to proceed in a more civilized manner. Are you willing to give it some thought?"

"With due respect, sir, I'll just give you my answer now. I don't think it's something I'll want to do."

There was a lengthy pause on the other end of the line. "I see. Would it make a difference if my daughter had asked me to call you?"

"I don't think she did."

"You're quite right, she didn't."

"Either way, my answer would have been the same."

"Sorry to have troubled you, Matt. I hope this won't interfere with your friendship with Leanna."

"I assure you it won't."

"If you change your mind, I'd be pleased to hear it."

After Sam hung up, Matt stared at the wall. Had the fact that she was blind entered into it? Here was a solution if money was truly the problem. Sam Bowmont had been highly uncomfortable making the offer, knowing full well that he was running the risk of appearing to purchase a relationship for his daughter.

He'd known Leanna for what, a month? Less. Kissed her one night, slept with her two nights later.

There was more to it than that, and he knew it. She'd been on his mind from the moment he'd seen her struggling by the roadway. He'd hated Curt Baylor on sight, and it had nothing to do with his being a cooker. Some kind of chemical something-or-other had happened between him and Leanna that had been a mad mixture of sweet and incendiary. He'd been preoccupied with her since he'd left Walden City, was having severely erotic dreams about her at all hours of the day, and hadn't been able to come up with a solution.

Her father had just offered to dump one in his lap, and he'd turned it down flat without giving it twenty minutes' thought. Hell, you took two months to decide on a car, he berated himself. He thought about it the rest of the day, as the old man knew he would.

Bowmont must consider Leanna pretty serious about him to make such an offer, which made him feel great, but somehow uncomfortable words crept into his equations, like "bought" and "kept." Big stumbling blocks. He had eight years on the force, a credible career, a promising future; a newspaper was an unknown animal. Being socially and politically responsible was another seven-day-a-week job. Hell, he didn't know a lot about anything other than being a cop, let alone taking on the weight of running a newspaper.

But the real issue was, what if it didn't work out with Leanna? He'd have to learn a whole new way of life. Seeing for both of them, anticipating her needs, fitting time with her into an overloaded schedule while he began a new career. Would she be willing to wait and worry like other men's wives? She hadn't lived twenty-four hours a day with him yet; what if she changed her mind and they didn't reach an "understanding"?

Unable to concentrate, he told Dino he was taking an early dinner and went for a walk. When he returned, he'd reached a decision to call Sam and go for it. So it cost him some pride; there was no way he was willing to give her up.

That evening, quite suddenly, Sam Bowmont died.

33

Promises kept . . .

    Matt arrived at the Bowmont mansion to offer his condolences. He rang the bell and reached into his pocket to finger a book of matches. Alice Faye, resplendent in black and diamonds, met him at the front door and escorted him into the living room. "My stepdaughter will be down in a few minutes," she said pleasantly. "We'll be leaving for the services as soon as she gets dressed. Actually, I'm glad to have a few minutes with you alone."

He met her probing glance but found no recognition of him; still, something in her tone sounded a warning.

"I understand from Parker that Sam had tentative discussions with you regarding the possibility of joining the staff at the *Bowmont Herald*."

"He offered me a job, yes. I've decided to take it."

"Mmmm. Unfortunately, now that he's gone I don't think that will continue to be possible," she said smoothly, and smiled up at him.

"Oh? Why is that?"

"In view of my stepdaughter's blindness, it's going to be necessary to appoint a trustee to run the paper, and personnel decisions will made by that person."

"Really. And I take it that person is going to be you, Mrs. Bow—excuse me, Alice Faye?"

"I don't see that it's any of your business, Detective Halston."

"You're rescinding my job offer, so I assume it's you. Can I ask when this is going to happen?"

"Very shortly, I assure you," she said stiffly.

Leanna came to the doorway, and Matt immediately crossed to greet her. She was drawn but composed and beautifully dressed in a soft rose wool dress; her eyes were hidden behind dark glasses. "You look wonderful," he said softly. "Sam would be real proud."

Alice Faye joined them. "It's your father's funeral. I thought you were going to wear the black dress," she observed icily.

"Dad never liked me in black," Leanna responded without turning toward her stepmother. "This was one of his favorites."

"Suit yourself. Black would have been more appropriate."

Matt looked away from Leanna long enough to tap Alice Faye on the wrist. She looked at him with irritation, affronted by his presumption. He slipped the book of matches from Nicholson's bar into her fingers. She glanced at it, blanched, and then stared up at him with sudden recognition. "Your son's in the kitchen, I think," he said quietly.

"Yes, I'm sure you're right." A pale Alice Faye left the room to find Parker.

"I'm sorry about your father."

"Thank you." Leanna stood in front of him; he noticed she was nearly his height in heels, and that she seemed to watch his face. "Dad told me he called you about the paper. He said he had a great deal of respect for you and he was worried that he'd made a mistake. I told him you wouldn't be upset."

"You were right. I wasn't. I'm not."

"What did you give Alice Faye?" she asked softly.

She took off her sunglasses, and when he looked into her eyes, shining with unshed tears, it hit him like a thunderbolt. "You can see me."

She nodded. "You have light brown eyes with steel gray rims, and your hair is the darkest brown I've ever seen."

She moved his hand slowly back and forth in front of her face and followed the action slowly, without focus. "What I see right now is light and shadow. I don't always have color yet, but they say it might be possible. It depends on how badly damaged the optic nerves have gotten from inactivity."

He was astounded, unable to express himself. She had described him pretty accurately. "How?" he managed finally.

"They don't know. Dr. Peachtree says it has something to do with the headaches, that's all they've been able to figure out. I've had a couple of flashes of pure sight. They want me come to Chicago so they can study me."

"Chicago?" he echoed crazily. "Are you going to do it?"

She nodded, her eyes on his face.

"How long?"

"Not too long. I have to find someone to help me run the paper."

"I think I might know someone. You need a place to stay?"

She nodded again and stood on tiptoe to kiss his open mouth, and he kissed her back, enjoying it immensely.

"Do you want to get married first?"

"Not necessarily."

"Good." He kissed her again and was still kissing her when Parker came to collect them.

Alice Faye rode to the service in a separate car.

Two days later Parker faced his truculent bride-to-be.

"I don't consider it any kind of a wedding with only thirty-five guests, and now that your father's gone, I don't see why we can't postpone it for a while. Why can't I have the wedding I want?"

"Because I don't know when I'm going to have time, Jolene. Between the real estate business and the insurance company, and managing my father's trust, I'll be lucky to have five minutes this next year. Sweetheart, I know you wanted a bigger wedding, I did too, but let's just do it now like we planned and get on with our lives."

"That's easy for you to say. You're not giving up anything. I'm giving up everything."

Parker sighed, exhausted with the conversation. "Look, I've just lost my father. I'm going to show up tomorrow prepared to say 'I do,' and if you want to marry me, you show up, too. Otherwise, you're giving up me, a new house, and a trip to Acapulco." That shut her up, as he knew it would, and he kissed her. "You can start booking real estate appointments for the middle of January when we get back. Now go buy a dress or something."

When she smiled at last, he walked out of the room to find peace in his father's library. He pushed open the door and saw Alice Faye crossing the room toward the fireplace with a batch of yellow papers. There was a small fire in the grate.

"What are you doing?" he demanded. "Those are Dad's papers."

"I'm perfectly aware of what they are. I'm his widow and I have a right to go through his papers."

"Going through them is fine. You're destroying them." He blocked her path and took the papers from her grasp. She tried to snatch them back and failed.

"Just because he decided to tie everything up with your name on it doesn't mean you can tell me what to do," she said furiously. " I don't care what I signed when I was twenty-two, I'm still your mother and I didn't spend all those years with him to wind up taking orders from you and Burt Holman."

"Dad put your share of his estate into a trust for tax reasons, Mother. It saves millions. We've been over this. You insisted I be his successor. Well, Dad apparently agreed with you. I'll never be unfair to you, so why don't we just—"

"I will not ask my son for spending money!"

"Unfortunately, Mother, you will. And I will give it to you." He glanced at the papers. "Why do you want to burn these?"

"Go ahead, read them," she warned grimly. "When you see what he's admitted to, you'll wish you hadn't."

It was a draft of a letter in his father's handwriting addressed to Burt Holman. He read through it, then handed the pages back to her. He made no move to stop her as she tossed the papers in the fire.

"Your father's money will leave this family," she

warned angrily, "over my dead body. There's nothing about this in his goddamn trust, and now there's no reason to worry about it."

"I'm not worried about it, Mother," he said heavily. "I happen to know Dad never discussed it with Burt, so you and I are the only people who know."

"I'll deny it ever existed." She stalked out of the room and left him staring at the ashes in the fireplace.

Early the next morning he drove to Annie Chatfield's.

Jay met him at the front door without rancor. "I'm sorry about your father." He glanced at his watch. "Aren't you getting married today?"

"Not until two o'clock. Can I come in?"

Parker followed him into the kitchen and accepted a cup of coffee. "Jolene said she invited you. Are you going to show up?"

"Is Jillian going to be there?"

Parker gave him an oblique look. "She's Jolene's maid of honor." He shook his head, confused. "Jillian?"

"Yes, Jillian. Sister of the bride. If she's there, I'll be there."

Parker stared at him, gaining understanding. "God, you do like living dangerously."

Jay shrugged. "What are you talking about? You're marrying Jolene."

Parker laughed heartily for the first time in weeks, and Jay joined in. Parker shook his head again. "Is there somewhere we can talk?"

They took their coffee onto the back porch and Parker settled onto the swing.

"I had a long talk with my father the night he died," he began, studying Jay's face. "He held you directly responsible for Leanna's regaining her sight, and he told me I should get used to you." He laughed and shook his head again. "If it's going to be you and my sister-in-law, I guess he was right."

Jay nodded without comment, waiting for him to continue.

"Dad gave me some very specific instructions where you're concerned. . . ." Parker blew out his breath in resignation and plunged in. Alice Faye was going to have a conniption. "And they are as follows. One, I'm to arrange full tuition for you at Traxx University starting next fall. Also for your brothers and sisters upon each of their graduations.

"Two, law school of your choice, including housing, books, whatever you need—I guess that would include a job. Whatever, we'll work it out. And three, a position in Burt Holman's firm when you pass the bar. There's one string. Two, actually. The first is that as a lawyer, you're to look after—"

Jay stopped him. "I already talked with your father about Leanna. There's no bill due me. I don't understand why you're doing this."

"I told you why—plus I gave my word. You agree to look after Bowmont interests," he continued. "Including Leanna's. And the second is that you and I bury the hatchet." He offered his hand. "Here's the second."

Jay reached out, wordless, and shook Parker's hand.

"What about the first?"

"What am I, crazy? Deal. Done." Jay paused. "I'd like to be friends with you as well."

"We'll never be friends because of Jolene."

"Hey, she's marrying you."

Parker got off the swing. "Yeah, I can afford her and you can't. Yet. I'll never trust her around you." He swung down off the porch. "Speaking of getting married, I guess I'd better get to the church. I assume I'll see you there."

Jay watched Parker walk around the corner of the house and waited until the whine of the Porsche had died away. Then he did something he'd never done in his life. A joyous "Yaaaahoooooo!" eddied across the lake and echoed back from the stand of spruce trees.

Inside, he danced Annie around the kitchen. "You're not gonna believe this."

Annie was greatly interested, but when she didn't seem terribly surprised, he stopped cold. "You told him. It had to be you because nobody else knew."

For the first time in his life, he saw Annie Chatfield blush. "Well, I might have mentioned your mother," she conceded. "We talked about a whole lot of stuff."

He stared at her. "And?"

"And, he smiled and said thank you."

Jay got to the church early, chose a seat with a clear view of where the maid of honor would stand, and waited impatiently for things to get going. He'd seen Leanna briefly a few minutes ago; there'd been no sign of Jillian, but he spied Matt Halston seated on the aisle and nodded hello. Guests had been waiting ten full minutes, and there were no late arrivals. If he knew Jolene, she was building the drama of her entrance.

Finally the organist got a signal from somewhere and shifted from a series of standard love songs to begin the distinctive notes of the traditional "Wedding March." Moments later the procession began, and he watched the attendants take measured steps down the aisle, a radiant Leanna reaching out without a pause the precise moment she passed Matt to touch hands with him.

Then came Jillian. A fabulous new Jillian, hair no longer blond but returned to the honeyed brown he remembered from high school and cut in a beautiful, feathery frame for her face. Her gown was somewhere between raspberry and a rich red wine in color. She looked positively delicious. Concentrating on her careful steps, she did not see him as she paced down the aisle.

Finally Jolene made her entrance, and he couldn't deny it, she looked absolutely beautiful. Dr. Llowell took his daughter's arm and began to escort her to meet Parker at the altar. Jay turned to Jillian and found her staring at him with a look of surprise. She looked away the instant he caught her and watched her sister's slow walk to the altar without once glancing at him again. He didn't care.

He studied her throughout the ceremony, saw her produce Parker's wedding band and hand it to Jolene at the appropriate moment, and her sigh of relief when her part in the proceeding was completed. From that point forward, he simply waited until it was over, marking time from the repetition of the vows to the moment they ducked the rice and drove to the reception at Dr. Llowell's country club. Somewhere in the middle, he chastely kissed the bride and shook Parker's hand in genuine congratulations.

When there was food, he ate. When there were toasts, he drank. When there was a ballad, he approached Jillian. "You owe me a dance," he said quietly. She came slowly, stiffly forward. And they danced.

At the end of the song, he stooped abruptly and gathered her into his arms, walking quickly out of the ballroom and through the lobby of the country club. At the front entrance, he caught the eye of the parking attendant, who immediately brought Annie's station wagon forward, and a second attendant opened the passenger door. Before Jillian could object, they were on the road to the bluff.

"Am I being kidnapped?" she asked in an odd voice.

"Not exactly." He looked at her, unable to decide if she was indignant or indifferent. "Well, yeah, sort of. Would you have agreed to come if I'd asked you?"

"Probably not," she answered honestly. "I've had about all the pain I need out of this relationship, and I don't think I'm interested in more, so—"

"Good, because I'm not, either."

The raspberry/wine dress rustled silkily as she turned to face him. "I'm not interested in being a stand-in for my sister. Not with you, not with my father. I'm through with it. I'm going back to New York next week."

"You hear me out and I'll drive you to the plane if that's what you want to do," he answered.

"Don't make me hope, Jay. Don't do that to me. Just let me go."

He reached the bluff at last and brought the car to a halt. "I've had a lot on my mind lately," he said carefully. "I'm not too sure I like being an adult. But, it is the situation, and I'm trying very hard to live up to it."

She looked at him with a stubborn chin.

He reached into the back and took a small tin box off the seat. "In here is every letter you ever wrote to me. I counted them this morning. I got out of bed to do it. Because I didn't really get it about you until somewhere around five A.M." He handed the box to her.

She looked inside and was suddenly teary. "Don't do this unless you mean it."

"Oh, I mean it, Jillie. There are forty-five. Twenty letters, four Christmas cards, four birthday cards, and seventeen postcards. There is nothing in there from

Jolene because I threw all of her letters away years ago. She must have known it, because she never sent another one. And you know what? I cannot remember the contents of any one of them."

Jillian's tears were spilling over. He took the tin from her, closed the lid, and tossed it onto the backseat.

"I had a thing for your sister that had nothing to do with love. It had to do with seventeen-year-old hormones and trying desperately to hold on to something in my life that was there when my parents were living . . . and doing every bloody thing I could to keep it from changing like everything else around me."

She looked away from him, silent and disbelieving, shutting him out. "And I didn't know I was doing it until the night with you. As hard as I tried to keep things the way I thought I wanted them, they changed on me. You changed them."

"I don't know why you're doing this. You wanted Jolene that night," she accused wearily. "You can't alter that now. I saw your face, Jay. I know what you felt. You wanted me to be her, and when you realized that I wasn't—"

"You have no idea what I was thinking."

"The hell I don't! You were astonished. Embarrassed. You couldn't even say anything to me."

"Yes, I was astonished," he agreed. "I couldn't believe it. And embarrassed, oh, God, Jillie, embarrassed. But not because of what happened between us," he said emphatically. "I couldn't believe I could make love to someone and not think about Jolene. Operative words, make love. It was the first time in my life that I didn't feel like I'd just had sex.

"I couldn't say anything to you because I didn't know how to tell you that I've had sex with other women but

I've never been able to do it without your sister some-where over my shoulder or in my head—except that night. How could I say something like that to you when *I* couldn't deal with it? And up until this morning, I was still having problems with it. And I finally got it. I love you. Not only that, I'm in love with you, and I probably have been since high school. I remember the first time I kissed you in front of Teddy Zeigler's old green Ford."

She was crying openly now, and he pulled her into his arms. "And I think you love me, too. I realized it the night you came to my room."

"No," she sobbed. "I never—"

"Yes, you did. I know it was you."

"Not me," she insisted.

"I know it was you because no two women are the same, even in the dark."

She punched him. "Not good enough."

He got serious. "Because she's the woman I want to be there from now on."

Jillian was silent a long time, but she stayed in his arms. He waited as long as he could stand it.

Then he kissed her.

AVAILABLE NOW

FOREVERMORE by Maura Seger
As the only surviving member of a family that had lived in the English village of Avebury for generations, Sarah Huxley was fated to protect the magical sanctuary of the tumbled stone circles and earthen mounds. But when a series of bizarre deaths at Avebury began to occur, Sarah met her match in William Devereux Faulkner, a level-headed Londoner, who had come to investigate. "Ms. Seger has a special magic touch with her lovers that makes her an enduring favorite with readers everywhere."—*Romantic Times*

PROMISES by Jeane Renick
From the award winning author of *Trust Me* and *Always* comes a sizzling novel set in a small Ohio town, featuring a beautiful blind heroine, her greedy fiancé, two sisters in love with the same man, a mysterious undercover police officer, and a holographic will.

KISSING COUSINS by Carol Jerina
Texas rancher meets English beauty in this witty follow-up to *The Bridegroom*. When Prescott Trefarrow learned that it was he who was the true Earl of St. Keverne, and not his twin brother, he went to Cornwall to claim his title, his castle, and a multitude of responsibilities. Reluctantly, he became immersed in life at Ravens Lair Castle—and the lovely Lucinda Trefarrow.

HUNTER'S HEART by Christina Hamlett
A romantic suspense novel featuring a mysterious millionaire and a woman determined to figure him out. Many things about wealthy industrialist Hunter O'Hare intrigue Victoria Cameron. First of all, why did O'Hare have his ancestral castle moved to Virginia from Ireland, stone by stone? Secondly, why does everyone else in the castle act as if they have something to hide? And last, but not least, what does Hunter want from Victoria?

THE LAW AND MISS PENNY by Sharon Ihle
When U.S. Marshal Morgan Slater suffered a head injury and woke up with no memory, Mariah Penny conveniently supplied him with a fabricated story so that he wouldn't run her family's medicine show out of town. As he traveled through Colorado Territory with the Pennys, he and Mariah fell in love. Everything seemed idyllic until the day the lawman's memory returned.

PRIMROSE by Clara Wimberly
A passionate historical tale of forbidden romance between a wealthy city girl and a fiercely independent local man in the wilds of the Tennessee mountains. Rosalyn Hunte's heart was torn between loyalty to her family and the love of a man who wanted to claim her for himself.

COMING NEXT MONTH

FLAME LILY by Candace Camp
Continuing the saga of the Tyrells begun in *Rain Lily,* another heart-tugging, passionate tale of love from bestselling author Candace Camp. Returning home after years at war, Confederate officer Hunter Tyrell dreamed only of marrying his sweetheart, Linette Sanders, and settling down. But when he discovered that Linette had wed another, he vowed never to love again—until he found out her heartbreaking secret.

ALL THAT GLITTERS by Ruth Ryan Langan
From a humble singing job in a Los Angeles bar, Alexandra Corday is discovered and propelled into stardom. Along the way her path crosses that of rising young photographer Adam Montrose. Just when it seems that Alex will finally have it all—a man she loves, a home for herself and her brother, and the family she has always yearned for—buried secrets threaten to destroy her.

THE WIND CASTS NO SHADOW by Roslynn Griffith
With an incredibly deft hand, Roslynn Griffith has combined Indian mythology and historical flavor in this compelling tale of love, betrayal, and murder deep in the heart of New Mexico territory.

UNQUIET HEARTS by Kathy Lynn Emerson
Tudor England comes back to life in this richly detailed historical romance. With the death of her mother, Thomasine Strangeways had no choice but to return to Catsholme Manor, the home where her mother was once employed as governess. There she was reunited with Nick Carrier, her childhood hero who had become the manor's steward. Meeting now as adults, they found the attraction between them instant and undeniable, but they were both guarding dangerous secrets.

STOLEN TREASURE by Catriona Flynt
A madcap romantic adventure set in 19th-century Arizona gold country. Neel Blade was rich, handsome, lucky, and thoroughly bored, until he met Cate Stewart, a feisty chemist who was trying to hold her world together while her father was in prison. He instantly fell in love with her, but if only he could remember who he was . . .

WILD CARD by Nancy Hutchinson
It is a dream come true for writer Sarah MacDonald when movie idol Ian Wild miraculously appears on her doorstep. This just doesn't happen to a typical widow who lives a quiet, unexciting life in a small college town. But when Ian convinces Sarah to go with him to his remote Montana ranch, she comes face to face with not only a life and a love more exciting than anything in the pages of her novels, but a shocking murder.

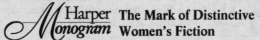 **Harper Monogram** **The Mark of Distinctive Women's Fiction**

LORD OF THE NIGHT
by Susan Wiggs
A Venetian lord dedicated to justice suspects a lucious beauty of being involved in a scandalous plot.

ORCHIDS IN MOONLIGHT
by Patricia Hagan
Caught in a web of intrigue in the dangerous West, a man and a woman fight to regain their overpowering dream of love.

A SEASON OF ANGELS
by Debbie Macomber
Three willing but wacky angels must teach their charges a lesson before granting a Christmas wish.
National Bestseller